Pippa Roscoe lives in Norfo... and makes daily promises to ... the day she'll leave her computer to take a long walk in the countryside. She can't remember a time when she wasn't dreaming about handsome heroes and innocent heroines. Totally her mother's fault, of course—she gave Pippa her first romance to read at the age of seven! She is inconceivably happy that she gets to share those daydreams with you. Follow her on Twitter @PippaRoscoe.

Melanie Milburne read her first Mills & Boon novel at the age of seventeen, in between studying for her final exams. After completing a Master's degree in education she decided to write a novel, and thus her career as a romance author was born. Melanie is an ambassador for the Australian Childhood Foundation and a keen dog-lover and trainer. She enjoys long walks in the Tasmanian bush. In 2015 Melanie won the HOLT Medallion, a prestigious award honouring outstanding literary talent.

Also by Pippa Roscoe

His Jet-Set Nights with the Innocent
In Bed with Her Billionaire Bodyguard
Twin Consequences of That Night
Forbidden Until Midnight

The Greek Groom Swap collection

Greek's Temporary 'I Do'

Also by Melanie Milburne

One Night in My Rival's Bed

Weddings Worth Billions miniseries

Cinderella's Invitation to Greece
Nine Months After That Night
Forbidden Until Their Snowbound Night

Discover more at millsandboon.co.uk.

RESISTING THE ITALIAN

PIPPA ROSCOE

MELANIE MILBURNE

MILLS & BOON

All rights reserved including the right of reproduction in whole or in part in any form. This edition is published by arrangement with Harlequin Enterprises ULC.

This is a work of fiction. Names, characters, places, locations and incidents are purely fictional and bear no relationship to any real life individuals, living or dead, or to any actual places, business establishments, locations, events or incidents. Any resemblance is entirely coincidental.

Without limiting the author's and publisher's exclusive rights, any unauthorized use of this publication to train generative artificial intelligence (AI) technologies is expressly prohibited. HarperCollins also exercise their rights under Article 4(3) of the Digital Single Market Directive 2019/790 and expressly reserve this publication from the text and data mining exception.

® and TM are trademarks owned and used by the trademark owner and/or its licensee. Trademarks marked with ® are registered with the United Kingdom Patent Office and/or the Office for Harmonisation in the Internal Market and in other countries.

First published in Great Britain 2025
by Mills & Boon, an imprint of HarperCollins*Publishers* Ltd,
1 London Bridge Street, London, SE1 9GF

www.harpercollins.co.uk

HarperCollins*Publishers*, Macken House, 39/40 Mayor Street Upper,
Dublin 1, D01 C9W8, Ireland

Resisting the Italian © 2025 Harlequin Enterprises ULC

Inconveniently Wed © 2025 Pippa Roscoe

Illicit Italian Nights © 2025 Melanie Milburne

ISBN: 978-0-263-34469-1

06/25

This book contains FSC™ certified paper
and other controlled sources to ensure responsible forest management.

For more information visit www.harpercollins.co.uk/green.

Printed and Bound in the UK using 100% Renewable Electricity
at CPI Group (UK) Ltd, Croydon, CR0 4YY

INCONVENIENTLY WED

PIPPA ROSCOE

MILLS & BOON

For Nella Giatrakou,

Your courage, your fortitude and your conviction are an inspiration, shaping the world around you for the better.

All my love.

Xx

PROLOGUE

Six years ago

MAYBE HE WOULDN'T SHOW. Maybe Antonio Gallo had come to his senses and decided to not go through with his crazy plan.

Nineteen-year-old Ivy McKellen shifted from foot to foot. She imagined she looked as uncomfortable as she felt, standing alone on the steps of a register office in South West London.

When Antonio had first asked her, she was sure the Italian businessman had been joking. Marriage? Him? To *her?* A *waitress?* Maybe the pressure of his high-powered job, whatever it was, had gone to his head. She'd offered him a glass of water and he'd laughed. The sound rich, luxurious, had rolled over her skin and made her blush.

'*It's simple,* cara. *I need a wife to get my grandfather off my back.*'

'You don't even know me.'

'Exactly! It's perfect.'

With a dad she hadn't seen in four years and a mum who had spent the last two years in Majorca bouncing between boyfriends, Ivy was the first to admit she wasn't an expert in what made a marriage work, but she was pretty sure it required *some* knowledge of each other.

It had been a Thursday afternoon at Affogato, the café where she worked in central London, the tables eerily quiet, which most likely meant that the pubs were full of the usual regulars. But Antonio was different from the city boys she was used to serving. No, he had a focus and a determination that had impressed her.

At least, until he turned that focus and determination on her.

He'd found her at a weak moment, on her break. And offered a solution that would benefit them both.

She'd shaken her head and turned to walk away when he'd reached out to grasp her wrist. And that was the first time Antonio Gallo touched her.

Sparks.

Heat.

'Please. Hear me out...'

He'd probably be shocked to hear that it had been the 'please' that had won her over. At least enough to listen to what he had to say. And what he'd had to say had been unimaginable.

He'd offered her a life-changing sum of money to marry him, all because his grandfather was pressuring him to marry his cousin. And in exchange? He'd give her two hundred and fifty thousand pounds.

Two hundred and fifty thousand pounds.

Her heart had missed a beat.

'Once we're married, you'll never have to see me again.'

With that amount of money, she could pay for her brother to get the help he needed. She could do that and *still* have enough money to put a deposit down on a flat so that when Jamie found his feet, he'd have somewhere safe to land. Somewhere secure. She might even be able to stop working for long enough to go to university.

She could breathe. She could dream again.

Ivy peered along the road to see if she could spot him, not realising that she was holding her breath. But amongst the faceless pedestrians hurrying back and forth, she couldn't catch even a glimpse of the tall, powerful Italian who would stand out amongst a crowd like this.

She smoothed a hand over the lace detail of the white dress she'd found in her local charity shop. It probably wasn't anything like what a real bride would wear, certainly not to marry someone like Antonio Gallo. But this wasn't a real wedding. Not really.

Unlike most young girls, Ivy had never daydreamed about big white dresses and meeting Prince Charming. Her parents' devastating arguments too vivid in her mind, the fear of being like her mother, of desperately looking for love in all the wrong places, too powerful a deterrent. No. Ivy McKellen had sworn never to get married.

But the sudden thought of Antonio *not* coming, the fear that she might lose her chance to help her brother, brought her out in a cold sweat.

Foolish. She'd been foolish to think Antonio would actually show.

'Ivy?'

She turned to find him standing right behind her, relief flooding her so quickly that she nearly stumbled into him.

Her swallowed inhale brought the scent of his aftershave to her, something earthy and expensive, fitting the severity of his features. The wind tussled the tamed waves of his dark hair and ruffled the lapel of his fine handmade suit. But despite all the trappings of wealth he wore, it was still *him* that was the most arresting. The sharp angles of his cheekbones almost painfully beautiful, a mouth so sensual it mocked Antonio's no-nonsense demeanour.

She braced herself against the luxury of him, standing there in a second-hand dress and simple make-up, feeling more naked than if she'd been wearing nothing. He was so overwhelming her heart struggled to beat in time.

'I have a meeting to get to, so...' He gestured for them to enter the register office.

'Of course,' she whispered and fell into step beside him.

His assistant, she'd been informed, had suggested the register office closest to her home address, and she'd thought that was sensible until Antonio was standing before her on the South London street, looking about as incongruous as a diamond in the dirt.

If Antonio thought anything of his surroundings, he thankfully didn't reveal it. No, the one thing that she had noticed about Antonio Gallo was that he wasn't a snob, unlike some of the other customers of the café where they'd met.

Unlike them, Antonio didn't try to pinch or grab at her, or peer down her shirt when she came to pick up empty cups and plates. He'd always treated her with respect, and it was only when he'd caught her feeling vulnerable after a particularly bad incident with her brother and he'd asked if she was okay that—to her horror—she'd admitted that she wasn't. That her brother was struggling and she was behind with the rent because...well, she'd not been able to say that her mother had stopped sending her money for the rent months ago. But Ivy didn't have to explain any further. He'd clearly recognised her dire situation for what it was. Near hopeless.

'Your boss can't help?' he'd asked.

He'd looked aghast when she'd explained that, with her other job, she'd not been able to take on more shifts.

'You have two jobs?'

She had three, but she didn't want to reveal that.

And that was when he'd suggested his crazy idea.

Their shoes clicked out a staccato tattoo on the tiled flooring of the register office, Antonio marching through the halls confidently, leaving Ivy to follow in his wake. They found the right office and Antonio entered without knocking. He introduced her to the lawyer who had not only organised everything but was also acting as a witness. The other was provided by the registrar.

In a daze, Ivy watched Antonio's lips mouth words promising to love, protect and honour her, feeling uneasy about the lie but knowing that the way this marriage would change her and her brother's life was incalculable.

'And do you, Ivy Jean McKellen, take Antonio Andrea Gallo as your lawful wedded husband?'

Love, honour, protect. In sickness and in health.

It was such a small thing, really. She knew Antonio didn't expect her to keep to the vows—she very much doubted *he* would. But for all that Antonio was offering, it seemed like such a small thing in exchange. And as she made her vows—ones she intended to keep—some of the guilt she felt about selling herself in marriage in this way, even if it was for a good cause, eased.

'I do.'

'You have decided to forego the rings,' the officiant said perfunctorily and Ivy blinked, quickly telling herself off for being silly for thinking that there would be rings. After all, Antonio had been very clear.

'It is a signature on a piece of paper. Nothing more.'

'I now pronounce you husband and wife. You may kiss the bride.'

She looked up at Antonio, just as he bent his head towards her. It would be the last time he touched her, she thought. His lips hovered above her skin, long enough for her to take a ragged breath, to feel the heat of his body against the curve of her neck, for him to see the way her pulse fluttered at her jaw, before he placed the most chaste of kisses on her cheek.

She bit her lip to stop it from trembling, suddenly overcome with a wave of longing for things to have been different. For this wedding to have been all the things it wasn't. To have been loved, to have been protected, to have been honoured. She folded her fingers into a little fist.

It *wasn't* different, but it would give her and her brother what they needed, and that was enough for her. It had to be.

Because within five minutes Antonio Gallo's car had arrived to pick him up and take him back into central London, while two hundred and fifty thousand—*thousand*—pounds had been transferred into her account. And there, from the side of the road, watching the car whisk Antonio away, Ivy made the call to the rehab centre to book her brother a place that would save his life.

CHAPTER ONE

ANTONIO ANDREA GALLO stalked down a South West London street towards an almost offensively bland building in Wandsworth, feeling a distinct sense of déjà vu. With his mobile phone glued to his ear and his eye assessing every single person on the street for nefarious intent, he tried to find the patience to not shout at his lawyer.

'This is what I pay your extortionate fees for, Simon,' he growled into the phone.

'It's never happened before,' the Englishman replied apologetically. If it hadn't been for Simon's obvious confusion, Antonio would have suspected that the man was on the take.

'Well, it's happening now.'

'It's highly irregular, sir. Highly. Is there maybe something you haven't told me?'

Only the fact that the words were forced through a significant amount of discomfort allowed Antonio to excuse the man for even suggesting that it was somehow *his* fault.

'I have told you everything,' he bit out.

'Then I don't know why Mr Justice Carmondy overruled our appeal. The divorce should have been granted before it could be put before him.'

They had fought the summons as hard as possible, convinced that the judge would give up long before now on a matter such as this. But he hadn't. Which was why, reluctantly and without any other option, Antonio was here.

'What does he want?' he demanded. 'Money?'

'No. And don't try to offer him any. The English courts are different to what you're used to,' his lawyer warned.

'Everyone wants something, Simon,' Antonio insisted, speaking from experience.

He checked his watch. He didn't have time for this. He'd flown to the closest private airfield that morning and needed to be back in Italy later that afternoon. The fallout from the reading of his grandfather's will had sent so many ripples into an already turbulent pool that if he hadn't already been dead, Antonio would have willingly murdered the man.

'The only thing he seems to want is to see you and Mrs Gallo—'

'Don't call her that,' Antonio snapped down the phone.

'You and *Ms McKellen* in his chambers to discuss reconciliation.'

'Reconciliation? I haven't seen the woman since the day we married, six years ago!'

'For heaven's sake, don't say that to the judge! If he thinks you tried to game the system—'

'I wasn't trying to game the system, I was trying to game my *grandfather*,' Antonio growled, just as he arrived at the unassuming concrete steps leading to the Wandsworth Courts where Simon, who had been waiting for him, put away his phone.

Antonio took a moment to glare between the tall bespectacled man and the court, as if that alone might bend them to his will. And when that didn't work, he turned and marched up the steps to fix this himself, stopping only when Simon didn't immediately follow behind.

'We're waiting for Ms McKellen,' Simon said in response to Antonio's raised brow.

Antonio glanced at his watch. There was still some time before their court appointment, but not for Antonio.

'I plan to have this resolved before she even gets here,' he said, continuing up the steps with determination.

The judge, however, had other plans and made him wait. First, outside his chambers, in a hallway where he was subjected to the curiosity of nearly every single passerby, as if he were some rare breed on display. Which, he conceded, was probably true, seeing as he doubted that many billionaires lived in this small London borough.

Antonio caught glimpses of the pale, balding man behind the desk every time someone entered and left the room. And each time they made adversarial eye contact to the point where Antonio firmly believed the judge was purposely wasting his time.

And then, even after Antonio and Simon had been 'invited' into the judge's office, they were made to wait as he sifted through various batches of paperwork. As someone who personally abhorred the stuff, Antonio should have felt some sympathy for him.

Should have. But didn't. Because this entire farce was a waste of his time.

'No Mrs Gallo?' the judge asked without preamble.

'She is on her way, Your Honour,' Simon answered.

The judge turned to glare at Antonio. A glare that Antonio was more than happy to hold for as long as it took. After all, he'd been practically raised by his grandfather—a man who had entwined authority and intent into a near lethal combination. Antonio had been the only person, ever, to defy Gio Gallo's commands and remain unscathed. But it seemed the old man had had the last laugh after all.

'You didn't come together?' the judge asked, peering over the top of his reading glasses.

'They have been separated for some time, Your Honour,' Simon replied for him.

The judge raised his eyebrow, as if he'd hoped to catch him out.

Antonio nearly laughed. He ate men like this for breakfast. Daily.

After Antonio's marriage to Ivy, his grandfather had actually believed that cutting Antonio off would bring him running back home. But instead it had freed him, and he'd flourished. He'd started his own company and that company had thrived. And so had the people Antonio *did* care for.

His mother. His cousin, Maria.

And now, aged twenty-nine, Antonio was the billionaire CEO of a multinational brokerage company. Alessina International was completely his, no investors, no board of directors, no meddling.

No one to bow to.

Eventually he'd reconciled, albeit grudgingly, with his grandfather. He'd won the man's respect, Antonio knew that. Which was why he hadn't expected the other man's last move. But he should have. Antonio had grown complacent, believing Gio's age had tempered him. He'd been wrong. Instead, Gio had plotted the future of his grandchildren and that of his company, Gallo Group, to an almost Machiavellian level. And as a consequence, he needed to divorce Ivy and marry Maria in order to meet the terms of Gio Gallo's last will and testament.

He would do this one last thing, for his cousin. And then he'd be done.

'Your Honour—' Simon started.

'Do you know what I dislike most about billionaires?' the judge asked, cutting him off.

Antonio wrestled with the urge to roll his eyes. Under any other circumstances, he would have laid down his terms, and an unhealthy amount of money, and walked off without another wasted second. But Simon was right, England was different. And while this particular judge didn't appear to want money, he clearly wanted to run him through the mill. And if that was what it took to get the divorce? He'd do it.

'It's the assumption that your wants and needs are superior to those of others.'

Having met a good number of billionaires, frankly, Antonio was of a similar opinion. Not that he'd admit such a thing to the man currently hellbent on ruining his day. He chose to nod sagely, which served only to irritate the older man. Really, the resemblance between the judge and his grandfather was striking.

There was a timid knock on the door to the cramped office, which did nothing to stop the judge mid-tirade. With half an ear on the judge, who was now compiling a list of faults of not only his wealth but his generation, Antonio glanced as the door pushed open and Ivy McKellen nudged her way into the room.

He half turned to greet her, when Carmondy expounded yet another unfounded objection to Antonio's apparent crimes, recalling his attention. From the corner of his eye, Antonio caught a glimpse of long, rich auburn hair.

He didn't remember that. In his lesser travelled memories, her hair was always swept back in a small efficient knot, as she shot him a conspiratorial smile, sharing her amusement with him at her Italian boss's increasingly outrageous but utterly harmless behaviour.

She'd been far too bright to be stuck serving customers who'd leered at her, keeping them at bay with a quick put-down that was gentle enough to soften the blow, but firm enough that they didn't get back up again.

She'd impressed him. And that had been hard to do at that point in his life. Undoubtably beautiful, she'd kept him at arm's length which, utterly without ego, was an unusual experience for him. And then had come the day he'd found her on a break, crying behind the café, and convinced her to tell him what was wrong.

The shameful confession of financial struggle, the desire to protect a sibling, the frustration at the heavy burden... the *shame*. Oh, Ivy had spoken obliquely, but he'd understood enough. And it had reminded him of his mother. Crying when she didn't think Antonio could hear her, struggling in the aftermath of her husband's desertion, all because of him.

Ivy, like his mother, was giving everything to protect her family. And just like that, he'd known. He'd known that she might be the *only* person who would go through with his mad scheme to win his freedom from his grandfather's pressure to marry his cousin. Ivy would agree because of her brother and her integrity meant she wouldn't betray their deal. And, in exchange, the money he would give her would allow her to radically change her life. It had been the perfect arrangement.

Until now.

Ivy shifted uncomfortably on her feet, and Antonio stared at his lawyer until Simon stood, gesturing for Ivy to take his seat. The judge continued to drone on about resources and invaluable time but Antonio couldn't focus as Ivy hooked the russet waterfall behind her ear. Antonio, who had always been sensitive to stimulation, took in all of her at once.

Delicate. Detailed. *Fine*.

The women he knew, his family, the staff at his office, were rich, expressive forces of nature, determined; they *wore* their femininity. Ivy seemed to shrink from it. She had been a little like that when he'd known her before, but not to this extent. Perhaps it was her discomfort at the setting but, despite her apparent intention to hide, she was still...*luminous*.

And then he dismissed the unusually elegiac fancy. He'd not seen or heard from her in six years. He'd not searched for her, looked her up or allowed himself to wonder about the waitress he'd met while spending three months working in London. Because she had been the means to an end, and that was all he'd needed her for.

Even now that she was sitting on a chair less than a foot away from him, she was still just that: a means to an end. She flicked a glance at him just as he looked back to the judge, whose penetrating gaze brightened with satisfaction.

'Now that we're all here,' the judge said by way of segue from one opinionated rant to another, 'I am ready to hear your application for divorce.'

'As both parties are in agreement—' Simon began, before the judge cut him off.

'Are they?' the judge asked Simon. 'Are you?' he demanded, looking between Antonio and Ivy.

Antonio nodded once, firm and decisive.

Several little bobs of Ivy's head confirmed her agreement.

'Really?' the judge demanded of her again.

All eyes turned to Ivy.

'Yes?' she answered hesitantly.

'That sounds more like a question than a statement, Mrs Gallo.'

Ivy blinked, as if surprised to hear herself addressed as such. She opened her mouth to speak but, once again, the judge cut in.

'Do you know what?' the judge asked them, apparently without requiring a response. 'I *believe* in marriage. I believe in the *sanctity* of it. I believe that once you make that binding declaration, your lives are entwined for ever,' he said, his finger striking his desk with each sentence. 'I'm not religious, and I'm not a legal zealot. But I believe in the importance and inviolability of giving your word to something.

'So, Antonio Gallo, are you a man whose word is not of value?' the judge demanded, much to the horror of his lawyer.

'Absolutely not,' Antonio replied indignantly.

'Yet you promised to love, protect and honour this woman,' the judge accused, pointing at Ivy. 'And nothing about your marriage, your time together or your *prenup* implies the slightest hint of that.'

Antonio frowned.

'A prenup which gives Mrs Gallo nothing, is that correct?'

'Yes.'

That had been their agreement. He had paid Ivy two hundred and fifty thousand pounds to marry him. She had agreed that she had no right to anything beyond that, and as such the divorce was supposed to have been easy. His lawyers had assured him of such a thing.

Clearly no one had expected Carmondy.

'You signed this willingly?' the judge asked, waving a piece of paper at Ivy.

She nodded.

'Did you have a lawyer present?'

She bit her lip before swallowing. 'I didn't need one, Your Honour. I knew what I was signing.'

The judge's gaze turned on Antonio accusatorily. 'When you married her, she became your family. She became *yours*, not to own, but to protect, to care for. It is a responsibility you have deeply neglected,' the judge stated.

'Hold on a minute—' Antonio said, nearly rising to his feet. He was enduring this entire farce precisely because he *was* trying to protect his family.

'Don't interrupt me,' the judge warned.

Antonio ground his teeth together so hard he'd need to see a dentist when he got back to Italy.

'I am sick to the back teeth of people marrying and divorcing willy nilly.'

Was the man having a stroke? Why was he talking about teeth? What on earth was a nilly? And what did it have to do with male anatomy?

'Are you okay?' Antonio asked.

The judge stared back at him. 'No! I am not. I am fed up with rich people who treat marriage like a tax haven, and the British Courts like a toll booth.'

'Well, that isn't prejudiced at all,' Antonio said sarcastically.

The judge opened and closed his mouth. But really, Antonio was only speaking the truth.

'Okay,' the judge said, finally finding his voice. 'I am refusing to grant this divorce, until it can be proved that you have both worked as hard as possible to rectify your differences.'

Antonio sat back in his chair in shock. He'd never heard of anything like it. Neither had his lawyer, as evidenced by the way Simon's mouth hung open.

'Your Honour, this is highly irregular,' Simon said when he finally found his voice.

'That it may be, but this is my decision. You will have three assessments with a court-appointed mediator in order to determine that you have genuinely given everything you can to make this marriage work, and yet still have irreconcilable differences.'

'Assessments?' Simon asked in confusion.

'Yes, assessments. Interview-based assessments. *Three of them*,' the judge demanded hotly.

'Where? In England? I can't stay here,' Antonio bit out at the ludicrous suggestion. 'I have business in Italy.'

'And your wife, Mr Gallo?' the judge demanded.

Antonio drew a blank.

The judge looked at Ivy, who winced. 'I have work too. Here,' she said, sealing his fate with yet another black mark against his name, apparently.

'The assessments can happen in Italy if you want to pay for the travel and accommodation of the mediator, and can negotiate that with Mrs Gallo, or you can stay in England. Make a decision, Mr Gallo. I have already made mine. Dismissed.'

Ivy McKellen wasn't quite sure exactly what had happened, only that it most definitely wasn't what Antonio Gallo had *wanted* to happen. And from the look on his face, that was as unique as a unicorn.

'We do *not* have time for this,' he said to the lawyer who, less than a month ago, had knocked on her door and deposited nearly half a tree's worth of legal paperwork with sticky tabs indicating where her signature would end her marriage.

Please sign, date and return.

That was how she had been informed of Antonio's intention to obtain a divorce.

Please sign, date and return.

She'd been taken a little by surprise at how much it had left her off-kilter. Of all the shocks she'd experienced in the last six years, really, her divorce shouldn't have even registered. Especially as she'd known that it would come eventually. Despite what he'd said, a man like Antonio Gallo couldn't remain in a convenient marriage for ever.

She'd wondered about the kind of person who had finally caught the notorious lone wolf of the financial world, the man who had often been referred to as the invisible hand behind the world's most lucrative business deals, and promptly stopped herself. It was none of her business. So she'd signed the papers and naïvely believed that was the last time she would see her name anywhere near his.

But yesterday she'd received an email informing her that she had to be in court. Today.

Just a formality.

As they emerged into the hallway outside the judge's office she wondered whether perhaps there might have been a different outcome if Antonio hadn't managed to antagonise the judge so much. An antagonism that seemed new. She certainly didn't remember that from before.

Ivy shifted, trying to ease the ache in her feet. She'd worn the nicest pair of shoes she owned, but they'd absolutely massacred her heels. She looked up as Antonio squinted down the hall. While she could practically see the cogs in his brain working, she searched his features for other changes the last six years had wrought. He was slimmer, yet somehow more imposing. Hard angles had replaced the traces of softness that she'd been able to see when they'd first met.

The cut of his suit displayed the breadth of his shoulders and a trim waist. The light-coloured linen fabric stood out like a beacon amongst the grey department store suits worn by nearly everyone else in the building. He'd commanded attention six years ago, even in the little, out of the way coffee shop in central London, but now the allure of him was impossible to deny. As evidenced when a woman tripped over her own feet as she did a double-take that had Ivy sending her a sympathetic smile.

'Can we go above his head?' Antonio asked his lawyer, having missed the interaction.

'It would take too long,' the lawyer replied miserably.

Of all the things she'd been worried about—seeing Antonio again, being summoned to court and, in her worst moments of fancy, being discovered and arrested for fraud—the last thing she'd expected was *this*.

Three court-appointed visits to assess their reconciliation attempts? How were they going to prove that? And where? In her flat-share in Apsley Road? The thought of Antonio's imposing frame squeezing into the little two-bed flat with Simon the lawyer, a court-appointed assessor and Sang Hee, her Korean flatmate, pushed her worryingly close to hysteria.

But it wasn't as if she could go to Italy. She had only just started her new job at the local library and couldn't take a holiday barely a month into it. And even if she *could* have, Ivy would never leave at such a critical time for the library. She'd been volunteering there for nearly a year now and they were finally about to raise enough money for the community's much-needed afterschool club. Government cuts to local councils had pushed them so far down the waiting list that Ivy and the other staff had been forced to take matters into their own hands. They'd had bake sales, they'd painted faces. They'd done everything they could to raise enough money and with their efforts matched by local businesses they were *so* close.

'The man is insane,' Antonio said of the judge, before turning back to Simon. 'I need you to find out exactly what these court assessments will involve.'

Simon nodded, looking increasingly more concerned. Ivy had met quite a few people like Judge Carmondy over the years, people who had been pushed a little too far for a little too long and who had finally decided to dig their heels in. And a part of her was sympathetic with his stance. She'd always felt uncomfortable having promised love and fidelity in exchange for money, even if they were both consenting adults under no illusions. But perhaps they shouldn't be able to cheat the system and get away with it.

Yet despite that, even now she would make the same choice again. In a heartbeat. Just the thought of her brother and the changes he'd been able to make to his life was enough for her to know that she wouldn't alter a single thing.

She felt Antonio's hawkish gaze on her.

'You've been well?' he asked perfunctorily, as if some ingrained sense of decorum prompted his question rather than genuine curiosity.

And, for a moment, all she could do was blink. Didn't he remember? Could he have forgotten that easily? Of course he had, Ivy realised, burying the hurt deep down to unpack later in private.

'Yes, thank you,' she said, hoping that he'd missed the brief hesitation before she answered. The millisecond's pause as she constructed an answer suitable to what he expected of her. 'And you?'

'*Sì*,' he replied, saying nothing of the grandfather she knew had passed four months ago, nor the million-dollar deal he was currently brokering between the Americans and the Chinese, a deal making waves around the world. Things she knew because, on not so rare occasions, she caught sight of headlines about her husband in name only. It was almost hard not to.

The large clock on the wall behind him clicked closer towards eleven and she bit back a curse. She was going to be late.

She opened her mouth to speak just as Antonio did.

'Do you have a passport?'

Taken aback, she replied without thinking. 'Yes.'

'Good. We're returning to Italy this afternoon,' he informed her imperiously.

Whether he'd become more presumptuous or she'd become more headstrong, Ivy couldn't tell, but she very much disliked this new side of his character.

'You are welcome to return to Italy, but I cannot.'

'Of course you can,' Antonio dismissed, pulling out his mobile phone and tapping on the screen.

'I can't,' Ivy stressed, trying—and most definitely failing—to ignore the way his jaw muscle flexed and his eyes glittered with warning.

'I don't remember you being this obstinate,' he observed.

'I wasn't,' she said, unsure whether to be proud of herself or horrified for answering back.

'It doesn't suit you,' he volleyed.

'And arrogance doesn't suit you,' she returned.

A gasp turned into a choke over Antonio's shoulder. His lawyer, looking almost as shocked as Ivy felt.

She turned to leave, half expecting to feel his hand around her wrist, the same way he had once done when she'd dismissed his proposal as a joke.

'This is important,' he said, his words stopping her departure instead.

She swallowed her impatience at his easy dismissal of her priorities and turned back to him. 'I am sure it feels that way to you, but there's not much I can do and it seems you both have this in hand.'

Antonio looked at her, appalled. 'Is that a joke?'

'Well, no. Not intentionally,' she said with a tilt of her head.

He ran a hand through his hair in frustration, before returning that burning gaze to hers. 'What would it take?' he asked, the words forced out through a jaw so tight it looked painful.

Ivy stared at him in confusion. 'What do you mean?'

'How much?'

'For what?' she asked, her patience fraying further.

'For you to come to Italy.' He looked at her, and what she saw in his eyes stopped her heart.

Disappointment. Inevitability. Resignation.

She took a moment to gather herself. She wanted to feel indignant, outraged even. But could she really expect him to think any better of her? After all, she had married him for money. It was no wonder he thought that money would get him what he wanted. But she was no longer that desperate nineteen-year-old and she wouldn't, *couldn't*, take any more of his money.

Shame painted red slashes on her cheeks as she shook her head. 'There is nothing, Mr Gallo. I can't come to Italy,' she said as firmly as she dared. Her job, her life—the life that she was only just beginning to get back on track—was here. And no amount of money would change that. Her phone buzzed, a message from work asking where she was. 'I want to help, I really do,' she said sincerely. 'But I must go. When you figure out how to make this work, please call?'

'I don't understand. Is that a question? Why is everything so complicated today?' he asked obtusely, the question clearly rhetorical.

'Mercury is in retrograde,' she offered with a touch of sarcasm, and allowed herself to relish the look on his face for a second before she hurried from the court.

She almost felt sorry for him. She doubted that Antonio Gallo was used to road blocks to his plans. Antonio might be the most aggressively handsome man that she'd ever encountered, but he was also the most ruthlessly selfish.

In the six years of their 'convenient' marriage, Ivy had reached out to him only once, three years ago. It had been the lowest point of her young life. She'd needed someone desperately. And, despite being called, he had not come. So she knew exactly what she meant to Antonio Gallo. Nothing. And it would remain that way. She would happily grant him the divorce they both needed, but she couldn't let it derail her own plans.

The only person she could rely on was herself. The only person who could choose her was her. She had learned that the hard way.

'This isn't over, Ms McKellen,' she heard him warn over her shoulder.

'I would imagine not,' she replied and hurried from the court to the bus that would take her to work, trying to ignore the way her feet burned with each step.

CHAPTER TWO

Ivy rubbed the ache at her left temple, hoping that the tension there was just that and nothing more. Her boss, the formidable Mrs Tenby, was still glaring disapprovingly at her after she had burst through the doors to the library nearly forty minutes late and soaking wet from the unexpected thunderstorm. Rain battered the large double-glazed windows, providing a light drumbeat over her fragile nerves.

Ivy was raiding the first aid box for a plaster for her heel when Mrs Tenby helpfully reminded her that if she'd hurt herself on the premises then it needed to be added to the first aid book.

'Yes, Mrs Tenby,' Ivy replied, feeling like an errant schoolchild for *nearly* misappropriating library resources.

She put the plaster back into the box and pulled the returns trolley into the stacks for reshelving, willing the quiet calm of the library to work its soothing magic after the sudden and shocking impact of that morning's events.

But, no matter how many books she tried to shelve, all she saw was Antonio. The sharp line of his cheekbone, proud above the dark shadow of stubble that made him look more rake than businessman. Raven's wing hair had glinted beneath the courthouse's strip lighting and he seemed as out of place as a peacock strutting amongst the pigeons of Trafalgar Square.

In her mind's eye she saw him looking after her as she walked away and guilt lashed at her conscience. She wanted to help him, truly she did, and she hated that she couldn't go to Italy with him at the click of his fingers. Because marriage to him had been exactly as life-changing as she'd imagined it would be.

She thought of the picture her brother had sent her just last night. Grinning at the camera with twenty other young men and women. In military fatigues covered in mud, with a Scottish mountain range behind them, Jamie was almost unrecognisable from the angry, wayward kid he'd been at fifteen.

Thinking back to that time six years ago, she remembered how she'd been near sick with worry every minute of every day, desperate to come up with any solution to the demons he'd wrestled with. Drink, drugs, and the extreme anger that came from the deeply rooted hurt and confusion left behind by their absent parents was all he had known and nothing she'd said or done had got through to him. The helplessness of watching him lose the fight with his addictions over and over and over again had been devastating. He'd only had her, and Ivy had had no one. Her mother had left two years before and not been back once.

And when she'd called from France, or Spain, or wherever she was, it was always the same story, no matter how much Ivy had begged for her to come home.

'Oh, love, I've just met this guy and he's amazing, so I can't leave now. *But don't worry. Jamie will be just fine! He's a fighter, that one.'*

And if Ivy asked for money...

'Sorry, love. You're just going to have to make do.'

So she had. Ivy had made do the best she could, and it still hadn't been enough. Jamie had continued to spiral...

until Antonio's proposal. She'd used the money from their marriage to send Jamie to an intensive residential rehab facility and put down a deposit on a small flat. For a man like Antonio Gallo, it was probably less money than he earned in a week, but to Ivy it had been a miracle.

Which was why she felt so terrible telling Antonio she couldn't go to Italy. She wanted to help him, she really did, but she couldn't risk losing this job. It had been made painfully clear to her by Mrs Tenby that the one condition of her appointment to the role was that she couldn't take her leave during the summer holidays because all the other staff were parents who needed that time for their children.

As much as she felt guilty, she also knew that she couldn't sacrifice her job for Antonio. Because when he got what he wanted he'd be out of her life and she'd never see him again. Just like her mother.

She shelved the last of the trolley's books, slowly breathing through the hurt from that painful time, and returned to the desk for the next, but stopped short at the sight of Anita, the assistant librarian, eyes rimmed red, and Mrs Tenby in an uncharacteristic display of kindness rubbing circles on her back.

'What happened?' Ivy asked, leaving the trolley and approaching the pair.

Anita shook her head, clearly incapable of words.

'Is it Tommy?' Ivy asked, fear curling her stomach at the thought of something happening to Anita's two-year-old boy.

'No, no. Nothing like that,' Mrs Tenby explained quickly.

'We lost Morrison,' Anita said through sobs. 'He's had to withdraw his funding.'

'No!' Ivy exclaimed.

'He's devastated but he lost one of his biggest clients and now can't afford to donate to the afterschool programme,' Anita explained as Ivy's heart sank. That was terrible news. Mr Morrison had been the biggest donor to the library's afterschool club.

'All the children we've promised places to…'

'They'll have nowhere to go,' Ivy finished, realising why Anita was so devastated.

'Oh, it's so silly. I don't know why I'm crying,' Anita said, waving her hands in front of her eyes. 'It's not his fault. And all the parents knew the places were conditional on funding. But the children were so excited, and it's such a shock. Especially having just secured the library association's agreement to match our donations.'

They'd been so close to meeting their target, but with Mr Morrison withdrawing nearly one hundred thousand pounds in donations, and government funding going elsewhere, they wouldn't be able to get the money they needed to get the afterschool club off the ground. It was something all three women had invested a lot of time, energy and belief into, each of them knowing how desperately needed this was for the local community.

'I don't know what we're going to do,' Anita said miserably.

'There will be a way,' Ivy said, forcing a determination she didn't feel into her words.

'How?' Anita asked hopelessly.

'How much? For you to come to Italy.'

'I'll think of something.' Ivy said, feeling torn.

The afterschool club was a vital resource for local families who worked multiple jobs that couldn't fit around school hours, let alone afford childcare. If there had been an afterschool club when she and Jamie were younger, he might have stayed away from vices that had turned to addictions. They might have had somewhere warm, bright, creative and full of art and people to go to, instead of a cold flat with no food in the fridge and a mother who wasn't home.

Ivy had been sixteen when her mother had first gone away. It was just a holiday, two weeks with her new boyfriend, and of course Ivy was old enough to look after her younger brother. Six months later, her mother was off again, only this time she didn't come back for a month. The next time had been even longer and Ivy couldn't let anyone know. Not school, not friends…because social services would come and they'd take Jamie away and she couldn't let that happen. She had to protect him.

There were some government services that were scarier and more dangerous than helpful, but the library wasn't one of them. And it twisted her heart to be so close yet so far from what was such an important part of the local community. She felt Mrs Tenby's intense glare warning her not to make promises she couldn't keep. But that was the thing. Ivy kept her promises. Every single time. Whatever it had taken. Because she'd been let down too badly by a mother whose promises had always been empty.

Antonio's question whispered inside her mind again, and no matter how hard she tried to force it down, it returned to her on a loop.

She bit her lip, returning to the stacks to shelve the returns on autopilot. Could she? Could she ask him for more money? Was she shameless enough to do it?

Not for herself. She could never have asked for herself. But this wasn't for her. It was for the library, the community, the parents who wouldn't have to choose between their job or their child. Thoughts crowded her brain and a wave of exhaustion overcame her. She'd already done a lot in one day, between the court visit, Antonio and now this. Her eyes began to ache.

Take things step by step and if you need a break, take that too, she told herself.

And promptly ignored it. She returned books to their shelves quicker and quicker as her mind turned over. She could ask him for the money—just for what they needed. It was less than he'd paid her to marry him. Although she baulked at the idea of extracting money from him, he'd offered it to her, hadn't he?

Yet she'd told him that there was nothing he could do, no amount he could pay her.

She pressed her teeth together, trying to ground herself, as she thought through how it would go. How she would, of course, be confirming every worst thought he had about her being a money-grabber. Because she'd seen it in his eyes when he'd offered her the money. The expectation that she was simply out for what she could get.

Ivy swallowed the feeling of nausea welling from deep within. She reminded herself of the good that she had done for Jamie with the money. The rehab centre that had turned him around and the flat they'd had—the home—even if it had just been for a few short years, it had been enough security to get him started on a new life path. She could do the same again. Use Antonio's money to help others. The determination, the plan forming in her mind soothed her jaded heartbeat and jagged breathing. It had worked before—it could work again.

Mrs Tenby might have refused her a holiday request so soon after starting, but if it would help them secure the funding they needed, surely that would be different?

All she'd have to do was ask Antonio for the money.

She was returning the trolley to the desk when she had a horrible thought. What if he'd already found a way to circumvent Judge Carmondy's requirements? What if he didn't need her to go to Italy any more? Suddenly the plans she'd begun to make in her head disappeared like the end of a road and she mentally screeched to a halt. Panic broke out in a cold sweat at the back of her neck.

Her phone buzzed in her pocket. Retrieving it, she scanned the message from the unknown number.

We need to meet.

A shiver of apprehension cut through her. The way that she'd been thinking of him when he'd messaged her was unnerving. Ivy didn't have to guess who it was from. Only Antonio Gallo would dare send such a message without even bothering to sign his name.

She typed back.

When?

Now.

She frowned and messaged back.

I'm working.

'As I said before, Ivy, this is more important,' Antonio said from behind her.

Antonio watched an entire range of emotions pass across Ivy's fine features. Shock, surprise, guilt...*hope*. With her hair swept back from her face in a knot atop her head, they were exquisitely on display and he wondered at them. A light dusting of freckles covered the bridge of a perfect nose, small enough and just slightly upturned enough to be considered cute.

He took in a small scar halfway along her jaw that hadn't been there when he'd known her six years. Seeing it set off a small twist in his memory, something he should have remembered but couldn't quite…

The thought disappeared before it could take hold as she bit into her bottom lip, slicked only with gloss that made it look simple, homely. All the things that the women he encountered on the rare occasions he socialised disguised in an attempt to garner his attention.

His lawyer had warned him not to go to the library where Ivy worked, fearing that Antonio's wife would recognise the power she held at that moment. But the one thing Antonio knew about Ivy was that she wasn't calculating in the least. Had she wanted to, she could have demanded twice as much six years ago. Negotiation hadn't even crossed her mind.

Yes, he'd been surprised that she'd denied his request—demand?—to follow him to Italy, and she'd baulked at his offer of money. But she didn't understand the severity of the situation for him. He'd come here to plead his case, but something had changed, he could tell. He didn't know what, and he didn't care. As long as it resulted in her agreement to pursue this farce of a plan the judge had cooked up.

Simon had informed him that the judge was beloved in the UK, which just went to show how crazy the English were, and that no one would be willing to either defy or circumvent his decision. They just had to get through these 'assessments' as quickly as possible—time was running out.

Antonio had one month to meet the requirements of the will. And only then would Maria finally be free to inherit the company she deserved more than anyone else. Gio might have entailed the whole of Gallo Group to Maria and Antonio on the occasion of their marriage, but Antonio had absolutely no intention of touching his grandfather's company. Maria was the one who had sacrificed blood, sweat and tears, she had danced to their grandfather's tune, and Antonio was determined to see that his cousin got what she deserved. Because if she didn't, the entire company would go to Micha Rufina, their grandfather's henchman, and while Antonio didn't care a single bit about the company, he *did* care about that.

Aside from his mother, Maria was the only person who had treated him like family from the very first, even when others hadn't. And he would do whatever it took to repay that kindness. So, he had come to the work address listed on Ivy's paperwork to convince her that she needed to come back to Italy with him.

Ivy took a step towards him and then stopped, claiming his focus.

'You can't be here,' she whispered, staring around her as if someone—her boss presumably—would come and tell her off.

Antonio bit back a sigh of impatience, frustrated that she was bothering to fight this. He just didn't have time. He opened his mouth to say as much when she cut him off.

'What would you do if I barged into your boardroom and demanded you return to England with me?' she pressed on.

Laugh.

He didn't have to say it. She knew the answer.

'Precisely,' she concluded, hugging the worn hardback to her chest as if it were armour.

He clenched his jaw, feeling the muscle flickering under the strain of holding back his frustration. In an ideal world he'd have liked to be less blunt, but he didn't have time for gentle. Brutal was perhaps the only way to get through to her.

'Ivy—let me be painfully clear. I need this divorce. A billion-dollar company hangs in the balance. It employs over four hundred thousand people globally, it has contracts with household name companies, and stocks and shares and subsidiaries that would make any businessman weep. So, forgive me for being crude, but your single job that can't pay much more than twenty-five thousand pounds is literally the definition of less important.'

Eyes widening as each word struck, outrage warred with shock, and then confusion.

'I didn't realise that Alessina International had grown so big,' she said, taking a step back.

This time, Antonio frowned. He wasn't talking about *his* company, but she was. She knew about that?

'It hasn't. I'm talking about Gallo Group,' he clarified.

She frowned, evidently taking in that piece of information. 'I'm sorry, I don't see how a divorce will help with that?' she said, doing that question/statement thing again that he found so hard to translate.

He paused, taking a breath, buying a few seconds to debate how much to tell her. He baulked at providing information that would give her power over him, reminded himself that she wasn't so much of a threat, remembered that looks could be deceiving, and finally concluded that, despite every instinct to the contrary, he needed to tell her the truth.

'I need to marry Maria.'

Her face did a strange scrunchy thing to express her confusion.

'The same Maria you married me to *avoid* marrying six years ago?' she asked, coming a step closer. 'Your cousin Maria?'

The irony was not lost on him. Six years ago, Antonio had believed the only way to escape his grandfather's demand that he marry his cousin in order to ensure the familial succession of Gallo Group was to remove himself completely from that scenario by marrying Ivy.

Finding a suitable successor had been an obsession for Gio Gallo. He had considered none of his five children remotely worthy and had, in fact, already disinherited one of them.

And despite any number of cousins and uncles and hangers-on who would have readily, nay, *gleefully*, welcomed taking on the mantle of Gallo Group, Gio had been firm; it would go to a grandchild.

Antonio had been ruled out, because even though he was the only child of Gio's eldest, he didn't have a single drop of Gallo blood. No, Antonio had been adopted and thus was *unsuitable*. Maria, by sole default of being female, was also *unsuitable*.

But in Gio Gallo's mind, if Antonio married his non-blood-related cousin Maria, their child would be of Gallo blood as well as being linked to his eldest child, and as such the child would be the *successor supreme*. And while it might be considered a unique example of two wrongs making a right, both he and Maria had, naturally, been horrified by the prospect, with neither feeling for the other anything remotely more than familial love.

Burying the deep sense of rejection and hurt caused by his grandfather's actions, Antonio had told no one of his plan to avoid Gio's manipulations. Not Maria, not his mother. He'd done it quickly and quietly, before anyone could stop him.

He'd come to England with two intentions: first, find a way to make it absolutely impossible for Gio to force the marriage between him and Maria. This had been achieved when he'd married Ivy and, as far as Antonio was concerned, Gio would just have to find someone else to take over Gallo Group.

And second, to start his own business. One that couldn't be taken away, bargained, bribed or used against him in any way. And at the age of twenty-nine, Antonio had done that. Six years of inconceivably hard work, long hours, sacrifice and self-determination. He had become utterly self-sufficient, financially independent, worth many millions in his own right, and had ensured security for his mother and, should she have wanted it, his cousin Maria.

But Maria had done the exact opposite. She had, instead, worked at Gallo Group for years. She had poured all her efforts and energy into it, hoping to eventually prove her worth to a grandfather who couldn't see beyond her chromosomes. And it hadn't meant a single thing. Gio had, in his last will and testament, left the company to her conditionally. And the outcome was that if they *didn't* marry the company would go straight to Micha, and neither he nor Maria would ever allow that to happen.

'Yes,' he said, finally acknowledging Ivy's question. 'I intend to marry my cousin, Maria.'

'Because a billion-dollar company hangs in the balance?' she asked.

'*Sì*,' he said, before contradicting himself. 'If we marry, the company comes to us. And then I can give it to Maria.'

'Why didn't he just leave it to you?'

His jaw ticked. 'Because I am not my mother's son by blood.'

Ivy frowned even deeper. 'What does *that* have to do with anything?'

'It was important to my grandfather.' *And my father.* It was an errant thought, ruthlessly pushed aside. 'The Gallos have strong feelings on legitimacy and blood ties.'

She frowned at him, as if wanting to disagree. But he'd long ago given up trying to understand his grandfather's motivations because, blood or not, Antonio *was* a Gallo—and it was a surname that meant everything to him.

'Okay, so why can't Maria inherit the company on her own then?'

'Because she is a woman.'

Ivy reared back and Antonio raised his hands in surrender. 'This is not how *I* feel, I assure you. But it is crucial that we marry so that she can inherit the company and prevent it from going elsewhere.'

'Where would elsewhere be?'

'To someone unworthy,' he said, utterly unaware how like his grandfather he sounded in that moment.

'Why don't you want it—Gallo Group?' she asked.

He stopped, surprised by her question.

'You said, "And then I can give it to Maria"?' she pressed.

Alert now that he had revealed too much and she had been quick enough to spot it, he hesitated before he answered. 'I don't need it,' he lied, choosing his words carefully. He refused to admit that the betrayal he'd felt at his grandfather's belief in his inferiority had poisoned his family's company for him for ever.

'But we are running out of time to meet the terms of the will,' he continued, pressing the issue.

'How long do you have?'

'One month.'

Ivy's mouth formed a little 'o'. Not in shock, almost a silent 'oh'. It confused him, the way she communicated. And when she looked back up at him the blue of her eyes caught him by surprise, just like they had the first time he'd seen her in the London café.

'Can you give me five minutes?'

Her question interrupted his train of thought, thankfully. *'Sì.'*

She nodded and walked past him, away from the shelves. His gaze followed her, almost unwillingly, and when he noticed the slight limp in her stride he frowned at the inflamed slash of red at her heel.

'You're bleeding,' he called after her.

She spun round, something like fear on her features, her hand rising to her eye, of all places.

'Your heel,' he explained, and she looked down.

'Oh. Yes.' And then, unfathomably, she turned and continued to walk away.

A headache pressed against his temples. He had already spent too long in London and didn't have time for the confusing roundabout ways of the English. Nothing was simple here. No one said what they meant and, after a childhood of misinformation and misdirection, after his grandfather's manipulations, he disliked that intensely.

Mindlessly, he scanned the bookshelves, distracting himself from the questions pouring through his mind. The only way he'd managed to achieve what he had in the last six years was to focus on what he wanted to the exclusion of everything else. Ruthlessly so, some had said. But it had worked, hadn't it?

Footsteps approached him and he turned to find Ivy, still holding the book to her, as if she'd forgotten it but needed it at the same time.

She cleared her throat, a pink flare filling the delicate hollow beneath her cheekbones.

She nodded before she spoke. 'I can come to Italy if...' She swallowed and he waited. There was always an if. It was inevitable and yet he dismissed the strange feeling of disappointment.

'If you can give me ninety thousand pounds,' she finished in a near whisper.

Ninety thousand...

He masked his surprise. Behind Ivy, at the end of the shelves, two women peered into the stacks, failing in their attempt to look inconspicuous.

Ninety thousand pounds?

She could have asked for anything. But Antonio was as confused as he was near offended by the insignificant amount. So much so that his natural inclination to barter, to haggle, absolutely disappeared. Before he remembered the poster at the reception desk that he'd passed on the way to find her.

Star Donator: Michael Morrison for providing ninety thousand pounds!

It couldn't be a coincidence. The exact same amount of money she was asking for. Was she not asking for herself?

Did it even matter? Not at that precise moment in time, no. What did matter was that he had everything he needed to meet Carmondy's ridiculous demands.

'So, to confirm. I will pay you ninety thousand pounds in exchange for two weeks of your time in Italy, to comply with whatever it takes to satisfy the terms of Judge Carmondy's assessor and however the assessor expects us to *prove* that we have given our marriage a true and proper 'go', before finally appearing before the judge again to ask for a divorce,' he stated succinctly.

Ivy, wide-eyed, nodded.

'Done,' he informed her.

'Really?' she asked, seemingly surprised to find it that easy.

'I can have it in your account in five minutes,' he announced. 'I just need your account details.'

'It's actually not my account,' Ivy said, wincing as if that might change his mind.

'Ivy, I don't care,' he said, almost truthfully. Because his curiosity *had* been piqued, but he could satisfy that on his own time. 'Now, can we go?'

Ivy threw some clothes into an old holdall of Jamie's. She'd explained to Mrs Tenby that she would only need two weeks of holiday, but the watery-eyed woman had insisted that she take as long as was needed. The fact that Ivy would be using it to secure enough funding to fill the hole left by Michael Morrison was enough to soften even her icy demeanour.

Ivy looked around her bedroom, wondering what else to take, painfully conscious that Antonio and his car were outside, waiting impatiently. She refused to think about what would happen when she got to Italy. She refused to wonder how they would prove that they were giving their marriage 'a go'. She knew from past experience she needed to take each day as it came, otherwise she would become overwhelmed to the point of stasis. And she couldn't do that. Not again.

Two beeps from a car horn sounded from outside.

Keys, passport, clothes, phone charger and, most importantly, camera. If she had those, she'd be fine, she promised herself.

The number for her doctor was in her phone. He'd insisted that she could travel when she'd taken a moment to call him before letting Antonio know she would come to Italy. At her request, the doctor had explained, for the hundredth time, that she was at no more risk than anyone else of the retinal detachment happening either in her good eye or worsening her bad eye. He'd reminded her that she knew the warning signs. But preventatively? There was nothing she could do but live her life.

Yet, despite that reassurance, her heart still pounded in her chest.

'Go to Italy. Make the most of it. Have fun,' the doctor had said.

Fun? Perhaps there were some people on the planet for whom having fun involved a private jet to a villa in Tuscany and spending time with a man like Antonio Gallo. But she knew first-hand how dangerous it was to build sandcastle dreams about the Italian billionaire. Because three years ago she'd learned *very* vividly that she was not important to him in the slightest.

Perhaps that was fair for a man who had never said otherwise. But at least she knew where she stood. It was a lesson she had learned first from her mother and then him. So no, she was under no illusions about Antonio. But he *had* paid her to do this and she would do it to the best of her ability.

She scribbled a note to the flatmate she barely saw and

left her mobile number in case of emergencies. It felt almost surreal to lock her front door, leave the flat and, after giving her bag to the driver, get into a car that would take her to a private airfield.

A car that had brought her and an impatient Antonio to her flat from the library. She hadn't missed the way that Antonio had peered up at the house her flat was part of. The way that he'd—albeit discreetly—raked his gaze over his surroundings, more wary than disdainful. But it had made her hyperaware of the fact that they came from very different worlds.

As she buckled herself back into the seat, the driver putting her very small bag in the boot of the town car, she felt the build-up of questions fill the car. So it wasn't surprising when Antonio finally asked the question, but she still felt his censure.

'Is there anything left of the money I originally gave you?' he said, his voice steely. With judgement, she wondered, or was she just being sensitive?

Ivy turned to look out of the window to see what he saw. It clearly wasn't anything like the luxury he was used to, but she refused to be ashamed of it. No, there wasn't any money left from what he'd given her six years ago. It had been used: spent or lost for reasons beyond her control. She had worked hard for every penny she now had and she was proud of that, but she wouldn't lie to him.

'No.'

A cool silence descended between them, until Antonio passed her a small box before returning his attention to his phone. Frowning, she opened the white plastic box to find a first aid kit inside.

Her heel.

She'd been in such a hurry to pack her clothes, she

hadn't even changed out of what she was wearing, or her shoes. She could change on the plane, and she'd deal with the cut then. To do so now, with Antonio so close, it felt too...personal. *Vulnerable.*

'Thank you,' she whispered and only the slight nod of his head told her that he'd heard.

The driver took them straight onto the tarmac of the airfield, where his jet was fuelled and ready to leave. Air staff brought the few bags they had onto the plane and checked them in on their flight path plan.

Ivy was still holding the first aid kit as she buckled herself into the seat on the opposite side of the cabin from him, but honestly, she was old enough to look after herself and he couldn't waste time worrying about a blister. Let alone whatever she'd spent the money he'd paid her to marry him on. Yes, he remembered that her brother had needed help, but a part of him was strangely disappointed. He'd expected that she'd have done more with it, and that he'd read her wrong was unsettling. But none of it was important and to distract himself with such curiosity was ridiculous.

He finally typed out a message to Maria.

I'm on my way.

What kept you?

A judge, a marriage and a librarian.

Is that a joke?

Sadly not.

He stole one last glance at the librarian in question before he opened his laptop. He wondered whether she was ready for what was about to come. Because, in truth, he wasn't entirely sure *he* was. To prove that they had given their marriage 'a go' would presumably require them to 'be married'. He didn't think even the judge was crass enough to suggest that they share a bed, but he had a sneaking suspicion that there would be marital hoops they would have to jump through, and that neither he, Ivy, nor anyone else involved would emerge unscathed.

CHAPTER THREE

Ivy squinted at the Italian countryside through tinted windows, passing at a rate of approximately seventy miles an hour. Antonio had spent almost the entire journey glued to his phone and she let the Italian wash over her in fits and starts.

Before the accident, she'd spent some time studying his language, inspired by Antonio and encouraged by her boss at Affogato, the job she'd kept to help pay the mortgage. Between the rehabilitation centre's fees and a deposit on a flat, the money Antonio had given her to marry him hadn't exactly been a free pass on living expenses, but it had been a measure of security and stability.

And those eighteen months had been some of the happiest she'd ever had. She'd even thought about going to university, maybe to study art like she'd always wanted to, but Jamie's addiction hadn't been a quick fix. He'd spent a year or two in and out of rehab, and another year getting himself fit to enrol in the army. She'd needed—*wanted*—to be there for him.

But Ivy still remembered some of her language lessons, so she was able to pick up some things Antonio had said into his phone and, while the business jargon was lost on her, it simply added just *more* to the fact that Ivy was in *Italy*. And, no matter what had brought her here, the sight of the tall cypress trees on the hill ridge in the distance, the patchwork quilt of farms and vineyards, the heat in the air, so different to anything she'd experienced in the UK, filled her with the kind of excitement that was foreign to her. She would make the most of this, she promised herself. For all she knew, it could be years before she had the money and the opportunity to leave England again.

Before long, the car turned off the main road, venturing deeper into the hills and valleys of the countryside and her curiosity as to what Antonio's home was like increased. He'd explained that she'd have her own room, and that he was going to be *very busy*—she'd all but heard capital letters—and that she could do whatever she wanted, as long as she was there for the appointed visits.

The lawyer, Simon, seemed to be working out the specifics and really, she didn't need to get involved in what she was sure was a complicated process. She certainly didn't want to mess it up.

'A billion-dollar company hangs in the balance... I need to marry Maria.'

She felt a little sorry for Antonio. Not just because he was, six years later, in almost exactly the same position as he had been. But also that he seemed perfectly fine with throwing marriage around as if it meant nothing.

She stared out at the patches of land covered in the blurry yellows of sunflowers or the sunburnt greens of tobacco plants. She'd had some time to think about what marriage meant to her in the last six years, and while nothing in her experience had caused her to change her mind, she still couldn't help but think that Antonio was just repeating a mistake he'd already made. But then, in some ways, wasn't she too? Perhaps Antonio was meant to marry Maria after all.

The car pulled off the road again and, to her delight, the

tree-lined avenue surpassed even her wildest dreams about Italy. Closing one eye to focus, she followed the winding track upwards and round a corner she caught the glimpse of a villa at the hill's peak and her mouth dropped open.

Eyes glued to the sight of it, her heart soared. She'd never seen anything more beautiful. Through the tall green slashes of cypress trees, glimpses of soft yellow walls and carved stone features called to her. Here and there, she caught glimpses of another building in soft grey stone rather than plaster. They peered down at the verdant hills and valleys below.

'It's beautiful,' she couldn't help saying. His attention turned on her like a touch and she felt gauche for being so impressed by something he saw every day. But even that couldn't take away from the awe she felt as they approached the villa.

The car drew to a halt and she got out as the driver, unable to discharge his duty to her, moved instead to open Antonio's door. She missed the disruption she'd caused to routine etiquette as she took in the sprawling building that could clearly and easily house twenty people at least.

It was stunning and her fingers itched to reach for the camera in her bag. To peer through the viewfinder, to frame the image in single focus, rather than the double vision that had plagued her ever since the accident. But, feeling the tension rolling off Antonio, she knew that now wasn't the time to ask.

Even with her vision impaired, the scale and breadth of Antonio's villa—his wealth—was astounding. He hadn't inherited this. She knew that he'd been cut off by his grandfather, presumably the moment Antonio had shown proof of his marriage to her. Even in the UK, news of the Italian tycoon's decision to disinherit his grandson had made the headlines.

She looked back at him to find him watching her, his expression unfathomable, and once again she felt naïve, foolish, but most of all fearful that he thought all she saw was the money, rather than the beauty in his home.

The proud jut of his chin was a warning. His shoulders, drawn in defensive slashes beneath his shirt. He didn't want her here. It was evident, but not because it was *her*. His discomfort didn't feel personal, it felt... Like *she'd* felt at the thought of him filling her cramped flat back in South West London.

'It's beautiful,' she told him again, this time purposely, hoping that he saw the truth of her words.

He nodded, and turned to pass through the open doors beneath dark grey stone mouldings. The buzz of his phone echoed around the foyer she followed him into, bouncing off the terracotta tiles beneath her feet. He answered while pointing at a discreetly dressed older lady waiting at the bottom of a staircase so grand she expected it to be cordoned off by a red velvet rope. In rapid Italian he both answered his phone and conveyed to the woman, who appeared to be a housekeeper, that she was to take Ivy to her room, before disappearing into what seemed to be an office.

Ivy smiled apologetically at the woman who, Ivy imagined, drew on her professionalism to conceal her shock either at Ivy's presence or simply her appearance.

'Le borse, signora?'

Before Ivy could answer, Antonio yelled from the room that she only had the one bag, not to worry about it and just to show her to her room.

Ivy pinned her lips between her teeth to prevent the smile at the older woman's huff, and was halfway up the stairs before a stream of loud curses turned the air blue.

***

Madonna mia, Antonio was going to kill his lawyer, burn this day to the ground and leave the ashes smoking, while he went to the *taverna* in the local village and drowned himself in a bottle of Valpolicella.

They could all go to hell. His family, his grandfather, the judge.

His housekeeper, Agata, began yelling at him before he'd even slammed down the phone, berating him for his coarse language with a few colourful terms of her own. He stalked back out into the foyer and found his housekeeper and his wife—*Ivy*—staring at him, one outraged, one concerned.

'What's wrong?' Ivy asked.

Antonio drew in a deep breath.

'It seems in his apparent hurry to ensure that our court-appointed visits are done with as soon as possible, Simon has arranged for the first assessment to take place in—' he checked his watch '—one hour and forty-five minutes.'

Antonio was becoming used to the way that shock widened Ivy's eyes enough to see even more of the bright blue irises. Now was not the time to notice the way that shards of gold flecked the blue, or the way that her skin flushed when she was surprised.

He cursed again, loudly. Earning himself another reprimand from Agata.

'But we only saw the judge this morning,' Ivy said, slowly coming down the stairs, holding onto the banister for support.

'I know.'

He *asked* his housekeeper to take Ivy's bag and unpack it in her room and gestured for Ivy to follow him. He made his way down the long corridor that split the ground floor down the middle, at the end of which was his favourite room in the whole villa.

He entered the kitchen, walking straight to the wine fridge, and retrieved a decent pale yellow Soave and grabbed two glasses. The Valpolicella would have to wait because Ivy looked as if it might knock her out. Thankful that she wasn't peppering him with a thousand questions like Maria would have, or whipping her emotions into a silent tornado, like his mother, he pushed open the back door and emerged into the oasis of the large pergola-covered patio, where he took a single moment to inhale the scents of home—bougainvillea, citrus and wild fennel—before nudging a chair out from the table for her with his foot and placing the glasses down.

'Did Simon find out what the assessments will entail?' she asked as she sat down. 'What is the assessor going to expect us to know?'

'I don't know. So, this is what we're going to do,' he explained to Ivy as he poured them each a glass and handed one to her. 'We're going to spend the next hour and forty minutes getting to know as much about each other as possible.'

Ivy's eyes were still huge. 'Are you sure that's a good idea?'

'Is there another option?'

'Food poisoning?' she offered, clearly only half joking.

And for a second he considered it, before dismissing it. 'From my private jet?'

'Fair enough. Okay. Just give me...' She held up her finger, brought the glass to her mouth and downed the entire contents.

The horror on his face must have shown.

'I'm sorry,' she said genuinely. 'I'm a really terrible liar.'

'And you tell me this now?' he demanded. '*After* extracting ninety thousand pounds from me?'

She winced. 'I thought I'd have more time to prepare. But if I'm drunk, then it will just look like I'm drunk. Isn't that better than being caught out for lying?'

He willed his mouth not to drop at her logic. And then poured her another glass. 'We'll do both,' he decided.

'If it's any consolation, I'm not much of a drinker, so it really shouldn't take long. Or waste too much of your alcohol,' she explained.

'It's not,' he replied. 'A consolation,' he clarified when she appeared confused by his response.

She shrugged apologetically and took another worryingly large mouthful.

'Okay,' he said, taking the glass from her. 'Slow down. We want drunk, not throwing up.'

He leaned back in the seat opposite her and tried to get his nerves under control. What was wrong with him? He didn't get flustered like this. It was her. Ivy. In his house. No one came to his house. Not even his mother, or his cousin.

He just needed to focus. That was all.

'We need to make it look like we did marry for love, but that it didn't work out. And that now our lives are so very different it would be untenable to continue with the marriage.'

'Right.' She nodded. 'So, it doesn't matter that we haven't been living together?'

'No,' Antonio said.

'But did we ever?'

'How much did you drink?' he asked her, suddenly worried.

'No, I mean, we're going to have to lie about our…history, right?'

'Yes,' he said, closing his eyes in understanding. 'Of course. *Sì*. Yes. We lived together in England. But not Italy.'

Ivy bobbed her head in agreement, the long chestnut layers of hair picking up the glimmer of the setting sun. 'I suppose the assessor is going to expect us to know things about each other?'

Antonio nodded, before abruptly shooting a question at her. 'What is your favourite colour?' he demanded.

'Red,' Ivy replied, trying not to let his rapidly fired question throw her. It had been the easiest colour for her to see following the accident. Rich, vibrant, lipstick red. 'You?'

'Blue,' he said, barely stopping to take a breath before asking, 'How do you take your coffee?'

'I don't,' she admitted. 'I don't really like the taste.'

Antonio spluttered. 'But you worked in a coffee shop.'

This time she couldn't help but laugh. 'Not because I like coffee, Antonio. I just needed the money,' she said.

He stared at her as if he were trying to reframe what he thought of her.

'*Va bene*. Family?' he pressed on.

'One brother, Jamie,' she said.

'Parents?'

She sighed; the topic of her parents was always difficult. 'We haven't heard from our father in about ten years now. And our mother...she remarried and lives abroad,' she replied, remembering the phone call from four years ago vividly.

'I got married! To Ted! Oh, love. He's just wonderful. He really is.'

'When?' was all Ivy had been able to ask.

'Last week. We didn't want to bother you about it. Especially as it would have been so far for you to come.'

'So far?'

'Boston. I'm in Boston! We have to be here because Ted needs to be near his daughter.'

A daughter only two years younger than Jamie. And six years younger than her. Ivy swallowed. Her mother hadn't even asked about Jamie, her own child. She hadn't even asked how Ivy was, what she was doing, whether they needed anything.

'You?' she asked him to stave off any further delving into her personal life.

'Family? Lots. Gio had five children. My mother, Alessia, was the eldest. The eldest son, also called Gio, passed away before I was born. Uncle Carlos was next, but he is unmarried with no children. There was Aunt Amalia, who Gio disinherited long before trying that on with me. She had the gall to marry an American actor, much to my grandfather's horror. She had a son, our cousin Enzo, who we met for the first time at the funeral. And then the youngest is Uncle Luca, who is Maria's father.'

Ivy swallowed. There was no way she was going to remember all that. And in the silence that settled between them, she wondered whether he realised that he'd listed his family by their importance to his grandfather.

'So why the library?'

'Mm?' she asked, catching up with the back and forth of the conversation.

'You work at the library. Is that just for money too?' he asked.

'Oh. No,' she replied, a small smile gracing her lips. 'Well, not *only* for the money,' she conceded. The library hadn't been where Ivy imagined she would end up working, end up finding her *purpose*. But it had been. 'It's an important part of the community,' she said judiciously to

Antonio. 'It's a place for people to come when they want to escape. It's a shelter. It's companionship.'

It's a haven.

'That's noble,' he mused.

'You say that like you don't believe in such a thing.'

Antonio shrugged, refusing to get drawn in further.

'And Alessina International? What exactly is a brokerage firm?' Ivy asked.

'I help negotiate between people who want to have something and people who want to sell something.'

Ivy could see how that worked. Money, transactions, she saw, were important to him.

'I'm proud of it,' he continued. 'We have offices in several major cities, employ over a thousand people and have a turnover that would make most businessmen weep,' he announced with a passion she could see was true and honest.

'Congratulations,' Ivy replied sincerely. 'I can't imagine how hard you had to work to make that happen. Especially in such a short amount of time.'

He nodded, accepting her praise, but she wasn't entirely sure he heard her. She'd meant it. Ivy really was impressed by what he'd achieved, knowing that it had been done in spite of his grandfather, rather than because of him.

But she couldn't help feeling that Antonio might be taking a wrong turn with what the assessor would be interested in.

'Do you think that the assessor might want to know other things, rather than what we know about each other?' Rather than each other's CVs, she thought privately, but stopped herself from saying that.

'No,' he dismissed. 'Honestly, this meeting will be a walk in the park. We'll just explain that we met in London—' he rolled his hand '—had a whirlwind romance—'

another roll '—we were young and wanted to be together, couldn't bear for it to end—'

He broke off as Ivy failed to stifle her laughter.

'What?' he demanded, for some reason moving her glass of wine slightly out of her reach.

'You might want to look a little less flippant when you say that,' she advised.

'Say what?'

'That we wanted to be together? It's undermined a little by the distaste so evident in your tone.'

Antonio's sigh of frustration as he sank back into the chair almost made Ivy feel sorry for him. Almost. She wondered whether his autocratic nature had increased because of the power and money he had amassed, or because people were intimidated by him and agreed to his every whim.

'Okay,' he said, leaning across the table and taking her hand. 'We were so young,' he said, repeating his earlier words, this time his tone like honey, pouring over her skin. 'We thought we were in love, unable to bear the agony of being apart.' The espresso-rich gaze bored into her, the intent furrow of his brow casting his face in shadow, emphasising the graze of stubble across his jawline.

Even though the dusk of the evening made it harder for her to see, Ivy was still hit by the near brutal impact of his masculinity. The shirt button, opened at his neck by frustrated impatient fingers, displayed a dusting of dark hair over olive skin, just enough to tease an underworked imagination. It had been years since she'd thought about men. Since she'd had the chance, or the inclination. After the accident, the little energy she did have was needed to simply get up and face the day.

'We married in a whirlwind,' he continued, drawing her

further into the fantasy he was weaving, utterly uncaring of the impact he was having on her, intentionally or otherwise. 'And for a few spectacular weeks it was perfection.'

She almost believed it herself, the sincerity in his voice, the way he was looking at her. As if…as if…

'But then reality hit, hard and fast. I had to return to Italy. You had to stay in England, and the relationship just petered out,' he concluded with a shrug.

Ivy nodded, willing her heartbeat to slow. Cleared her throat. 'Yes,' she whispered. 'I think that will be enough.'

'Signor Gallo? C'è qualcuno qui che vuole vederla.'

Ivy jumped at Agata's statement, wondering how long she had been standing in the doorway.

'The assessor is here. She's early,' he commented.

Ivy nodded, and cast a look at the remaining wine in her glass. It hadn't been a great idea—alcohol on top of the exhaustion and unfamiliarity of the location. She'd probably bump into a wall or something, but at least both Antonio and the assessor would only think she was tipsy.

'Shall I bring her outside?' Agata asked in Italian.

'Would it be better to take this inside? It's getting quite dark.' Ivy intervened before Antonio could make his decree.

Antonio looked at her, frowning as if she had said something unexpected, his eyes beginning to narrow. She looked away, and Agata cleared her throat. *'Signor?'*

'Salotto.'

Relief swept through Ivy as she followed him to the living room. He turned back to her, as if he were about to ask her a question, when clipped, determined footsteps claimed their attention.

They turned, unknowingly in unison, to watch the approach of a grey-clad no-nonsense woman in her late fifties. Steel-grey hair pulled back in a bun that appeared more brutal than efficient.

Ivy's heart sank. The woman immediately reminded her of Mrs Tenby and Judge Carmondy combined. There was no way that they'd be able to convince her of anything. She reached for Antonio's arm, trying to call his attention to her, wanting to warn him, because she was absolutely convinced that this—perhaps for the first time in his life—was a woman he wouldn't be able to charm. But he shook her off gently and went to greet the woman with a smile.

'Please forgive my lawyer, he was rude enough not to share your name with me,' Antonio explained with his hand outstretched.

The assessor stared at it for a beat longer than necessary—just enough to try and put a man like Antonio Gallo in his place—before taking it.

Ivy swallowed. This was going to be a total disaster.

This was going to be fine, Antonio told himself. All they had to do was get this woman on side, and that was something he excelled at.

He turned to the assessor as Ivy came to stand beside him.

'Would you like something to drink, Mrs—?'

'It's Ms Quell,' she informed him curtly.

Antonio swallowed his dislike of her tone. 'A drink, Ms Quell?'

'No. I would prefer to get this first assessment done as soon as possible, thank you.'

He nodded to Agata who—despite what most people thought—could speak fluent English when she wanted to and had practically done all his childhood homework with him. She withdrew from the room, leaving the three of them alone. He gestured for Ms Quell to take a seat and she took the middle of the sofa, retrieving an obscene amount of paperwork from her deceptively sized handbag. Ivy was forced to assume the place next to him on the opposite sofa.

'So, have you—?' he began.

'Mr Gallo, I assure you this will go much quicker if you let me take the lead,' Ms Quell interrupted.

'Absolutely,' he said, raising his hands in surrender.

He leaned back, his arm draped across the back of the sofa, perilously close to the thin column of Ivy's neck. But to remove his arm would be a display of discomfort and this woman, he thought, eyeing Ms Quell, was a shark. If she hadn't irritated him so much, he'd be offering her a job.

'Mr and Mrs Gallo. His Honour Judge Carmondy has ordered there to be three assessment interviews to take place over the next two weeks. These assessments will be in the form of three interviews—of which this is one—and one additional written assessment in the form of a questionnaire to be completed ahead of the next court date.

'The intention of these sessions is to verify that you have both given this marriage due and proper consideration before a divorce can be granted. Furthermore, as these sessions are court-appointed, they, and I, should be treated with all due respect. Do you both understand?'

'Yes,' they answered in unison.

'Mrs Gallo,' she said, turning to Ivy without any further delay.

Ivy blinked, eyes wider than necessary, and sat up straight.

'Why don't you tell me how you two met?'

'I was working in Affogato, a café in central London, when M… Antonio was in the country on business,' she began. Antonio winced at the near slip that would have—he was ninety percent sure—been 'Mr Gallo', and the least likely thing a wife would call her husband. She was going to ruin it.

'I couldn't take my eyes off her,' he said, intervening in the car crash that was about to happen. 'She's beautiful,' he said without having to lie.

Ms Quell acknowledged this with a tilt of her head.

'And beyond that, what most drew you to Mrs Gallo?' Ms Quell asked.

His mind blanked. Impossible. It had never before happened, but there was nothing.

'He's too shy to say,' Ivy confided, leaning towards Ms Quell conspiratorially. 'But I won him over with my espresso,' she teased. 'Impossible for a mere Englishwoman to be capable of matching the best coffee in the world. *Impossible*,' she said with a rather worryingly accurate mimicry of him.

For a moment he thought Ms Quell might actually smile.

'And you? What drew you to your husband?'

Something passed across Ivy's features—he only caught a glimpse of it, sitting beside her, but then he became distracted by her answer.

'He came to my rescue,' she said simply.

'Not literally.'

'Yes, literally,' Ivy said with a laugh that for some reason squeezed his stomach in a vice. 'I was being harassed by a difficult customer. It had been a hard, long day. I'm sure you can imagine. And you know what men can be like. The customer was being belligerent, and Antonio came to my aid. He was my hero,' she said, turning a glistening gaze on him.

If Ivy was a terrible liar, he'd eat his hat.

'Why was there such a rush for the marriage?' Ms Quell asked, scribbling notes down on the notepad in her lap.

'We were worried about family intervention,' Antonio supplied, also truthful.

'And once married, did you visit Italy?'

'Of course, I live here,' Antonio replied brusquely.

'I was asking *Mrs* Gallo.'

Ivy shook her head slowly. A slight wince in her eye made him wonder if something was wrong. A headache, perhaps? They had covered quite a lot of ground in one day, which couldn't have been usual for her.

Ms Quell frowned. 'How did you feel about that?' she asked, turning on him in the blink of an eye.

'Feel?' he repeated.

'Yes, Mr Gallo. How did you *feel* when Ivy wasn't able to follow you to Italy?'

'Frustrated,' he lied. 'I would have liked her to join me, but it wasn't possible. There were family matters to attend to.'

'Family matters that excluded your wife?' Ms Quell asked.

Antonio took a breath and suddenly felt Ivy's hand on his where it lay between them on the sofa, a warning.

'I didn't want my new wife to see my family the way that they were behaving at that time,' he forced through his teeth. Also, not an untruth.

'You were protecting her from your family,' Ms Quell clarified.

'*Si*. Yes.'

'And since then?'

Antonio opened his mouth.

'I'm not sure if you're aware, Ms Quell,' Ivy interrupted. 'But that was a difficult time for my husband. He was estranged from his grandfather for a significant period of time following the news of our marriage. Emotionally and financially. Antonio has spent the intervening years working harder than anyone alive to make the company he founded with nothing but grit and determination a multinational success. And I am so very proud of him for that. Truly. Even if it came at the cost of our marriage. A marriage that I will never regret. But we are no longer *in* a relationship and to pretend as such would be dishonourable, not only to Judge Carmondy but to each other,' Ivy concluded, shocking the words right out of Antonio's mind.

'I appreciate your words, Mrs Gallo. Mr Gallo should too, as they are clearly a very kind interpretation of what appears to have passed between you. But let me be clear. While this is a highly unusual situation and while I may be far more familiar with custody battles, alimony disputes, and the wants and needs of small children,' she said, peering directly at him with intent, 'I assure you, I take my job very seriously.

'I have been sent here to assess how you have tried to *repair* your marriage. Not grade how well you know each other, or identify what caused the rift. Tell me—*show* me—what you've done to try and bridge it,' she said, putting the monumental amount of paperwork back into her bag. 'You have two more sessions to show me this.'

On that note, Ms Quell left, and Ivy, deflated, sank back on the sofa beside him.

In that moment, Antonio Gallo was forced to admit to himself that he had greatly underestimated the ease with which they would navigate these 'assessments'. But there was no other option than to rise to the occasion if he was going to ensure that Maria got what she wanted.

CHAPTER FOUR

Ivy woke up in a panic, not knowing where she was. Her vision was worse than usual, and she knew that was because yesterday had been a lot. A lot more than she was used to at least. It came back to her in flashes and all jumbled in order. The judge, Antonio at the library, Ms Quell, Anita crying, a scribbled note to her flatmate. And two glasses of wine on an empty stomach.

She groaned as she turned on her side and, squinting at the clock, realised that it was seven-thirty in the morning. All she had eaten since the sandwich she'd hastily swallowed between the court and the library yesterday was a flapjack she'd found in her bag last night.

She would have asked Agata after Ms Quell left, and Antonio had locked himself in his office, but she'd not been able to find the housekeeper. And with no clue where the light switch was, Ivy had made it up here last night, frustrated and embarrassed that she'd had to feel around the walls like a woman with no sight. Which wasn't true. She was a woman with three-quarters of her sight, so she could stop feeling sorry for herself and get on with things. The problem was that she didn't know what 'things' she was supposed to be getting on with here in Antonio's Tuscan villa.

She threw back the covers and wandered over to the windows, pulling back the largest curtains she'd ever seen to gasp at the sight through the window. Pressing one hand to her chest and squinting through her good eye, the sun stretched lazy morning rays over rows and rows of grape vines, before rolling green hills reached a small town over in the distance. She could just make out the terracotta roofs and tall church towers.

She grabbed her camera from her bag and held it up in front of the window. Even when she was alone, it felt more natural to hold the viewfinder up and for her to be able to see the world entirely as she wanted it to be.

The sight in her good eye was still excellent. But the damage done by the first retinal detachment from the trauma of the accident had been compounded by a second detachment. She'd been lucky in that a visiting specialist from Greece had treated her and performed miracles according to the medical community. Her case was now taught at hospitals around the world, and she was at least—in some part—thankful that some good had come out of the shocking bicycle accident that had left her reeling when it had dramatically changed her life as she knew it.

And while there was still a possibility that her brain would eventually adjust to the differences in the information that each eye provided, for three years she had lived in a world that had one strong image, superimposed by a second, shadow image just a few millimetres out, and that was unlikely to change now. There were times when it was harder than others, but none were as awful as the moment that the darkness had slowly come down over one eye as the second detachment had occurred. The inching black had struck a fear so severe into her heart that she still felt the echoes of it even now. But she knew better than to give in to that fear. It had claimed nearly a year of her life following the accident, and she wouldn't let it claim any more.

She made her way to an en suite bathroom so beautiful she thought she could live in it, showered, and dried off with the fluffiest of towels as she reconciled the incongruity of seeing her toothbrush and paste in such splendour. She ran her fingers through her hair, relishing the heat of Italy that made it possible to dry it naturally. She pulled on a fresh change of clothes and went in search of food.

Ivy followed the stairs back down to the large beautiful kitchen. In the morning light she was able to see it much better than she had yesterday, when they'd simply passed through it on the way to the garden.

She found Agata bustling around the pristine space.

'Cosa le porto, signora?'

Ivy was about to answer when Agata's offer to get her something was translated into English from behind her. She turned to find Antonio, clean-shaven, hair as damp as her own, looking fresh and crisp and all the things that she didn't quite feel.

In a blue shirt and tan linen trousers, he was almost enough to make her forget Agata's question.

'I'll have a herbal tea if you have one? Or mint? I noticed there was some in your garden last night,' she said, turning to Agata. 'That would be lovely, but I can make it?'

Agata fussed and shook off her offer, and Ivy realised that Agata spoke at least as much English as Ivy spoke Italian.

'Grazie,' Ivy said with a smile as the housekeeper disappeared into the garden.

She braced herself before turning back to Antonio. Really, the sight of him had blown apart her defences and she needed to gather them before facing him again. Her dreams last night had been intense, and erotic and full of him, and she simply wasn't used to it. He had filled her nights in the months following their marriage, but time had dulled them to occasional harmless occurrences. But being back in his presence...

He held a small espresso cup in his hand, his gaze assessing on hers.

'I am prepared to admit that I might have made an error in judgement last night.'

Ivy pinned her lips between her teeth, hoping he couldn't see her smile. It must be hard for a man like Antonio to admit a mistake. That he did proved that the man she had once known—albeit briefly—was still in there.

'I can see now that I was wrong to think this would go away easily, and I have a *new* plan.'

Ivy nodded, almost entirely sure that she wasn't going to like where this was going.

'You have an appointment this afternoon in Siena.'

She nodded again, wondering why he was telling her about his meeting in Siena if—

'Wait...*me*?'

'Sì.' He nodded.

'*You* got things wrong and *I'm* the one with the appointment?' she asked, not to be obtuse, but because she was very confused.

'Ivy,' he said as if with the greatest of patience. 'If we are going to prove that we gave this a 'go', then we are going to need to be *seen* 'giving this a go'. We will start with dinner tonight. We will do some sightseeing tomorrow and later in the week we will be attending a gallery opening.'

'A gallery opening,' Ivy repeated, her lips numb.

She blinked and pressed a thumb to a temple that had started aching with each step of his plan. Starting with her appointment.

'What's in Siena?'

* * *

Precisely one hour later, Ivy was thrust through the glass doors of one of Italy's most exclusive salons, feeling more nervous than she had done before her last ophthalmologist's appointment.

She looked about her at the empty salon, wondering if the driver had brought her to the right place.

A statuesque man emerged from the back with a disarming smile that put Ivy instantly at ease. 'Ms McKellen?' he asked.

'*Buongiorno*,' she said by way of greeting.

'It's a pleasure to meet you,' the stylist continued in English.

She looked about her again. 'I'm sorry, are you closed? I can come back when it's better for you?' she offered, and the man looked at her, confused.

'Closed? No, this is all for you,' he said with a dramatic sweep of his arms to encompass the entire beautiful salon. '*Venga, venga,*' he called, and from behind him emerged what looked to Ivy like a small army.

She took a step back, a little overwhelmed by it all, and couldn't help but wonder whether Antonio had arranged this for privacy or efficiency. It was most likely to be the latter, but Ivy couldn't help the small wish that burst into being that for once someone might have wanted to do something like this for *her*. As a treat. As something special.

'Signor Gallo told us to take extra special care of you, and that is exactly what we're going to do,' the man promised, clearly not realising that *'Signor Gallo'* had failed to bother to tell her what 'special care' actually meant.

Ivy had presumed a haircut—which she was, admittedly, in need of—but when a diminutive woman pulled out a clothes rack, Ivy's pulse jerked again in panic.

Gavvi, as he finally introduced himself, ushered her into a chair in front of a mirror, where she was poked and prodded, assessed, and found wanting. After an intense three minutes of a stream of Italian she only caught single words from, Gavvi clapped his hands once.

'Are we in agreement?'

Ivy shook her head in denial—she hadn't agreed to anything yet!—but no one was actually looking at her.

A glass of sparkling wine was thrust into her hand.

'È *champagne, non prosecco,*' one of Gavvi's assistants explained with a sniff of disparagement as the others complained about the English drowning themselves in buckets of the inferior sparkling wine. It was so inconceivably extravagant that Ivy couldn't help the quiet giggle that emerged from her mouth. The moment she did, one assistant gasped and the other pointed.

'I knew it!' Gavvi exclaimed. 'A true beauty is somewhere in there, beneath the drab,' he said, delicately brushing imaginary lint from the perfectly fine grey long-sleeved top she was wearing. 'Even if it *does* make your eyes look like silver,' he whispered in her ear.

Ivy couldn't help but smile at the compliment, wondering how much extra Antonio had paid for her to be charmed. Maybe she simply could enjoy this? After all, it wasn't as if she got to do this every day, or maybe even ever again. And as another assistant removed the cloth covering *another* clothing rack and she saw bursts of colour that she would never dare to wear in England, she took a deep breath. She could do this. And she would.

After all, he had bought her. *Twice*. It wouldn't happen again. He might be able to afford it, but she couldn't. She couldn't get used to it. Because all of this? It wasn't real. And the moment that he got his divorce, she'd be back in her flat in South West London, with only herself to rely on, once again.

Antonio drummed his fingers on the white cloth of the small square table in the central square in Siena, the Piazza del Campo. He looked at his watch, his gaze narrowing on the time. She was late. His phone buzzed in his pocket and he resisted the urge to check the email notification that was surely just more bluster from the Americans, panicking about what promised to be one of the largest business deals of the century so far. It was a bold claim. One he intended to make true.

But the Americans were accusing him of being distracted. He could understand why they might feel that way, between his grandfather, his wife and his future fiancée. But Antonio would never let such things impact his work, not even for a single moment. The Chinese were trying to renegotiate already agreed upon terms. They needed to be seen putting up a fight to their shareholders and both he and the Americans could wait. But Maria couldn't.

Already, Gallo Group was beginning to buckle beneath the lack of clear leadership. They'd just lost another VP, and while Maria was in the office every single day, working all the hours God sent to keep the roof on tight, Micha, someone he'd once considered a friend, the man that their grandfather had threatened to give the company to, was nowhere to be seen. Although his mother was of the belief that he would be at the family party at the end of the week. A family party that Antonio had absolutely no intention of attending. He rolled his shoulders subtly, trying to ease the tension in his neck, aware of the attention he was drawing.

But hadn't that been the entire point? Sitting in one of the busiest squares in Tuscany, a place no normal Italian would be seen dead in during the summer. Tourists flocked to the region from all over the world, while Italians counted down the days until they left again and it returned to being their home. Others clung to the industry, making their money in short intervals through the year—hoping it would be enough to pay the bills through the off season.

Antonio might have never known poverty personally. But the possibility of it had always been there. A shadow life of what could have been, had he not been adopted. And it had left its mark. It was a knowing that the others of his circle couldn't imagine. Because they were there by birth. He was there by grace, and never had he been allowed to forget it. First by his adoptive father, then his grandfather. And as for his biological parents? One of them had seen fit to abandon him not only once, but twice.

His fingers gripped the stem of the wine glass, which wobbled precariously as tension fought with condensation.

'Scusi, Signor Gallo, posso offrirle qualcosa?'

Antonio dismissed the offer of another drink with a grimace and a shake of his head. Until recently, his life had been as close to perfect as it could get. He'd worked at his business hard, demanding only what he gave himself: excellence and dedication. He'd started with little more than a handful of contacts and what was in his personal bank account, and he'd made it a multinational, billion-dollar industry. He'd paid his mother back beyond measure, and he hadn't looked back.

Until his grandfather had passed. And since then, everything he sought to do was frustrated by incompetence and other people's agendas. If he were religious, he'd think his grandfather was purposely tormenting him from beyond the grave.

He missed him, Antonio realised, the miserable, autocratic bastard. He missed verbally sparring with him, finding ways to wind the old man up, to shock him, or best him. He'd been the longest, strongest, male figure in his life and, *Dio mio*. He was rocked by a sliver of grief rippling through his chest and lungs.

It hurt. The absence of a man Antonio had genuinely thought would survive the apocalypse. He knew Maria felt similarly, though she wrestled with it for different reasons. Their grandfather had always thought her less because she was a woman, and Antonio had never been able to side with that way of thinking. Maria was, in all likelihood, a better businessman than them all.

And if his grandfather would have just acknowledged that, they wouldn't be in this mess at all. Everyone knew that the last thing either cousin felt for the other was sexual attraction. But Gio had refused to see it. Determined to keep the business in the family, and unwilling to leave it to him—who had not a single drop of Gallo blood in his veins—this had been Gio's ultimate goal, no matter who it hurt.

Back when they'd been teenagers, Antonio had always thought that Maria would end up with Micha. The three of them had been inseparable, but Maria and Micha, they'd had something different. Something special. Until Micha had left, severing all contact, leaving Antonio confused and Maria utterly distraught. Antonio would never forgive Micha for the hurt he'd caused, his anger crowding out the possibility that Gio had sent Micha away because he threatened to interfere with Gio's plans for Gallo Group's successor. No, deep down, Antonio feared that, like his mother, Maria had paid a heavy price for caring for him. That had she not, Gio would never have even thought of his crazy scheme to marry them off.

Antonio took a sip of his wine, to swallow down the ache in his throat, and was distracted by the sight of a slash of vibrant red. Even before he could see what it was, it made him think of Ivy.

Her favourite colour.

And as he remembered that, he also recalled how she'd rubbed her temple the night before. How she had thought it was dark when the sun was still in the sky—low, but still there. Strange.

The slash of red appeared in his peripheral vision again, distracting him, and several male tourists, from the looks of things. Heads turned, eyes peered, following the glimpse of crimson, the same way he did. And then the crowds parted and his hand jerked, sloshing wine over the rim and onto the cloth.

Ivy's hair fell in loosely curled layers around her face, shoulders and arms. *Bare* arms that held a camera up to her eye. A straight, low neckline between two solid red straps pressed against breasts that arced near indecently over the top and Antonio had to work harder than he'd care to admit to avert his gaze. The corset hugged her torso lovingly and the skirt flared from her waist, falling elegantly to a mid-calf point that seemed only to emphasise the shape of her legs in a way that Antonio had never seen before.

Dio mio.

Arousal hit him so hard, and so fast, that he was simply unprepared for the assault. Need surged throughout his entire body from a single pump of his heart. Breath punched from his lungs from a strike to the gut so hard, so deep it left bruises. He hadn't been expecting it.

Not the red. He'd thought that a trip to the salon would make Ivy more presentable, less...*librarian*. Not a siren, not sensual, not irresistible.

The waiter who had served him earlier was frozen, gawping, as Ivy approached their table, having returned her camera to the small bag hanging from the crook of her arm, apparently ignorant to the trail of near destruction she was leaving in her path.

As she came closer to the tables, one hand hovered outstretched by her thigh as if unconsciously balancing herself as she slowly wove between the tables. *That was new*. One of the things he'd remembered—almost against his will—was how Ivy had woven between the tables of Affogato, taking orders and sweeping away used coffee cups as if it were a performance. She'd been *graceful*.

Perhaps it was the shoes, he thought, taking in the thin four inches of matching red stilettos on her feet. His gaze zeroed in on her heels, wondering about the plaster he had given her yesterday...until those same feet came to a stop beside the table.

Following, at his leisure, the turn of her ankle, the shape of her calf, the warm cream tone of her skin, bright against the shocking carnal red—innocence and sin—and skating over the span of her waist and the press of her chest against a neckline he struggled not to find fascinating, he finally reached her face, catching on her concerned expression.

'Do I look okay?' she asked self-consciously.

Antonio cleared his throat. 'No, *cara*. You do not look "okay",' he replied truthfully. 'You look magnificent.'

Ivy's heart lurched.

Foolish, she called herself, as she sat in the chair the waiter had pulled out for her. They were in public on purpose, she had been made over, on purpose. All this was part of the plan to *show* Ms Quell that they were giving their marriage a go. 'Date night' had been Antonio's idea, and he was simply following what normal date etiquette was, she presumed. She'd never actually been on a date.

Perhaps if he'd held her gaze she'd have been able to see in his eyes whether it was the truth or an exaggeration. It might have given her some of the confidence she'd felt at the salon, where the team had *oohed* and *aahed* at her appearance from the dressing room.

After nearly four hours in their company, she had relaxed enough to enjoy the process, and been talked into a suitcase full of clothes that she would never be able to wear in England but had been informed were mandatory while in Italy.

But, of all the things that had happened that afternoon, it was her hair and make-up that actually struck her the most. She'd taken the time, in the privacy of the dressing room, to close one eye and inspect herself closely. The make-up was perfect. A smoky eye that the artist had made her copy until Ivy was accomplished to their satisfaction. And a stained lip that was more durable for the day to early evening, Ivy had been assured, than lipstick.

But it was the soft highlights put in her hair, which enriched copper undertones she'd not even known were there, that really caught her attention. Instead of drawing on the cooler tones of the blue in her eyes like the grey top had, now even she could see the gold flecks that glittered in her irises. They made something so damaged look so beautiful.

She swallowed. 'Thank you,' she said to Antonio, sitting across the table from her, flicking his gaze between her and the menu.

'For?' he said, almost dismissively.

She bit back a sigh of impatience. He'd done this. He'd given her something. That it didn't mean anything to him was fine, but it didn't give him the right to diminish what it did mean to her.

'For supplying me with the accoutrements required for the job you have hired me for,' she bit out impulsively. She was blaming the dress. Apparently, the red was impacting her self-control.

Antonio raised an eyebrow, and honestly Ivy was half convinced she heard a female customer behind her sigh, enraptured by the sight.

'You don't like it?' he asked, pushing the menu aside.

'I love it,' she insisted truthfully.

'Then what is the problem?'

It was a good question. But how could she even begin to explain the twists and turns of the emotional rollercoaster she'd been on in the last twenty-four hours? Was it normal for a librarian from south London, used to store-bought clothes and charity shops, to feel overwhelmed at being transported to the most beautiful places in Tuscany, styled and clothed by creative geniuses and forced to eat with an Italian billionaire who looked like some Adonis?

She rubbed at her temple, her left eyelid flickering unconsciously.

'Nothing,' she said, shaking her head and forcing a smile to her lips. She stared at her hands, hoping to reduce the visual stimuli from her field of sight.

The waiter appeared and Ivy let Antonio order for her without intervening. He hadn't asked her what she wanted for dinner, but that hadn't mattered at any other point so far, so why would it now? And besides, she reluctantly admitted, she would really very much like to have the *gnudi*, ever since she'd seen the spinach gnocchi on a cooking show at home.

She could probably do with something in her stomach as she'd only been able to nibble at the salon. And not much before that either. She told herself off. She knew better than that. She had to take care of herself better.

She reached for the basket of bread and dipped a piece into the small bowl of oil and vinegar, sighing, almost exactly the same way as the woman behind her had, from the pleasure of the soft yeasty bite of bread and the sharp tang of the balsamic. She closed her eyes and let herself enjoy it.

Antonio cleared his throat. 'Did you have fun?'

She opened her eyes but kept them narrowed, considering his question. 'I'm not sure *fun* would be how I'd describe it, but the people from the salon were lovely,' she insisted, worried that he might not approve of their choices. 'And now I have an ensemble fit to be seen in.'

The slash of brow shaded Antonio's gaze. 'That's not what...well, it's not entirely why I sent you there. We will be attending events and places that you weren't prepared for, and I wanted to make sure that you didn't feel uncomfortable.'

'Oh,' Ivy replied, blinking at the explanation of her visit to the salon.

There was a moment of uncomfortable silence before she forced herself to ask, 'Did you have a nice day?'

The question was perfunctory even to her own ears, but they couldn't sit there in silence for the entire evening.

'I'm not sure *nice* would be how I'd describe it,' he said, mirroring her words, and she smiled, this time easily and genuinely.

'Are you going to make the deal between the Chinese and the Americans?'

The surprise across his features told her she'd revealed too much.

'It was in the papers,' she said to explain her knowledge of him. His fame, surely, enough to cover the fact that, in reality, she'd always looked out for information about him. Even after the accident.

He looked around them at the public place and replied, 'Maybe.' She understood his inability to answer in a place where they could be overheard.

'Top secret work stuff,' she said, and he nodded, the smallest curve pulling at his lips.

The waiter brought their plates, topped up their glasses and left.

A waft of sharp Parmesan rose from the ricotta and spinach dumplings sitting on a bed of rich tomato sauce, her stomach grumbling loud enough for Antonio to hear. She cut into one of the three mounds and luxuriated in the tangy comfort of the delicious mouthful. Distracted by the food, she reached for her glass, missed and knocked it from the table, the smash echoing around the diners in the square, causing a ripple of sarcastic applause from the tourists on nearby tables.

Shock and embarrassment painted her cheeks in red slashes as the waiter rushed over to clear up the mess. She was half out of her chair, reaching for the shards of glass, when Antonio's hand wrapped around hers, pulling her back from the sharp edge of a piece that would have cut her.

'No, no, no, *signora*, allow me,' the waiter said, efficiently brushing up the broken glass into a pan while another waiter replaced her glass without fuss.

Ivy sank back into her chair, rubbing her hands together, feeling instantly vulnerable in a way that even the red dress couldn't combat. The restaurant diners slowly resumed their conversations and Antonio waited for the waiter to leave. But she was still rocked from the shock of the accident and the distinct air of tension between them.

'Is there something wrong?'

'No, not at all,' she tried to evade.

'I mean, is there an issue with your sight? Last night you thought it was dark when it was not. Today you were unsteady as you walked between tables similar to those I saw you navigate perfectly six years ago, and now you just nearly cut yourself on a piece of glass that was right in front of you. So,' he said, before repeating, 'is there an issue with your sight?'

Any trace of hunger fled. It wasn't that she was embarrassed. She was proud of how she'd coped, what she'd overcome to live as she did, to continue as normally as possible. But his question reminded her of before she'd been that way. Of when she'd been in the hospital, terrified and alone. It reminded her of when the nurse had informed her that they'd left a message with her next of kin: that they'd called her *husband*. Of the way she'd felt relief. Hope even.

Until she'd tried to call him herself.

'Yes. From the accident,' she said.

'The accident? What accident?'

CHAPTER FIVE

Ivy struggled with the wave of anger that snapped at her heart. Praying for patience, she asked, 'You really don't remember?'

But his blank look only hurt more.

She tried not to be devastated by the fact that one of the worst days of her life wasn't even a memory for him. She tried to focus on the fact that she had survived, both the accident *and* the realisation of just how unimportant she was to a man who had married her in name only. It wasn't his fault. But it still hurt.

'Three years ago, I was crossing a road when I was hit by a cyclist. I was knocked unconscious for a short time and taken to hospital,' she said, trying to ignore the way he'd tensed in his seat. 'When I came round, the nurse told me that they'd tried to call you because you're listed as my next of kin,' she explained, fighting the memory of how hopeful she'd been when she'd heard that. Of how terrified she'd been in that hospital, bruised and battered, her sight so damaged, and just how desperately she'd wanted someone to be there with her. 'I came round before you could call back,' she said, pressing on.

A muscle flexed in his jaw, but his gaze remained unreadable.

'So I called you myself,' she confessed, looking at her hands.

She'd called him and she'd so very nearly asked, begged and pleaded for him to come. If he could. Just for a short while. Just so she wasn't alone.

'I got your secretary and...'

She'd been such a fool. She should have known better. He hadn't promised to be there for her, he hadn't ever pretended to be a real husband. So no, it was not Antonio's fault that she had imagined that he might be even remotely concerned about her.

After what she'd heard him say, she'd realised that she had to stop. Stop waiting for people to start caring about her.

'Three years ago...' Antonio trailed off.

Three years ago, he'd been at the tail-end of negotiations on a deal that was crucial to Alessina International. They'd been back and forth for three days straight. No one had slept, they'd barely eaten and they'd been surviving on coffee and adrenaline alone. It was a deal that had *made* his company.

'There's a call from England, Signor Gallo. They say it's about your wife?'

He remembered now. It had been on the tip of his tongue to say that he didn't have a wife. But he did. He'd told his assistant to take down the number.

He'd said that he'd call back. But then...

'Ms McKellen is calling from London.'

'What is it?' he'd shouted. *'I cannot keep having these interruptions. Is it important?'* he'd asked.

'No, signor. She says it's not.'

That he remembered the call in bits and pieces was telling of how distracted he had been—not that it was in any way an excuse. Whether the marriage was in name only or not, he should have called her back. She had been in *hospital*, she had been *unconscious* and *alone*, and he had asked if it was *important*.

Bastardo.

He fisted the napkin in a white-knuckled grip, wishing it was his own throat. For all his superiority about protecting his family and being better than the men in his life, he was just the same. If not worse, because he'd actually thought himself better than that.

When you married her, she became your family. She became yours, not to own but to protect, to care for.

'Ivy, I am sorry,' he said to her now, and he was, truly and deeply. 'I should have called you back. I should have...'

Been there for you.

'It wasn't your fault,' she said graciously. 'And I was fine.'

'You were hurt,' he stressed, taking in the little scar on her jaw in a new light. He'd seen it. His subconscious had tried to remind him.

Ivy's inhale shuddered in her chest. She didn't want to talk about it, that was evident, but...this woman, his *wife*... she could have died and he'd not... He'd...

He swallowed.

'I *thought* I was fine,' she clarified. 'Just cuts and bruises,' she said with a shrug—as if it could offset the way her entire body had tensed as she told the story. 'But while I was in hospital the vision in my left eye became very blurry, with dark spots. I was told that my retina had detached, but that it was okay—they would take me for surgery and repair it. No one was overly worried,' Ivy added.

Surgery? *Dio mio.*

'It was a success and I was discharged from hospital.

But three days later, my vision was troubling me again. There was this flash—not like a camera flash, but enough to make me rush back to hospital. I was waiting for the doctor when—' her hand came up to her left eye '—it was like a…blind slowly coming down over one eye. And…' She didn't have to finish her sentence. He could see the fear in her eyes. She shook her head and shrugged again.

'I was lucky, actually,' Ivy pressed on, with forced positivity in her voice. 'There was a specialist visiting from Greece. He explained how severe it was, but he told me how good he was,' she said with a smile. 'And he was true to his word. My sight will never be fully back, but he gave me more than I thought I would get.'

Antonio *knew* Ivy was downplaying how dangerous and terrifying it must have been.

'And now? What is it like for you now?' he forced himself to ask.

She took her time answering. 'It's better now. I struggled. Before,' she said, avoiding his gaze. 'But now it's better. I have double vision all the time, though. My brain can't seem to marry the information from both eyes,' she admitted, taking another deep breath. 'If I close my left eye then my right is okay, but it's a lot of strain on one eye.'

She pushed the food around her plate as if her hunger had fled as much as his.

'You struggled?' he dared to ask.

She pinned her lip with her teeth. 'I was on my own,' she confessed defiantly, as if he might judge her somehow.

'Where were your family?'

She looked at him as if he were crazy. 'My brother had just started Basic Training with the army, and I told you yesterday that my mother was abroad…' She looked off to the side. 'In America, I think.'

'She didn't come for you?'

Like I didn't come for you? he thought, guilt a fierce punch to the gut.

'No,' she said, wincing a little. 'The last I heard, she'd split from Ted, changed her number and moved on.' Ivy offered him a small smile. 'She was always terrible at being alone.'

He wanted to tell her that her mother hadn't been alone—that she had two children—but he knew that Ivy already knew that.

The waiter arrived and took their plates away, saying something about dessert that Antonio didn't catch as he stared at this woman who had battled so much for so long in silence.

'Was there enough money left over from what I gave you to cushion you?' He hoped to God the question didn't sound crass, but he wanted—needed to know, that something he'd done had helped her.

He watched her swallow before answering, looking off to the side as if she could hide the emotions behind her words.

'I used the money you gave me to pay for my brother's rehabilitation,' she said with a true smile. Small, but true. 'I think I told you that he got into trouble when he was younger?'

'You told me a little about it, that day in the café,' he admitted.

Ivy caught his gaze, then looked away.

'I shouldn't have,' she said, as if she felt ashamed for having shared her burden.

'I'm glad you did,' he said truthfully, admiring the woman he had married beyond anything he could have imagined.

Antonio swallowed in her silence.

'It took a few years,' she pressed on, 'but he's sober. And he fights for that, every single day,' she said, a gleam of pride bringing life to her eyes once more.

'And you? Did you use the money for yourself?' he asked, guilt settling uneasily into his gut. He'd judged her for not doing more with the money, when in actual fact she deserved praise for achieving what she *had*.

Dio mio. What had he done?

'I was able to put down a deposit on a flat for us and that would never have happened were it not for you. That was security and stability that neither I nor Jamie had ever experienced, and you made that happen.'

'He came to my rescue.'

Antonio clenched his jaw. But he hadn't, had he? He had paid her to marry him and then he had forgotten about her in his determination to make something of himself, to prove himself to his family. He hadn't been there for her when she'd needed him most.

'And that's the flat you share now?' he asked.

She didn't want to lie to him, but she didn't want to admit the truth. That in the months following the accident things had got so bad that she'd been forced to sell it. But now was not the time to be squeamish. She had gone this far, she might as well tell him everything.

'After the accident I couldn't work for a while, so I wasn't able to keep up with the mortgage payments.'

It had been terrible. Days, weeks, months lost to a kind of emotional detachment that had mirrored the physical one. Adjusting to the alteration in her eyesight had been so much more emotional than physical. While there had been no pain, there was a kind of grief to navigate—grief over a loss that was a might-have-been: a life she could have had. And while she had been so damn thankful that this was all that the accident had cost her, the true devastation had been the near constant battle with the fear that had consumed her life.

Fear that she could lose the sight in her other eye, fear that she would never not know fear, fear that this misery was all that she would feel for the rest of her life. And that was before you got to the basics of everyday life. Fear of getting on the wrong bus, of getting lost and having no one there to help. Fear of not being able to work. Fear of the loss of her self-reliance.

And then some of those fears had come true.

'I had to sell the flat,' she admitted, the pain of losing her home a dim echo of the deep wound it had once been. 'The housing market wasn't the same as when I'd bought it, but there was enough left over to help me until I was able to get back to work,' she finished, not wanting him to think that she was completely terrible with money. Yes, there was still a sense of shame attached to the fact she hadn't done *better*, but she had done what she needed, when she'd needed to. And she wanted Antonio to know that it hadn't been a complete loss.

'And now things are much better. I have a lovely little flat-share, and I love my job, and...'

Was she trying too hard? Could he tell?

Dessert appeared in front of them. Rich, chocolate, extravagant, and she suddenly wanted to cry.

'*Cara*,' he said, his voice low, gravel thick, as he reached across the table for her hand.

She let him take her hand but couldn't meet his gaze. She didn't want to see what was in his eyes. Didn't want to see what he thought or felt. But she would let him offer the silent comfort she needed, just for now. It was part of his apology, she knew. It wasn't something she could rely on in the future, but just for now, God, she wanted it so badly.

'If you need more money—'

'No,' she replied, shaking her head.

'I know the money you've asked for is for the library and not for yourself.'

She nearly laughed. It sounded like an admonishment.

'I don't need your money, Antonio,' she said with more determination.

If her flat-out refusal surprised him, it didn't show. But no, she couldn't take money for herself again. Not like that. She wasn't sure she ever wanted to own a house again. The pressure of meeting the mortgage payments had weighed on her so heavily, the bills she'd not been able to keep up with because she'd not been able to work...the responsibility... What if something happened again? She wasn't sure she could survive losing her home twice. It had nearly destroyed her last time.

She took a bite of the rich chocolate dessert, not tasting a single bit of it.

'I'm glad that you're okay,' he said, the words stilted, and she smiled sadly.

Yes. She *was* okay.

'Thank you,' she replied, before taking another mouthful she didn't really notice.

Antonio left his untouched, but waited patiently until she'd forced herself to finish the dessert because it would have been rude not to. He paid for the meal and escorted her to where the car waited to take them back to the villa in a pensive kind of silence that Ivy didn't feel the need to break. It wasn't uncomfortable, just an awareness.

But that awareness became something more as he

opened the car door for her. As they made the journey back and he didn't reach for his phone to check emails. She tried not to let her glance slide to the way that the moonlight outside the car landed on the angles and planes of his face—that he was sitting on her right side made it easier. Subtle hints of his aftershave reached her from across the car and she was struck, viscerally, by the way he'd kissed her cheek at the wedding ceremony. A timely reminder that she shouldn't build sandcastle dreams about this man.

No, she hadn't really expected him to come for her when she'd been in hospital. He'd never said that he would, or intimated that he even could. That wasn't really the problem, she realised now. The problem was that she'd *wanted* him to.

Antonio glared, bleary-eyed, at the espresso Agata had just put in front of him. Last night, he'd watched Ivy head up the stairs towards the room he'd given her down the hall from his own, and returned to his office. But for the first time in years, it wasn't to check emails or business reports.

Instead, it was to research everything he could on retinal detachment. He'd even found a reference to Ivy's case in some paywall protected journal, but it was enough to get the name of the 'specialist' she'd mentioned. From there it had been a simple matter of sending a few 'urgent' emails so that he could discover as much as possible about what had happened to her.

He had been inconceivably arrogant. Not in terms of ego, but in terms of believing that his needs—the needs of his loved ones—overrode all else. And while he still had his eye firmly on the goal of marrying Maria to meet the ridiculous terms of his grandfather's will, it didn't mean that he couldn't find a way to make up for the fact that Ivy had been alone, in a very desperate state, and he'd chosen to ignore her.

There had only been one moment in his life when he'd felt that way—alone. Truly alone and utterly helpless. And the fact that he'd left Ivy feeling that way was a deeply bitter pill to swallow. Self-loathing was sharp, hard and swift.

In the kitchen, he noticed the makings of Ivy's herbal tea by the sink and frowned.

'Dov'è Ivy?' he asked Agata.

She nodded out into the garden, where he could just see her sitting by the pool's edge, the early morning sun kissing her skin where she wasn't covered by a cream and fuchsia kaftan. Her face was lifted to the sky and suddenly he had an image of her from six years ago, on a break from Affogato, that same peaceful smile as she'd turned page after page of an art book she'd been reading.

But from the information he'd gleaned, both from his research last night and what she'd told him, reading would be hard for her now. And, just like that, where he'd once seen a means to an end, all he saw now were questions.

Did she still read? Was working in a library hard for her? Why hadn't she asked for money for herself when he'd offered it? He could have given her anything. What was money to him? he wondered carelessly. He had what he wanted, didn't he? If not, then it was certainly within reach—thanks to Ivy.

As an orphan who had been abandoned by his biological parents and rejected by his adoptive father, Antonio knew better than to ask about her parents beyond what she'd told him, refusing to tread into emotionally painful areas for her.

He picked up the espresso and made his way out towards the pool, welcoming the scents of home on the breeze, the warmth of the sun-soaked ground evaporating the last traces of the past night's mist. And yet, despite all these things that Antonio usually relished, he only had eyes for Ivy.

'I can see why you like it here,' she said as he approached, keeping her face tilted to the sky. She wore a pair of sunglasses that must have been bought yesterday, because they were from an Italian designer that hadn't made it over to the UK yet. She sat on a blanket with her mint tea and her camera within easy reach.

It was surprising, the wave of satisfaction he felt at knowing that she was dressed in things he'd bought for her. Primal, in a way he didn't have a right to feel about the woman he was in the process of divorcing.

He looked around, the view stretching far below into undulating verdant valleys in almost all directions. In the distance he could see the rooftops of San Gimignano, but the beauty, the peace of it, the *sight* of it, struck him somehow as so much more precious than it had yesterday morning.

'My mother rented this villa just after her husband left us, when I was eight years old,' he admitted. 'We escaped the fallout of the press and the wrath of my grandfather who, despite how much he adored my mother, still struggled with the notion of a divorce.'

Ivy frowned. 'He seemed to have got over that notion if he was happy enough for you to divorce me to marry Maria?'

Antonio sighed. 'It was impressive just how much Gio could get over, in order to get what he wanted,' he admitted, taking a seat on the cushioned chaise near to where she sat on the warm patio. He frowned, feeling incredibly overdressed in his suit trousers, shirt and loafers, next to her soft, gentle cover-up that wasn't really doing as advertised.

He caught glimpses of shapely thighs and a high-cut bikini and was so distracted that he didn't realise Ivy had stopped looking at the sky and her watchful gaze was now on him.

'I'm sorry.'

'For my mother's husband? Or my grandfather?' he asked.

'Both.'

He shrugged dismissively, but she didn't buy it. The knowing curve of her lips told him that much. The way she looked at him was different to the way other women looked at him. It was as if she were trying to see behind his words, rather than wanting nothing beyond his bank account. Everything about Ivy said that she didn't want that from him, even if it would help her considerably. That made him distinctly uncomfortable.

He pulled at the collar of his shirt, eyeing up the crystal-clear water in the pool. He noticed Ivy looking longingly at it too.

'You should go in. It looks blissful,' Ivy said wistfully.

'You're the one dressed for it,' he pointed out.

'I haven't been in the water since...' She trailed off with a sigh. 'I don't know how unbalanced it would make me feel,' she said, her eyes narrowing to express both thought and concern at the same time.

'I'm here. You could...hold on to me.'

His offer was stilted, and so uncomfortably delivered Ivy wanted to laugh, but when she tore her gaze away from the pool, back to him, the laughter died on her tongue. His words might have been clumsy, but his eyes were intent. As if he were determined, half against his wishes.

And the problem was that she *did* want to. Her skin,

warmed to the point of hot by the rays of the sun, would luxuriate in the cool temperature of the water. It would feel like heaven to slip into the pool and have an anchor.

She was surprised to find that she didn't feel self-conscious with Antonio, the way that she did with other people—even her brother to a point. There was a wariness about the way they were around her, waiting for her to walk into something, or get something wrong, waiting for her to need them.

An excuse was forming on the tip of her tongue when Antonio started undoing the buttons at his cuffs. And that was the precise moment she realised she'd made a very dangerous mistake.

She'd been thinking about how she would feel about being in the water.

Not how she'd feel about being in the water with *him*.

'I don't—'

'Chicken,' he said, standing and pulling the shirt out from his waistband and beginning to unbutton it from the neck.

'Did you just call me a chicken?' Ivy asked, trying to focus on the matter at hand while inch after glorious inch of one of the most spectacular torsos she'd ever seen was revealed.

'Yes,' he said with a smirk that, horrifyingly, made him even more handsome.

A blush rose to her cheeks. What on earth was wrong with her? Why couldn't she get her body's reaction to him under control? It was just a pool, after all.

But when he shucked his shirt and his thumbs hooked into his waistband, she turned her gaze firmly back to the pool.

'You're wearing a swimming costume?' she asked in a voice far too breathy for her liking.

'No, but I am wearing briefs, and cotton dries,' he said, before she saw him move to the edge of the pool in her peripheral vision. For one, heart stopping moment, he came into unique focus, and the sight of it sent a flare around her entire body, jolting her pulse into an irregular rhythm, before he dived perfectly into the mirror-smooth surface.

Heartbeat pounding in her chest, she thought of all the reasons not to do this. Of all the things that would usually stop her. And thought, *Please. Just once. Let me have this.*

She stood up, hoping that he couldn't see the way her legs trembled. She took short careful steps to the edge of the pool, which was silly, she told herself. She could walk perfectly fine, but the knowledge of how easy it would be to misjudge the distance and fall in kept her on guard.

Antonio surfaced powerfully at the other end of the pool and trod water while keeping his gaze on hers. She was thankful that, rather than rushing her, or peppering her with questions, he was letting her adjust to the idea in her own time.

She sat on the edge of the pool, drawing the kaftan over her head and casting it aside, and slid into the pool before she could change her mind. Her fingers white-knuckled the curve of the pool's edge, anchoring her in place so that she could let herself adjust to the way the water undulated around her.

Breath whooshed out of her lungs as she tried to find her balance on her feet in the shallow side of the pool and ignored the way that Antonio closed the distance between them with a lazy breaststroke.

'How is it?' he asked as he stayed a respectable distance from her.

Goosebumps pebbled the skin on her arms as she let the cool water soothe her heated skin. Although the way the water lapped at her made her nervous, she unexpectedly felt relief. There was no falling over here. Yes, she could crash into the side of the pool, but she wasn't racing the hundred metres.

Freedom, she realised. Freedom in closing her eyes and letting the water move her. In the water, she didn't have to worry about knocking something over, breaking it, trying to decipher it. If she tried too hard to focus on the waterline it made her a little dizzy, but if she ignored it…yes, freedom, she realised. And with Antonio here, she knew he wouldn't let anything happen to her. She knew that viscerally.

She smiled, opening her eyes. 'It's amazing,' she admitted.

He nodded, satisfied with his all-knowing, all-seeing prowess.

'Don't let it go to your head,' she warned with mock severity.

'My shoulders are strong enough to support my ego,' he replied easily, his confidence making her laugh.

She skated her hand across the water, sending a sharp wave towards his face and ducking beneath the surface before he could retaliate in kind.

There, sound muffled, water pressing around her head, her giggle emerged as water bubbles streaming their way to the surface. She waited for as long as she could, before gingerly emerging to what she was sure would be a sneak attack.

She frowned, not seeing him in the pool, and then screamed out loud when she realised he was right behind her. He grabbed her waist and she slithered in his hands, nearly swallowing a mouthful of water.

It was the best kind of scare—one that was as much delight as it was heart-stopping and so different to what she'd felt three years ago. Oh, God, it was *joyous*. She spun in his arms to face him, her hand coming over her heart and a smile on her face that made her cheeks ache in the best of ways.

She couldn't help it, the laugh peeled out of her.

'Va bene?' he asked, making sure she was okay, and it was all Ivy could do not to grab hold of him.

'Yes…' She nodded before realising that she was so close she was practically rubbing up against him.

Now that she wasn't distracted by her fear of being in the water, all of her senses exploded with *him*. She watched a drop of water glide down his cheek from the slicked-back hair, the breadth of his shoulders somehow enlarged by the nakedness of his torso.

Shivers trembled her body, her heart stuttering, and for a moment—just a moment—he looked down at her in the way she'd imagined a husband might, before his eyes became shadowed by a furrowed brow.

'What is—?'

'Ms Quell—we weren't expecting you,' Antonio stated over her shoulder, cutting Ivy off mid-sentence.

Ivy swallowed. How long had she been standing there? And how much of what had just happened between them had been for show? Just how far was Antonio willing to go to prove that he'd tried to make this marriage work?

As far as it took was the answer she didn't need to search for. Her heart sank as she stepped away from him and to the safety of the side of the pool.

CHAPTER SIX

ANTONIO DIDN'T KNOW whether to believe that Ms Quell had been 'forced' to bring forward the second assessment or not. They shouldn't have met with her for at least another six days. But her frostily delivered explanation of being needed in court for another client *'whose time is just as important as yours'* had been delivered with the sole purpose of putting him in his place.

The interview had gone from bad to worse from there, and no matter how much both he and Ivy had tried to suggest that two days was simply not enough time to achieve what Ms Quell was asking for, it did not help their cause.

'It's not the big things that make a marriage work, Mr Gallo, it's the little things. Like knowing what skincare brand she uses, what perfume. How she likes her coffee.'

Ivy didn't even like coffee.

Frustration had held him by the throat, and Ivy's hand on his had been both restraint and warning in one. He'd focused on simply hoping to survive this second assessment, until Ms Quell asked if Ivy would be going with him to the Gallo family party at the end of the week.

Dio mio, he cursed the press and their fascination with his family. Ivy had done well to hide her surprise when he'd replied that *of course* Ivy would be going to the family party with him. So, instead of taking Ivy to a gallery opening, he now found himself obliged to attend a party he'd intended to avoid.

Three days later, he still wanted to add Ms Quell to the list of people he would wilfully murder, as he changed gear with a little more force than strictly necessary and punched the gas with his foot. The engine roared satisfyingly beneath him as he palmed the wheel and hugged a familiar corner of the road. But instead of the thrill he usually felt, he was overwhelmingly aware of the tension emanating from Ivy in the passenger seat beside him. He eased off the accelerator.

'Is my driving making you uncomfortable?' he asked.

Ivy smiled apologetically. 'It's the twists and turns. When we straighten out it's fine.'

The way she said 'fine' made him think of the way he felt about paperwork, and he barked a laugh.

'Ivy, you can tell me if you don't like something. You don't have to be polite.'

'Okay,' she hedged. 'I really don't like your driving,' she informed him primly, her hands in her lap, over the skirt of the dress she wore.

Antonio couldn't help the smile that curved his lips and he shook his head, marvelling how quickly he could flit between murderous anger, amusement and then…how *was* it he felt about the upcoming visit with his mother's family?

It would be good to see Maria and his mother, but for the rest…? He could happily never see or hear from them ever again. Gio's siblings, and there were many, had been as profligate as their brother, and more proliferate. Every single one of them wanted a piece of Gallo Group, and when they discovered that they weren't going to get it they would be out for blood. Mainly his and Maria's. But if Micha chose to show his face, things could get very interesting.

'What are you brooding about?' Ivy asked.

'Brooding?' he repeated, changing down gear to take another corner. Slowly.

'Yes, you get this—' she stopped to gesture with her hands, as if she were rolling a ball between her palms '—look about you.'

He glanced at her hands and back to the road.

'Cogs turning,' she explained of her gesture. 'Thinking too hard.'

He sighed. 'We shouldn't be doing this,' he admitted.

Ivy crinkled her nose. 'Ms Quell seemed to imply that it was a vital part of the assessment.'

'I think she's got it in for us.'

'Do your family know? That we're married? *Why* we're married?' Ivy asked hesitantly.

'My mother and Maria know, as did my grandfather. But it was not the business of anyone else,' he concluded in clipped tones. 'It would be best for the rest of the family to believe, like Ms Quell, that we married for love and are considering reconciliation. That way, when we divorce, it won't be so surprising and it won't give them a reason to challenge the will when it's made public.'

Since Gio's death, the members of the Gallo family had been like wild dogs: rabid and desperate.

'But they know the terms of the will?'

'No. Only the four of us—myself, Maria, my mother and Micha—know the terms of the will.'

'Micha?' Ivy asked, turning to look at him with a frown.

'Micha Rufina. He was once a childhood friend. He's worked for my grandfather most of his life and stands to inherit Gallo Group if Maria and I don't marry.'

Ivy bit her lip and nodded, before looking out of the window, squinting into the distance.

'So your family *don't* know about your forthcoming marriage to Maria?'

'No. It will probably come as a surprise and there will most definitely be rumours, but nothing we haven't navigated before.'

She tucked a strand of hair behind her ear, and Antonio was momentarily distracted. She'd been leaving her hair down ever since the salon, and it was making it difficult for him to keep her in his mind as the waitress he'd married for convenience. And then, after the pool, a few days ago? *Cazzo*, he'd not been able to put her back in that box at all.

She'd looked at that pool like he'd seen financial advisors look at his company's bottom line—with naked lust—and he'd wanted her to have what she wanted. And yes, he might have been just a little jealous. Of a swimming pool. But that wasn't why he'd enticed her into it.

Now that he knew about her sight loss, he could just as easily see the bars on the cage she had tucked herself into. And it was wrong. Wrong to see her like that. She was different from the person she was six years ago, they both were. But what was missing was a sense of…he struggled to find the right word…*ease*. Her sense of self had been *easy*. Yes, there had been cares and concerns hidden in her gaze, but her laughter had been *easy*. She'd had an innate sense of grounding. But all of those things seemed to be different now.

And for a moment in the pool he'd seen a glimmer of that woman he'd married. Before her eyes had turned on him and he'd felt it.

Heat.

Want.

Desire.

Oh, it had disappeared pretty quickly once Ms Quell had arrived on the scene. But he couldn't get it out of his head. It ran on a loop in his mind, catching him by surprise whenever his guard was down. Like at night. Or in the shower. He'd remember the feel of her skin slipping through his palms, or against his chest and thighs. The way her eyes sparkled, shards of gold in a sea of blue, like glimpses of underwater treasure.

'Is Maria going to be there?' Ivy asked, her fingers playing with the hem of the white skirt that had ridden up along her thigh.

'*Sì*,' Antonio replied, ignoring the spread of heat through his body and locking his gaze on the road ahead. 'She knows you're coming. She knows we're trying to get a divorce as quickly as possible, and she also knows that she won't be able to get her hands on Gallo Group without all this, which includes your help. *She's* not the enemy.'

'If she's not, then who is?'

The muscle in his jaw flickered. 'The rest of them.'

If Ivy had thought that Antonio's villa was impressive, it was nothing compared to Villa Alessia. She'd gasped out loud as they'd rounded the gravel drive, lined with artfully manicured box trees in terracotta pots, her fingers itching for her camera. The stone walls sprawled over several floors and stretched out across and around a magnificent courtyard she caught glimpses of as Antonio parked the car.

He'd explained that he'd bought his mother the villa shortly after his first international deal with Alessina. And without needing to hear it, Ivy had understood that he'd wanted his mother to have something that was hers, and not given to her by Gio—something that couldn't be taken away, like Antonio's inheritance had been. That it was important to him that his mother always had a home melted her heart a little. Especially as someone who knew how much that meant.

He waited for her patiently as she tried to take it all in, squinting a little unintentionally. The unmistakable sounds of a party carried on a gentle breeze and even the late hour of the afternoon hadn't dulled the heat of the summer's day.

Antonio gestured with a flick of his dark head to follow him and she rounded the car, her wedge sandals crunching on the gravel. The breeze continued to play with the calf-length skirt Ivy was sure she would stain before long, but it was pretty. It made her *feel* pretty and she hoped that might be enough to give her the confidence she needed to face Antonio's family.

Stepping carefully on the path that would have, six years ago, been thoughtlessly easy, but now required just a little more attention, she followed Antonio's thankfully slow footsteps as they rounded the building and came to an open courtyard filled with nearly fifty people.

Ivy came to a halt. '*This* is your family?'

Antonio turned, frowning at her. 'Not all. There are more coming later for the meal.'

Ivy blinked. She couldn't imagine being related to so many people. And the glamour! Diamonds and gold glinted in the setting sun, enough to remind her of the flashes she'd seen as the detachment claimed part of her eyesight.

And for the first time since the clothes had arrived from the salon, she was truly thankful that Antonio had bought her such fine things to wear. Certainly, the things she'd brought with her from London would have drawn nothing but scorn. As it was, she felt everyone's attention on her and it wasn't entirely comfortable.

Unconsciously, she scanned the faces, looking for one in particular.

Micha Rufina.

Ivy was aware that she should have told Antonio she knew him. Or had at least met him, one year ago. But instinctively, she'd been trying to protect him, knowing that the context surrounding her meeting with Micha would undermine whatever peace he'd found with his grandfather in the last few years. Micha had only approached her on Gio Gallo's behalf. And once she'd sent him away, Ivy had put it firmly out of her mind, unwilling to travel down that path.

She'd never thought she'd see Micha, or Antonio, again for that matter. But now…

A beautiful dark-haired woman dressed in an exceptionally flattering ornate black dress detached herself from the crowd. And while they might not have been blood-related, there was something about the way that she moved which reminded Ivy of Antonio. Regal. Determined. Powerful.

Those things might not be genetic, but they had most definitely been nurtured.

'Mamma,' Antonio said in English. 'This is Ivy McKellen.'

'It's wonderful to meet you, Mrs Gallo,' Ivy said with a nervous smile.

'Alessia, please,' she insisted easily. 'It is very brave of you to be willing to face the Gallos. If my son hasn't thanked you profusely for agreeing to be dragged into this farce, then I will,' she said, glaring at her son in disapproval, while not making Ivy feel slighted in the least.

'That's not necessary, but thank you,' Ivy said, fighting the incongruous urge to curtsey.

Alessia smiled, dark lashes framing a pair of startling blue eyes, so markedly different to Antonio's dark brown.

Antonio produced a slim velvet box from inside his jacket and gave it to his mother, along with a kiss on her cheek.

'Antonio, *figlio mio*, please, you don't need to do this,' she said, casting a little glance of embarrassment in Ivy's direction.

'But I wanted to. You deserve it, Mamma,' he said of the gift, squeezing her hand.

Alessia accepted it with grace. 'My apologies for being rude, Ivy, but I just need a word with my son.'

'Of course,' Ivy said, and stepped back to give them some privacy.

Strings of tiny lights had been twisted into the vines wrapped around a pergola that covered a section of the large courtyard and garden beyond, making it look almost magical. Music drifted gently around the space, over which could be heard a multitude of conversations. But as she stood there, taking as much in as possible, she couldn't fail to miss the sideways looks cast her way, and the way that others had even gone so far as to turn their backs on Antonio.

Ivy was rocked by the sense of outrage she felt on his behalf. That his family would treat him this way, just because he'd been adopted. It was enough to give her the strength to meet the curious gaze of an older gentleman head-on, who broke first, much to her satisfaction.

And then in the background she heard Antonio say, *'Non è possibile,'* drawing her back to where he stood with his mother. *'C'è un letto soltanto?'* Antonio demanded.

'Only one bed for what?' Ivy asked, having translated Antonio's response, alarm in her voice.

'To sleep,' his mother answered.

Antonio asked, 'You understood that?' at the same time.

'Yes,' she answered. 'Only one bed?' she repeated.

This time Antonio demanded, 'You speak Italian?'

'A little,' she admitted.

'Since when?'

'Is that really more important than there being one bedroom for us? To *share*?' she said pointedly.

'No, it is ridiculous,' Antonio dismissed, turning back to his mother. 'I'll sleep on the sofa.'

Ivy flinched, while Alessia slapped her son's arm, more sharp than hard.

'You will do no such thing,' she whisper-hissed in Italian. 'I'll not have my son sleeping on the furniture while his wife is in another room. There will be no more gossip for these vultures.' At least Ivy was pretty sure the translation was vulture. '*You* decided to go down this path,' she warned him, clearly speaking of their marriage. 'You will be living—*and sleeping*—with the consequences, Antonio.'

'Mamma—'

'Don't "Mamma" me,' she chided with a pointed finger in his chest.

And while part of Ivy was calculating how on earth she was going to survive a night in the same room as Antonio, another part of her was delighted by how he had transformed into a naughty schoolboy before her very eyes.

'Now, Ivy, come,' his mother commanded and drew her away from Antonio and into the throng.

Antonio watched his mother and Ivy, arm in arm, for as long as he could before they disappeared from sight, unease curling in his chest. He didn't want her here. He didn't want to subject her to the kind of disdain and vitriol his family were capable of.

He tensed as a hand clamped possessively across his shoulders, and then eased, realising that it was Maria.

'Are we having fun yet?' she demanded, as if it was his fault that the party was so stiff.

'Just waiting on *you*,' he said, leaning into her side, and she pushed him away. He took her in—a riot of dark lazy curls that framed high cheekbones, a button nose, a perfect bowed lip and an arched eyebrow that bored daggers into him.

Much to her apparent frustration, Maria had grown into a very beautiful woman who clearly hated that it made it harder for men to take her seriously. Especially in the boardroom. Not that they thought that way for long. But while Maria had inherited her beauty from her mother, she had inherited her grandfather's cut-throat business acumen.

In the hierarchy of the family, she might be considered to be at the bottom rung of the ladder, but Antonio anticipated the day when they would realise she was the best heir to the Gallo throne. It was just a shame that she needed to marry him to prove that.

'Is that her?' Maria asked, nodding towards where his mother stood.

'Mm,' he acknowledged, picking his mother and his wife out of the crowd.

'She's pretty,' Maria observed.

'Mm,' Antonio conceded with a smirk that Maria seemed to find funny.

'You *like* her.'

He turned and glared at his cousin.

Her smile dropped a little. 'Do you *like* her, like her?'

'Why can no one speak in sentences any more?' he demanded, tossing his hands in the air before stalking towards the bar to get himself a drink.

'Antonio—' she stopped him with a hand on his arm '—is this a problem? Should I be worried?'

It was the first hint of vulnerability he'd ever seen her display, which was enough to remind him of what was at stake for her. Everything.

He closed the distance he'd put between them. 'No, it's not. The plan is the same. We're just here to fulfil the requirements of an asinine judge before he grants us a divorce.'

Maria closed her eyes and nodded. *'Va bene.'* And when she opened them again she was smiling as if nothing had happened.

'Ah, there you both are!' his mother called from over his shoulder and this time he was the one that grimaced.

Per l'amor di Dio, he just wanted a drink.

He turned to watch them approach, feeling more than a few curious gazes on them.

'Ivy, may I introduce Maria?' he said, turning to Maria. 'Maria, this is Ivy.'

'There. See? It wasn't so bad,' his mother whispered before slipping back into the crowds.

Antonio sighed, while Maria's smile was big, beautiful and confident.

'It's lovely to meet you, Ivy. I've heard a lot about you,' she said, her hand outstretched.

Ivy smiled and took the offered hand. 'I imagine that would be quite hard, but that you've heard about me at all bodes well.'

'You work in a library?' Maria asked, leading them over to the bar where finally, thankfully, Antonio could get a drink.

He let their conversation drift over him, parsing it for anything alarming while he scanned the rest of the guests. He saw the familiar disdain in the side glances, felt the whispers and the hostility towards someone who wasn't 'of their blood'.

He didn't care. Truthfully. These people didn't mean anything to him. But while they didn't own Gallo Group, they certainly sat on the board and benefitted from it. And that was important to Maria, so he'd play their game.

Until he got Maria what she deserved.

An elaborate dinner began at about the time Ivy was used to going to bed and she resisted the urge for another glass of wine, knowing she would have to keep her wits about her. They were outside, at an impossibly long table beneath a pergola from which hung luscious vines hiding grapes within their leaves.

She'd tried to make conversation with the woman beside her, but had given up soon after it became painfully clear that she wasn't the least bit interested. Instead, Ivy turned her attention back to Antonio, who had asked if she was okay with the lighting.

It was rather dark, but she'd assured him that she was fine. Throughout the day she'd felt his solicitous attention, which only served to unnerve her more. As they tucked into beef Carpaccio, Ivy willed herself to eat, even though what Antonio's mother had told her earlier that afternoon had left her stomach quivering with emotion.

'They have a special relationship,' she'd said of Maria and Antonio as she had led her away from the party, looking for somewhere private to talk. 'Maria was there for him when his own father couldn't be. My husband was a man who underestimated himself, and when confronted with his own failures decided to run from them rather than stay and fight.' Alessia had lowered her head in shame.

'One night, Antonio overheard my husband saying that he regretted ever adopting him... Antonio ran away. We searched for him for hours, but couldn't find him. My husband, he...he said that he couldn't live like this. He couldn't bear to be a man who didn't want his wife's child, and if he stayed that's all he would ever be: despicable and unworthy. The man I married had been a kind, loving man. But Antonio was an affront to his masculinity and in an environment where that was paramount, he crumbled. So he left, before we'd even found Antonio.'

A sliver of hurt had cut Ivy deep. 'How did you find him?' she asked.

'Luca, Maria's father, called, saying that Maria knew where he was. She, Antonio and Micha would often play in a nearby forest and she was sure that's where he would be. She wouldn't stop screaming until we let her take us there to find him.'

Ivy's had chest stirred. 'How old was he when this happened?'

'Eight. Maria, six. He'd been there for several hours before Maria led us to him.'

Ivy had cursed silently; an image of Jamie had popped into her head and the rage she felt was fierce and swift. And she couldn't help the question that fell from her lips. 'What happened to your husband?'

'I don't know and I don't care,' Alessia had said, with a sad determination in her gaze. 'Which is precisely why I changed our surnames back to Gallo. He is nothing to us, *no*?' Alessia said, and Ivy understood completely.

'I don't say this easily,' Antonio's mother continued, 'but I say this because I think you should know this about my son. He is fiercely loyal to those who love him and he seems to think that's all he needs. But I believe he needs more.'

And something in Ivy's heart ached. Ached that Antonio had a mother who wanted more for her son. Ached that Alessia was the kind of mother Ivy would have wanted growing up. One who had chosen to stay instead of leave—fight for her family instead of surrender it. One who loved her child above other more selfish wants.

The clatter of cutlery drew Ivy back to the dinner and she cast a look at Antonio beside her, his profile a study in chiaroscuro, his features slashes of shades of darkness and light.

Plates were taken, and course after course continued, as Ivy thought over what Alessia had said. Remembering the way Antonio had looked at her when he'd realised she'd been alone at the hospital when he'd ignored her call. She'd been an adult when that had happened to her, but what about him? He'd only been a child when he'd been abandoned by the very people who should have cared for him the most. And she knew—*knew*—the kind of wound that inflicted. The hurt...the pain.

She felt Antonio's arm come across the back of her chair, unknowingly offering her reassurance and comfort for the ache she felt for *him*.

'Are you okay?' he whispered in her ear.

She nodded, even as her heart turned for him. She smiled up at him and, in doing so, caught the snide gaze of a family member. A mean giggle cut across the table. The hostility surprised her and angered her in equal measure. How could they be so openly cruel? How could Antonio have put up with this for his entire life?

Antonio flicked a gaze between Ivy and his cousin, and

tossed his napkin onto his plate. He turned to his mother on his other side and said something, before getting to his feet and holding his hand for her to take.

Silence descended over the table, dinner hadn't finished yet, but he only had eyes for her. Right now, she held onto that, ignoring the rest of the family the same way he did. She took his hand and let him lead her away from the table and back into the sprawling villa that she would most certainly have got lost in had she not been guided by him.

They passed through gently lit hallways with stone flooring and ancient wooden beams above. The colours of muted plaster and soft terracotta passed in a blur as Antonio led her into the heart of the villa.

They came to a stop outside a door at the end of a corridor. He pushed it open and gestured for her to go inside. 'I don't care what my mother said,' he told her, waiting at the door. 'I'll find somewhere else to sleep.'

Ivy bit her lip. 'Actually, can you stay?'

His face was a mask, disguising his thoughts, but she wouldn't regret asking him. She didn't want to be alone in this unfamiliar mansion. His wound had opened hers and she felt vulnerable in a way she couldn't put words to.

'Are you sure?'

'We're both adults, Antonio,' she said with more conviction than she felt, passing him to enter the room.

The bed was large and dominated the entire back wall. It sat against exposed brickwork that looked traditional, while sleek fittings in light touches made the space feel modern and open. The room was lit with gentle up-lights, making the most of the high ceilings, but really, all Ivy saw was the bed.

Her bag was next to his, beside a chaise longue that was too small for either of them and she wandered over to the window that looked out on the opposite side of the villa to where they had been having dinner.

'Tired?' he asked from behind her.

'Yes,' she lied, already doubting that she'd get even a minute of sleep lying next to Antonio Gallo.

An uncomfortable silence filled the room. Neither of them moved from where they stood.

'Can I ask you a question?' she said before she could stop herself.

'*Sì.*'

She turned to face him. 'Do you want to get married?'

He watched her carefully. 'I *am* married,' he said slowly—as if wary about where this could be going.

Ivy bit back an impatient sigh. 'One day. Not to Maria. If that was all sorted out, would you want to get married? To someone you fell in love with?' she asked.

He huffed out a laugh. *'Non è possibile.'*

'Of course it's possible,' Ivy shot back, trying to hide her frustration.

'No, Ivy. I won't get married. A ring? A vow? A piece of paper? Meaningless. In my experience, paperwork is no guarantee of feelings, of *love*, of *safety*,' he said scornfully. 'It didn't mean anything when my mother's husband legally adopted me, and it didn't mean anything when he then went on to divorce her,' he said, as she tried not to flinch at the vehemence in his tone. 'So, no. *Non è possibile*,' he repeated, stressing his previous words.

Ivy opened her mouth to protest, but he cut her off.

'Would you like to use the bathroom first?' he offered politely, as if he hadn't just ripped open a wound for her to see.

She hovered, wondering whether to press the issue, but the determined bent to his gaze told her it was a fool's errand. She slipped into the en suite bathroom, went to the sink and braced her hands either side of it.

Her heart ached for him. For all the things that he'd not said and for the things that he had. In that moment, she thanked God for Maria, that she had been there for Antonio, and that his mother had loved Antonio enough to stay. Ivy understood why he was so determined to help Maria inherit Gallo Group now, and she silently promised to do whatever she could to assist them both.

Rolling her shoulders, she stepped beneath the blissful jets of the shower, lathering soap to wash away the imprints of sadness and hurt for Antonio, who was now old enough to look after himself.

She wondered what he was doing right this minute. Pacing the room, checking his phone? Getting ready for bed...? Soap bubbles slid over sensitive skin, and pulse points throbbed in places she'd nearly forgotten. In her mind, she saw him unbuttoning his shirt, the way he'd done by the pool the other day, and shivered. She felt his hands around her waist and trembled.

She shook her head. This was madness. She should *never* have asked him to stay. She'd get out of the shower and tell him she'd made a mistake. He'd understand, she knew he would. She dried off and stepped into her silk pyjamas, jaw clenched with tension, want in a turf war with need inside her chest. She'd just tell him she'd been feeling overtired and now that she was in the room he could—

She opened the door to find Antonio, eyes closed and arms crossed behind his head, already in the bed—his clothes in a neat pile on the chaise longue.

Oh.

Her breath stopped in her lungs.

He wasn't asleep. She knew that much. But he was shutting her out. She stole one last moment to take him in. The bulge of his biceps, the breadth of his chest, the whorls of hair that dusted pectorals and bisected abdominal muscles. Her hungry gaze gathered as much of him to her memory as it could.

'Get into bed, Ivy,' he ordered, his eyes still closed.

Mortified, her cheeks on fire, she slipped beneath the smooth covers on the opposite side of the bed to him. More aware of her body than she had *ever* been before in her life, she gripped the edge of the mattress with white knuckles, hoping that she wouldn't move from there in her sleep.

She willed her pulse to slow and her breathing to calm and after ten minutes she was nearly there, when Antonio asked, 'What about you? Would you marry again?'

She bit her lip. 'No,' she told him. But for a reason she wasn't able or willing to put into words just then.

CHAPTER SEVEN

ANTONIO HAD WOKEN three times during the night. That he'd even *fallen* asleep was miraculous. He'd been driven near out of his mind when he'd heard the shower turn on. Images, conjured from a mix of fantasy and memories from their time in the pool, provided such a vivid impression that he'd had to adjust himself in his briefs.

The first time he'd woken, he'd found himself pressed against Ivy's back, one hand fisting the sheet by his thigh and the other pinned beneath his head. He'd carefully removed himself and retreated to the other side of the bed.

The second time he'd woken to find that she'd turned to face him, her head tucked into his chest, and the arm that had previously been pinned beneath his head was now free to hold her to his side.

The third time, the final time, he'd blinked his eyes open and she was gone. And after a shocking moment of regret, he was relieved. Relieved and thankful. By that afternoon they'd be heading back to his villa, where there were two totally separate beds for them to sleep in.

But that didn't help his present state of arousal. He cursed, throwing his head back on the pillow. It had been far too long since he'd last shared pleasure with a woman. He didn't have to rack his brain. He didn't even have to question when. It had been over six years earlier.

Antonio hadn't initially intended to keep to his marriage vow to forsake all others, not consciously anyway. Back then he'd still, whether he wanted to admit it or not, been reeling from the discovery that the woman he'd been seeing was more interested in his bank account than his personality. Yes, he was self-aware enough to understand the irony. Poor little rich boy. But she'd hidden it better than the other women he'd encountered in his life. Of course, when Gio had threatened to cut him off she'd disappeared, just like all the others.

That was one of the reasons why Ivy had appealed to him. Because he'd known what she wanted from the beginning. Just the money. The terms had been agreed, there was no ulterior motive, nothing to be uncovered. Nothing to catch him by surprise. He was the one in control. And then, when Gio had cut him off, Antonio had thrown himself into the hard work that was needed to make his business as successful as it was. He'd pulled eighteen, nineteen-hour days, seven days a week, for years. And thinking on it now, this was the longest time he'd had away from work. Ever.

Women hadn't even factored in those first few years, and then he'd realised that life had just been easier without them in it. Less risk, more reward. But for the first time in those six and a bit years, he knew that taking himself in hand wouldn't even begin to satisfy the need coursing through his veins, courtesy of his deeply inconvenient wife.

He threw back the covers, stalked to the bathroom. He glared at himself in the mirror, the dark smudges beneath his eyes advertising his restless sleep. He tried to ignore Ivy's open toiletries bag and the mismatch of skincare containers.

'...it's the little things. Like knowing what skincare brand she uses...'

He didn't want to know. He didn't want Ivy creeping into his life even more than she had already.

Biting back a curse, he turned on the shower and stepped beneath the powerful jets of water. The frigid temperature might have numbed his skin, but it did nothing to touch the heat bubbling beneath the surface. Leaning one hand against the cool tiles, he took himself in the other with long, powerful strokes. His head fell back, open to the water as it pounded against his face, the pleasure an unsatisfying imitation of what he really wanted.

Ivy.

Ivy smiled at Maria as she searched the breakfast buffet that was big enough to feed the army that was the Gallo family. She was looking for herbal tea, but craving the fresh mint that Agata made so well.

'How did you sleep?' Maria asked by way of greeting.

Terribly.

Amazingly.

Not that Ivy would even think of telling Maria what it was like to wake up to feel Antonio beside her. How that, for the first time in ages, despite the way her body lit up like a firework, she'd also slept the most sound, deep sleep she'd had in what felt like years. Yet, even though she was utterly rested, she was restless and agitated.

'Good, thank you. And you?'

Maria gave a graceful shrug. 'I drank too much,' she admitted freely, and Ivy couldn't help but smile. There was something infectious about the energy Maria had. It was powerful. 'But you must have the *cornetti*—they're homemade and divine,' she added, before her eyes landed on the pot of coffee on the other end of the table and she disappeared, leaving only a moan in her wake.

Ivy smiled to herself as she wandered further along the table, seeing the pastries Maria had mentioned. She picked up a plate just as someone else picked up the tongs.

'Allow me, *signora*.'

Ivy's gaze flickered to the face of the man who had offered to help her to some pastries and stopped. 'Micha!' she exclaimed in a whisper.

'It is good to see you again, Ivy.'

It was silly, she knew that, but she cast her gaze around, knowing that Antonio wouldn't like her talking to him.

'I had hoped to be here last night, but work kept me away,' he said, picking up a *cornetto* and putting it on her plate. 'Alessia was kind enough to extend an invitation to me,' Micha explained as if she would have queried his presence.

The tension she felt shifted to compassion, sensing that he too was not entirely at home here.

'I'm sorry about Signor Gallo,' she said to him, and something flashed in his gaze. She imagined that most people thought Micha's relationship with Antonio's grandfather was that of employee and employer, but when he had approached her in London last year, Ivy had seen it to be more than that.

'*Grazie,*' he said, and he meant it, she could tell. 'How is the—?' He broke off and tapped beside his eye.

Ivy smiled, knowing that he'd been concerned for her when they'd met. Apparently, Gio Gallo had a full dossier compiled on her and knew full well about her accident and her eye. Gio, she assumed, was a man who'd wanted to *'know thine enemy'*. But by the time she'd met Micha, Ivy had been well on the way to recovery.

'It's about the same,' she admitted, 'but I'm working again and that feels good.'

Micha's face was expressionless, but still she felt something shift.

'Was Signor Gallo angry when you went back to Italy?' she asked, wondering what had happened after he'd left London. 'When I refused his request?'

Micha pouted and shrugged. 'More surprised. You impressed him.'

That hadn't been her intention. Although it might have been shocking to the Gallos to have someone considerably less wealthy refuse such a request, Ivy hadn't even needed to think about it. She had given Antonio her vow. He was the only one who could ask her to break it.

'Not enough to make him change his will,' Ivy pointed out, despite the small burst of pride that she'd managed to impress Antonio's grandfather.

'No. Signor Gallo was consistent in one thing. He wanted his company to stay in the family. It was…important to him. He did many things to ensure it happened the way he wanted.'

There were shadows and a story in Micha's eyes, but now wasn't the place nor the time for it. Ivy wondered, as Micha bowed his head and left her to breakfast, if many people took the time to look beyond the forbidding façade he showed the world. But as she encountered the curious, sometimes hostile, mainly disdainful looks on the faces of the Gallo family, she doubted it. She might have hated growing up with an absent father and a mother who cared only about her own wants and needs, but at least she'd had Jamie. And that had to have been better than growing up in the viper den that was the Gallo family.

She went to sit at one of the smaller tables and was halfway through a mouthful of the—as advertised—*divine* pastry, when a ball hit her ankles. A little girl with a riot of dark brown hair and startlingly blue eyes careened towards her in a way that suggested she hadn't long since learned to walk. And before she knew it, Ivy was embroiled in a game with three children, a puppy and a ball, so much so that she was completely unaware of Antonio approaching Micha after their encounter.

'What the hell was that?' Antonio growled into Micha's ear, having stalked across the garden.

'I have no idea what you're talking about,' Micha replied, not even bothering to look at him as he picked up the espresso cup by its rim, with his thumb and forefinger. Antonio wanted to bat the thing out of his hand.

'Don't. Not today. Not now,' Antonio demanded. 'How do you know Ivy?'

Rage was pouring through his veins, thick, hot, heavy, sending him out of his mind. A distant part of him recognised that he was close to losing control. It whispered for restraint, but all he could think of was the insidious idea that Micha, Gio and Ivy had colluded somehow, for some nefarious purpose. That there *had* been an ulterior motive all along. Even though he couldn't see how anyone would gain from it, the thought had taken hold.

This couldn't be happening. Not again.

Micha cast a look over Antonio's shoulder. 'You're causing a scene.'

'You think *this* is causing a scene?' he demanded, not bothering to lower his voice. 'Keep it up, Micha, it's just the beginning.'

'And how would your mother feel about that?' Micha chided.

'Vaffanculo—'

'Watch your language. There are children present.'

Outrage poured through Antonio. Micha had the gall to scold *him*?

Micha gestured for him to follow as he turned away from the family gathering over breakfast and towards one of the old barns on the property. The moment they were out of sight of the family, Antonio gripped Micha by the shirt and pushed him up against a building.

The only thing that stopped this from going further was the fact that Micha wasn't fighting back. Not even pushing. No, instead, the bastard was laughing.

'*Calmati*, Antonio. Seriously. What's got into you?'

It was a damn good question. Antonio released his grip, stepping back in disgust, whether for himself or for Micha he didn't know.

'Tell me how you know her,' he ordered.

'What makes you think—?'

'I saw you both talking. That wasn't a "hi, nice to meet you" conversation.'

Micha looked at him, assessing, debating.

'Just spit it out.'

'Okay,' Micha said, arms raised in surrender. 'Are you sure you want to know?'

Antonio's stomach turned. If Ivy was like everyone else, if she had somehow used him…betrayed him… Then, yes. He needed to know. For himself. For his sanity. When had she become so important to him, enough to make him so reckless as to physically assault someone? He couldn't say. But the idea that she had wanted to use him—

'Whatever it is you're thinking, you're wrong,' Micha said, dusting his hands off each other. He looked out into the distance and pulled loose the tie at his throat. Then he shook his head. 'Gio asked me to find her.'

'When?' The question shot out of him.

'Last year.'

'What? Why?' Antonio demanded.

'He wanted to pay her off to divorce you.'

'What?'

Shock nearly buckled his knees. His mouth fell open with a thousand questions, but nothing came out.

Micha squinted in the morning sun. 'Gio knew he wasn't well and he was desperate. He wanted to see you married to Maria. He wanted that damn company to stay *in the family* and was willing to do whatever it took.'

'Including paying Ivy off?' he said. 'Is that why she's here? Is she going to collect money from the will or something?'

'What?' Micha asked, confused. '*Imbecille*. She said no,' he announced, pulling the sleeves of his shirt down by his cuffs.

'She said no.'

'Antonio, how is it that you have a multinational corporation, when all you do is parrot what I say?' Micha demanded as if he were thick. 'She said no, I left, that's it.'

'How much was she offered?' Antonio asked, his eyes closed, as if that would somehow soften the blow of his monumental misjudgement of her.

'Half a million.'

Breath shot out of his lungs. He'd only given her half that much to marry him in the first place.

'She said no?' Antonio repeated. 'Why?' he asked incredulously.

'You will have to ask your wife,' Micha said disdainfully.

'Half a million,' Antonio repeated, stunned, opening his eyes to find Micha looking at him accusatorily.

'Yes. Half a million. And I know how much you paid

her, don't think I don't. I also know what she could have done with that money too,' Micha warned, and Antonio was struck by the sense that Micha Rufina knew more about his wife than he had seven days ago. 'I'd not really thought you were a bastard, until then,' Micha said, shocking Antonio with the vehemence in his tone. 'She deserves better than you. And one day I hope she finds it.'

With that parting shot, Micha left Antonio reeling.

Something was different about Antonio when he came to find her later that morning.

'We're leaving,' he announced in a clipped tone.

She looked up at him, immediately worried. 'Has something happened?'

'No.'

'Did I do something wrong?' she asked in a whisper, aware of the attention his behaviour was drawing.

He simply stared at her, his expression heated but unreadable.

'What about the assessment?' she asked as he led her away from the courtyard where the little group of children she'd been playing with were waving after her. 'Do we need proof that I was here?'

'There'll be photographs. We have done as was asked. We can now truthfully say that you have met my family. You certainly seem to have made an impression,' he said, opening the passenger door of his car for her with more force than was strictly necessary.

'Antonio—'

'Not here. They are still looking,' Antonio said of his family, some of whom she saw pretending not to stare when she cast her gaze back to them.

It nearly gave her a headache, having to spin the threads

of lies into a rug thick enough to stand on. She didn't know how Antonio and Maria had grown up like this. Micha too. Ivy wasn't quite sure how he'd fitted into their childhood—clearly, at some point there was a severed connection. And she couldn't help but think that Gio Gallo was the hand that had wielded that knife too.

And not for the first time, she found herself thinking uncharitably of the man whose hand reached beyond the grave and into the present to achieve his own ends. Yes, she understood wanting to protect family—after all, she was here precisely because she had wanted to help Jamie. But at some point people had to live their own lives.

Did you?

The question caught her by surprise. Had *she* lived her own life? Losing her sight and her flat after the accident had thrown her off her path. But now? What did she want for her life now?

Antonio manoeuvred the car down the gravel drive, away from his mother, who had come to stand at the front door to bid them farewell, the same unreadable expression on the older woman's gaze as worn by her son. They might not be blood, but their bond was irrefutable.

'I believe he needs more.'

Her words echoed in Ivy's mind on a loop. She felt the same way, but she just didn't know what it would take for him to feel that way too. And right now? Tension coiled like a rope through the body of the man beside her, the sleeves rolled up on his forearms revealing the power he used each time he changed gear.

'Antonio—' she tried, but he cut her off before she could finish.

'I need to concentrate on the drive,' he announced

through his teeth, and she wondered what demons he was battling.

It was an uncomfortable forty-minute drive back to the villa.

She didn't want to have done something wrong, she realised. She didn't want to disappoint him. The hostility she'd felt directed towards him from some members of his family was horrible and unjust, whether it was because he was adopted or just because he stood to inherit half a business that they wanted to get their hands on themselves.

He might have been watching out for her throughout the visit with his family, but she'd been paying him just as much attention. She'd seen the way he'd been with Maria and his mother. She'd seen the way he'd been easy with those he'd got on with, and polite even with those who he hadn't.

She liked him. Admired him—how he handled himself. She might not agree with how he went about things—she still wasn't sure that using marriage as if it was part of some business deal was okay. But she understood why he was doing it now. Understood what Maria meant to him.

But understanding Antonio and what made him tick was a double-edged sword, deepening her already risky feelings for him while at the very same time making it heartbreakingly clear that he would never feel the same way about her. Because his bond with the people he had chosen to be loyal to, his mother, Maria—*his family*—the very thing that she admired most about him, would always come before her.

When the car finally pulled up at the villa, the winding drive strangely familiar and welcome, Antonio turned off the engine and neither of them moved. They sat in silence as the car engine ticked. But while the car cooled, the tension in the air between them heated. Not like the heat from last night, but a different kind of heat. Angry, restless, but unsure and dangerous.

Ivy got out of the car first, heart bruised already, and was halfway towards the villa when she heard Antonio's car door open.

'Why didn't you tell me about Micha?' she heard him ask from over her shoulder.

Breath shuddered in her lungs and she dropped her head. She huffed out a small laugh.

Why hadn't she told him that Gio had tried to buy her off?

She wasn't sure he'd actually believe her if she told him that it was because she hadn't wanted to hurt him. That she had been keeping her vow to protect him. Because she knew. She knew that you could cut ties and still be hurt by the people who should have loved you the most.

And no matter what she'd felt waiting in that hospital room, hoping against all hope that he might come for her. No matter what she'd felt then, Antonio had never deserved what Gio Gallo had tried to do.

She turned and took in the sight of him. Halfway out of the car, his arm braced across the top of the door, his sunglasses hiding his gaze from her view, he was even more unreadable than usual. But she saw it. The tic in his jaw, the tension. The hurt.

'I didn't want to make things worse between you and your grandfather,' she admitted.

He took off his sunglasses and a part of her wished he hadn't. Confusion, hurt and frustration were quickly masked, as if the strength of his feelings was finally enough to make cracks in his usually unbreakable mask.

The grip he had on the top of the car door was white-knuckled and she wanted to go to him.

But she couldn't move. Not if she had any dignity left. Because if she did go to him, she might actually beg, plead with him to lift that mask. To let her see the real Antonio beneath it, because the glimpses she was beginning to see here and there were enough for her to half fall in love with him.

'What did Micha say? When he approached you.'

'Why do you need to know?' she asked.

'I just do,' he demanded belligerently.

She shook her head. The sun setting behind the villa reached out a warm glow across the rolling hills dropping away in the background, but picked Antonio out in near perfect detail. Unconsciously, her left eye closed just to take him in, in single form, but she blinked her eyes back open when it became too much.

Noticing the flicker in her left eye, Antonio extricated himself from the car, closed the door and went to stand before her. Boosted up by a few steps from where he stood, they were at eye level. And he needed that. He needed to see her expressive features up close, to see behind the words she carefully chose. Because no matter how hard Ivy tried to conceal it, her expressions made the truth as clear to him as a person's future to a palm reader.

'Micha found me about a year ago at the library. He introduced himself as working on behalf of your grandfather. He explained that they understood that we were married, but that it was only one of convenience. That Gio believed your point had been made, but he was still adamant that you should marry Maria.'

Antonio nodded, barely able to keep himself in check as he asked his next question. 'Did they threaten you?'

The quick flicker of confusion and disbelief across Ivy's face were answer enough, even before she spoke.

'No. My dealings with Micha were...' she shrugged '... cordial? I like him, actually.'

This time it was Antonio's turn to be full of disbelief. 'You *like* him? Micha?' he demanded, unable to stem the sudden burst of jealousy that poured through him like a freshly tapped oilwell. 'He's arrogant and manipulative,' he pointed out. 'He's mulish and disrespectful. I do not see what there is to like.'

Ivy smirked, her eyebrow artfully disdainful of his observation, and for some reason the look was breathtaking on her.

'Really? I found him quite similar in personality to you, actually.'

'Take that back,' Antonio demanded, wholly aware that he was sounding like a petulant teenager and absolutely unable to stop himself.

'You don't see it?' she questioned instead, the smile on delicately pink lips playful.

And in that moment he did see it. Not the similarity between him and the man who had been, at one point, almost as close to him as Maria. What Antonio saw was Ivy's beauty. Somewhere along the way it had wrapped around his chest and taken hold.

There, in the dusk, as the sun played off the golden shards in her eyes and the caramel embers in her chestnut locks, he realised just how beautiful she was. Heat spread through him, pushing at the anger and burning into darkness, bringing light to long-forgotten places.

'He is disloyal,' Antonio said, thinking of their childhood friendship and desperately holding onto the thread of their conversation rather than his body's reaction to her proximity.

'I...' she narrowed her eyes in consideration '... I don't think that's true. It's just that perhaps his loyalty is not to those *you* are loyal to.'

Internally, Antonio flinched. Ivy's keen observation of the dynamics of his family surprised him. Micha owed a debt to Gio Gallo, and had done even when they were younger. But that wasn't what Antonio was really interested in.

'Why didn't you say yes? Why didn't you take the money?' he asked. She'd been offered twice what he'd given her six years ago. She hadn't taken that for herself, but she'd taken ninety thousand for her library? The woman had no sense at all.

Discomfort clouded her gaze and in a quiet voice she said, 'I don't want the money. And I made my vows to you, not to Micha or your grandfather.'

She might as well have knocked him to the floor.

'The only person who had the right to ask me for a divorce was you,' she continued.

'And what if I'd never asked you for one?' he demanded, lips numb.

For the first time, there was nothing in her gaze. Everything stilled, Ivy apparently having learned to be wary just when he wanted to see her most. Her silence was her answer.

'Would you never have wanted a divorce for yourself? What if you met someone?' he asked, his curiosity suddenly inflamed. This woman was self-sacrificing to her own detriment. She could have bought herself a home outright with half a million. Security. She could have met someone and... He found himself growling at the thought before he could stop himself.

'Okay, I no longer understand what you're mad about,' Ivy announced. 'That I didn't want to divorce you? Or that I didn't tell you they'd tried to pay me to?'

'Both.'

'Why?' she demanded just as hotly as he'd replied.

'Because you refuse to do even the most basic things to protect yourself, and this world is not kind to people like that,' he said, unable to help himself.

'How dare you say that?' she hurled back, as if outraged. 'Everything I have done for the past three years was about clawing my way back from the darkest of days. Every day, every hour, every minute fought for, battled, and won. Even if it was just an inch. Even if it was just getting out of bed in the early days. So don't you dare tell me that I can't protect myself, just because I chose to do it in ways you don't recognise.'

Her finger prodded at his sternum accusatorily, but it was the truth she spoke that struck the real blow.

Because she was right. The knife sticking in his gut and twisting was the fact that, for all his words about having to protect his loved ones, Maria and his mother, for being a better man than his father, and his grandfather... the truth was that all this time it was *Ivy* who had been protecting *him*.

CHAPTER EIGHT

Ivy's cheeks burned with shock and shame. The finger that had been poking into Antonio's firm chest shook as she withdrew it to press it against her lips.

'I'm... I'm so sorry,' she said, and would have turned and fled had it not been for the arm that shot out and snared her by the waist, anchoring her, turning her.

Head bent, 'I should never have said that,' she confessed. The vulnerability arcing between them was painful. Because hadn't he been right? Wasn't she afraid of wanting things for herself, only to lose them all over again? Her home, her security, her sight. But it was more than that. It was the future. It was the future she'd thought she had.

'Look at me?'

It was a question, not a demand or a statement in the way he usually offered them. His voice was harsh, rasping, as if the words had been caught on gravel. But it was his gaze that undid her. Raw, unfiltered, powerful and... oh, so expressive. She saw it all. The want, the desire, the contest, and the recognition of truth.

The breath whooshed out of her lungs.

All the energy seemed to pour away from their argument, their fight, and he caught the dip of her head with his own, pressing his forehead against hers in near surrender. They were perilously close to the line drawn in the sand by their situation. But there was still time to walk this back. There was still time to leave.

Antonio's hands flexed around her waist, as if divining her thoughts, preventing her from running away.

Their breaths punched the air between them, she could feel his sharp exhale on her lips. Her heart pounded in her chest and coherent thought fled. She *wanted*. It was nothing more complicated than that and it was as undefinable. She just wanted…

'I need to marry Maria,' Antonio said, but it sounded more like a reminder to them both than an excuse.

'I know.'

'I can't let her down. Not now, not with so much at stake.'

She heard it. Felt the same warring twisting her gut. It was madness to put whatever this was above everything he'd worked for and everything she needed. But oh, God, she wanted to.

'I understand,' Ivy said truthfully. 'I really do.'

She hated that she did, but also knew it was one of the things that she most admired about him.

'But this…' he said, raising his head just enough to look her in the eye. 'But you…' He trailed off. His hand came to brush a lock of hair back behind her ear and stayed to cup her cheek.

Oh.

The heat of his hand, the feel of it against her skin. She wanted to lean into it. To take what it offered, to know what it felt like, what *he* felt like. She wanted the power of him, the security. She wanted, *needed* it, like the way she needed her next breath. Because if she walked away from this, without knowing what it felt like, she would spend the rest of her life wondering 'what if' and she knew exactly how damaging that was. What if she hadn't been struck by the cyclist? What if the first operation had worked? What if her parents had stayed?

'What ifs' were torment where regret was pain. But somehow, she knew that, no matter what happened between her and Antonio, she would never regret it.

She ground her teeth together to stop herself from saying as much. He couldn't be with her. Wouldn't. So she needed to walk away. She swallowed and turned, but he cursed and, before she could react, he had pulled her back to him and claimed her mouth with his.

The moan of pure want poured from her into him, setting them both ablaze.

He held her to him and she opened for him, without question or hesitation. She luxuriated in the way his tongue filled her, possessing her completely and utterly in a way she'd never known was even possible. She clung to him, her hands fisting in his shirt, a passion, an untapped femininity unleashed. Just for him. Just *by* him.

Her body flared with a single united pulse as he took her under his control.

Mindless and dizzy, she didn't fear the sensations; he would catch her if she fell. Oh, not for ever, not beyond this. She wasn't naïve enough to hope for more. But this was what she wanted. No regrets. No doubts.

This.

Him.

Antonio tried to hold onto the twisting wildfire that Ivy became in his hands, but could only touch and grasp. He didn't know who had been more shocked by the kiss, him or Ivy, but once that first barrier had been breached, once his lips had tasted hers, there was no going back. Not unless she willed it.

But for him? It was like finding something he'd never known he'd lost. Yet at the same time it was like being found. And then Ivy's gasp reached deep within him and put an end to any kind of coherent thought.

He walked them into the house without breaking the kiss. It wasn't as if there were prying eyes, but he needed… wanted… He prised open an eye and aimed for the side table.

He lifted her onto it, pushing between her legs, relishing the way she leaned forward into him. Here, not anywhere else, but *here* she fought him and matched him with every kind of fervour he could think to want for. Powerful, demanding, utterly unrestrained, it was the most glorious thing he'd ever seen or experienced.

'Agata?' Ivy asked against his lips, not even the thought of his housekeeper enough to bring a halt to her desire.

'Away. All of them are away,' he said of the staff.

Her hand swept into his hair, short nails scraping gently against his scalp as her mouth opened even more for him to possess. Harder than he'd ever been in his life, he needed more, more, more. The refrain pulsed through his veins maddeningly. But just as he was reconciling himself with the idea of slowing things down, Ivy yanked the shirt from his trousers and cool little hands swept over his sensitive skin. His body reacted instinctively, his hands reaching around her to pull her firmly against the hard length of him.

Ivy, leaning back against the wall, stared at him with eyes so carnal, so lustful, so damn wanton he would never, for as long as he lived, forget her like that.

'Incredible…' The word fell from his lips and her eyes glowed.

He throbbed for her and never, not even as an untested youth had he felt so helpless to stop himself. But he would. For her. Because she had to understand. She had to know.

And even if it would put an end to things right now, he would still ask her. She had to have power in that.

'Ivy, this changes nothing,' he confessed, forcing himself to look her in the eye.

'I know. And I still don't want to stop,' she said, meeting his gaze, understanding and determination clear in her eyes.

'Are you sure? Because—'

'If you're going to tell me I can change my mind, stop at any time, I appreciate that, Antonio, I really do. But,' she said, her body quivering as she inhaled, 'I want this. I want *a few spectacular weeks*—the ones we never had when we first married,' she said, referring to the lie that they had carved from reality.

'It will only be days, Ivy. We have so little time.'

'I still want them,' she said, a plea in her gaze.

Antonio's breath caught in his throat. Because he wanted them too. With a ferocity that should have scared him. And perhaps if he hadn't been half out of his mind with lust, he might have listened to that fear. But instead, he was helpless to resist.

'Then your wish is my command.'

Her body leaned instinctively towards his, but he shook his head slowly as he raked his gaze over her. Hair dishevelled, lips kiss-bruised, breasts heaving with every inhale—breasts he would come back to, he vowed—but he knew where he needed to be.

His fingers flexed around the backs of her knees and palmed smooth thighs as he ruched the material of her skirt. His eyes on hers caught the moment she realised— caught the anticipation, the shock, the want.

'Is this okay?' he asked, sinking to his knees.

She swallowed and nodded, and he doubted she even

realised how her tongue came out to sweep across her bottom lip, before pinning it with her teeth. He hid his smile. He'd help her find her voice, even if it was the only thing he could do for her before they parted.

Cazzo, she was beautiful.

He loved watching her every thought pulse in her eyes, her every want. And yes, she wanted this, but not as much as he wanted to do it.

Gently lifting her legs over his shoulders, he settled between them and, unable to wait, he pressed an open-mouthed kiss to her core. She shifted restlessly around him, her knickers soaked now from both sides, the faint taste of her on his tongue not even beginning to be enough.

He teased her, thumb pressing against her entrance, blocked by the thin cotton barrier, driving them both wild, until he couldn't take it any more. Too impatient, he simply moved her panties aside and claimed her with his mouth.

Gasps of pleasure filled the large hallway, melting into moans. His fingers massaged her thighs as he drew his tongue in one long strike across the length of her core, before he teased the little bundle of nerves that drove her wild around him.

He hummed his own pleasure against her delicate flesh as she writhed for him. He hooked his thumb against her entrance, pulling down so very gently, before turning his hand and teasing her with his forefinger. She arched forward, away from the wall, and he reached a hand up to hold her back, his palm flattening on her sternum between her breasts.

She was delicious. Everything about her was a damn delicacy.

A second finger joined the first, and he filled her and teased her with his tongue and his hands. Her pleas became desperate, her moans like music to his ears as he drew her closer and closer to a peak he could almost taste.

Her whole body pulsed with an energy that he felt in his own, throbbed in time with the pounding of his heart. His name on her lips was a mantra in his soul. She was so close, he could tell, all he had to do was… He took that little bundle of nerves into his mouth and sucked, hard, and Ivy fell apart, on *his* tongue, around *his* fingers, in *his* arms, in the hallway of *his* home. The possessive roar that filled his body as aftershocks flickered through hers should have shocked him, should have sent him running for the hills. But instead, he just wanted more.

Ivy saw flashes of light against the backs of her eyes and for the first time in three years she wasn't scared, she didn't fear for her sight, herself or her future. No. Right at that moment, Antonio anchored her in the present, to bliss, to a sense of something that was nearly beyond description. Her body *sang*. It had bowed to his name, it had bucked to his command and she was free within that. Absolutely unrestrained and free.

She owed nothing, was responsible for nothing, feared *nothing*, and it was a liberation her body had known would happen before her mind had. He'd held her as the shocks had receded from her body, cradled in his arms, *protected*. He'd ensured her pleasure before his own and that made her feel special. Oh, she knew it was dangerous to think like that, but just for tonight, just for now, she wanted to indulge in the fantasy that Antonio was hers and he wanted her just as much as she wanted him.

'Are you okay, *cara*?' he asked, rising to his feet and pressing his forehead gently against hers.

She nodded, and hummed her answer, not quite ready

for coherent sentences yet. She looked up to catch the trace of a satisfied smirk pulling his lips, before she was distracted by the intensity of his gaze.

Heat. Heat and more heat. It burned her already sensitive skin and when he pulled her against him she felt the hard press of his arousal against her core.

He encouraged her to lock her ankles around his waist and, once she'd done so, he picked her up as if she weighed nothing. Boneless, she draped herself around him, her head falling forward, her cheek pressed to the crook of his neck, where the scent of his cologne filled each breath. Every inhale brought her back to her senses which, shockingly, were already beginning to want more.

She shifted in his arms and felt the gentle chuckle undulate through him into her. 'Patience, *cara*. I'm not going to let the first time I take you be in the hallway, on a side table,' he promised her.

If he noticed the way she'd stilled at his mention of 'first', he chose to ignore it. God, could it be? Might there be more than just tonight? Ivy filed away the thought, along with the hope that flared within her. Just this. Just now, she told herself. That was all that mattered.

He reached the landing and carried her into his room, on the opposite side of the staircase from hers. He laid her gently on the bed, and she marvelled that they were both still fully clothed.

His eyes, hot and steady on hers, teased as he slowly began to undo the buttons of his shirt. She leaned back on her forearms, content to watch the display of masculine beauty. This was for her, for them. Antonio's near brutal efficiency would have seen all their clothes removed in a heartbeat, she imagined. But he wanted this, she could tell. He wanted her to see him like this.

He threw his shirt aside, letting her consume the sight of him to her heart's content. He kicked out of his shoes and socks, and the belt slid from his trousers with a slick slap that had her pinning her lips between her teeth.

Predatory. That was how he was looking at her. But not as if she were some vulnerable prey, simpering in the shadows, hoping to hide. No. She felt equal to him, he let her feel that, encouraged it. Spurred on by the challenge in his gaze, she began to draw her skirt up her legs and thighs, relishing the way she had captured his hungry attention. The slide of the soft material rose goosebumps on her flesh as she realised the double-edged sword of her sensual play worked both ways: on him *and* her.

Antonio flicked open the button of his trousers, and without taking his eyes from hers, he removed them and his briefs together. Fascinated, her gaze feasted upon the dips and curves of his muscles, the restraint he'd shown in prioritising her needs reflected in the tension beneath his skin. She was speechless. Just looking at him made her hot and wanton.

Suddenly now frustrated with the clothes covering her body, she slipped the silk cami up and over her head, throwing it aside as he took a step closer. She pushed the skirt away from her waist and down her legs, along with her knickers, and carelessly tossed the expensive clothes away from them.

Ivy tried not to but she couldn't help herself, sliding her legs against each other, desperate to ease the ache that was beginning all over again, just from the power of his gaze.

He knelt on the bed at her feet.

'This is what you do to me, *cara*. Know that. Just you. No one else.'

While she hadn't needed to hear that, it touched a part

of her, it fed a hungry, yearning part of her that she didn't recognise. And when he came down over her, he whispered in her ear. He told her the things he wanted to do to her, *with* her, in both English and Italian. He slipped the strap of her bra from her shoulder, following it with his kisses, before removing it deftly with one hand, all the while the other worshipped and teased her nipples.

Her head fell back as he lay between her legs, as he feasted on her breasts, and she just let him. Just enjoyed the feel of him consuming her piece by piece, inch by inch, pulse by pulse. He owned her completely and she just didn't care. Because it was the most exquisite feeling in the world.

She knew he took as much pleasure from this as she did. She could hear it in the words of praise he peppered her with, in between licks and sucks and guttural moans of delight.

But soon the pressure began to build and she grew restless beneath him, wanting more, wanting him, needing him to fill her, truly and completely. As if reading her body's needs, without removing his attention from her breast, he reached to the bedside table and retrieved a condom.

She watched, fascinated, as he tore the foil with his teeth and then sheathed himself, his hand fisting the base of his length and making her flush with desire.

'*Cara*—' he started, but she interrupted him.

'I want this, Antonio. I want you,' she said, insistent. 'I want to feel you inside me, and I want the next time I hear my name from your mouth to be as you come, deep within me.'

His eyes blazed at her bold words. The muscle at his jaw flickering, he huffed out a breath as if shocked, as if stunned. And she was pleased, because at least it meant that he was feeling just a little of what she was feeling.

She'd found her power. It was still a little unfamiliar, but she wanted him to be the first she shared that with. The first to know it and feel it with her.

As he settled between her legs, lined himself up with her entrance, and spread her with his girth where, inch by glorious inch, he filled her, her breath was sobbing in her chest from sheer euphoria. And in that moment she knew that she'd never be the same again.

The feel of Ivy encasing him launched Antonio out of his mind. Everything but her felt intangible, everything but her felt ephemeral and inconsequential. He'd never experienced anything like it, and while a part of him recognised that it had been some time since he'd shared his bed with a woman, this was not like that. The two things were incomparable.

He gave himself over to her, to pure sensation. They moved together as if they were the same tide, brushing up against the shore, Ivy's breaths the sound of the ocean and his body the current, pushing and pulling with no destination in mind other than bliss.

And while his mind would have held him back, like an anchor dropped into the seabed, reminding him of the limits of what they could be to each other, the magic they were making eclipsed all rationality.

The erotic sounds of her pleasure drenched him in sweat, heightening his sensitivity and making him only want to hear more. Once again, his own needs were brushed aside, because all he wanted was her. All he sought was her.

He took her hips and pulled her further onto him, obsessively watching as her head fell back, lost to the sensations between them. He ground against her and she cried out as he bit back a feral groan of his own. He held her there with one hand while the other came to the sensitive bundle of nerves just above where they were joined. His thumb strummed delicately over it, sending a cascade of shivers across her body, and he was rewarded with a carnal cry.

Over and over again, he stroked her, revelling in the slick slide of his length, deep within her. Pinned by his hand on her hip, Ivy drew her legs up, and he watched himself enter her and withdraw. Curses and prayers filled his mind in equal measure and he felt her eyes on him, knew she was watching him watch them.

A dark flush heated his cheeks as he flicked his gaze between her and where they came together, and tension gripped the base of his spine. As if mirroring his own, Ivy's body tightened around his length, pushing him further towards his own orgasm, but he held back. Teeth bared, hands white-knuckled, he wanted to feel her fall apart once again, he needed her to find her pleasure first. But every flutter of her muscles encouraged his own, back and forth, until they were both hurled into the depth of a midnight sea and lost on the waves of pleasure that nearly drowned them both.

Antonio collapsed back, taking her with him and draping her over him, unable to bear not touching her for even a moment. He should get up, he should take them into the shower, he should…

'Stop thinking,' Ivy murmured.

He bit back a smile. 'How did you—'

'I can hear it from here. The whirr of your brain. Just stop thinking,' she said.

So he did, deciding that Ivy didn't need help finding her voice. It was right there, and he was really enjoying it.

CHAPTER NINE

'I DON'T UNDERSTAND why you wanted to come *here*, of all places,' Antonio said, looking around the busy market stretching the seams of the square in Umbertide. 'I could have literally taken you anywhere. Rome, Orvieto, Puglia, if you like the sea, Positano even!'

All incredible locations she had heard of. And maybe, one day, she might see them all. But what she wanted now? She'd wanted to visit somewhere that she might never see without him. Somewhere without tourists, without money. That was what she'd asked for, and he'd brought her here.

Ivy laughed. 'You're such a snob.'

'I am not!' Antonio spun to face her, outrage in red slashes on his cheeks as he scanned the surrounding people to make sure they hadn't heard. 'I am *not*,' he insisted again in a whisper.

She laughed and hooked her free arm in his, the other holding her precious camera one-handed easily enough.

'I know. It's just too easy to tease you.' She smiled as they wove between shards of sunlight, tourists and locals, and cloth-covered stalls containing everything from fresh vegetables, multi-packs of underwear, second-hand books and kitchen utensils. It was *full* of people, of life, of noise and scents, and if she hadn't been with Antonio she'd have been utterly overwhelmed, but being here with him, *lean-*

ing on him, letting him protect her...it was the perfect way to spend her second to last day.

Tomorrow they would face the last assessment with Ms Quell, who had finally returned to Italy, but she didn't want to waste what precious little time she had left with Antonio dwelling on the misery that made her feel. She just wanted to enjoy every moment she could. And Antonio, it seemed, felt the same: determined to cling onto what they had with both hands, determined to try and satiate this need that had grown between them.

Since coming back from his mother's party a week ago they had spent almost the entire time in bed, learning, discovering, teasing and indulging.

Hiding, a quiet part of herself whispered.

Was that so bad? Really? The day after tomorrow, she would be back home in her South West London flat, getting ready to go to work, probably wondering if it had all been a dream. At some point in the future, she imagined herself confiding to a disbelieving friend that she'd once been married to an Italian billionaire and spent a wild two weeks in Tuscany. It was a strange feeling. As if part of her were living this now and part was already in the future, desperately clinging to the memory of it, even as it happened.

A flash of colour caught her eye and she drew to a stop, raising the camera and peering through the viewfinder, her bad eye naturally closing and the world coming into stark, beautiful, near shocking focus and her pulse slowed in appreciation.

She snapped the scene multiple times, marvelling when she'd finished that Antonio had remained patiently by her side until she was ready to move on. She hadn't even thought of it until she was done. She looked up at him, surprised, and he smiled down at her as if it had been the most natural thing in the world.

They walked from stall to stall, Ivy alternating between taking photographs and buying small things. A handful of fresh tomatoes that smelled like plums and basil, and some gorgeous bread. Antonio chose some cheese and dressed salads and salivated over artichokes and olives.

They stopped at a small artisan store run by a young woman selling handmade soaps, incense and essential oils, even little bottles of perfume. Antonio offered a few for her to try that made her nose scrunch. She wasn't a fan of the sweeter, more flowery scents, but there was an earthier one that reminded her of summer. Of Italy. Of *him*. And when Antonio wasn't looking, she bought a small sample of the perfume, knowing that when she was back in England it would remind her of this moment.

Ivy spent a while taking photographs of an older couple manning a lace stall, the story of their lives played out in wrinkles on their skin and sparkles in their eyes. Their love for each other was a privilege to see and she spent a long time gossiping with them in her half-forgotten Italian and listening to their stories of grandbabies and even great-grandbabies.

She thanked them and turned to find Antonio, who had procured a large wool blanket and an ice-cold bottle of wine.

'Can I see?' he asked, trying to peer at the screen on her camera.

She pulled it away from his prying gaze. 'No,' she said determinedly, but with good humour. The pictures were hers. Hers and perhaps the older couple's. But no, they were very much hers.

'Picnic?' he asked, not offended in the least by her response.

She honestly couldn't think of anything more perfect.

A short drive back towards his villa, Antonio found a spot near the woods that he'd once played in as a child, with Maria and Micha. He'd spent so long focused on the present, on building his own company, that only now did he realise just how much he'd avoided memories of his childhood. And while it was bittersweet, he went willingly to a spot that Ivy would love.

He parked up and they walked a short distance through the dappled light and fresh pine scents of the trees, until the dense foliage opened up into a glade. Ivy's gasp of delight was enough to tell him that he'd been right to trust his instincts. Even at the very beginning when he'd first met her, he realised now. He'd never felt that about another person. Never *known* them in the way he felt he knew Ivy. But he wanted more. More answers to the questions that sprang up from the bits and pieces he drew together to form the picture of Ivy he held deep within him.

He spread out the large blanket he'd happily paid a small fortune for—the market stall owner recognising a wealthy mark. Ivy sat, trying to unpack the things they'd bought for lunch and take in her surroundings at the same time.

He laughed and told her to go, shooing her away from the lunch preparations while she went to explore. Her camera was back out almost before the words had left his mouth.

When he was done, he stretched out, leaning back on his elbows and watching her walk in a slow circle around the glade. Lost completely to her pursuit, she moved more like she had done when he'd first met her. The sensual weave around the glade reminded him of when she had first caught his eye, slipping through the little tables and chairs of Affogato.

'What is it about taking pictures you like so much?' he asked, not needing to raise his voice much to reach her in the stillness of their surroundings.

There was a pause to her movements, her camera dropped a little as if she was considering how best to answer his question. She raised it to snap a few pictures of something he couldn't see and turned to him, firing off one of him, catching him a little off-guard. He wondered what she'd captured in him. His curiosity about her? His desire? Each as unquenchable as the other.

She smiled, lowering her camera and making her way towards him, losing just a little of that ease she'd had only moments before.

She came to sit on the blanket and he handed her wine in the glass she'd teased him about buying from the market so that they could be civilised with their picnic. She raised a wry brow at the glass but took a sip, pleasure breaking out over her features as she tasted the cool white Orvieto.

He waited. He knew she'd answer when she was ready. There was, he had discovered, no use trying to rush her.

'Photography was one of the lessons I took at the library following the accident,' she said with a small smile, which grew wider as she spoke. 'And it was amazing. I realised that the camera was the perfect solution for me. When I look through the viewfinder, my brain only has to deal with the information coming from that one eye—there's no double vision as it struggles to process the two conflicting images. It's wonderful. I'm not self-conscious—'

'You're self-conscious?' he asked, not liking that she

was. And he remembered all the things he'd made her do. Being the centre of what he'd thought was nothing more than a pampering session must have been hard, not to mention the dinner in the restaurant, and then meeting his family.

'A little, yes,' she admitted. 'I don't walk with the same security others do, or the way I used to. I don't orientate myself in the world the same way. When I'm tired my eyesight gets worse, and I have to squint more, or close my bad eye more. I tire more easily, over things that others don't. It's different, *I'm* different now. And no one likes that. Not really,' she said.

He bit his lip, self-recrimination a powerful force in his chest.

'But the camera,' she said with a smile, leaning in to give a small demure shrug, 'it lets me see what you see. One eye to the viewfinder is all I need and I'm not different any more. It's not noticeable that I'm tired—it's obvious *why* I'm squinting,' she said, the joy in her eyes something to behold.

'And you get to control what you see,' he intuited.

She smiled again. 'I'm not surprised that you see it that way, but yes. I *love* seeing the world again.'

She took a sip of her wine and stole an olive, squinting into the sunlight. 'So,' she said delicately, around the olive in her mouth, 'is this where you bring all your lovers?'

He nearly choked on his wine. 'No,' he spluttered with a laugh. If she only knew how few and far between those lovers had been she might get the wrong impression. 'No, I haven't been back here since...' He trailed off, realising just when it had been. His gut clenched as the sun disappeared behind a cloud.

'Since?' Ivy asked gently.

His gaze narrowed on his hands. 'Since I was eighteen,' he said, nodding to himself. 'I didn't realise it had been that long.'

'Yes, because you're such an *old* man,' Ivy teased, giving him an out, he realised. Giving him the chance to change the subject. He could do it. If he wanted to. But she had been vulnerable with him, truthful with him. She deserved only the same in return.

He dropped his head, a small smile failing to pull his lips into submission, before they flattened.

'I last came here after I met my mother,' he admitted, and it took Ivy a moment to realise that he wasn't talking about Alessia.

'I didn't… I didn't know you'd met your biological parents,' she said.

'Parent. Just the one.' He shrugged, before looking back up at her. The pain in his gaze was masked quickly. 'And no one knows. Alessia *never* will,' he said, the warning clear in his voice.

'We don't have to talk about it,' she assured him, but he shrugged, nonchalantly, though it was clear that the ripples from the meeting had become waves that had changed things for ever.

'At eighteen, my adoption records were unsealed. After my mother's husband had left, I…' He clenched his jaw. 'I stupidly thought that I'd like to meet them. I was handed the paperwork and, for the first time, I had the name of the woman who had given birth to me.'

Ivy waited, her hand having found its way to his shin—the small touch barely there, but enough to connect them.

'When I met her, the first thing she asked me was "What do you want?" And in the space of a heartbeat, I saw her take in my appearance, my clothing, and that question morphed into "What can I get?"' Antonio said, his swallow hard.

'She wanted money?' Ivy asked, her heart breaking for him, unable to imagine how deeply that must have cut. Her mother had left them, chosen someone else over her own children. But Antonio's mother? She had *used* him, *taken* from him. Anger and pain shook her from deep within.

He nodded.

'And you didn't give it to her,' Ivy stated, not even beginning to comprehend what that must have felt like.

'I did,' he said, much to her surprise. 'I gave her what she wanted. It meant nothing to me, and everything to her,' he replied dispassionately.

But he was wrong, Ivy realised. It *had* meant something to him. It had cost him a piece of himself. And he'd borne it alone with no one knowing. No one there to support him or help him. He'd been left with a scar, a wound, that he carried with him still. Because that was how Antonio controlled the world around him. Money. Paying people to do things—her to marry him. Paying people back—his mother with the house he'd bought her, Maria with the company he'd help her get through marriage to him.

Every relationship for him had been transactional.

'Why didn't you take the money? Why didn't you want the money for yourself?'

The questions he'd asked her took on new meaning then, because she'd confounded him by not playing by the rules he understood. Because he'd never allowed anyone to care for him without an exchange, without something specific and tangible to justify that care, that love.

'Antonio, I—'

He shook his head, raised his hand between them as if to ward off what she was about to say.

It hurt, yes. But she understood why he felt unable to hear the words she would have given him freely. She understood that it wasn't about her, and chose to shelve the pain that caused. The prick of a thorn that would bleed and ache more in the time to come.

Ivy couldn't give him what he wouldn't accept, but there was something she could give him. Something that he welcomed from her. And as she looked around this magical glade, the place he'd brought her to, she realised that she *could* remake his memories of this place. Refocus and reframe this part of his world for him.

She reached for his hand and pressed her mouth to his palm, the tenderness of the gesture spreading warmth between the two of them. Warmth enough to melt the ice that had held Antonio stiff.

The hardness in his gaze softened into heat, and he reached for her, pulling her across him and arranging her legs either side of him. Straddling him like this, she relished the feel of the hard length of him, his need for her so much more obvious but equal to her own. She reached for his other hand and pressed it against her breast, Antonio not needing any further encouragement to palm it and then tease her nipple taut with deft fingers.

He reared up to take that same breast in his mouth, hot, wet, over her linen shirt, his arms wrapped around her, holding her to him desperately. In these moments it was impossible to remember that there was no future for them, that there was no love, because what else was this when she felt worshipped by him? Wanted to the point of madness. Desired in a way that made her see herself differently.

A hand swept up beneath her skirt, stroking the outside

of her thigh, sweeping between them to find the ache at her core, sparking quivers that pulsed and throbbed and fizzed and hissed across her entire body.

He swept aside her panties and teased her, keeping her on the exquisite edge of pleasure. Her body rose to meet him, to take what it needed, urged on by some hedonistic instinct. Sensations were all she knew, the feel of his mouth around her breast, his hand between her legs, his length beneath her, impatient and straining.

He thrust from beneath her, mimicking what she wanted more than her next breath, and he growled as she moaned, his mouth finally moving up from her breast to her lips as his tongue took full possession of her. Her hands flew to his hair, holding him in place, needing just this moment... a kiss, to taste, to tease, to fill him as much as he filled her. To show him what he meant to her.

His hands stilled on her body as if he—just for this moment—was willing to let her show him, let her body tell him, what he refused to hear in words. Cradling his head between her hands she kissed him, possessed him, consumed him as he had done her. Her fingers scratched against his skull, unable to rest until they had shaped his head then, hungry for more—just like her lips—explored the rest of him.

She pulled his shirt free and tore the buttons, needing to feel him, to memorise every inch of his body. The dips and hollows of his collarbone, the swirls of hair over his pectorals... Her hands followed it down to the buckle of his belt. She pulled it apart and reached further still, wanting to feel him, hold him, grasp him. He growled into her mouth as she took him in her hand, squeezing as he thrust into her palm. She wanted him to feel this, needed him to feel what she felt for him.

* * *

Antonio let her have her way with him for as long as possible. It had taken all his restraint to let her lead, let her explore...but the moment she wrapped those cool fingers around his length, the shivers that rippled across his skin became a violent need. To participate, to act, to taste, to touch, to possess.

Antonio drew her shirt to the side and bared Ivy's breast to his mouth. Heaven. He was in heaven.

'Up,' he commanded, the words pressed against her lips. 'Up,' he repeated with gentle impatience.

He helped her rise to her knees as he pulled her knickers down her thighs, supporting her as he slid them from her legs. He fisted her panties in his hand and thrust them into his pocket, before retrieving his wallet and the condom from within.

'*Cara*, you have me behaving like an untested youth,' he complained as he tore the corner of the foil packet with his teeth. 'Taking you here? Amongst the trees and the grass?'

She looked down at him, settled further back on his thighs as he covered himself with the condom.

'I wouldn't have it any other way,' she said, and he felt it. The truth of her words. He wanted to tell her that neither would he. That she was the most beautiful woman he'd ever been with and that he was half convinced that she'd ruined him for ever, but the words clogged his throat, unable to get out. He couldn't give her the words she needed, the ones she so deserved to hear. But he could give her this...he could give everything he had to *this*.

He lined himself up and despite everything in him urging him to possess, to take, to have, he forced himself to show restraint. Slowly, taking in every single change of expression on Ivy's face, he entered her, filling her, stretching her, luxuriating in the way she came down onto him, taking what she wanted… He'd let her. He'd let her take all that he could give, even if he couldn't give her more than that.

Her head fell back and he pressed open-mouthed kisses to the long slender column of her neck, his hands palming her breasts as she moved over him, driving him out of his mind. His hands, desperate for more, fell away from her breasts and anchored on her hips, holding her in place, in that one precise point that made her breath hitch and her cries moans and her body tremble and her muscles tighten around him. And there, under the clear blue sky, there was no one but him to see how glorious Ivy was as she rode him to the end of an orgasm so sweet he'd feel it even after she had left Italy for England.

CHAPTER TEN

Ivy frowned, folding a beautiful cream jumper with flashes of fuchsia woven into it. It was gorgeous. But would she wear it back home? The thought of it in her tiny little shared flat made her quite sad. And she told herself off for being foolish.

She'd take it because it was beautiful, *pretty*, and it would make her happy. But some of the others…the red dress she'd worn to their first dinner out, that would stay behind.

'What are you doing?'

She felt his presence hover in the doorframe of the room she'd slept in only a handful of times while she'd been here.

Forcing a smile on her face, she turned and said, 'Packing,' with an ease she didn't feel. He watched her with hooded eyes. He'd been like that since they'd returned from the glade yesterday. Guarded. Resolved.

She bit back the breath that shuddered in her lungs. The hurt. It wasn't his fault that she'd fallen in love with him. He looked away as if he'd somehow read her thoughts, seeming to take in the clothes on the bed.

'You're not taking the red dress?' he asked, stepping into the room.

'No,' she replied. 'It's not exactly suitable for an assistant librarian to wear to shelve books, clean up after kids and help people find their email accounts on the shared computers,' she said wryly, before adding, 'as much as I'd like to see it.'

'And this?' Antonio said, picking up a navy-blue jumpsuit with a deep V neck.

It had been her favourite piece, one she'd not got to wear. 'It can go back,' she explained. 'It still has the tags.'

'These were bought for you. You should take them with you,' he said, as if speaking to a recalcitrant child. She didn't understand why he was getting so upset.

'They are beautiful clothes, I would love to keep them all. But I don't have the space to fit them. Or,' she said, placing a hand on his arm to try and soothe him, 'the lifestyle to wear them.'

His gaze narrowed, as if he wanted to argue but couldn't.

'When will Ms Quell be here?' she forced herself to ask.

'About an hour,' he said without looking at his watch.

She nodded and folded a pretty linen wrap skirt that she couldn't bear to part with into the suitcase. It would come in handy in England, she told herself. On one of the rare hot days they might be lucky enough to get.

Already she had an extra bag to take home with her, and then she laughed as Antonio had arranged for her to return on his private jet, so it wasn't as if she had to worry about baggage allowance.

'What has you so amused?' he asked.

'Nothing. Absolutely nothing,' she replied and went to the bathroom to get her toiletries, inappropriate tears pressing at the corner of her eyes.

Antonio paced the room, his hands fisting his hair. Why did this all feel so wrong? Ms Quell would come, they'd have the final assessment, he'd get the divorce he needed—

for Maria. It was for Maria. He owed her that. For staying by his side when no one else had.

What about Ivy? She stayed by your side. Even from the UK. Even when you didn't do the same for her.

He couldn't keep his thoughts straight and an anger that had begun to build yesterday in the glade was near constant now, making his heart pound, making him flinch at any small thing, making him clumsy and drop things, break things.

He was spinning out of control. He just needed the divorce. Just needed to marry Maria. *Then* he could figure out what to do about Ivy, could figure out a way to help her. Not the library, not some other family member, but *her*. He wanted her to have the security that she so richly deserved. He wanted her to have the lifestyle where she could wear that dress. He wanted her to travel the world, taking photographs of the people and things that caught her eye. He wanted to see that world, the way she saw it…

Dio mio.

What was wrong with him?

Ivy came out of the bathroom and he couldn't stop himself.

'Do you have to do that now?' he demanded, very much sounding like the frustrated husband he had never been.

She looked at him warily. 'Yes,' she said, putting her toiletries into the small carry-on she had brought with her.

'Why?' he asked, sounding petulant even to his own ears.

She turned to him, arms across her chest, and he wondered whether it was ironic that perhaps for the first time in their six-year marriage they finally looked like a husband and wife.

'Because I think it's better that I leave with Ms Quell,' she said, levelling him with a gaze.

'No.'

Ivy opened her mouth.

'No, absolutely not,' he repeated, slashing the air with his hand.

She huffed out a frustrated breath of air. 'Antonio—'

He turned his back to her, more to stop himself sounding even more like an irrational ass than to silence her.

He heard the bed dip as Ivy sat.

'Are you okay?' she asked quietly.

He turned to stare at her. '*Dio mio*, Ivy, *sto bene*. I just don't see why you're being difficult and why you have to leave,' he said, unable to stop the words pouring out of him. He punctuated the whole thing with a dismissive shrug.

Ivy raised her brows the moment he accused her of being difficult and he knew he was messing this up.

'You're fine? Behaving like a child is fine for you? Because it's not fine for me,' she replied hotly. 'I'm trying to keep things civil. I'm trying to do what we agreed to do, in order for you to get the divorce you want.'

'Well, stop it. Stop trying to do all these things.'

'Really? And what then, Antonio? What is this about? If you don't want me to do this, if you don't want me to help you get this divorce, what do you want?' she demanded.

He couldn't say it. He knew it. *She* knew it. She saw it in his eyes and nodded.

'I'll be down in a minute,' she informed him curtly.

He had been dismissed.

'Ivy—'

'I'll be down in a minute,' she repeated, as if clinging onto the last thread of her patience.

By the time that Ivy came downstairs Agata was showing Ms Quell into the room where they'd first met. She paused on the last step, inhaling slowly and deeply, trying to remember the run of the argument she and Antonio had planned and practised over the last few days in order to convince Ms Quell that they had done their best but still needed a divorce.

She thought that perhaps it wouldn't be such a reach to 'fake' an argument between them right now. She could see that Antonio was struggling, she knew that he didn't want her to leave. But that wasn't enough any more. She could never stay here and watch him marry another person, even if he did ask her to.

Because it wasn't really about the marriage. It was about the fact that he would always prioritise Maria over her. She understood why...oh, God, did she. But understanding didn't make it any easier, and she *had* to choose herself this time. Not her brother. Not the library. Not Antonio even. She couldn't continue to be the woman who'd waited in a hospital bed wishing things were different.

And she wasn't. Not any more. Whether he had intended it or not, coming here to Italy had been...liberating for her. Before, Ivy had lived in fear of stepping out of the unknown: she took the same route to work, she worked in the same place she volunteered, knowing the layout of the building, and with the people she liked. She stayed in her flat, she watched her pennies, she lived within her means... But she wasn't really *living*. She'd always thought that after Jamie was settled, perhaps she'd travel. She'd find something for herself. But then the accident happened and... she'd been scared.

But now? Okay, yes, she had been chauffeured around Italy without having to spend a single penny, but she had travelled. She had seen Siena, she had visited a bustling market, she had swum in a pool and had her hair and makeup done at the fanciest of salons. She was living again. So perhaps she didn't quite have to go back to the same home she had left. Perhaps she could begin to make small changes that led to travelling elsewhere one day. Perhaps she could start to *live* again.

Steeling her spine, she went to join Antonio and Ms Quell, who were sitting in stony silence, facing each other with a kind of grim resolve.

She pasted a smile on her lips. 'Ms Quell,' she greeted.

Ms Quell nodded. 'Ms McKellen,' she acknowledged, gesturing for her to take a seat beside Antonio, which instinctively she knew would enrage him in his own home. The sharp inhale only confirmed it.

Ivy made sure to sit further away from him than she would have chosen to, which drew a single flicker from Antonio's jaw muscle.

'How have you been?' Ms Quell asked.

Ivy paused before answering. 'Tested,' she said ruefully. 'By both this process,' she said of the assessments, 'and my husband.' There was no heat in her words, only resignation. After all, this was a goodbye, whether Antonio willed it or not.

Ms Quell nodded. Ivy thought there was a flash of sympathy in the other woman's gaze. And she wondered whether Ms Quell's bluster was similar to Antonio's—a form of self-defence. Instinctively softening, Ivy asked, 'And how are you? I hope your flight here was okay.'

Ms Quell nodded, eyeing Antonio suspiciously. 'It was very…quick. Thank you,' she added belatedly, as if pained by it.

Antonio dismissed the generosity of making his private jet available for the assessments as if it were nothing, his casual display of wealth clearly irritating Ms Quell, as intended, Ivy was sure. If it wasn't that so much was riding on the outcome of this meeting, Ivy would probably have found their exchanges funny. Two similar personalities butting heads.

There was no meanness or malice in it at all. Just both wrestling for control.

'You attended the family event together last weekend?'

Antonio nodded, apparently clinging to his sulk and insisting on speaking as little as possible.

'Yes,' Ivy embellished. 'It was…good. Difficult, but good.'

'Difficult in what way?' Ms Quell asked.

'Every family has their own dynamics. It was always going to be hard, me being English and not quite fitting in. Alessia, Antonio's mother, made a real effort but… as much as a marriage does require the support of family and friends, really, if the issue between the two people concerned is irreconcilable…' Ivy trailed off in a shrug.

This was the point where Antonio was supposed to interrupt and accuse her of being cold and standoffish with his family, just as they had planned. But he said nothing.

Ms Quell looked between them and Ivy shifted uncomfortably.

'Did you want to add anything?' Ivy asked Antonio pointedly.

He looked at her, his gaze mulish. 'No.'

Now it was Ivy's turn to get angry. *He* needed this. *He* was making her do this.

'And now you see what I have been dealing with,' she appealed to Ms Quell. 'He does this. Just shuts down when he doesn't get his way.'

'Well, it's not as if my way was horrible or difficult,' Antonio interjected.

'No. But it was about what suited you. Not me. And I need, sometimes, for things to suit *me*.'

He glared at her as if that was what he'd been trying to say to her all along and, all of a sudden, she was turning this back on him. 'That is not fair,' he accused.

'Nothing about this is fair,' she shot back.

'I have done everything in my power, Ivy. If there was something else, I would try it,' he insisted, pleading with her with his eyes.

'And I've told you. I understand. I'm not blaming you. There isn't any blame to give. Not here.'

Ms Quell watched them like a tennis match, back and forth, over the net of a subtext she didn't understand and perhaps didn't need to.

'I don't think we gave this enough time,' Antonio said, shocking both her and Ms Quell, but perhaps not in equal measure.

'What do you mean?' Ivy demanded, the ground shifting beneath her feet and throwing her off-kilter. He wasn't playing by the rules. He wasn't following what they'd agreed to say.

'I'm just wondering if there was something more we could do?' he asked, the words forced through his teeth as if he were fighting himself and a whole army of past hurts.

'You think that there is something more we could do to try and make this marriage work?' Ivy demanded slowly and succinctly, making sure that she—and Ms Quell—were understanding him correctly.

He thrust a hand through his hair impatiently. 'Yes? I don't know,' he said infuriatingly.

Why was he doing this? They had an agreement. He was supposed to marry Maria—it was the only way he could help her get what she needed. Ivy was supposed to go home, back to England, and be happy. Not battle with this seesawing of emotion, with a future brighter and more beautiful than she could have ever imagined for herself going in and out of focus at Antonio's whim. He couldn't play with her like this. She couldn't handle it.

Her heart broke beneath the two fractured futures—one of her at home in her flat, and one of her here, with him.

'You think you might want to give this marriage a go?' she repeated, forcing him to be clear, the quiver in her voice as much despair as it was anger.

He looked at her, his eyes widening.

It was too much. He couldn't do this to her. It was a cry from deep within her soul.

'I have,' she confessed, 'spent my entire life loving people who are, in one way or another, too selfish to love me back.' It was painful to admit, but it was true. 'My brother. Certainly, my parents,' she said, her inhale shaky before she continued. 'I don't think they did it by choice. Addiction made my brother inescapably selfish and my parents?' She bit her lip. 'I don't think they actively set out not to love us, not to prioritise us, or care for us like parents should,' she acknowledged through the pain of a shattering heart. 'But that's what happened. My father left and my mother chose someone else's child over her own. I can't do it any more,' she said, as much to herself as to the others in the room. 'I can't keep waiting for someone to choose me. And I can't do that with you,' she declared, turning to Antonio.

'Do you love me?' she asked. Because that was why they were here, no? That was why he was digging his heels in and why her heart was breaking. And just like that, she was all the versions of herself that had waited for so long, hoping that someone would come for her, hoping that someone would choose her, *love* her.

He sat, clenched jawed and silent, and glaring at her. If he wanted to he could say yes and end this all right now.

But he didn't.

Heart shattering into a thousand pieces, Ivy turned to Ms Quell. 'Is that sufficient?' she asked.

'Yes,' Ms Quell said with a sad nod of her head.

'Okay then.'

Antonio watched Ivy stand from the sofa, knowing that it wasn't because he'd been unable to stop her but that he'd been unwilling to do so. She'd done that. Forced his hand. And he'd made the choice he'd told her he would. He'd chosen family, which was right, wasn't it?

Vaguely, he was aware of Ms Quell informing him that she would email him the final written assessment to be completed before someone from the judge's chambers would be in touch with the last court date, which he would have to attend. But, all being well, his divorce could be finalised before the end of the following week.

He should be elated, but instead he sat there in numb silence, watching Ivy and Ms Quell leave the room together. He didn't even stand to see them out. He heard their footsteps click across the tiled hallway and out of his life— *and he should be pleased.*

And he would be, he believed. He just needed to wait until the ringing stopped sounding in his head. It was high-pitched and oddly like a tension headache, but that couldn't be, because he had what he wanted, right? And really, that was only thanks to Ivy. Because he'd nearly blown the whole damn thing.

'I don't think we gave this enough time.'

He let out a bitter laugh for no one to hear. Some last-ditch attempt to slake his insatiable lust for her, perhaps. No more. Surely no more.

'Do you love me?'

It was a question that was still rattling around his brain three days later as he wandered aimlessly from his office into the kitchen in search of the whisky. He'd completed the damn paperwork for Judge Carmondy, answering asinine questions like *Would you agree with the statement that you have given your all to your marriage?* and *Do you recognise that the failings are of equal measure or do you feel otherwise?* which Antonio was half convinced had been asked solely for the purposes of annoying him.

The American deal with the Chinese had gone through. And he couldn't bring himself to care. He'd told Maria about the outcome of the assessment and tried to be enthused as she'd thanked him, and when she'd talked about making plans for their wedding he'd told her to go ahead. He'd do whatever was needed.

Agata looked up at him and scowled.

'C'è qualche problema?' he demanded.

'No, signor, nessun problema,' she said, and left the room muttering about him turning into a neanderthal.

He rubbed at what had been stubble a few days ago and was now the beginnings of a beard. He might keep it. It was easier, after all, than shaving every morning. He reached for a glass and filled it with ice.

'We're out of whisky,' he shouted after Agata.

'Lo so!' she yelled back.

Antonio frowned, wondering why his housekeeper had become so intractable all of a sudden. If she'd known they were out of whisky, why hadn't she bought a new bottle?

He put the empty one on the counter and opened the wine fridge to extract a bottle.

'It's a little early for that, isn't it?'

He closed his eyes and slowly closed the fridge door.

'*Ciao* Mamma,' he said, forcing a smile to his lips.

'Don't *Ciao Mamma* me,' she replied, coming to clip him round the back of the head and pull him into a hug at the same time. Usually, he had his wits about him and would have successfully navigated his way out of both, but he was being unusually slow at the moment.

His mother had a package in her hand that she put on the table.

'What are you doing here?' he asked, aiming for congenial rather than the petulance he felt the full force of at the moment.

'You haven't been answering my calls.'

'For a day—'

'For *three* days. And I know I didn't raise you to be that disrespectful, you ungrateful brat.'

'Mamma—'

Her hands bracketed his face as she angled it to peer at him, cutting off his complaint.

'You don't need any more to drink,' she decided for him, and released him, only to put the wine back in the fridge and the empty whisky bottle in the bin. 'Open that while I fix you something to drink,' she ordered.

He peered at the package. 'What is it?' he asked.

'I don't know. It was on the side table when I came in.'

He looked at the address and noticed that it had come from England. The return address, South West London.

Ivy.

Even while he calculated the risks of opening this in

front of his mother, his fingers had already slipped beneath the seal and torn open the package.

A note slipped out from a stack of printed photographs.

For you

There was no signature, no other words. Nothing that could be read, obsessed over, analysed. Her handwriting was prettily sloped and he stared at it like a lovesick teenager.

His mother put down a glass of water beside him and picked up the silky photographs that he'd not even spared a glance at yet.

'*Oh...*'

The word slipped from his mother in surprise and he peered over her shoulder to see the image she was looking at. It was from the party. Of him, his mother and Maria all laughing together.

One by one she leafed through the pictures, all beautiful, intimate moments captured perfectly by Ivy's skill and masterful eye.

'I saw her with the camera, but I didn't expect... I didn't think...' His mother trailed off as she gazed at one of Maria talking to her father, with Micha looking on in the background—the look on his face unfathomable. 'Hmm,' she said, before turning to the last one. The picture Ivy had taken of him in the glade, the day before she'd left. 'Oh, Antonio,' she said, turning to him.

But all his attention was on the photographs.

'She said that this was how she saw the world,' he explained as he looked at picture after picture. They were good. Really good. There was a picture of him with the old couple laughing from the lace stall at the market. And once he reached the end, he went back to the beginning again.

'What are you looking for?' his mother asked.

He was about to say that he didn't know, but then he realised that he did. He was looking for a picture of her. But she wasn't in any of them.

He shook his head, thinning his lips purposely to stop them from trembling with an unnamed emotion.

She took the pictures back from him and looked at them sadly.

'What is it?' he asked.

'You say this is how she sees the world?'

'Sì.'

'Then what do these pictures tell you?' she asked.

He frowned. 'What do you mean?'

His mother looked at him pityingly. 'You. You're in nearly every single one of these pictures. You *are* that world.'

That sudden realisation shot a sliver of pain so deep into his heart, he struggled to catch his breath.

Oddio.

He heaved a breath in, and his mother began to look panicked.

'Antonio, please, you're scaring me,' she cried. 'Talk to me, *tesoro.*'

'I can't afford to love her, Mamma,' he said, the confession wrenched deep from within his heart.

'Why not, Antonio?'

'There is nothing equal to her love. Nothing valuable enough that I could ever give her in return.'

'*Mio cuore,*' his mother said, 'in all the years I've loved you and cared for you, I've not once wanted anything in return. You may have thought I did, you may have pre-empted what you thought might be a request, but I've never wanted anything other than your happiness. You've bought me a house, jewellery, clothes, holidays—things I don't want, because *all* I want is for you to be happy,' she said with tears gathering in her eyes. 'It breaks my heart that you think love is an exchange. I wish I'd never taken a thing from you if I taught you such a thing.'

'No, Mamma, it wasn't you,' he said, unable to bear the tears she shed.

'I'll *never* forgive my husband for not being the man I thought he was. But Ivy is nothing like him. I saw that at the party and I see it with these. *You* are enough. You,' she said, holding him with a fierce grip, 'are equal to her love. Just give her yourself. That is all she needs.'

'How do you know?'

'Because it's all I ever needed from you and I love you more than life itself.'

Antonio's heart thundered in his chest at his mother's words, from her love. From the fear of taking the risk to open his heart and hope that perhaps he was worthy of love without condition or transaction. That he might just be enough by himself.

But he'd let her go. He'd seen how devastated Ivy had been as she'd asked him if he loved her. He knew what asking that had cost her and he'd forced her to do it.

'What have I done?'

'Nothing you can't undo, *figlio mio*.'

Dio mio, he hoped his mother was right.

CHAPTER ELEVEN

'Shouldn't you better get going?' Mrs Tenby asked gently.

Ivy peered at the clock on the computer and sighed. 'Yes, thank you, Mrs Tenby.'

The woman had softened towards her once she'd realised that Ivy wasn't some 'young upstart' hoping to come in and take over the library with plans for 'modernisation'. Of course, the money she had secured had also helped.

Antonio had been better than his word and by the time Ivy had returned to work the day after the flight that had brought her and Ms Quell back from Tuscany, the library association had matched the funds he'd donated and Mrs Tenby had been given the green light to move forward with the afterschool club.

Ivy had not been as surprised as Mrs Tenby that the donation from Antonio was in fact more than double what had originally been promised, but she was immensely pleased that it allowed for the employment of another staff member, so that they could provide even more places for local children. The generosity and the momentum it brought had made the staff happy and optimistic, excited for the future plans and programmes they could now explore.

It shouldn't have made it harder for Ivy, but it did. Everything did.

Apparently, the moment she had set foot back into her old life, the hopeful, determined Ivy who had stood proud and powerful in Antonio's living room facing a future without him had faded like a suntan, leaving the old, pale Ivy feeling heartbroken.

Oh, she was still determined to do the things that she'd realised she wanted to do: to travel the world, to continue to take photographs. But that pervasive sense of loneliness was hard to ignore.

It was a cycle of emotions that she would have to process. She knew the drill. Yes, it hurt, but it wouldn't be for ever. And she clung desperately with both hands to the fact that she was doing the right thing, that demanding more for herself *was* healing.

Only there wasn't a painkiller for this. There wasn't something that could take this ache away. Especially as there were reminders of Antonio everywhere. Each question on the paperwork Ms Quell had given her on the flight home had burned like a brand, punctuating all that she'd had so very briefly and all that she'd lost. And when she'd tried to unpack the clothes from Italy, she'd realised that she'd never be able to wear them. Not as Ivy McKellen. Because they belonged only to Mrs Antonio Gallo.

As she got on the bus to take her to the courthouse, her phone buzzed with another message from Jamie. He'd been a little surprised when she'd told him that he couldn't stay with her this time while he was on leave, but very understanding. And, strangely, he'd thanked her for all she'd already done for him.

It wasn't that he'd been wilfully obtuse about it, but it was quite amazing how positively he'd responded to the boundary she'd put in place. And then she wondered if perhaps she'd done that sooner, he might have had the opportunity to show her that he could respect it sooner.

The thought made her slightly sad for herself and for Jamie, but also hopeful for the kind of relationship that they might have in the future. He really had turned himself around and Ivy knew that wouldn't have been possible without Antonio.

He had changed her life in so many ways and now, Ivy thought, it was time to take that life and do something with it. And if in her mind's eye she saw that future being in Italy, or travelling around the world, Antonio within reach, protecting her, steadying her while she took photographs, while they touched and kissed and laughed and loved…

She swallowed the painful lump that had formed in her throat.

That was just a dream. Nothing more than the remnants of a fantasy of what could have been.

The ding of the bus bell signalled it was stopping near the court and Ivy rose to her feet, waiting for others to get off before she stepped out onto the pavement. Despite the fact that it was summer, that only a week and a half ago she'd been in Italy where the sun had kissed her skin and warmed the world around her, England felt cold, and what passed for warm here sent a shiver down her spine. She longed for the days when she could wear sunglasses that would hide how she squinted at the world, and smiled at the fanciful idea of moving to a warmer country just for that. She had been spoilt and she just needed to get over it, she told herself firmly.

But the moment she saw Antonio's lawyer in the hallway outside the courtroom, Ivy knew that all the thoughts that had filled her head had been nothing more than a distraction. Because suddenly she was a hair's breadth from bursting into tears.

He'd chosen Maria. He'd chosen someone else over her and God, it hurt. It really hurt. Because she loved him so damn much. Her breath quivered in her lungs and she had to stop, had to turn to face the wall and get herself together. She fisted her hands, her nails forming crescent moons deep into her palms.

You can do this. You have to.

She took one deep breath and then another before making her way towards Simon. She wasn't capable of a smile, but she greeted him the best she could.

'Ms McKellen,' he said, looking slightly harried. 'This way, please.'

He gestured for her to follow him through a door and Ivy was startled to find herself in an actual court this time, not the judge's chambers.

It didn't quite look like the courts she'd seen in TV dramas, but then again, this was South West London. There was no rich mahogany, no barristers in wigs. Instead, there was pine and plain red cotton seat cushions, though Judge Carmondy, sitting in the middle of the raised dais, still wore his black gown.

Simon showed her to a seat behind a table and proceeded to take the one beside her.

'Where's Antonio?' she asked in a whisper.

'Coming.'

'Shouldn't you be sitting with him?' she asked.

'No. He fired me and hired me for you.'

'What? He fired you? Why?' she demanded, confused and off-balance.

Simon made a quieting gesture as the door opened and Antonio stalked in.

Her hungry gaze devoured him. He refused to look her way, but that only allowed her free rein to indulge in all the things that she'd been missing. Oh, she had been starved of him. She'd nearly convinced herself that she'd imagined his perfection. But she hadn't. Her whole body hummed in his presence. It recognised him as a part of her and her heart ached even more.

And that hurt made her a little nauseous.

She watched Antonio take a seat on the opposite side of the room, wanting him to look her way. But she couldn't be sure that she wouldn't break into a thousand pieces if he did. Judge Carmondy cleared his throat as one of the women in the court announced that they were now in session.

Antonio couldn't remember ever being more nervous in his life. Partly because until now there had been nothing nearly so valuable to him as Ivy. As *this*.

'I have received the reports from the assessment from Ms Quell and read over both of your written assessments,' Judge Carmondy began, peering between his papers and acknowledging Ms Quell, who sat just behind Antonio in the courtroom.

'Thank you both for your concerted effort to prove that you have taken this matter seriously. It is appreciated,' he said with a long hard stare at Antonio. Finally relenting, he leaned back in his chair, as if already moving on to his next case. 'I take it we are ready to proceed with your divorce?' he asked.

'No, Your Honour,' Antonio said.

'I beg your pardon?'

'You're pardoned,' Antonio replied, confused by the judge's response.

'Don't get smart with me, Mr Gallo. Do you or do you not want a divorce from Ms McKellen? Which I was on the verge of granting, may I say.'

'No. I don't want a divorce.'

He felt the shockwaves ripple out from where Ivy, his wife—the woman he loved—sat, but he couldn't risk looking at her. Not yet. If he did, he might never get through what he needed to say.

'Explain yourself. Quickly and succinctly, or I shall find you in contempt of court,' Judge Carmondy warned.

'I hate paperwork,' Antonio began.

Carmondy side-eyed him a warning glance.

'All of it. I hate the things I have to sign as a business owner, I hate receiving it, I hate it as documentation and if I never sign another piece of paper in my life it would make me extremely happy.'

'Mr Gallo. Get to the point. Soon.'

'You accused me of not taking this marriage seriously. And I didn't, Your Honour. You were absolutely right,' he confessed. 'Marriage, to me, was just another piece of paper, certainly not holding any greater importance to me than simply a means to an end. My marriage to Ivy McKellen was everything you thought it was.'

He could practically see the steam rising from Carmondy's ears.

'Almost,' Antonio added before the judge could, as he'd threatened, find him in contempt. 'My dislike of paperwork was hard learned. It started with the biological parents who signed away their rights to me on papers just like these,' he said, pointing to the file of legal documents on the table in front of him. 'And then, with two signatures on more paperwork, I was claimed by adoption papers. For a while. Until yet another signature on even more paperwork removed my mother from her husband as his wife, and me from him as a son. My grandfather,' Antonio said with a rueful laugh, 'he cut me from his legacy, striking my name from his paperwork. So, Your Honour. I'd like to think that I have, as you would say, *just cause* to have an issue with paperwork.'

Judge Carmondy acknowledged it with a nod, his hard eyes softening just a little, enough to encourage Antonio to continue.

'When we first met, you said that you believed in the sanctity of marriage. I didn't,' he said, shaking his head. 'I didn't understand what marriage was. I didn't see how it could be anything other than a transaction. And when the terms weren't met, the marriage ended. That's what happened for my birth parents and my adoptive parents.

'I just didn't know it could be otherwise. I didn't know what it meant to work towards someone else's happiness without fear of them not wanting to do the same for you. I believed that love was a debt to be paid, and I didn't even know how to begin to pay for Ivy's love,' he admitted with deep pain.

'And, as Ms Quell rightly recognised, I didn't see that marriage takes a million small things each day. Choices, commitments, actions.'

He turned to Ms Quell and smiled wryly. 'Ivy doesn't have one particular skincare brand,' he said, finally answering the question she'd asked back in their second assessment. 'I didn't ask her, but I'm pretty sure it's because she buys only what she needs when she needs it and when it is most cost-effective. She uses cleanser, toner, eye cream and skin cream. She's terrible at using sun cream, but she is English so that's probably just because she's not used to it.

'For perfume, she prefers earthy scents to floral ones,

partly because floral scents are too sweet for her, and anything that connects to a memory for her is the one that she will choose first. Deep down, she wants to dress in bright, beautiful colours, but doesn't feel that she could do so here in England. When she *does* dress in bright, beautiful colours, Your Honour,' he said, briefly turning back to Judge Carmondy, 'it is a sight to behold, I assure you.

'Oh, and Ms Quell, Ivy hates coffee and I will spend the rest of my life not understanding this.'

Antonio turned back to Judge Carmondy. 'You told me I promised to love, protect and honour this woman. I did promise those things and I failed to do any of them, spectacularly, and I will never forgive myself for this,' he admitted truthfully.

He would regret for ever not returning the hospital's call that day. He would regret for ever not taking the call she'd made following that. He would regret for ever forsaking the vow he'd made.

Whatever his motivation behind the marriage had been, he should have stayed true to that vow. He'd thought—naïvely and incorrectly—that his duty had been done when he'd paid her for her hand in marriage. But he'd been wrong. He had learned from that mistake, but at a cost to Ivy that was unforgivable.

Oddio, he wanted to look at her so much, but he couldn't. Not yet.

'In the last two weeks I spent with Ivy McKellen, I learned that she's a far better person than I am. She is strong, and wilful, even in the face of a more powerful force—like me,' he said without a hint of irony, 'or the accident that almost stole the future she had imagined for herself, or the parents that abandoned her with a younger sibling to care for, or the husband who abandoned her for his own self-interest.

'She experienced all of those things and is *still* someone who puts others first. The library where she works, the brother who needed her and the husband who didn't deserve her. I love the way she thinks about others but I wish she'd think about herself even half as much. I love the way she moves through the world with a fierce determination and, despite many setbacks, she is hopeful and optimistic. I admire her. And I love her. And, should she let me, I will tell her every day how wonderful she is, how much she is loved, and I will protect her and prioritise her *always*,' he added as his heart beat ferociously in his chest.

'It is up to her whether she chooses to accept the love that I willingly and freely give to her. But I want her to know that, whatever happens, there is a house in her name with a bank account to cover bills, expenses and whatever is needed to run that house for the rest of her life. She should know that. There is even paperwork,' he said ruefully but sincerely. Because no matter what happened between them, he wanted—*needed*—her to have security and safety and permanence in her life.

'Well, Ms McKellen?' The judge asked. 'Do you accept this man's love?'

For the first time since entering the court, Antonio allowed himself to risk a glance in her direction. She was looking straight at him, her eyes glistening. He dared to believe, to hope...

Ivy's heart pounded in her chest, stunned by all that Antonio had said. He loved her? Admired her? Those things seemed incredible to her when she felt exactly the same for him.

Was she dreaming? All this couldn't really be for her, could it?

Simon beckoned her to him so that he could whisper in her ear. 'You don't have to say yes. I've looked over the documents. The house is all set up. And even if you sell it, the account is for you, so it comes with you if you buy a new house. It is important to Mr Gallo that you understand this and you don't feel pressured. He also said—' he paused, as if trying to remember the correct words '—this is not a gift, or a trade, or a purchase,' Simon quoted. 'Does that make sense to you?'

It did. It absolutely did. She nodded, realising that, whatever her answer, Antonio was willing to protect her and give her the security she'd always wanted. He was prioritising her, over his own wants and needs.

She felt Simon's eyes on her, the judge's gaze, too. And this time, when she looked back at Antonio, she finally found him looking at her. She saw it then. All of it. He was a man who had made concealing his emotions an art form, who had hidden his wants and needs behind trades and payoffs, but everything had been laid at her feet.

His love, his promise, his vows. She didn't need a piece of paper to tell her that, to make her his, or him hers. She didn't need a ring or a celebration, a party or even a house—she had him. And he was her world.

'I do, Your Honour,' she said as tears rolled down her cheeks, turning back to Antonio in time to see him grip the table in white-knuckled relief.

The judge sighed, though for a heartbeat Ivy thought that he might have been just a little pleased. 'Then I suppose I declare you husband and wife. *Again*. Now, please kiss your bride and never return to this court,' he commanded.

Antonio made his way past a ridiculous number of chairs to reach her.

'Oh, and Mr Gallo? I will be fining you seven thousand pounds for wasting the court's time.'

'Yes, Your Honour,' he said without complaint.

'Case dismissed!'

By the time Antonio reached her she was a little unsteady on her feet, but the moment his hands held hers, the moment he wrapped her in his arms, she felt grounded, protected, *safe*.

His lips found hers and it was heaven. Antonio's kiss, at first half frantic, soon gentled to one of reverence and it was the most perfect thing, until the judge banged his gavel and told them to clear out of the court before he could fine Antonio for 'lewd conduct'.

Antonio led her out into the hallway, where she caught a glimpse of Simon looking rather pleased with the outcome before Antonio kissed her again.

'Antonio,' she whispered against his lips.

'Again,' he commanded without breaking the kiss.

She smiled, his mouth shifting around hers to try and capture it. 'Antonio,' she said again, and he relaxed against her as if all he'd needed was his name on her lips.

She loved him.

She loved him and was free in that love and it filled her and just kept filling her. There was no end to it. It was not finite. It just poured from her in waves that she would never want to stop.

'I love you,' she said, finally pulling back from the temptation of his lips and looking up into the deep brown eyes that had hypnotised her from the very beginning, before he looked down.

'I don't know if I'll ever be worthy enough to—'

'You don't have to earn anything from me. Not my admiration, not my respect, not my love. These feelings for you aren't based on your worth or your value to me,' she said, clinging to his shirt front with a vehemence she hoped he understood.

'I left you in that hospital.'

'I was the one who said it was not important,' she said sadly, realising how much he had punished himself over this.

'I made it impossible for you to say otherwise,' he insisted. 'I should have come for you.'

'What would you have done? If you'd been there at the hospital?'

'I would have made sure you got the best medical help.'

'I *did* get the best medical help. And the rest was on me.'

'But your home…'

'Was mine for the time I needed it,' she said simply. 'You? You are my home *for ever*,' she said.

He took her hand and flattened her palm against his heart, placing his own over hers, and pressed his forehead against hers, his breath shuddering out of his chest in a sigh that felt as if it had been held for years.

'*Dio mio*, I love you, and I promise to show you just how much, every single day for the rest of my life.'

Her heart soared in her chest, just one thought coming back to anchor her. 'Antonio, what about Maria? What's going to happen to her? And Gallo Group? Will it go to Micha?'

He swallowed. 'I honestly don't know. But we'll make sure that, whatever happens, she'll be okay,' he said, the words another vow that Ivy felt to her bones, and one that she echoed. She wasn't sure how she'd be able to help, but if there was anything she could do, she'd do it. Maria was Antonio's family. Her family now.

She looked back up at him. 'Yes, we will,' she told him. 'But what do we do *now*?' she asked in a whisper, realising that they were beginning to draw attention, wrapped up in each other in the middle of the court corridor. He finally released her but held out his arm for her to take and began to lead them out of the courthouse.

'How do you feel about children?' Antonio asked as if he were inviting her out for dinner.

Simon spluttered behind them.

'Four,' Ivy replied easily and instinctively.

'Oh, at least,' Antonio replied with a smile on his face that stole her breath.

This was her husband. The man she had married six years ago for all the wrong reasons, but who had returned to her to show her the true power of love.

EPILOGUE

Ten years later...

ANTONIO HAD BEEN right when he'd said that marriage took a million small things each day, Ivy thought as she stepped out into the garden of their villa in Tuscany. The sun was high in the sky, the dappled light being filtered through the leaves rustling on the breeze. Ivy was extremely happy as she placed the cool jug of lemonade on the long wooden table that was big enough to seat their entire sprawling family. Though they were considering adding another smaller table to the garden for all the children.

As well as the four children she and Antonio had, there were Maria and Micha's three, and Enzo, Gio's other grandson, would be bringing his three children and his wife Erin, who was pregnant *again* with their fourth. It seemed that the Gallos' proliferation was still rife in the family.

And Ivy loved it. With every new child there was even more love to give. And while it wasn't always easy, there were many hands to make light work of it all. Maria and Micha had bought some land nearby and were halfway through their villa's build. Enzo had visited in time for Ivy and Antonio's marriage blessing and he'd fallen in love with the area. And for a man who had never really settled in one place for more than three months, it was perhaps telling that he had bought a villa on the other side of Antonio's land and was currently spending summers here in Tuscany.

Ivy was happy to have Erin so close. While Ivy's Italian was now as good as it could be, it was refreshing to be able to come back to speaking English every now and then. It was also helpful with the children, who they were raising as bilingual. With Enzo as much American as he was Italian, there was an even split and she didn't feel as outnumbered as she'd originally feared she might.

Every year they came together for the long, hot summer months of the children's holiday. Especially as it coincided with Antonio and Ivy's anniversary.

Nine years ago, they'd gathered the people who meant the most to them, family or friend, blood or bond, and celebrated their love for each other. They had carved out their own way of honouring their relationship—one that wasn't bound up in paperwork, or hollow vows, or rings… though Antonio had been somewhat surprisingly insistent that she wore a huge white puffy wedding dress—that secretly Ivy hadn't been so mad about.

With words and promises that they'd written themselves, they'd shared their love, their honour, their worship of each other with their nearest and dearest, and then revealed the fine line, intricate tattoos on their fourth fingers, their commitment to each other indelibly marked on their bodies.

It had been a beautiful day, and one they marked each year with a huge celebration with the family members they wanted to have with them. And then towards the start of autumn they would return to London, where Ivy continued to volunteer at the library. It gave her the flexibility to travel elsewhere when they had the time, and prevented her from being a drain on the library's precious resources. And the moment they were free from the school timetable they would return to Italy. Return to their home and their family.

Jamie had even visited briefly with his wife when his leave had permitted. And she'd been finally at peace to see him settled, finding his feet and a family in the army, with a structure that he'd always needed.

About three years ago they'd received word that their father had passed and together they had gone along to a funeral full of strangers, for a man they barely remembered but felt some obligation towards. It had been hard for her but Antonio had been waiting for her when she'd got home. He'd offered to go with her, but she'd wanted it to just be her and Jamie. It had brought up a few things for them both, but with patience and support, and the love Antonio poured into her and their family, she'd been able to get through it as well as she could have hoped.

She felt his arms wrap around her now, pulling her gently back against him as a summer breeze swept the scents of rosemary and mint through the garden.

'Mmm...' she sighed, feeling herself relax into the husband she loved more and more each day.

'Are you ready?' he asked, nudging her head slightly to the side so that he could place little kisses on her neck.

She shivered appreciatively. 'Ready for what?'

'The Gallo clan chaos.'

She laughed. 'No one is ever ready for that,' she confessed. 'Is it bad that I'm thankful that it's just *us*? That your mother is the only one who entertains the rest of them?'

Ivy wouldn't have them there by choice, never forgiving them for the way they had treated her husband. But Antonio did...

'No, *cara*. That's not bad of you at all. You know I wouldn't want them in the house,' he assured her and she was happy.

Alessia was due to arrive soon and Maria would be hot on her heels, not wanting to miss out at all. Ivy had liked the woman she'd met ten years ago on sight, but in the months and years that followed, they had become like sisters, the same as with Erin, who would also arrive soon with her husband and children.

'Then I will always be ready for the Gallo clan chaos,' Ivy replied happily and confidently.

Dio mio, he loved his wife, Antonio thought as he placed a kiss on the curve of her neck and deeply inhaled the soft scent of her. If he could bottle it...he'd never share it. He'd hoard it like a man obsessed, he admitted wryly to himself.

He'd never imagined the kind of happiness, the kind of *completeness* she had brought to his life. Ivy had shown him what love really was when she'd slipped into his heart and healed the hurts he'd been trying to ignore for years.

And when she'd nervously told him that she'd like to adopt he'd been hit with a punch of emotion so powerful he'd been stunned into silence. It wasn't something he'd ever thought consciously about. It wasn't something he'd even planned for his own future—the idea of children and a wife being almost inconceivable to him. But the moment she had voiced her desire he'd known how right it was.

Not that they'd gone into it blindly. If anything, he'd been overly cautious, consulting every resource to ensure that he was best placed to look after children who would need a huge amount of emotional sensitivity. He'd spent six months with a therapist, ensuring that he was prepared not only emotionally himself, but for the kinds of emotions that his future children might experience too. Ivy had been by his side, encouraging and supportive, and had joined him for some sessions.

The first night their first child had spent under their roof had been one of the most terrifying and wonderful moments of his entire life and there wasn't a single person in the world Antonio would have chosen to share it with other than Ivy.

'Have I told you today how much I love you?' he whispered into her ear.

'Well, this morning you told me you loved that thing I did with my—'

'Ivy Gallo, there are children present,' he warned, loving the way he felt her smile vibrate through her body.

'You can tell me again if you like?' she offered.

'I love you more and more with every single moment that passes, *amore*.'

She turned in his arms, looked up at him with such conviction in her gaze his heart stopped. 'You are the love of my life. The only one. Ever. My heart is yours, Antonio,' she said, bringing a dampness to his eyes that he could never be ashamed of.

'What are you doing next August?' he asked, gently pulling her into a sway timed to the music drifting out from the kitchen, where Agata was making lemonade and mint tea.

'Here, I think. Why?'

'I was wondering if we could get our wedding blessed.'

'Again?' Ivy asked on a laugh, confusion in her eyes. 'Why?'

'Because it will be our tenth anniversary,' he said with

a smile. 'And because, *cara*,' he confided in a whisper, 'I want to peel the biggest, puffiest white dress from your body again. Once was not enough,' he admitted, feeling their bodies stir from his words. 'And then, when we're naked and together, you can do that thing I love with your—'

Ivy cut him off with a kiss just as their eldest son came running around the corner with his younger sister and brother hot on his heels and in a heartbeat the words *Mamma* and *Papà* were mixed with kisses and laughter that both Antonio and Ivy would remember for the rest of their lives.

Friends and family always marvelled at their happiness, and whenever he was asked what his secret was, Antonio would reply, *'A judge, a marriage and a librarian.'*

* * * * *

If you couldn't put Inconveniently Wed *down,*

then be sure to look out for the next instalment in the Filthy Rich Italians trilogy, coming soon!

And why not try these other stories by Pippa Roscoe?

His Jet-Set Nights with the Innocent
In Bed with Her Billionaire Bodyguard
Twin Consequences of That Night
Greek's Temporary 'I Do'
Forbidden Until Midnight

Available now!

ILLICIT ITALIAN NIGHTS

MELANIE MILBURNE

MILLS & BOON

In loving memory of my beautiful miniature poodle
Lily, who crossed the Rainbow Bridge
during the beginning stages of this novel.

I wrote so many novels with her asleep on the sofa
behind me.

I was the first person to hold her when she was born
and the last as she passed away.

Such a beautiful girl from start to finish. xxxx

CHAPTER ONE

ADDIE WAS BRUSHING her teeth at nine thirty at night when her phone vibrated on the bedside table. She paused for a moment… She hated late-night phone calls from her mother, complaining about how she had put on half a kilo and had to get it off before her next photo shoot. Or calling to tell Addie she was kicking her latest lover out of her luxury home in the Bahamas.

She came out of her tiny bathroom and glanced over at the phone, deciding whether or not to ignore it. Suddenly she recognised the number. Her heart banged against her breastbone like an out-of-control pendulum.

She snatched up the phone and answered, 'Hewwo?' Unfortunately, she hadn't had time to empty her mouth of its minty contents.

'Addison? It's Vic Jacobetti.'

Addie couldn't speak—and not because her mouth was still full of toothpaste. Mumbling unintelligibly, she left her phone on the bed, dashing to the bathroom to spit and rinse.

She came back and snatched up the phone and answered breathlessly, 'Sorry about that. You caught me at an awkward moment.'

'My apologies. Is there someone with you?' That

deep gravel-rough voice did something strange to the floor of her belly, making it flutter like the wings of a moth.

'Erm...no...' The thing was, there was never anyone with her at this time of night. She hadn't had a date in years. She couldn't even remember the last time she was kissed. That Vic Jacobetti thought she might be with someone was laughable to say the least. But perhaps her brother, Marcus, and Vic's half-sister, Isabella—who happened to be her sister-in-law and the mother of her adorable little niece, Katerina—hadn't mentioned her lack of a love life.

'Marcus called a moment ago.' Vic's voice had an element of gravitas that sent a wave of uneasiness through her. 'He and Isabella are stuck in New Zealand due to a severe storm and flooding that occurred as a result. They can't get back in time to relieve the nanny they engaged. They want us to take care of Katerina until they can get home.'

Addie licked her suddenly dry lips. 'Us?'

'We're her godparents and they thought she'd be happiest with us.'

'But why can't the nanny stay on?' Addie loved kids. All kids. But she had never been left in charge of one. Her specialty was animals. Her work as a vet nurse was a perfect fit for her. Her mother thought it was weird that Addie had zero interest in fashion and had no desire to be in the spotlight like her as a world-famous swimsuit model. She didn't even own a swimsuit. She loved nothing better than tending to sick and wounded or aging animals. Or the cute little puppies and kittens that come in for their vaccinations with their proud owners. Addie loved the trust the animals had in her, the love they showed even when they were sick or stressed. They didn't judge her for the clothes she wore—she wore scrubs, anyway—or her makeup-free face and pulled-back hair. They saw her for what she was.

'The nanny has another job she can't postpone. Marcus and Isabella were only going to be away four days for their friends' wedding. Katerina is at my villa in Lake Como, where Marcus and Isabella were planning to join her and have a family holiday there. But the nanny is insisting on leaving, so we'll fly there immediately to take over.'

She gulped. 'Immediately?'

'I'll send a car for you. It'll be there in half an hour.'

'But I have to call my boss and let them know, but it's late at night and—'

'You can do that on the way. Pack a bag and be ready. And don't forget your passport.' His tone was commanding as if he was used to issuing orders and having them obeyed without question. The only question Addie had was: Why hadn't her brother called her? She knew he was seven years older than her, but he was still her brother—not that they were particularly close.

Marcus was her mother's favourite child and being so much older than Addie he had been away at boarding school or university or working abroad while she was growing up. She couldn't recall a single instance of her mother berating her in front of Marcus, or anyone for that matter. It was a private thing that somehow made her feel even more isolated. Who would ever believe the charming and gorgeous Solange could be cruel and insensitive to the needs of a small, insecure and shy child?

As if Vic read her mind he added, 'Marcus told me to tell you he'd call you when he gets a chance. The power was out, and his phone was running out of battery.'

'Okay. Just as long as they're both safe and out of harm's way.'

'They're fine but it might be a day or two before we hear from them.'

Addie put the phone down once the call ended and chewed at her lip. That was quite easily the longest conversation she had shared with Vic Jacobetti. She met him first at Marcus and Isabella's engagement party and formed an immediate crush on him. She couldn't explain it other than there would be very few women on the earth who wouldn't be knocked off their feet by his gorgeous Italian features. Tall, dark and handsome didn't adequately describe the utter perfection of him. And droves of women obviously agreed with her because he was rarely without a glamorous lover hanging off one of his gym-toned arms. Of course, her crush on him made her tongue-tied and awkward and ridiculously gauche around him, which didn't improve the second time she saw him at Marcus and Isabella's wedding. She drank way too much champagne to cover her introversion. She was not particularly keen on social gatherings, especially society weddings. The wedding of Isabella, as the half-sister of hotel billionaire Ludovico Jacobetti, and Addie's brother, Marcus, the firstborn and golden child of supermodel Solange Featherstone was a big deal. A very big deal. Hundreds and hundreds of guests, including royalty and celebrities and paparazzi buzzing around like a swarm of locusts of biblical proportions. She was just thankful she hadn't been asked to be in the bridal party so she could fade into the background. She was not so much a wallflower but wallpaper. Beige wallpaper.

The third time she met Vic was at Katerina's christening. Given that she and Marcus weren't super close, she was still truly honoured to be asked to be his little daughter's godmother, but Addie was gobsmacked to find she was sharing the responsibility with Vic. They stood there, side by side in the church and made their vows. Heat rushed past the roots of her hair to her corpus callosum because she was thinking of how wonderful it would be to be making other vows together one day. Ridiculous. What would someone like Vic Jacobetti ever see in her?

And now she was going to be spending who knew how many days and nights with him at his private villa in Lake Como. The fact that their nineteen-month-old niece would be there with them acting as chaperone was beside the point.

Addie went to her wardrobe and stared at the contents for a few moments. She shook her head. Her mother had a walk-in wardrobe that was as big as Addie's entire flat. It was practically a drive-in wardrobe. Unlike her mother's colourful wardrobe, hers only contained neutral-coloured garments. Brown, beige, white and grey and black. Background tones that suited her…

well, she was not sure if they suited her colouring or not but she was most comfortable in them. Her mother regularly dropped off bags of her clothes that 'she had only worn once and wouldn't be seen dead in twice', but Addie had a different build from her mother, a fact she had been informing her of since she was six years old.

Addie stuffed a few things in a small suitcase and packed her duckling pyjamas and piglet slippers. She was an animal lover. Her night attire was a little more colourful than her day clothes, but that was because no one ever saw her in them. And she meant no one. She tried not to dwell on the fact that she was still a virgin at the ripe old age of twenty-eight. It was embarrassing for one thing, but she found dating difficult. She was not good at small talk; she didn't know how to flirt and flutter her eyelashes or whatever anyone had to do to attract a man's attention. Call her old-fashioned, but she positively refused to try one of those dating apps. Her mother, on the other hand, was a professional at dating. If there was an award for it, Solange would get a gold medal. Addie had lost count of the number of partners she'd had. Her dad was the first of five husbands, but Solange got sick of paying legal fees, so now only stayed with a guy a few weeks or one or two months. Oh, and Solange wasn't her real name, either—it was Susan but she thought that was too common and not sophisticated enough.

Addie was still packing her few toiletries when the doorbell rang. Toothbrush, hairbrush, a couple of hair ties, moisturiser, lip gloss, and industrial-strength sunscreen. The last thing she needed was more freckles.

She opened the door and her breath stalled in her throat. Vic Jacobetti was much taller than she remembered, or maybe that was because on the three formal occasions she had met him she had been wearing heels. Boy, did she need a pair of heels right then. Or a ladder. Or a crane. She looked up, up, up to meet his dark brown eyes. Her eyes were brown too, but nothing like the colour of his. Hers were a bland sort of brown, neither light nor dark but something in between. His were so dark, Addie could barely make out where his pupils began and ended, and they were fringed with ink-black lashes far longer than hers. His eyebrows were prominent, his nose straight and his mouth… Oh, dear Lord in heaven, his mouth would have sent Michelangelo dashing off to sharpen his chisels. Sculptured with a full lower lip that was both sensual and utterly masculine. Vic hadn't recently shaved and the dark stubble along his chiselled jaw and around his mouth made her mouth water. He was dressed in dark blue suit trousers and a light blue business shirt that emphasised the olive tan of his skin, the cuffs folded back from his strong wrists, the neck open to reveal a dusting of hair on his chest—curly, thick, black, dangerously male.

'Ready, *cara*?' His casually delivered term of endearment should not have drawn her eyes back to his mouth. It should not have made her heart skip and her pulse trip. It should not have made her think she was anything special because she had heard him say it to lots of women. But…no one had ever called her that before.

'Erm, yes…sort of…' She was trying not to show how flustered she was. And not just because six foot four of male perfection was standing in the frame of her front door addressing her with an Italian term of endearment. Here was the thing—at work, she was fabulous in an emergency and never got flustered. She stayed calm and never allowed her emotions to get the better of her. Of course, some of the incidents at work were gut-wrenchingly sad but she held herself together until she got home. But being in Vic Jacobetti's presence was enough to send her pulse racing and her heart to bounce around her chest like a yo-yo having a tantrum. Her crush to this point, on a scale of one to ten, had been a five. Now it was a six.

'Is that your only luggage?' Vic looked at the small overnight case she had packed and placed near the door; a frown pulling at his brow.

'Yes.'

He raised his eyebrows in what she took to be an expression of faint surprise and picked up her bag. 'Let's go. The car is waiting.'

Addie locked her door and followed him to the long sleek car parked on the street. A driver was behind the wheel and there was a glass partition between him and the passenger section. The driver got out of the vehicle and swiftly opened the door for her, giving her a polite nod. 'Good evening, Miss Featherstone.'

'Good evening.' She smiled and got in with as much grace as she could muster, but she couldn't help wondering if both the driver and Vic were comparing her to her mother. Most people did. Needless to say, her mother was excellent at entering and alighting from luxury vehicles. She, on the other hand, was so worried she might trip or bump her head, she usually ended up doing one or both. But miraculously, this time she managed to get in without making a fool of herself.

Once Vic had taken his seat and closed the door, the driver closed the panel dividing him from them, and smoothly pulled away from the curb and entered the night-time traffic.

Addie was suddenly aware of being alone with Vic Jacobetti. He was sitting within touching distance. She could smell the citrus and woodsy notes of his aftershave. She could see the long length of his legs, and she could hear the rustle of his shirt as he reached for some papers in a leather briefcase on the floor at his Italian leather–clad feet. He sat back in his seat with the papers resting on his lap and glanced at her. The dark interior of the car made his eyes so black she was mesmerised by them. Hypnotised like someone being put under a spell.

'Is everything all right, *bella*?'

She rapid-blinked. If only she didn't have the propensity to blush. *Bella*. Now, that was taking the endearments a little too far. She did not for one moment consider herself beautiful. Hopefully the subdued lighting would disguise the heat crawling across her cheeks. 'Of course. It's just been a bit of a rush, that's all.'

One side of his mouth lifted in a grimace, and he looked back down at his papers and began to shuffle through them. 'Tell me about it.'

There was an echoing silence.

'What did you have to cancel in order to take care of Katerina? A hot date with a supermodel or super-famous actress?' She wanted to bite her tongue. She wanted to slap the side of her head for being such a fool for showing any interest in his love life. She wanted to sink to the floor and disappear under the seat like a lost coin. She hated this about herself, but sometimes when she was flustered, she didn't clam up as you'd expect someone shy to do, but instead she would blurt out the first thing that came to her mind. It was like the more uncomfortable and out of her depth she felt, the more likely her tongue would flap its way into territory it would never normally dare to go. This was such a time.

Vic's eyes came back to hers with a glint that did nothing to quell her skittering pulse and cool her hot cheeks. 'No. I've taken myself off the market for a while.'

Her brows rose. 'Oh?'

He tapped the paperwork on his lap with his long and tanned fingers. 'I have a lot of work on at the moment. I'm about to begin a new hotel development.'

She tried not to show her surprise at his choice of temporary celibacy. It was rare for a week or two to go by without a gossip magazine or social media platform documenting his latest love interest. For all she knew, there was probably a waiting list of women desperate to date him. 'So, where is this new development?' she asked.

'Lake Como.'

'Near your villa?'

'As close as you can get.' He gave a wry half smile and added, 'It is my villa. I'm turning it into a hotel, or I will be once Katerina and her parents finish their holiday there.'

'How long have you lived there?'

'I haven't lived there since I was a child.' He turned over another page and then glanced at her again with an inscrutable expression and continued, 'Isabella and Marcus use it more than I do. I've only been there two times in the past year. I mostly travel between my hotels or stay in my London apartment.' He looked back down at his paperwork, his expression now set in taut lines of almost fierce concentration.

'You don't feel any sentimentality about the place?'

'None.'

For some reason, she wasn't fooled by that brusque response. Sensing an undercurrent of bitterness contained in that single-word answer, she kept quiet. She had heard via Marcus that Vic had lost his father when he was young, and his mother had remarried a couple of years later. Isabella was born the following year. Losing a parent at any age was devastating, but for a young child it was life changing. So too was divorce, but she didn't want to think too much about her parents' acrimonious divorce, and she certainly didn't want to talk about it. With anyone. Even Marcus and she had made a tacit agreement to never discuss it.

'How long did you live there as a child?'

'Until I was seven.'

'Where did you live then?'

'Boarding school. In England.'

She stared at him with a concerned frown. 'But surely you came home for holidays?'

'Not often. I was mostly shipped off to my aunt's place in Florence.'

'But you were so young,' she said, still frowning. 'Your mother must have wanted to see you more than only occasionally?'

Vic's mouth had a cynical twist to it and his eyes were as hard as black marble. 'My mother was not one to defy her husband's orders. Besides, she was busy once Isabella came along.'

'So, you don't get on with your stepfather?' It was hardly a wild guess on her part. She could sense the hatred and resentment coming off him in soundless waves.

A muscle tensed in his jaw and a lightning flash went through his gaze. 'I tolerate him for the sake of my mother and sister.'

'I saw your mother and your stepfather at the wedding and the christening. They seemed happy enough together.'

Vic looked at her again with that cynical half smile she was becoming to know as his default setting. 'Is any marriage happy all the time?'

Licking her parchment-dry lips, she shifted her gaze to the tote bag on her lap. 'None of my mother's have been, but I like to hope that some people get lucky.'

'So, it's all down to luck in your opinion?'

His question drew her gaze back to his. Her cheeks heated. If only she had the sophistication to hold his gaze without blushing like a shy schoolgirl. 'I like to think true love exists, but I suspect it's something you have to work at like any other relationship. The two parties have to make a commitment to be there for each other in good times and bad.'

The cynical slant to his mouth tilted further. 'And how lucky have you been in love, *tesore*?'

Uh-oh, another spine-tingling endearment. How was she going to keep her crush at level six if Vic kept uttering those gorgeous words to her? The heat in her cheeks threatened to fog up the car windows. She tried to hold his penetrating gaze, but she simply couldn't do it. She turned to stare at the glass panel in front of her that separated them from the driver. 'Not lucky at all.'

'No current partner?'

'No.'

'When did you last have one?'

She tightened her hands around her tote bag until her knuckles became white. 'I suppose you've been talking to my brother, have you?'

'About what?'

She kept her gaze fixed on the glass panel, but she could see his reflection in it as well as her own. He was looking at her with a quiet intensity she found a little unnerving. 'I haven't dated for a while.'

'How long a while?'

She sat there for an infinitesimal moment and lamented the fact that if she had been an honours student of small talk, she would have thought of something witty to say that would have deftly swung the subject in another direction. But instead, she answered, 'It's… complicated.'

'Aren't most people's love-lives?'

She let out a serrated sigh and glanced in his direction. He was frowning at her like he had never seen anyone like her before. But then, he probably hadn't. There were not many twenty-eight-year-old virgins floating around these days. Or at least, not in the circles he swam in.

Addie turned back to fix her gaze on her bag on her lap. 'I'm…picky.' It wasn't the whole truth, but it would do for now. She hadn't told anyone about The Incident. Who was she going to tell? Her mother? Solange wasn't the type of mother to sit with her arm around you while you recounted the worst night of your life. Especially when it was her mother's popularity and beauty and fame that had turned Addie into a sexual trophy at only fifteen years of age. She was fortunate she found out in time that the boy she thought was in love with her and she with him, only wanted to sleep with her so he could gain street cred with his friends. Talk about mortifying. To this day, every time she was naked, she'd think of that awful moment when that horrible realisation dawned. How could she have been so foolish to think anyone would want her for *her*?

'Nothing wrong with being a little picky.' There was a quality to Vic's voice that made her glance at him again. He let out a rueful-sounding sigh and added, 'Maybe I should follow your example.' He looked back down at his paperwork with a small frown between his brows.

'What? You're not finding the playboy lifestyle fulfilling any more now Marcus isn't out on the town slaying hearts with you?' She affected a teasing tone.

He gave a half smile that didn't reach his eyes. They were unreadable pools of black mystery that made her more and more intrigued by him. He reminded her of a deep body of still water. What you saw on the surface gave no clue to the dangers or the delights below. You simply had to take the risk to find out. She was not a risk-taker, so…maybe she'd never find out. Pity.

'I'm not into breaking hearts. I've always been clear on what I can and cannot bring to a relationship.'

'I hate to be pedantic, but is it still called a relationship if it's only a one-night hook-up?'

'Isn't any interaction with another human being, no matter how short, a relationship of sorts?'

She found it hard to hold his gaze even as inscrutable as it was. The philosophical turn the conversation had taken secretly delighted her. She loved nothing better than a deep and meaningful discussion, hence her aversion to shallow small talk.

'Good point,' she said, nodding slowly in agreement. 'But how do you keep your feelings out of it? Asking for a friend.'

His smile was like a light coming on after a blackout. It transformed his face, softening his stern features, making him seem younger and far less intimidating.

'Tell your friend that it takes less work as the years roll on. I don't even think about it now when I hook up with someone. It's purely a physical thing.'

There was one part of her that was sitting there wondering what the hell she was doing talking about hookups with Vic Jacobetti, but another part was fascinated by his ability to control his feelings to that degree.

She was good at controlling her feelings too, but they were still there under the surface, even if she didn't show it on her face. She *felt* them. She was *always* conscious of them. They were deep down inside her, as deep as a kelp forest anchored to the ocean floor, its long fronds waving and flowing and twisting and turning with the tides of life. Sometimes, when she was alone, they could softly brush at her ankles, that brief touch setting off a panic she had to work hard to shut down otherwise she could become entangled and pulled under. Even that imagined touch of the tentacle-like fronds was a visceral reminder of their lurking presence, their power to drown her.

She couldn't imagine getting naked with someone and not feeling anything…well, apart from shame, but of course she didn't want to talk about that.

Vic was trying not to think about all the work he had to put on hold while he accompanied Addie Featherstone to look after their goddaughter, Katerina. He was also trying not to think about how sweet and shy and unassuming Addie was, especially compared to the women he associated with in his so-called private life. His life was not as private as he would have liked—it was too hard to avoid the attention when he owned one of the most successful hotel chains in the world. But success was his badge of honour, the way he honoured the memory of his late father who had founded the company.

Spending a few days at his Lake Como villa with Addie was the only solution he could come up with at short notice. The only solution he knew Marcus and Isabella would be content with given Marcus and Addie's mother was not the grandmotherly type. It was hard to believe Addie was Solange's daughter. Addie was not unattractive by any means, but she didn't have the stop-the-clock features and figure of her mother. Her quieter beauty and personality were strangely soothing to be around.

The first time he met her he had been shocked at how different she was from her mother. Shocked in a nice way, that was. Solange was over-the-top in everything she did—how she looked, how she acted, how she made sure she was the centre of attention. But Addie was nothing like that. She was so reserved and buttoned-up and yet he couldn't help noticing the way she revealed things about herself in a touchingly unguarded way. He suspected he intimidated her, which was certainly not his intention, but then many people found him intimidating. He didn't apologise for it. He made no allowances for it. He wouldn't have achieved the things he had achieved without being a little ruthless and hard-headed at times. But Addie's lack of artifice and guile was refreshing, a change from the artfully sophisticated women he bedded on a regular basis. Not that he was going to bed Addie, of course. That would be crossing a line he did not intend to cross. She was his friend's little sister. Forbidden. Off limits. Not on his radar. Not his type. And yet… something about her intrigued him, made him keen to know more about her. Like why she was so understated about her appearance, why she seemed so determined to melt into the background rather than be noticed.

But he had noticed.

He had to keep his head buried in his paperwork to stop himself studying her elfin features, to stop himself staring at the sweet contour of her full-lipped mouth, the gentle slopes of her cheeks and her retroussé nose with its sprinkling of freckles like nutmeg on a dessert.

Yes, he had noticed her, but it didn't mean he was going to do anything.

Addie Featherstone was forbidden. Tempting, alluring, intriguing but forbidden.

CHAPTER TWO

THEY ARRIVED AT the airport a few minutes later but Addie soon realised Vic hadn't booked them on a commercial flight. They whipped through check-in and security in record time. She'd been on private jets a few times before with her mother, so this was not exactly a new experience. It wasn't as over-the-top as other jets she had been on, but it certainly was luxurious in a simple and understated way.

Sinking into the plush leather seat opposite Vic's, she wondered if she should have taken the one next to him so she wouldn't be in his direct line of vision. She had never spent so much time alone with him before. She found him intriguing but intimidating because he was so difficult to read. Was he thinking how unlike her stunning mother she was? Her mother was an exotic flamingo. Addie was a common brown sparrow. Was he thinking how socially inept she was compared to her older brother? Her brother could work a room like it was a sport and he was the current world champion. She, on the other hand, melted into the background and left the room as quickly as she could.

'Is this the way you always travel?' she asked, more for the desire to fill the silence than needing to know.

'Yes. I'm not fond of commercial flights.' Vic looked down to click his seatbelt into place and looking at her again, continued with an arch of one dark brow. 'You don't approve?'

Addie gave a tiny shrug of one shoulder. 'I'm hardly in a position to criticise. I've flown on private jets with my mother a few times.' She twisted her mouth and added, 'Mostly because my father changed his mind about having me to stay with him and she didn't have enough time to make other arrangements.'

His dark eyebrows moved closer together over his even darker eyes. 'Their divorce wasn't amicable?'

She gave a tinkle of laughter, but even to her own ears it sounded fake, which it was. 'Understatement. But I'm sure Marcus has told you all about it.'

'He's told me surprisingly little.'

It was her turn to frown. 'Aren't you two close friends?'

'There are some things even close friends don't talk about.'

'Well, I wouldn't know because I don't have a lot of close friends.' She bit her lip, immediately regretting her unfiltered admission. Why was she making an idiot of herself by telling Vic Jacobetti about her lack of a close network of friends to hang out with after work and on weekends? She spent most weekends alone or worked extra shifts at the clinic so the other staff could spend time with their loved ones. Besides, the companionship of animals comforted her, gave her a purpose she lacked in her private life. She had no fear of animals turning against her or using her as a means to an end like that boyfriend tried to do when she was fifteen. With animals, what you saw is what you got. They didn't have agendas or devious plans to manipulate you. They took you as you were, accepted you and trusted you to take care of them. She was proud of her ability to soothe a distressed dog or cat in the emergency clinic. She always handled the so called 'difficult' ones. She didn't find them difficult at all. They were sensitive and they were hurting, and she knew how to help them feel safe and nurtured while under her care.

The jet began to move, and the pilot addressed them from the cockpit about travelling time and weather conditions on arrival. The interruption gave her a moment or two to compose herself, but she could still feel the burn of a blush lingering in her cheeks.

The jet took off and she looked out the window to see the winding and crinkled silver of the River Thames and the city of London in miniature. It looked like a fairyland at this time of night with its array of sparkling lights.

Vic stretched out his long legs and crossed his ankles, his gaze unwavering on her. 'Why don't you have any close friends?'

She rolled her lips together and they made a soft popping sound when she stopped. 'It's a long story.'

'We have a couple of hours.'

She tried not to squirm under his scrutiny. 'Shouldn't we be discussing how we're going to take care of Katerina? I mean, do you have any experience with small children?' She wanted to steer clear of any more embarrassing true confessions.

'Not much. I was at boarding school when Isabella was young. I only saw her occasionally on visits home. And I've only seen Katerina a handful of times since the christening. That's why I thought you should do this with me. Marcus told me you've seen her a fair bit.'

'Yes, enough for her to know who I am, but Isabella or Marcus were always there too. My specialty is small animals, not small children, but I figure since I was a small kid once, it can't be too hard, right?'

Vic's sensual mouth lifted in a slanted smile and her heart gave a sudden lurch. 'I'm not sure it works that way, *cara*.'

Gulp. She was losing count of how many times he'd addressed her with those delicious Italian endearments. 'Yes, well, I guess we'll muddle through somehow. But the poor little munchkin will be missing her parents, surely? I mean, she's not yet two. Did they leave instructions on her routine and that sort of thing?'

'The nanny will hopefully have informed my housekeeper of all that when she handed her over today.'

She frowned in concern. 'But surely the nanny could've stayed until we got there? Poor little Katerina, she must be so confused and frightened to be suddenly left with a total stranger.' She knew how her niece would be feeling because she had experienced it herself. Too many times to count. More times than she wanted to remember.

'My housekeeper is more than capable of looking after her until we get there,' Vic said. 'She's had four children and has several grandchildren of her own.'

She chewed at her lip, picturing the little toddler

dumped off like a parcel with someone who was almost a stranger to take care of her and reassure her. She could still recall her own terrifying sense of abandonment all these years on from similar drop-offs. 'But how well do you know your housekeeper? You said you'd only been to your villa a couple of times in the past year. She might be a wonderful housekeeper but a terrible childminder, even if she has grandchildren of her own. Child rearing practices have changed so much over the years. She might be doing or saying all sorts of things that are wrong by today's standards.'

'Katerina will be fine. Stop worrying. You're forgetting she's met Lucia many times before when Marcus and Isabella have stayed at the villa.'

'But what about your mother and stepfather? They're Katerina's grandparents, or at least your mother is,' Addie said.

Vic made a derisive sound at the back of his throat. 'My stepfather isn't fond of little kids.'

'What about your mother?'

'She adores Katerina.'

'So why doesn't she—?'

'Because my stepfather makes sure my mother is too busy to be available to anyone but him.'

Addie sat back in her seat and frowned. It wasn't hard to notice the bitterness in Vic's tone and it made her wonder exactly what his childhood had been like once his stepfather came on the scene.

'My stepfather isn't fond of little kids.'

There was so much packed in that sentence and yet Vic's half-sister seemed extremely fond of her father.

Marcus and Isabella's wedding had made Addie envious when she saw Isabella's proud father walking her down the aisle. Addie's father hadn't even come to any of her school functions or birthdays. It seemed pretty unlikely he'd want to walk her down the aisle if by some miracle she did one day get married.

Addie tried to remember if Isabella or Marcus had ever mentioned the housekeeper, Lucia. She'd had nice housekeepers and nannies too, but it didn't mean she was any less frightened to be suddenly without one or both of her parents. Children needed security and the slightest change could make them feel uneasy, uncertain and unloved. Addie's mother, as the other grandmother, was clearly not available. Solange had even refused when Katerina was born to be called anything but *Solange*. No *grandma*, *granny* or *nanny* for her—it was too aging and not good for her brand. Solange would be the last person Marcus and Isabella could call on in an emergency, which was why Addie knew it was up to her to comfort and protect her little niece until her parents returned. But doing it with Vic Jacobetti was something she was not quite prepared for. But how could she prepare for something so outside her lived experience? He was a playboy. She was practically a nun.

'Addie.' It was the first time she had heard Vic call her by her preferred name and the sound of his deep and mellifluous voice with his Italian accent sent a fluttery sensation to her core. He pronounced Addie with a slight accentuation on the second syllable—Ad-*dee*.

How could someone simply saying her name make her go weak at the knees?

She released her savaged lip and met his gaze. 'It'll be hours before we get there. Have you spoken to Lucia to see how Katerina is settling in?'

'There hasn't been time.' A look of frustration crossed his face. 'I had to cancel so many commitments in order to get there as it is.'

'I'm sure Marcus and Isabella appreciate you sacrificing your valuable time.' She hadn't intended to be as sarcastic as she sounded—it just came out that way.

There was a moment or two of silence.

'I understand you too had to cancel your own commitments,' Vic said in a less impatient tone. 'I appreciate you coming with me at such short notice, but I knew Marcus and Isabella would prefer us to do this together.'

'Do this together...'

Somehow those words had an intimate sound to them that stirred her body into heightened awareness. An awareness that tingled through her blood like a mind-altering drug. Vic Jacobetti was such a worldly and experienced and sophisticated man. She was a shy and socially awkward virgin who hadn't been kissed in years.

'Yes, well, it's not as if they can call on my mother,' Addie said with a side eye. 'She refuses to even tell anyone she has a grandchild.'

'Why is that?'

'Not good for her image.'

Vic's top lip curled, but he didn't respond, however,

Addie felt a strange alliance with him. A sense that he understood more about her background than most people, making her feel less alone and isolated. Was it because he was close to Marcus and knew how difficult some aspects of their childhood had been? Or was it because Vic was an astute businessman who knew the foibles of self-obsessed and vain people? Or a bit of both?

The flight attendant came out from the front section of the jet to serve them drinks and a light supper. Addie was glad of the distraction from where her thoughts were taking her. She declined the offer of champagne, mentally cringing at how she had overindulged at her brother's wedding. She sipped at some orange juice and turned down the delicious looking food on the tray. The attendant slipped out of sight again.

'Not hungry?' Vic asked, reaching for his coffee cup.

'Not at this time of night. It's way past my bedtime.' Eek. Why had she mentioned anything to do with bed?

'There's a bed down the back.' Vic nodded towards the area behind her. 'Why don't you have a nap before we arrive? We still have to get to Lake Como, so it'll be a late night.'

She tried but failed to suppress a yawn. 'No, it's okay. It'll only make me feel worse if I nap now.' She could only imagine how dishevelled she would look waking up from a sleep, even if it was on a private jet bed. Besides, the thought of Vic watching her while she slept was a little disconcerting. What if she snored? She bet none of his glamourous dates *ever* snored. 'Will we drive to Lake Como straightaway?'

'Yes, I have a driver organised to take us as soon as we clear customs.'

She took another sip of her orange juice, acutely aware of Vic's every movement. She watched as he leaned forward to put his coffee cup on the table between them. He leaned back to reach for the papers he'd brought with him. If he was tired, he certainly wasn't showing it. His face, while unshaven, did not have lines of exhaustion and his eyes were clear and unshadowed. Her eyes were gritty, and it was becoming increasingly difficult to sit upright. Oh, how she longed to lie flat and close her eyes for just a moment or two…

She blinked and sat up straighter in the luxurious leather seat. 'I guess you're pretty used to late nights.'

He gave a glinting crooked smile that sent a dart to her heart. 'Because I'm a playboy as you call it or because I run a global chain of hotels?'

'Both, I guess.'

He leaned back, his smile still causing havoc with her heart rhythm. 'I'm not afraid of hard work.'

'Or hard play, as rumour has it.' She gave herself a mental slap as soon as the words left her mouth. She had no business speculating on his private life, although it had to be said, his private life was reported publicly more times than not. But guess that's what happens to you when you're a super wealthy and spectacularly handsome man. Everyone wants to know what you're doing and with whom you are doing it.

His gaze held hers in a lock that sent a hot shiver rolling down her spine like a current of electricity. 'I definitely play hard.'

She disguised a gulp. She could only imagine how hard. And she was not talking hard drinking or partying because she knew from her brother—and she had witnessed it herself on the three occasions she had met him—that Vic never overindulged in alcohol. 'I can only imagine…' Her hot cheeks were betraying her yet again, but she had no control over that. 'My life must seem terribly boring compared to yours.'

Vic leaned forward again, this time to pick up a glass of water. He leaned back, holding the glass without bringing it to his mouth, his gaze unwavering on hers. 'Tell me about your life. What do you do in your spare time?'

Okay, so this was going to be embarrassing. 'I knit.'

One of his eyebrows lifted ever so slightly. 'Knit? Like sweaters? Scarves?'

'Coats. Dog coats.' She put her half-finished orange juice on the table and sat back. 'I volunteer at a rescue shelter. Some breeds of dogs, particularly the smaller short-haired ones, feel the cold.'

'That's a very noble thing to do.'

She studied him for a long moment, trying to gauge whether he was being serious or mocking her behind the unreadable screen of his gaze. 'It sounds pretty tame compared to what you get up to in your spare time, but I find it fulfilling.'

'Who taught you to knit? Not your mother, I'm guessing.'

She couldn't hold back a wry laugh. 'No, definitely not my mother. One of the senior vets taught me before she retired a couple of years ago. I find it quite meditative, actually.'

'What made you decide to become a vet nurse?'

'I love animals.'

'More than people?'

'More than some people.'

Vic smiled again and her pulse tripped. 'Did you have a pet growing up? Marcus has never mentioned one.'

'No, we weren't allowed pets.' She let out a tiny sigh and continued before she could put the brakes on her tongue, 'I think it would have helped me to have one, though, especially after the divorce.'

'It was a tough time for you?' The question was delivered in a gentle and empathetic manner, not probing or intrusive at all.

'I'd just started school, so it was unsettling to have to spend time with my dad who had moved to a house two hours away. His new partner wasn't great with kids.' Oh, man, what an understatement that was.

'Were you close to your father?'

'I was until he met Fernella.' Her shoulders slumped. She shouldn't have started talking about the dramas of her childhood, but somehow it was pouring out of her. Was it because it was way past her bedtime? Or was it because Vic Jacobetti had a magnetic impact on her? She was drawn to him, revealing parts of herself she revealed to no one. 'Not that my mother was great with kids either. In fact, she and Fernella were a bit alike in that regard.'

'I'm sorry to hear that.' He put his papers to one side

again and gave her his full attention. 'Is your father still with your stepmother?'

'No, they eventually broke up, but he keeps partnering with the same type of women. The self-absorbed, obsessed-about-their-appearance type.' Her shoulders dropped on a sigh. 'It's like he's trying to replace my mother but why? She made his life a living hell. I don't think she ever truly loved him. The only thing in the end she liked about him was his name, so she kept it.'

'Some people follow a pattern that was set in childhood. They go looking for something in a partner they recognised in their parent, but it usually ends in tears.'

'What was your father like?'

He paused for a long moment, and she wondered if he was going to change the subject, but then he finally spoke. 'He was loving and warm and kind and steadfast—all the things a child needs a father to be.' There was a sad wistfulness about Vic's expression as if he still found talking about his father painful in spite of the passage of time.

'I can only imagine how devastating it would've been to lose him so young.'

'It was.' He flicked her a brief glance and continued, 'I never really understood why my mother married again so quickly, but I think she was so lonely raising me by herself. And of course, the hotel business was overwhelming to her, and at six years old, I was too young to help.' His mouth twisted in an embittered way. 'My stepfather was a handy solution, or at least he made himself appear that way. He would take over the running of the business until I came of age and solve her loneliness in one fell swoop.'

'But that didn't happen.'

'No.' He brushed some imaginary lint off his sleeve and continued, 'He all but destroyed the business my father had worked so hard to build up. My mother was powerless to stop him. But as soon as I came of age, I made it my mission to buy out my stepfather and rebuild my father's business into one of the leading hotel brands on the globe.'

'And you've done it. The Jacobetti chain is one of the most luxurious chains of hotels in the world. You must feel so satisfied.'

There was a beat or two of silence.

'But you're not, are you?' she asked, studying his brooding expression.

A muscle flickered in his jaw. 'The only way I can ever feel satisfied is to break the hold my stepfather has over my mother, but she can see no wrong in him. Nor can Isabella.'

She frowned. 'But how does your mother explain the business all but collapsing until you were old enough to step in?'

Vic gave a cynical smile that made his eyes go as hard as onyx. 'He painted it as bad luck, the global economic downturn and so on. She took his word over mine. Still does.'

She could now see why he shied away from long-term relationships. He didn't trust love as an emotion. 'Maybe they see things in him you can't see. I mean, he's obviously nothing like your father, but he must have some good qualities, otherwise why would your mother and sister still love him?'

He sent her a sideways glance. 'Love is blind, that's why.'

'Which is why you want nothing to do with it.' She framed it as a statement not as a question.

'Got it in one.'

It was late by the time they got through customs in Milan, later still by the time they were on the road to Vic's villa at Lake Como. Addie's eyelids were weighted with anvils, and she fought the desire to sleep with a steely resolve she hadn't realised she was capable of. But at some point, that steely resolve must have finally rusted, because when the car eventually came to a stop, she opened her eyes to find herself slumped across Vic Jacobetti's lap. She could feel the firm strength of his thighs against her cheek, and she scrambled into an upright position, pushing her hair away from her face. Oh, dear God, how could she have fallen asleep on him? What must he think of her? Did he think she was throwing herself at him like all those other women? She couldn't bring herself to meet his gaze. But then her eyes drifted sideways, and widened with excruciating embarrassment as she saw the patch of dribble on his trousers close to his bent knee.

'I'm so sorry…' She bit her lip, conscious of heat flooding into her cheeks. 'I must've nodded off.'

'No need to apologise.' He gave a smile that sent her pulses skittering. 'At least you didn't snore.'

She grimaced. 'But I drooled on your trousers. I—I'll pay to have them dry-cleaned.'

'Don't be silly. I've had plenty of people drool over me before.'

'I can only imagine how many.' And now she was one of them. Eek. Was it possible to actually die of embarrassment? What sort of idiot was she to drape herself across his lap and slobber all over his thigh? Arrgh. Talk about unsophisticated. Why had she let her guard down so much? She would never normally relax in a man's company to the point of falling asleep on his lap. She hadn't touched a man other than her father and brother in years. Her father got the most perfunctory air kiss from her on the rare occasions she saw him. Her brother wasn't much of a hugger, but since he'd been with Isabella, he had become better at it. But now she had relaxed to the point of draping herself across Vic Jacobetti's lap and drooling, yes, *drooling* all over his designer trousers.

Shoot me now.

Vic reached out with his hand and gently stroked her burning cheek with a lazy finger, his eyes holding hers. 'Why do you blush around me so much, *tesore*?'

Her cheeks turned up the heat like he had pressed a button on her. But then, he had pressed a button on her. The lust button. It was heating not just her cheeks but other parts of her body. Secret parts. Parts that pulsed and liquified with silky warmth that made it hard for her to think of anything but him. The idle stroke of his finger, the shape of his mouth, the scent of his body—that heady combination of wood and citrus and maleness. An exotic scent to someone like her who was so inexperienced.

'Erm…am I blushing? I—it's hot in here.' She mock-fanned her face with her hand. 'The driver must have the heating on…or something…' She sounded as pathetic as she was. A naive innocent alone with a cynical playboy and feeling way out of her depth…like a little goldfish suddenly flung out of her tiny glass bowl and tossed in the wide deep ocean with who knew what dangers lurked beneath.

'I only have to look at you and you blush.' His voice was deep and held a trace of amusement that she could see reflected in his impossibly dark brown eyes.

'Erm… Do I?' She ran the tip of her tongue across her lips, watching as he followed the movement with his gaze. Something fell from a high shelf in her stomach. Heat pooled in her feminine core. Molten heat that made her aware of every beat of her heart because its echo was pounding between her thighs. She had not been this close to a man in a very long time. She could see the texture of his skin, the way it was stretched over the long straight blade of his nose. She could see the flare of his nostrils as if he too was taking in her scent like a wild animal does a mate. She could see the sculptured perfection of his mouth, the sexy contours hinting at consummate sensuality. A sensuality she suddenly craved to experience with every cell in her body.

Vic's gaze came back to hers in an unwavering lock. 'You do. You did at the engagement party and the wedding and Katerina's christening.'

She lowered her gaze a fraction. 'Does it…does it annoy you?'

He gave a crooked smile. 'Not at all.'

'It annoys me.'

'That you blush so easily?'

She nodded without meeting his gaze. 'I wish…' She squeezed her hands together in her lap and went on, 'I wish I could control it, but I can't. I've always been terribly self-conscious, much to my mother's immense frustration. Marcus got the outgoing genes in our family, which is why she—' She clamped down on her lower lip with her teeth before she revealed the full extent of her mother issues.

The driver slid back the panel at that moment, which gave her a chance to compose herself. He spoke in Italian to Vic and although she couldn't speak the language, she could pick up the gist of the exchange.

Vic got out of the car and came around to open her door. She stepped out and looked around the moonlit scene. The villa was huge, set in beautiful gardens with formal hedges and flowing fountains and interesting pathways that drew your eye further. The three-storey villa was situated on the edge of the lake with stunning views of the water and the looming mountains on the other side. The moon was high in the sky like a silver eye casting its luminous beam over the lake. A light breeze scented with mimosa toyed with her hair and she closed her eyes and listened to the distant but still audible slap of water against the shore. It was so peaceful, so serene and magical it was like being transported into a fairytale.

Watch it, Cinderella. This is no fairytale; this is real life, and you have a job to do that involves a small and no doubt bewildered toddler.

She gave herself a stern lecture before she got too enraptured. But wait...she was hardly Cinderella, was she? The fairytale she most identified with was *The Ugly Duckling*, but she couldn't see herself turning into a graceful swan anytime soon.

Vic closed the door of the car and placed his hand at her elbow. 'Come this way. Careful of the cobblestones, they can be a little tricky to negotiate at any time, much less when you've had no sleep.'

'But I did sleep. You didn't.'

He glanced down at her with another knee-weakening smile. 'I nodded off once or twice.'

'I wonder what Marcus would say if he heard we'd slept together.' There was another fact about her—she never made flippant and flirty comments. Never. But the words were out before she could monitor her tongue. Heat rushed through her. She could feel it burning like fire across her face. She could only put it down to lack of sleep and being in Vic's disturbing but alluring company.

Vic looked at her in the moonlight, his expression inscrutable. 'I think he'd be very surprised.' His voice was so deep it sent a shiver coursing over her body.

She forced herself to hold his gaze. 'Yes, well, I'm hardly the type of woman you normally date, am I?'

'No, you're not.' His voice was still deep, but something changed in his expression. A subtle change that brought his eyebrows together in a slight frown, as if he were suddenly seeing her in a different light. Thinking about possibilities he had never considered before. Possibilities she had thought about from the moment she first met him. Truth be told, she didn't think he had ever seen her in moonlight before, so there was a chance it was doing her a huge favour. She was photoshopped, filtered by the silvery moonbeams. Yay.

Out of the corner of her eye she saw a light brown moth fly towards one of the outside lights next to the villa. It was dazzled, disoriented by the bright glow, just as she was by Vic Jacobetti. If she allowed herself to be any more attracted to him, she was going to be like that poor defenceless moth—smashed beyond repair.

CHAPTER THREE

THE DOOR OF the grand villa opened behind them, and she turned around to see a woman of about seventy looking at them as if they were angels who had arrived to rescue her from being left alone with a rabid monster. She spoke in rapid Italian that Addie couldn't follow at all, but could sense she was agitated, tired and overwrought. Vic responded to her calmly and reassuringly, his air of command-and-control reassuring to Addie too.

But as soon as they entered the villa, she could hear Katerina wailing from upstairs. Addie didn't have time to take in the imposing surroundings. She barely noticed the works of art on the walls or the high ceilings with their heavy crystal chandeliers hanging with sparkling grandeur. She was hardly conscious when her flying footsteps left the cold, echoing marble of the foyer and landed on the ankle-deep carpet on the winding staircase. She gave the second floor a cursory glance without taking anything much in other than it looked a little faded, like an olden days Hollywood film star that had let herself go now the spotlight was no longer centred on her. The piteous cries tore at her heart like sharp claws, and she bolted upstairs, not waiting to ask directions or permission. Something about those desperate cries called out to her wounded inner child. The child that had spent hours crying alone without anyone coming to comfort her. Nothing and no one were going to stop her going to Katerina. That child needed comforting, and she needed it now.

She found her three floors up, standing up in a cot that looked like it might once have belonged to Vic or Isabella. Her eyes were streaming, and her face was bright red, her dark curls mussed around her head like a black halo. She was sobbing but as soon as she saw Addie the sobs stopped and only her little chin quivered. She reached her pudgy little arms and starburst hands out, and Addie scooped her up and held her close, breathing in the sweet warm human smell of her.

'It's okay, sweetie, I'm here now. I've got you.' She stroked her little back and snuggled her face close to hers. 'You're missing your mummy and daddy, aren't you? But they'll be back soon, and Uncle Vic and I'll take good care of you until then.' She rocked from side to side in a soothing manner. 'I'm sorry I couldn't get here any sooner, but I'm here now. There, there, precious. I've got you now.'

She heard a footfall and turned with the child still in her arms to see Vic enter the nursery. Her heart almost stopped at how handsome he looked standing there with concern etched on his dark features.

'Lucia said Katerina has been awake and upset for hours. She wasn't able to settle her once the nanny left.' He spoke quietly but it made his voice sound even sexier.

Addie could sense the child relaxing a little against her and kept her voice to a whisper. 'Is it any wonder? The poor little darling must've been so scared to be left with a virtual stranger.' She kept rocking from side to side and was pleased and immensely relieved to feel Katerina nestle further into her, a little sigh escaping her tiny mouth. If she had been screaming for hours, then she would be exhausted and would hopefully soon fall asleep in her arms.

'Lucia is hardly a stranger. Katerina has been here several times in the last year.'

'Maybe, but did she look after her? Play with her? Babysit her?' She didn't know why she was firing such rapid questions in a fierce undertone at him but something about the whole situation irked her. The child was clearly not used to being left alone with Lucia. And from the brief glimpse she'd got of Lucia when they arrived, it was clear the housekeeper wasn't that comfortable around small upset children. It didn't matter how many children or grandchildren a person had, they had to have patience and understanding and compassion for little kids who were missing their parents. Some people didn't have the skill set. She should know. She could write a PhD thesis on feeling abandoned by supposedly well-qualified minders.

Vic scraped a hand through his hair in a distracted manner and she got the feeling he was feeling as uncomfortable as she was about poor little Katerina's crying jag. He came closer and stood looking down at the toddler in her arms.

'Is she falling asleep?' His voice too was a low whisper.

'Getting there, I think, but I might wake her if I put her down straight away.'

He reached out and touched the toddler's plump little tear-stained cheek with his finger, but the child didn't stir. Addie was intensely conscious of how close he was standing to her. She could see the individual pinpricks of dark stubble on his face—the bone-tingling reminder of the potent male hormones that surged in his blood. Her blood was surging too, making her heartbeats rapid and uneven like she'd just run up three flights of stairs...well, she *had* just run up three flights of stairs, but still. Being anywhere near Vic Jacobetti was enough to send her pulses racing off into the stratosphere. She looked at his mouth while his gaze was focussed on Katerina. It had a soft wistful curve that she had never seen there before.

'You like kids, huh?' she whispered.

His eyes met hers and a jolt went through her like a lightning bolt. 'Of course, but it doesn't mean I want them myself.' His lips moved in a flat and firm way that suggested the decision was one he made a long time ago and would not, under any circumstances, be reversed.

She stroked a gentle hand down over Katerina's silky head of black curls, rocking from side to side to comfort her in case she was still awake. At least she had stopped crying. Who knew she was a such a fabulous toddler whisperer? Maybe animals weren't her only forte. Yay for her. 'Why not?'

'The short answer is I'm a selfish man who likes his freedom too much.' He moved a step or two away towards the cot and straightened the rumpled bed linen. His back was to her, but to be honest, his back view was almost as delectable as his front. Strong muscles framed his upper body and tapered down to a trim waist and lean hips and a taut behind. Oh, man, she wished she could stop being such a hopeless romantic at times like this. She knew in her bones he was not interested in someone like her. *No one* was interested in someone like her. Well, if they were, it was only so they could get an introduction to her mother and/or her agent or her money or all three.

'And the long answer?' she prompted.

Vic turned to face her again and she had to remind herself to take a breath. Even though it was close to dawn outside, the low light of the nursery with the blackout blinds pulled and only the nightlight on gave him a look that was straight out of a Regency romance. Irresistibly handsome and brooding and yet inscrutable too. 'Is a conversation for another time. Do you want me to take her for you? She's not very big but then, neither are you.'

She blinked at him owlishly for a heartbeat or two. She, tiny? She knew lots of young women had body issues due to unrealistic photos on social media and so on, but she'd had body issues since she was six. 'I wish my mother could hear you say that. She thinks I need to go down a dress size.'

'You mother needs to grow a brain.' He said in such a way that made her wonder if he was one of the few—

the very few—people on the earth who didn't worship at the shrine of her stunningly beautiful and impossibly slim mother.

He came back over to her and gently took Katerina from her arms. Now, this sort of manoeuvre always looked so easy and effortless when parents did it, even grandparents. But when two almost strangers did it, it was almost impossible to do without touching the other person. She was so close she could see his chocolate-brown eyes and the thick and long lashes that fringed them so attractively. She could smell his citrus and sage and woodsy aftershave, and she could feel the warm waft of his breath on her face as gentle and fresh as a summer breeze. She could feel the strength of his arms as he took Katerina from her and held the sleeping toddler against his broad chest.

'You look like you've done this before,' she said.

He gave a half-smile. 'It's my first time putting a kid to bed.'

'You're a natural.'

'Let's see if I manage to get her to stay asleep first.'

He laid Katerina down on the mattress with such care that Addie found herself choked with sudden emotion. Of course, she didn't remember much about her early infancy, but she knew as a young child she was rarely put to bed by either of her parents. And she didn't have loving and involved godparents or grandparents either. Vic covered the toddler up with the light cotton duvet and stood back, looking down at her.

'So far, so good.' His voice was still a husky whisper that sent shivers down her spine.

He walked backwards from the cot, wincing when his large foot hit a creaky floorboard. He stopped still, like he was playing a game of Pirate's Treasure or something. Then he continued until he was close to Addie again, near the door of the nursery. He turned and looked at her with a smile of victory on his face. 'Mission accomplished.' He held up his hand in a high five and she lifted hers to meet it. It was the lightest touch—no loud clap but a simple touch of male flesh on female flesh. But their hands met in a tingle of electricity that shot sparks of heat to her feminine core.

She lowered her hand and tucked it close to her side, but it was still fizzing like a firework. 'I know this sounds terribly British of me, but I could do with a cup of tea.'

'Well, it is just about morning. I'll get Lucia to send one up to your room.'

'Oh, please don't ask her to do that. She looked ready to drop when we arrived. I can make my own tea. Where am I to sleep?'

'You're in the blue room three doors down from here.'

'Is there a closer room? It's just your villa is huge, and I might not hear Katerina during the night.'

'My room is next door to hers.' He pointed to the master bedroom she hadn't noticed on her dash up the stairs earlier.

'Oh, right then.' She moistened her lips and asked, 'Are you a light sleeper?'

'I'm sure I'll hear a toddler crying. That kid's got a set of lungs on her like an opera singer.'

They were still whispering because they were just inside the door of the nursery. It was very hard to whisper-laugh but somehow, she managed it. 'Indeed, she does.'

'But to put your mind at ease, the nanny brought a portable monitor with her. We can download the app on our phones and check on Katerina whenever we want. It will also alert us if she cries.'

He told her the name of the app and she quickly downloaded it. It was reassuring to know she could check on Katerina to make sure she wasn't crying all alone like she used to do.

Vic took Addie's elbow and gently led her out of the nursery, partially closing the door. 'Come. We'll have that cup of tea and then catch a few winks of sleep before Katerina wakes.'

She tried but failed to smother a yawn as she followed him downstairs.

He glanced at her with a concerned frown. 'Tired?'

'A little, I guess. Maybe it's the jet lag but I feel a bit like I've stumbled into another universe.'

He made a sound of soft agreement in his throat. 'You've been to Italy before, though?'

'Once or twice with my mother as a child but not this far north.'

They came to the kitchen and Vic filled the kettle. 'Are you a mug or a cup girl?'

'Cup.'

A ghost of a smile twitched at his mouth as he sourced cups and a teapot from a cupboard.

'You're making real tea? Not tea bags?' she asked in mock surprise.

'You look like a real tea person.' He had his back to her again as he was spooning tea leaves into the pot so she couldn't read his expression.

'How did you decide that?'

Vic turned and set the teapot and then two china cups and saucers on the island bench in between them. He gave a one-shoulder shrug. 'Just a lucky guess. Milk? Sugar?'

'Why don't you guess?'

He studied her for a moment, his dark eyes making her knees turn to liquid. 'A dash of milk, no sugar.'

'I'm getting a little freaked-out by you.'

'So, I'm right?' He pushed the cup towards her with another devastating smile.

'Yes.' She picked up the teaspoon she didn't need but stirred her tea anyway. She watched the tiny whirlpool the action created and tried to get her heart rate to slow down. 'My mother didn't allow a packet of sugar in the house while I was growing up.' She kept her gaze on the swirling contents of her cup and continued, 'She was always on some sort of diet. I was put on one of her cleansing diets when I was six. I ended up needing an iron infusion.'

Vic put his cup down on the saucer with a little clatter. He was frowning so heavily there was a trench between his eyes. 'Marcus hasn't told me a lot about his childhood, but I can read between the lines. I've met your mother's type before.' He picked up his cup again and looked at her over the rim as he held it next to his mouth. 'My stepfather, for instance.' An embittered look came over his face like brooding clouds.

'What don't you like about him? I mean, apart from his mismanagement of your father's business.'

'I still don't understand why my mother married him. He's nothing like my father. Total opposite, in fact.' He drained the contents of his cup and put it back down on the bench.

'I guess she must have been so lonely without your dad.' She put her teaspoon back on the saucer and added, 'Perhaps she was concerned about providing a father for you. A role model if you like.'

Vic gave a harsh laugh that was nowhere in the vicinity of humour. 'Some role model he turned out to be.'

'But he's a good father to Isabella, right? I mean, they seem to have a good relationship. He led her down the aisle and gave a lovely speech and—'

'Isabella doesn't know him the way I know him. She's his blood child. I am not. He will do anything for her, but he has made my life difficult from day one.' His mouth tightened and he continued, 'I was sent to boarding school because he didn't want me in the house. He didn't like sharing me with my mother. When I did come home for rare visits, he made my life a living hell. Not in front of my mother or sister. He was too clever, too devious for that.'

She hugged her arms around her body, feeling cold all of a sudden even though it was summer. Before The Incident, she had considered herself a good judge of character, but since that night, she always doubted her ability to read a person's motives. She had liked Vic's stepfather on the three occasions she met him. He had been charming and friendly without being creepy. And Isabella had been so warm and adoring towards him, which to be honest, had made her feel a bit jealous. She couldn't remember the last time she even saw her father, much less got a hug from him. 'Oh, Vic, I'm so sorry, I never realised. Marcus only said you didn't get on with your stepfather. He didn't go into any details. Does Isabella know how difficult things were between you and her father?'

He moved away from the bench and went to the window to watch the sun come up over the horizon. 'She's nine years younger than me. There's a lot she was too young to remember. I didn't want to destroy her relationship with him. Anyway, she's got Marcus now.'

'And you have no one.' She said the words without thinking but in a way, they described her as well as him.

He turned to look at her with an unreadable expression. He reminded her of a fortress with the drawbridge pulled up. 'I don't need anyone.'

'Is that something you've taught yourself over the years? Not to need anyone?'

Vic's gaze held hers like he was waiting for her to break the lock first. She fought hard not to look away, but it took a mammoth effort. 'Don't feel sorry for me, Addie.' His tone was as cautionary as his keep-away-from-me expression.

'I—I don't feel sorry for you. I can relate to you, that's all.'

Something in his expression softened—the drawbridge lowering a fraction. 'Because of your mother?'

She gave him a grim look. 'You've met her. You don't need me to tell you all the gory details of our relationship.'

'But I'd like to hear all the same.'

Should she tell him some of the things she hated most about being her mother's daughter? It wasn't something she talked about. To anyone. Not even her brother. But Vic had opened up to her about his difficult stepfather. She could tell that wasn't easy for him, so surely, she could be courageous enough to share a little bit about herself. She picked up her teacup, closing her fingers around the fine bone china, but she didn't bring it to her mouth. 'I hated and still hate being compared to her. I'm not beautiful. I'm not vivacious and charming. I'm not a party girl who loves being the centre of attention. I'm a huge disappointment to my mother for not measuring up to her.' She hadn't realised how firmly she was holding her teacup until Vic gently removed it from her clenched fingers and put it back on the saucer on the island bench with a soft little clink. She hadn't even realised he'd moved closer—she was too fixated on listing her shortcomings. She looked up and met his gaze and something with soft wings fluttered in one of the ventricles of her heart.

Vic lifted a hand to her face and brushed a strand of hair away from her cheek, his touch as light as the brush of a feather. 'But you are beautiful.' His voice had a gravel and honey combination that sent a shiver racing over her flesh. He was standing almost toe to toe with her, and it made every cell of her body tighten with awareness. And a tingle of anxiety. She wasn't used to being the focus of someone's attention. She wasn't used to intimacy of any kind. It was a battle inside her, a war between two wants—one to get away and the other to come close. But she hardly knew Vic. He was a playboy, a man about town, and she was a homespun, boring, and bland and shy woman who had zero experience. Even though a part of her loved hearing Vic's compliments, she didn't for a moment believe them. How could she? They were just words. And she had heard them before on the night of The Incident. She was told by her boyfriend a whole heap of compliments and she had basked in them like someone who had never experienced the warmth of sunshine on their body. But there was the kicker—once he saw her naked body, he began comparing it to her mother's and the truth came out. He only wanted to sleep with her to crow about it to his mates.

She licked her dry lips and tried to disguise a swallow. 'Your jet lag must be far worse than I thought if you think I'm beautiful.' She injected a note of self-deprecating humour in her tone.

He gently tipped up her chin and her heart did a jerky somersault. She had always secretly dreamed of someone doing that to her—touching her so softly, so tenderly, their gaze focussed on her as if she was the most captivating person in the world. But how could she be sure Vic was really captivated by her? She was nothing like his casual lovers. They were flamingos like her mother. She was a barnyard fowl.

'Everything about you is beautiful, not just your looks. You have a sweet and kind nature too.'

'But you hardly know me. How can you tell what my nature is like?'

Vic was still holding her chin between his thumb and index finger. The warmth of his touch surprised her, delighted her, excited her. But a flicker of fear still lurked in the back of her mind. She wanted to be wanted for *her*. Heat seeped from his skin into hers, stirring her flesh into a deep longing for more of his touch. She stared at his mouth, the sculptured contours mesmerising to her. She wanted him to kiss her. She *needed* him to kiss her. She wanted to taste him, to feel those sensual lips moving against her own. But she had not been kissed in years. She had forgotten the moves, the cues, and she didn't have the confidence to ask outright. And what if he kissed her and it was a disaster? What if she pulled away out of fear and anxiety?

'I don't have to know someone for long to know what sort of person they are.' His hand released her chin, but his index finger moved in a slow stroke across her cheek.

'Making a quick character assessment must be part of the skill set of a playboy,' she said, trying to keep things light.

A frown appeared on his forehead, his mouth tightened a fraction and his hand fell away from her face. 'I'm not trying to get it on with you, if that's what you're thinking.'

Her eyes opened wide. 'I—I wasn't thinking any

such thing. Mostly because no one like you could ever be interested in someone like me.'

There was a pulsing silence. All she could hear was the sound of her breathing and the soft humming of the French door fridge.

Vic's eyes moved back and forth between each of hers, searchingly, searingly. 'Why do you say that?'

'I'm too ordinary. Plain, boring, conservative.' She swallowed and added in a lower, barely audible tone, 'Inexperienced.'

A flicker of shock passed through his gaze and his frown deepened. 'How inexperienced?' His voice was so low and deep it sounded like the bass chord of a pipe organ.

She turned to pick up her cup, mainly for something to do with her hands and her mouth before they got any further out of control. There was only a sip left in the cup and it was lukewarm, but she drank it anyway. Yuck, and it had tea leaves in it. Maybe she should have read them instead of swallowed them.

Vic's hand came down on her right shoulder, gently turning her to face him again. 'Are you telling me you're a virgin?' His expression was so incredulous it made her feel even more of a gauche fool.

Her mouth twisted. 'Isn't it funny that one hundred years ago, I would've been considered the ideal, the norm. Now I am a pariah. A misfit.'

Vic's hand released her shoulder, but he didn't step back from her. He stood looking down at her with a grave expression on his face. 'Is your inexperience by choice or circumstance?'

She let out a breath in a slow stream and shifted her gaze from the penetrating heat of his. 'A bit of both.'

There was another beat of silence.

'Do you want to talk about it?' Vic's voice had a raspy edge that made her flesh tingle.

She turned away again, this time to clear away the cups. 'I think it's time I got some sleep. I've already told you more than I've told anyone in years.'

'Yeah, well, same goes.' There was a wry note to his tone.

She stopped stacking the cups and glanced at him. 'About your stepfather, you mean?'

He gave a grim nod and rubbed at the back of his neck with one of his hands. 'I think it's being back here. It brings up a lot of things I'd rather forget.'

'Which is why you want to redevelop the place.'

'Yes.'

'But don't you have good memories too? Of living here before your father died?'

'The good memories have been tainted by the years that followed my father's death. This is not a family home, not any more. It'll do far better as a hotel.'

'What does Isabella think of your decision to turn it into a hotel?'

A flicker of tension moved across his face—a tightening of his jaw, a flattening of his mouth, a stubborn light hardening his eyes. 'It belongs to me, not Isabella. It's my decision and my decision alone what to do with it.'

She frowned. 'But why then did Isabella and Marcus ask us to mind Katerina here until they get back?

Was that their decision or yours?' She still hadn't had a chance to talk to Marcus or Isabella herself due to travelling and time differences.

'They were planning to come here for a summer holiday after their friend's wedding. They've holidayed here a few times even before Katerina was born. Isabella wanted Katerina to enjoy her childhood home one last time. She's far more sentimental about the place than I am.'

'And yet, you're still going to redevelop it?'

The intractable set to his features made her realise that once he had decided something, it was final. There would be no backing down, no matter what. 'It was left to me by my father. It was the one thing my stepfather couldn't take away from me. I'm going to make it into the most successful hotel in my company.'

She was in no doubt of that, but was his decision the right one?

Vic held her gaze for a long beat. 'You don't approve?'

'It's none of my business to approve or disapprove.'

His mouth quirked. 'Don't be too mad at me, *tesore*. This is purely a business decision. I never allow my emotions too much involvement.'

His casually delivered Italian endearment sent a wave of heat cascading down her spine. She needed to build up some immunity to him and fast. She couldn't allow herself to melt at his feet in a pool of longing. 'I—I think I'll go to bed if you don't mind. I want to be in a reasonable state to look after Katerina when she wakes.'

'I'll walk you up.'

'No, please,' She held up both of her hands like twin stop signs. 'I can find my way.'

'As you wish.'

Her exit would have been a whole lot more dignified if she hadn't bumped into one of the kitchen stools as she went. She swore under her breath and righted the stool, glancing back at Vic, but he wasn't even looking her way. He was staring out the windows at the golden rays of the sun coming up over the horizon with a brooding frown on his forehead.

Vic stared at the view without really seeing it. His mind was reeling with the shock of Addie's revelation. A virgin? Not that there was anything wrong with that if it was a personal choice, but he suspected there was more to her situation than she had let on. He had lost his so long ago he could barely remember the circumstances other than it was rushed and awkward, especially as his partner had far more experience than he. But what was holding Addie back from exploring her sexuality? Was it her shyness? Her introverted personality? Or had growing up with an extroverted and undoubtedly sexually active and stunning mother made her feel inadequate? Vic had read enough about Solange Featherstone in the gossip pages over the years to realise Addie was nothing like her. Marcus hadn't told him much about his childhood, but Vic had picked up enough to realise it hadn't been an easy ride for either Marcus or Addie. But Marcus was more outgoing and had lived life in the fast lane until he met Isabella. Vic had unintentionally been the matchmaker and while he was happy for them that they were building a life together, married life wasn't for him. While divorce had not brought about the destruction of Vic's parents' marriage, death had come out of the blue and destroyed the stability and happiness that had defined his childhood until the age of seven. The finality of it, the cruel hammer blow of grief that had consumed him haunted him to this day. There were no guarantees in life and love. Love didn't always last, but death was an inescapable certainty. There was no avoiding it. It would find you eventually, either in early years or later ones. He figured the longer you waited for it to claim those you loved, the more damage it did to you. He had only had seven years with his father and yet he still missed him and always would. There were so many milestones his father had missed, so many things he never got to experience because fate had swept in and taken him away. But Vic hadn't just lost his father, but his mother too. His stepfather had taken her away, changed her focus so it was trained on her new husband and not on her grieving son, essentially leaving Vic to cope alone. Vic didn't want to love someone only to lose them. Loving someone was asking for immeasurable, incurable pain and he wanted no part of it. Which was why he had no business showing any interest in Addie Featherstone. She was the sort of young woman who deserved to be valued and loved and appreciated. He was the last person who should be thinking about her, much less feeling flickers, and spine-tingling pulses of desire. He wasn't into breaking hearts, and she was exactly the sort of woman who would get hurt if he took things further. In a strange sort of way, he felt like he would corrupt her by taking away her innocence. He considered her as forbidden and it had to stay that way. It had to otherwise… He blinked hard and shook his head, trying to reprogram his thoughts, but somehow his body and mind were at war.

His mind said *no* but his body said, *why not?*

CHAPTER FOUR

ADDIE WOKE TO sunshine shining through a gap in the curtains like the beam of a laser. For a moment she was completely disoriented. But then she suddenly realised where she was and that she was supposed to be minding Katerina. She quickly glanced at her phone to see the time. How could she have slept in till 9:00 a.m.? Where was her sense of responsibility? Here she was criticising her childhood caregivers for being slack in how they took care of her and yet, here she was lolling about in bed three hours past her normal wake-up time.

She tossed off the bed covers and threw on her cotton wrap over her duckling pyjamas and stuffed her feet into her piglet slippers. She padded as quickly as she could to the nursery, but she found the room and the cot empty. She turned and made her way toward Vic's bedroom, her pulse pounding the closer she got. But the door was open, and the bed was so neat it looked like it hadn't been slept in at all. She continued down the wide corridor and then down to the lower floor, listening for the sound of Katerina's chirpy little voice and Vic's deep one. She glanced into the formal sitting room, but there was no one in there.

A glossy black grand piano was positioned in front

of the large bank of windows overlooking Lake Como, the heavy white-and-gold-embossed curtains draped along either side giving the appearance of the beautiful instrument being on a stage. And with the stunning backdrop of the lake and blue-tinged mountains in the distance, what grander stage could there be? But apart from the piano and the collection of sofas and side tables and lamps and artwork, there was no one in sight. She was not sure what compelled her to slowly walk towards the piano. It was as if it spoke to her in the echoing silence of that faded but still beautiful room. She stood in front of the black and white keys, her fingers reaching down to softly play a progression of C major chords. The tinkling notes broke the silence like the sound of a trickling waterfall. The piano was in surprisingly good tune and its tone was exquisitely enhanced by the acoustics of the room.

She heard a firm footfall behind her and guiltily pulled her hands away from the piano and turned around to see Vic standing in the doorway. He was freshly showered and shaved and dressed in dark blue denim jeans, brown loafers and a casual white shirt that highlighted his tanned complexion. She could only imagine how ridiculous she looked in her duckling pyjamas and piglet slippers with her hair in a sleep-mussed tangle.

'You play?' he asked.

'Erm…not well enough to do that old girl justice.'

'I'm sure you're being way too modest.' He walked further into the room towards her, the sunlight from the windows catching the glinting light in his eyes.

Was he laughing at her outfit? The silly little chord progression? At her?

'I'm not being modest at all...' She crossed her arms across her body. 'How is Katerina? I'm sorry I overslept. I should've been up hours ago. Why didn't you wake me?'

'Katerina is having her second breakfast with Lucia,' Vic said with a crooked smile. 'She had her first with me.'

She ran her eyes over his pristine white shirt and then met his gaze. 'You look surprisingly immaculate given you were recently involved in feeding a toddler.'

He flashed a smile that was as white as his shirt, and her heart did a funny little skip. 'I changed just now. Breakfast number one was...how shall I say...a messy affair?'

'A messy affair...'

Those words rang a warning bell in her head. If she allowed her crush on Vic Jacobetti to get any further out of hand, she would end up in a mess that would not be so easily cleaned by a simple change of clothes. She had to stop herself from picturing him shrugging of his soiled shirt. Stop herself from thinking about the breadth of his shoulders, the toned perfection of his pectoral muscles and washboard abs. She had to stop herself from thinking about running her hands down the warm satin of his olive toned skin.

She. Had. To. Stop.

She also had to bring herself back to the conversation with an effort. 'I think it's kind of cute how Isabella and Marcus let Katerina explore food for herself.'

'Exploring?' One ink-black eyebrow arched but his glittering smile was still in place. 'Is that what you call it?'

A smile began to pull at the corners of her mouth. 'I did warn you that parenting practices have changed significantly since we were kids.'

A shadow passed through his gaze and the light faded from his eyes. 'One would hope so.' There was a cryptic quality to his voice that made her want to know more about his painful childhood. She wanted to know why he was so keen to avoid long-term relationships. Why he didn't believe in for ever love. Why he didn't want children, a family of his own. He was clearly a devoted uncle, anyone watching him with Katerina could tell that. She had closed her weary eyes last night with the image of him holding his little niece in his arms. He had been so gentle with her, so caring and kind and yes, loving.

Vic moved closer to the piano, close enough for her to smell the clean sharp lemon-based notes of his aftershave. His thick black hair was still slightly damp as she could see the groove marks of a comb in the dark strands. He looked down at the keys for a pensive moment, then turned to look at her. 'Feel free to play any time you want. It's been a while since it's been played properly.'

'Thank you, but I don't want you to get your hopes up. I'm not much of a performer, I'm afraid. I get too nervous when I know someone's watching.' She couldn't stop from moistening her lips—they suddenly felt as dry as the faded fabric on the sofas. She couldn't stop staring into his espresso coffee eyes. They seemed to hold hers with a mesmerising power she couldn't withstand.

Vic lifted his right hand to her face and softly traced his index finger down the slope of her nose. No one had ever caressed her like that before. Who knew a nose could be so sensitive? The nerves were still jumping and dancing beneath her skin where his fingertip had lain so briefly.

'You have to start believing in yourself, *cara*.' His voice was low and as deep as the bass notes on the piano.

She could scarcely get her lungs to inflate enough to draw in a breath. She dipped her shoulders and moved away before she made a complete fool of herself and begged him to kiss her. She found it *so* hard not to stare at his mouth. Or his eyes. 'Yes, well, I think confidence is something you probably have to learn as a child. I might have missed a few lessons here and there.'

Vic was about to say something, but the sound of Katerina in the corridor outside made him close his mouth and turn to the door. She turned as well to see Katerina coming in with Lucia, the housekeeper in flustered pursuit. Lucia was trying to keep up with the toddler, but Katerina was too quick and too determined. She came bounding towards Addie with a beaming smile that made her heart contract. Addie scooped her up and planted a kiss on her chubby cheek, which tasted like strawberries, possibly because she had given herself a strawberry facial over breakfast number two.

Lucia exchanged a few words with Vic and then bustled out of the room with even more haste than she had come in. Addie got the feeling the housekeeper was glad to escape for a while, leaving Addie and Vic in charge.

'Pay pano.' Katerina pointed to the instrument and squirmed in Addie's arms to get down.

Addie sat on the piano stool and positioned Katerina on her lap so she could reach the keys. 'I hope your hands are clean because Uncle Vic might not like strawberry juice all over his beautiful piano,' she said, glancing up at him.

His indulgent smile made her heart contract all over again. 'I don't mind at all.'

She looked back at Katerina, balanced on her lap, her hands slamming down on the keys in discordant glee. Addie let her go for it, enjoying her enjoyment, secretly thrilled the little tot loved music as much as she did. But then Katerina grabbed one of her hands and pushed it to the keys.

'You want me to play?' Addie asked.

Katerina gave an affirmative nod. Of course, she had heard Addie play before. She had entertained her a number of times by playing various nursery rhyme tunes to her on her visits. And while she had sometimes played in front of Marcus and Isabella when she'd been visiting Katerina, she much preferred to play alone. Story of her life…but let's not go *there*.

'Okay, so let's see…' She caught her bottom lip between her teeth and began to play 'Twinkle, Twinkle Little Star' with some of Mozart's variations.

Katerina bounced up and down on her knee in excitement.

'Sing!' Katerina said, twisting to look up at her.

'Not today, sweetie. I'll just play the tune,' she said, acutely conscious of the adult audience.

Vic stepped up beside them. 'How about I sing it for you?'

She looked up at him in surprise. 'I didn't know you could sing.'

'Can't everyone sing?'

'I guess so…' She bit her lip again. Terrible habit. Dead giveaway of being ridiculously shy and nervous. She placed her fingers back on the keys and started playing again. Vic began to sing 'Twinkle, Twinkle Little Star' in Italian and shivers cascaded down her spine at the richness of his baritone voice.

Bella stella dimmu tu
Cosa vedi da lassu
Da quassu io vedo te
Da quassu io vedo te
Bella stella dimmu tu
Cosa vedi da lassu.

Once he finished, Katerina clapped her hands. 'Again!'

Vic laughed. 'You're a glutton for punishment.'

'Will you translate it for me?' Addie asked.

Actually, she was close to begging him to sing it again. How she envied Katerina's unabashed enthusiasm. She felt it on the inside but couldn't show it on the outside.

'Sure.'

Vic started as soon as she put her fingers to the keys. She knew the tune so well she didn't have to look at the piano so looked at him instead. He held her gaze as he sang and Addie was transfixed, transported, tempted to dream of a future with him, because music was something, another thing, they had in common.

Beautiful star, tell me
What you see from up there
From up here I see you
From up here I see you
Beautiful star, tell me
What you see from up there.

Vic gave a low bow and straightened with a self-deprecating smile. 'That's about the extent of my nursery rhyme repertoire, I'm afraid.'

She smiled back over the top of Katerina's dark head. 'I'll have to teach you some more songs.'

He held her gaze for a beat that she felt in her lower body. 'I'll look forward to some private lessons.'

Private lessons…sounded scarily intimate. Was he flirting with her? A frisson went through her at the thought of Vic touching her body. Would he compare it to all the other female bodies he had touched? Would she be found wanting as she had been by her first and last and only boyfriend? She had avoided being intimate with anyone. Years of her life had gone by, years she could not get back. She was nudging thirty and she still didn't know what it was like to have a man's arms hold her close.

Would she *ever* have the courage to stop avoiding and start embracing?

She looked back at the child on her lap, unable to hold Vic's satirical gaze. Katerina banged at the piano again, captured by the joy of making musical sounds. But like all toddlers, she soon lost interest and clambered off Addie's lap to explore the room.

'Is it okay for her to play in here?' she asked Vic.

He looked at Katerina playing peekaboo behind the skirts of the floor-to-ceiling curtains with a wistful expression on his face, as if he was looking back in time and seeing himself do the very same thing as a young and carefree and uninhibited child. It was a moment or two before he looked back at her. 'Of course. This used to be my favourite room as a child.'

She shifted slightly on the piano stool so she could study his expression. 'Who played the piano? Your mother?'

A shadow passed through his gaze. 'My father.'

'Do you play?'

His lips moved in a rueful twist. 'I haven't played in years.'

'Why?'

He gave a shrug of one broad shoulder. 'No time.' He ran a hand over the closed lid of the piano and then let it hang by his side. 'To be good at something, you have to put the time in. I use my limited free time in other ways.'

The gossip columns were full of what Vic did in his free time and she didn't want to be reminded of it. For years she'd read all about his sexual conquests—the hot dates with beautiful women, the flings that never went anywhere because he was not the settling down type.

Why was she crushing on someone so out of reach? Was she recreating her childhood fantasy of wanting to be loved, but because of the emotional wasteland of her early years, she had set her sights on someone who, like her mother, couldn't love her back?

Addie kept an eye on Katerina who was now playing with the foot switch of the standard lamp, giggling when she was able to turn it on and off. Addie rose from the piano stool and went over to hold the stem of the lamp steady in case it toppled over. She looked back at Vic who was still standing near the piano, looking down at it with an unreadable expression on his face.

'Vic?'

His eyes met hers across the distance of the room. 'The answer is no.'

She frowned. 'You don't even know what I was about to ask.'

His mouth grew tight. 'I do because I know how your mind works.'

Yikes. He had better not be able to read her mind otherwise she was going to be seriously embarrassed. 'What was I going to ask, then?'

'You were going to ask me to play the piano.'

She let out an uneven breath. 'Actually, I wasn't,' she lied. She wrinkled her nose and glanced at Katerina who was now in a squatting position with a look of fierce concentration on her little face. Her little primal grunts could mean only one thing. Eek! She had a phobia when it came to kid's nappies. Babies, she could handle. Toddlers not so much.

Vic frowned. 'Does she need—?'

'Yes, she needs changing.' She swallowed and tried not to breathe through her nose. 'Can you do it? I—I have a weak stomach.'

His eyebrows arched upwards. 'But you're a vet nurse.'

'I can handle animals, but humans are another thing.'

'That's ridiculous.'

'I know, but I can't help it.'

'What are you going to do when you have children of your own?' he asked.

She stared at him blankly for a moment. She hadn't even had a lover, how was she ever going to have children? She wasn't even sure if she wanted them. She hadn't had the easiest of childhoods, what if she didn't turn out to be a good mother? She hadn't had a great role model. What if she repeated her mother's mistakes without even meaning to? Wasn't that the story behind generational trauma? People did what was done to them because of social modelling. It took an enormous effort and conscious control not to fall into the same patterns of behaviour.

'I—I haven't thought about it that much,' she said, smoothing her damp hands down her pyjamas. 'Anyway, I'd have to find a husband first.'

Katerina straightened and waddled over to play with the tassel on a cushion, seemingly oblivious to the change of atmosphere her little body had caused in the room.

'I'll get Lucia to see to it,' Vic said and turned for the door.

Addie bit her lip and looked back at little Katerina.

She knew from listening to Isabella and Marcus describe what a wrangle nappy changing could be that it would be a challenge. Katerina did not like staying still for the time it took to remove her nappy and get a new one on. Things got a whole lot more complicated when it wasn't just a wet nappy. How could an elderly woman like Lucia manage it? She could barely keep up with Katerina as it was.

'I don't think Lucia can manage,' she said. 'Katerina hates having her nappy changed. We'll have to do it.'

'We?'

'We're in this together, right?'

He rubbed a hand down his face. 'I don't recall nappy changing as being part of our commitment as godparents.'

'No, but we are currently in loco parentis, so...' Painting a brave smile on her face, she hoped she could get through this episode without disgracing herself. Thank God, she hadn't yet had breakfast. 'Let's get on with it.'

Vic released a sigh and walked over and scooped up Katerina off the floor, his nose wrinkling as hers had just moments ago. Katerina giggled and patted his cleanly shaven cheek with a dimpled hand. He captured her tiny hand in his large one and Addie just about melted on the spot. He frowned at her over the top of Katerina's head of dark curls. 'I can't believe I agreed to this,' he growled.

'Nor can I.' She smothered a laugh and followed him out of the room.

CHAPTER FIVE

ONCE THEY HAD dealt with Katerina's nappy, Addie left Katerina with Vic while she had a shower and got changed. As much as she loved having a cosy pyjama day at home, there was no way she was going to spend any more time wandering around in her piglet PJs and duckling slippers in front of Vic Jacobetti. Sheesh. Talk about embarrassing.

She found Vic and Katerina out in one of the garden sections closest to the villa. The lush green lawn was framed on three sides by a waist-high hedge, providing a safe and relatively enclosed space for Katerina to run around in the bright sunshine. A trickling fountain nearby and the chorus of the birds in the shrubbery and the delighted squeals of the toddler filled the summer air and made her wonder why Vic was so intent on turning the villa into a hotel when it was such a wonderful place for a family. Large, of course, but what kid didn't want plenty of space to run around and explore?

Vic must have sensed her presence as he turned from watching Katerina and the moment his eyes met hers, she tingled from head to foot. 'Feel better?' he asked.

'Much.'

His gaze lightly scanned her casual attire—beige linen trousers and a white linen shirt and she wondered if he was comparing her to all the sophisticated and colourful and dazzling women he had dated.

'Do you have a swimsuit with you?' he asked.

Addie looked at him blankly. 'A…a *swimsuit*?'

She said the word like it was something completely alien to her…which it was. She had spent the last twenty or so years avoiding swimsuits. She hadn't worn once since she was a child.

'I should have told you to pack one. No problem. We can pick one up at the shops later.'

She swallowed. 'I—I don't need a swimsuit.'

Vic studied her for a brief moment. She worked hard to keep her features neutral, but it took an enormous effort. She could feel herself break into a sweat, fine beads of it forming on her upper lip and between her shoulder blades.

'There's a pool on the level below this. I thought we could have a splash with Katerina.'

She folded her arms across her middle, her eyes assiduously avoiding his probing ones. 'I'm happy to watch. I'm not much of a swimmer.'

Katerina toddled over and tugged on her linen trousers. 'Simming! Want to go simming!'

Addie looked down at her chocolate-brown eyes sparkling with anticipation. She knew her brother and sister-in-law had regularly taken her to parent-child swimming lessons; she had even gone to watch once and marvelled at Katerina's ability, not to mention her lack of fear. How was she going to get out of this?

'We'll go swimming after lunch and your nap, *mia piccola*,' Vic said to Katerina.

'Want to go now!' Katerina wailed.

Addie crouched down in front of her and took her chubby hands in hers. 'Sweetie, I know you're frustrated because you want to go right now, but we need to have lunch, and you'll enjoy it so much more after you've had a sleep.'

'No fleep. No fleep.' Katerina's chin protruded in an obstinate manner, her eyes bright with defiance.

Scooping the toddler up in her arms, Addie began to straighten, but just then, Vic's hand took her by the arm and helped her the rest of the way. His touch was light and yet she could sense the strength in his fingers, the power and potency of his touch sending her senses reeling. Katerina was not too happy about being carried indoors and Addie could sense a full-blown tantrum coming on. The toddler was tired and hungry, and Addie didn't want to get her so worked up that she began to ask for her parents. What could they tell her? They still had no idea of when Katerina's parents would be able to get to her and relieve them of their responsibility.

Fortunately, Lucia had food ready for them set up on the shady terrace. Addie strapped Katerina into her highchair, and she was soon busy sampling the array of tasty dishes set before her. She watched her enjoy her food and tried not to think of all the times her mother tried to control what she ate.

Vic pulled out a chair for her and she sat, glad of the leafy shade over them. She picked up a glass of ice-cold mineral water and took a refreshing sip. 'I could get used to this,' she said, sighing as she looked at the stunning view from the terrace. 'Work seems a long way away right now.'

Vic leaned forward to hand Katerina her sippy cup. She took it from him with both hands, her enthusiastic guzzling sounds making him smile. 'Yes, it's certainly a long way from what I normally do.' He sat back in his chair and looked at Addie. 'We can leave Katerina with Lucia for a couple of hours while she naps and get you a swimsuit.'

Shifting her gaze from his, she put her glass down with an unsteady hand. 'I hope you're up to date on first aid because I can't remember the last time I went into the water. I'm strictly a stay-in-the-shallows girl. Anything over my ankles is out of my depth.' But wasn't she already out of her depth sitting here in the dappled shade having lunch with a notorious playboy? She had stepped in over her head the minute she agreed to come with Vic Jacobetti to Lake Como.

'Don't worry, I'll keep you safe.'

Half an hour later they were walking along Via Vittoria Emanuele II, one of the main shopping areas in medieval Como. At the north end, the main street linked with Piazza de Duomo, the pedestrian-only area running for about four hundred metres until tapering out at Saint Vitale Tower and the end of the historic centre.

Addie was immediately aware of some of the shoppers and tourists doing double takes at Vic as they walked through the area. A couple of people even stopped and took photos of them with their phones. As she walked past a couple of women, she heard one woman speculate on whether she was Vic's latest lover. Her companion shook her head and insisted she wasn't pretty enough. Addie turned her face away, heat storming her cheeks, but Vic seemed oblivious to the attention they were drawing and if he'd heard what the two women had said, he gave no indication of it.

'Let's try here,' Vic said, gently guiding her by the elbow into a boutique.

The cool temperature of the air conditioning was a welcome relief from the warmth outside, but it wasn't the type of shop she frequented. Unlike her mother, she didn't have a taste for designer gear. Vic spoke in Italian to the female attendant, and she was soon ushered into a change room with an array of swimsuits to choose from. She stood there staring at the collection of bikinis and maillots and spaghetti-strapped one-pieces, the colours as vibrant and bright as spring flowers. She stripped off her clothes and tried on a sleek black maillot and studied her reflection, trying to silence the critical voice that had taken up residence in her head since she was a kid.

You're fat. You're plain. You're ugly. You're boring.

'How are you going in there?' Vic's deep voice made her jump out of her self-critical assessment.

'Erm… I need a little longer…'

'Take your time.'

She let out an uneven breath and peeled off the maillot and then reached for a hot pink string bikini. She couldn't explain why she was trying on such a notice-me colour other than she was tempted. Tempted to step out of her beige stage and live on the bright side for a while. She tied the strings of the bikini and looked at herself in the mirror. She had never worn anything so daring, so minimal…so *sexy*. A frisson passed over her flesh. By trying on the bikini, she was allowing herself to embrace a side of herself she hadn't known existed. A side who didn't hide in the shadows but stepped into the spotlight. A side who didn't walk in the shallows but dived in the deep end.

Addie took off the bikini and got dressed again. She couldn't help cringing at her beige outfit. After the vibrancy of the hot-pink bikini, her bland outfit did nothing for her colouring. It washed out her features and hid her slight curves like a sack. The attendant approached, asking if she needed help with anything. She found herself asking her for some separates, some casual outfits that would enhance her figure and colouring.

It was like the old her stepped into that change room but a new her stepped out. She put her beige clothes in one of the shopping bags and dressed in one of her new outfits—a fire-engine red top teamed with slim-fitting white capri pants.

She came out to join Vic and his gaze swept over her appreciatively. 'Wow. Red suits you.'

'I don't usually wear it. I think the only red thing I had in my wardrobe until now is a hair tie.'

He smiled a lazy smile. 'Go you.'

She went towards the attendant to pay but Vic stalled her by touching her on the arm. 'I've already paid.'

Addie's eyes widened. 'But I bought much more than a swimsuit.'

'No matter. Consider it a gift for coming all this way to help me with Katerina.'

'But I can pay for my own clothes. I don't expect you to—'

'Indulge me, Addie.'

'By allowing you to indulge me?'

He flicked her cheek with a feather-light touch of his finger. 'Don't you deserve to be spoilt now and again? Hmm?'

She moistened her suddenly dry lips. 'I'm not sure why you'd want to spoil me.'

There was a long moment of silence.

A frown began to form on his forehead. 'Don't read too much into it, *cara*.'

'What could I read into it?' She gave a mock laugh. 'No one would ever think you and I were…were…anything other than casual acquaintances.'

His frown deepened and he guided her out of the store. 'So, you heard that woman earlier.'

Her shoulders slumped. 'Yes.'

Vic tipped up her chin with his finger, locking his gaze on hers. 'You don't need beautiful clothes, *cara*. You are beautiful no matter what you're wearing.'

She lowered her gaze and stepped back from him. 'That's not the message I've been hearing most of my life. I've lost count of how many times people have said I look nothing like my mother.'

'But you hide your beauty, *cara*. You don't allow yourself to be seen. You hide in the shadows.'

She momentarily bit her lip, then released it to add, 'My mother says it the most often. It's like she still can't work out why someone as stunning as her gave birth to such a plain Jane. I'm an embarrassment to her.'

A deep frown brought his ink-black eyebrows closer together. 'Has she ever said that to you? Those exact words?'

'Once or twice when I was younger.'

There was a silence.

'Perhaps your way of gaining some power in the relationship was to downplay your assets to irk her.' His unwavering gaze unsettled her more than she wanted to admit. So too did his insightful assessment of the tricky dynamic between her mother and her.

Addie gave a noncommittal shrug, her cheeks feeling hot as if she were a child who had been caught out in a silly game they had hoped no one had noticed them playing. 'Perhaps.' She had never thought of herself as having any power in her relationship with either of her parents, but maybe Vic was right. She had for as long as she could remember distanced herself from the glamour and glitz and gaiety of her mother's life. She had fashioned herself into someone the opposite—bland and boring and beige. But was that truly who she was? Sure, she was far more reserved than her mother, but that didn't mean she had to hide away for the rest of her life. And wasn't that what she'd been doing? Hiding away, living in the shadows, trying not to be noticed. Trying not to be noticed and judged and found wanting.

But Vic Jacobetti *had* noticed her. The real her. It

was a disquieting realisation for now she had allowed a little spark of light into her life, how would she be satisfied with living without it once this time in Italy was over?

'Come.' He put a gentle hand beneath her elbow to lead her out of the suddenly bright glare of the sun. 'Let's grab a drink before we head back to take charge of Katerina.'

A few minutes later, they were sitting at an outdoor café, under some brightly coloured umbrellas that kept the sun off them. Vic took a sip of his espresso and she found herself mesmerised by the sensual shape of his mouth. She started, not for the first time, to wonder what his lips would feel like pressed to her own… But then she sat up straighter in her seat and frowned, annoyed with the path her thoughts were leading her down. She had heard, and so had everyone else nearby, including Vic, that she was not pretty enough to be his latest lover. She was out of his league in so many ways, but she couldn't seem to stop the desire that was smouldering inside her. A desire to feel his touch, his intimate touch, the stroke and glide of his hands on her body. She was not a teenager any more—she was an adult scarily close to thirty years old. If she didn't step out of the shadows soon and grasp life with two hands, she was going to find herself a lonely old woman with a houseful of cats. Or dogs, or birds or hamsters. Well, maybe not hamsters.

Vic put his cup down and met her gaze, one of his eyebrows going up in a questioning arc. 'Ready?'

She put her cup down on its saucer with a clumsy

little clatter. She'd been holding it for the last few minutes even though it was empty. 'Sure. I'd like to be there before Katerina wakes up. Sometimes little kids can get disoriented after a deep sleep. She might forget where she is and start crying for her parents. Have you heard from either of them?'

'Not today.'

They fell into step beside each other on the walk back to his villa. 'I wonder how long they'll be?' She gave him a sideways look to find him frowning.

'Hopefully not too much longer.'

She chewed at her lower lip, not sure how to interpret his comment. She was torn between wanting her brother and sister-in-law back as soon as possible for Katerina's sake, but the other part of her wanted a bit more time with Vic Jacobetti. It was a strange state to be in, a state of conflicting desires and temptations she had never allowed herself to dabble in before. 'I guess it can't be doing your playboy reputation any good to be seen with me and a small child for days on end,' she said to fill the silence.

He glanced at her, still frowning. 'Everyone knows Katerina is my half-sister's child, not mine.' His gaze dipped to her mouth for a brief moment and a trickle of something molten hot pooled in her core. His dark gaze came back to hers and her heart gave a somersault in her chest. 'But as for you...' He let out a long breath and gave a crooked smile that made her pulse suddenly race. 'Does it bother you that people might assume we're involved?'

She could feel her cheeks burning as if she had the

worst case of sunburn in her life. 'You heard what that tourist said. No one would ever believe you'd have a fling with someone like me.'

Vic's hand came up and his long, tanned index finger stroked a slow and exquisitely sensual pathway down her fiery cheek. Every nerve in her skin danced in delight and her heart skipped and tripped. His gaze darkened to a glinting pitch and went back to her mouth. 'Ah, yes, but there's always a first time for everything, *sì*?' His deep baritone voice had a rough edge that sent a wave of longing through her flesh.

She sent the tip of her tongue out to deposit a layer of moisture on her cobblestone-dry lips. 'Are you…' she hesitated over the choice of the word '…mocking me?'

His brows snapped together in a tight frown. 'Why would I do that?'

She flapped one of her hands in a distracted manner. 'You can't possibly be interested in me like…' she gulped '…*that*.'

Images popped into her head of him kissing her, touching her, worshipping her body the way it longed to be worshipped. Erotic images that made the possibility of it happening all the more exciting.

She saw the exact moment those forbidden thoughts entered his mind. A flash of something hot and liquid in his gaze, a flicker of something move across his face like a sudden breeze across a deep body of water. His mouth tightened, then loosened, then tightened again, a tension in his jaw that hadn't been there before, as if he was fighting his most primal instincts and not enjoying the process.

'We both know why that can never happen.' His tone was adamant but for some reason she sensed he was doing it more for his own benefit, not hers. Because she already knew it couldn't happen, right? They lived in completely different worlds—worlds that only rarely intersected because of their little niece. They had so little in common and yet…and yet…there was a beat of something in the air, a background humming that tightened and charged the atmosphere.

Addie couldn't hold the broodingly dark intensity of his gaze. 'You're right, of course.' She gave a light laugh that nearly choked her. 'I shouldn't have allowed the thought any traction inside my head.' She went to take another step, but his hand came down on her forearm to stall her. She raised her gaze back up to his, her pulse fluttering, her heart stuttering, her body secretly smouldering.

'Wait… Are you saying you *want* it to happen?' There was no escaping his gaze, it held her fast with its probing heat.

So, her moment of truth had arrived. An hour ago, she had tried on clothes, changed her clothes like shedding a skin and morphing into someone else. The moth had left its dusty brown camouflaging cocoon to become a colourful butterfly. She could continue to deny her needs as she had for all of her adult life, but she no longer wanted to. It seemed…dishonest, disingenuous, delusional even to pretend her attraction to him didn't exist. It did and she was going to own it.

The sun beat down on the top of her head like the

spotlight was finally on her. Nature's spotlight, sending the shadows she normally took shelter in scattering.

She looked up into Vic's now inscrutable expression, her new-found courage wavering for a moment, but thankfully not completely failing. 'Do you find that surprising? That I might enjoy a...a fling like everyone else?' She was proud of how modern and hip and cool she sounded about it, in spite of her vocal stumble over the word. A fling was no big deal. Just about everyone had them these days. And if she didn't do something about her sexual stasis, when would she ever get a chance as good as this?

Vic drew in a sharp-sounding breath and one of his hands raked a crooked pathway through the thickness of his hair. Subtle clues he was not quite as in command of himself as he had sounded. 'You're a *virgin*, for God's sake, Addie.' He said the word like it was something he had never encountered before. But then maybe he hadn't. He was used to liaisons with women who dated casually like him. Women who were experienced in the no-strings, no expectation hook-ups and flings that satisfied a physical need without engaging any emotional ones.

'But that's why I think you're the right person for me. I mean, not for ever, but at this point in my life, to help me get started, so to speak,' she said.

He held her gaze for a long moment. She could almost hear the cogs of his brain running through the list of pros and cons. She wasn't so innocent and naive that she couldn't see there were negatives and positives about any liaison between them—there were, lots of them. How would they keep it a secret? *Could* they keep it a secret? Did she want to be known as yet another one of Vic's casual lovers? She was used to flying under the radar but if she got involved with Vic, the press would find out sooner or later. They may have already done so. Everyone had a camera phone, and everyone knew who Vic was.

Vic let out another breath in a forceful stream. 'And what do you think your brother and my sister would think of it?'

'Does it matter what anyone thinks? It's between us, as two consenting adults.'

Vic glanced at her mouth and then back to her eyes, but she could see his gaze hardening with resolve. 'I didn't buy those clothes as some sort of bribe to get you into my bed.' There was a thread of anger woven through his tone, but she wasn't sure if it was directed at her or himself. 'Let's get back to Katerina. We can talk about this at some other time.'

She walked back with him to the villa, her thoughts in turmoil. Had she made a prize fool of herself? It was so hard to know with Vic. Although she wasn't experienced, she could still sense his attraction to her. The way he looked at her mouth all the time, the flare of his pupils, the heat in his gaze—weren't those telltale signs of male desire? Or was she kidding herself? Was her crush on him distorting her perception and making her see things that weren't actually there?

Vic had to stop himself from taking up Addie's invitation. What business did he have to *even* consider the possibility? He was totally wrong for her. He was a playboy for pity's sake. A man who had lost count of the number of women he had bedded. Addie had never been intimate with anyone. She was completely innocent and yet she had offered herself to him. But what could he offer her other than a fling? She wasn't the fling type. Didn't she deserve better than that, especially when it was her first foray into sex? He glanced at her as they walked back to the villa. Her girl-next-door attractiveness grew on him the more time he spent with her. He noticed things about her he had missed in the past: the sweet curve of her mouth, the way her lower lip was full and pillowy, the top one beautifully defined. The creamy texture of her skin, notwithstanding those cute freckles made her appear younger than twenty-eight. Whenever she smiled it was like a punch to the heart. Her smile lit up her tawny brown eyes and indented her cheeks with tiny dimples.

But while he knew he couldn't offer Addie anything permanent, he was worried about her giving herself to someone who wouldn't appreciate her or take care of her given how innocent she was. What if they only bedded her for the novelty of having slept with the daughter of the stunning and sultry Solange?

Vic enjoyed Addie's company more than he thought he would. He loved watching her interact with Katerina. She was patient and loving and kind and was wise in a way many people these days were not. She had an intuitive sense of what Katerina needed and responded accordingly to those needs. She would make a wonderful mother one day in spite of the way she had been mothered. It was wrong of him to even consider the possibility of indulging in a fling with her. Not going to happen. Never.

You want her.

Vic pushed the thought back. Closed the door on it. Locked. Bolted. But like smoke, it drifted out and swirled around his consciousness, tempting him to touch her, to taste her, to tantalise her with the sensual delights of passion. The gentle breeze sent a waft of her perfume his way and his lower body tensed and tightened with primal lust. Why was he so damn obsessed with her? Was it because of their forced proximity? Had their being thrust together like this stirred feelings in him he would not normally experience when other people were around?

He had met her three times before this trip to Lake Como and while he had noticed her, he had not once on any of those occasions felt this potent tug of desire. A flicker, yes, because he was human and she was beautiful and cute in a refreshing way, but nothing like this primal stirring that refused to go away. It was as if the more he told himself she was forbidden, the more his body wanted her. Acting on it was out of the question. Unlike every other fling, this was not the sort of relationship he could walk away from with a clear conscience. Sure, he could show her a good time, introduce her to the delights of sensuality but he wasn't interested in anything but a short-term relationship, and even *that* would come with its own minefield. He couldn't erase her from his life like he could with an acquaintance or a stranger. Addie was connected to him through the marriage of her brother to his half-sister. They were co-godparents to Katerina. There was a bond there that meant they would not be able to avoid each other. Sleeping with Addie would change everything. The dynamic between them would be different, inescapably different. For one thing, he would always be her first lover. It was dangerous to even consider the possibility.

Dangerous and unwise and yet so very tempting.

CHAPTER SIX

KATERINA WAS STIRRING from her nap just as Addie came into the room. Vic had mumbled something about an important call he had to make and left her as soon as they got back to the villa. He had seemed preoccupied on the walk back, a brooding frown appearing on his forehead, and he had seemed disinclined to talk. Had she embarrassed him by offering herself to him?

The more she thought about it, the more she wanted him to be her first lover. It would be so much less threatening to sleep with him rather than a stranger. How did people do that these days? She couldn't imagine hooking up with someone for sex. She needed to know the person, to like and admire them at the very least. She needed to be attracted to them both physically and emotionally. She needed to trust them, to feel confident they wouldn't exploit her or use her. That's why Vic was a perfect candidate. He ticked all the boxes. He would treat her with the utmost respect and while he might not promise anything long-term, she knew she could rely on him to make her first sexual experience a wonderful one. The chemistry between them was unmistakable—her skin tingled when he touched her, his eyes meeting hers sent a thrill through her entire body. No one had ever made her feel that way before.

Addie scooped Katerina up out of her cot and held her against her chest, her little chubby arms snaking their way around her neck.

'Want Mummy.' The hint of a wobble in the toddler's voice plucked at her heartstrings, making them vibrate with a melancholic melody that reverberated all the way back to her lonely childhood.

'I know, poppet,' she said in a soothing tone, stroking the back of Katerina's silky head of sweaty curls. 'But she and Daddy will be back as soon as they can get here. And I'm sure they'll video call you as soon as they can. That would make you feel better, wouldn't it? To see their faces and to talk to them?' She had already witnessed on many occasions Katerina's adeptness at using her mother's or father's phone. Katerina had actually called her on a couple of occasions, much to her parents' delight and immense pride. Katerina had probably only stumbled across her number in the call history by accident, but Isabella insisted her brilliant little daughter had not only recognised the number but Addie's name, as well. Addie wondered if her own mother had ever been proud of her. Had there ever been a time or instance where she had done or said something that had made her mother swell with pride?

Katerina pulled away from cuddling into her neck to look at her with big woebegone chocolate-brown eyes. Her lashes were as long as spider legs and her bottom lip was pushed out in a little pout. Addie had never considered herself a particularly maternal person. Animals were her thing—puppies and kittens were her kryptonite but looking into Katerina's eyes and holding her soft little body against her sent a ripple of maternal longing through her that took her completely and utterly by surprise. But then doubts trickled into her head, doubts that she would measure up. What sort of mother would she be? She hadn't had the best role model. Solange wasn't interested in being a grandmother to Marcus's child, why would she be any different if Addie were to have a baby? And who on earth would she get to father her child? Vic was dead set against having children of his own.

Vic? The father of her imagined child? Who was she kidding? Her outrageously out of character suggestion of having a fling with him had hardly been met with enthusiasm, how enthusiastically would he embrace the suggestion of shared parenthood?

There was a sound behind her, and she turned with Katerina still in her arms to see Vic coming in. He smiled at the toddler and her heart did a flip-turn in her chest. She held her breath as he came closer and held out his arms to the toddler. Katerina buried her head into her neck and gripped Addie all the tighter, but not before a cheeky giggle escaped from her rosebud mouth. Addie was going to faint from lack of oxygen if she didn't take a breath soon or Katerina didn't ease up her stranglehold. Or maybe her lack of oxygen was more to do with how devastatingly attractive Vic was when he smiled.

'Ah, I see how it goes,' Vic said in a lighthearted tone. 'But I thought we agreed on a swim this afternoon, *si*?'

Katerina lifted her head up and beamed at him. 'Simming!'

Even though Addie had a brand-new, designer no less, swimsuit upstairs, she was not so enthusiastic about the upcoming swimming session. It was one thing changing into a swimsuit behind the privacy of the change room curtains, quite another thing wearing said swimsuit when a tall, dark and deliciously handsome man was present. A man she was ridiculously attracted to. 'I can see I'm going to be outnumbered here,' she said.

Vic arched one of his eyebrows. 'Not having second thoughts, are you?'

'And third and fourth and fifth.' She chewed at the inside of her mouth for a moment. 'But I don't want to spoil it for Katerina.'

'There's my girl,' Vic said with a slanted smile that sent a shower of sparks through her blood.

But she wasn't his girl, was she? Nor did he want her to be. And she had better not forget it anytime soon.

Addie changed Katerina into a waterproof nappy and cute little lemon and white frilled swimsuit, and lathered her with sunscreen, even though that was the hardest part of the process but somehow, she got through it without tears. Katerina was clearly no fan of the sunsmart standards Addie adhered to, but no way was she going to allow her little goddaughter to get horribly sunburned on her watch. She had too many agonising memories of blisters and peeling skin and then more freckles than she wanted. She then took Katerina to Vic who was waiting down by the pool.

Her eyes drank in the sight of him standing waist deep in the clear blue water. His skin was tanned, his body toned with muscles in all the right places. Places she could only dream about touching—the sculptured perfection of his chest, the masculine bulge of beautifully toned biceps, the ridged washboard of his abdomen… She tried not to stare, but her eyes seemed to have their own agenda and drifted down below the waterline to study him. He was wearing black swimming trunks that clung unapologetically to his male form. A trail of black hair arrowed from the whorl of his bellybutton to disappear below his swimwear. It sent her imagination into overdrive, her wayward mind conjuring up images of what he looked like without the barrier of his trunks. She disguised a gulp as she handed Katerina down to his outstretched arms.

'Careful, she's slippery as an eel,' she said, trying not to touch him in the handover. 'She wasn't keen on wearing sunscreen, but we came to an agreement of sorts.'

'I heard the protest from down here.' His lazy smile sent her heart rate off the charts, so too the gentle way he held the small child, tucking her on his lean hip.

Katerina was keen to show off her swimming prowess, but Vic was wise enough to not let her go. The child kicked and splashed and giggled with glee and Addie watched in vicarious enjoyment. And, truth be told, a bit of envy. A *lot* of envy. But wasn't that the story of her life? Sitting on the sidelines watching as everyone else had a good time.

Vic looked up at her at one point, Katerina now

perched up on his broad shoulders. 'Aren't you coming in?'

She took a step back from the inviting pool and shrugged in a dismissive manner. 'Maybe I'll try it another day.'

His eyebrow quirked again. 'When was the last time you got in a pool?'

She compressed her lips for a moment, not sure her memory went back that far. Or even wanted to. 'I'm not sure.'

'No excuses, Addie, you have a swimsuit, now go and put it on so you can join us.' There was a commanding quality to his voice that would have annoyed her under a different set of circumstances, but she knew she needed a little push to get herself in that pool. Okay, maybe even a big push. It wasn't the temperature of the water; it wasn't the exposure to the sun because she had industrial-strength sunscreen. It wasn't the thought of sharing the pool with Vic because that was the part she was secretly longing to do. It was the thought of baring her body to his appraisal. What if he didn't like what he saw? What if he compared her to every woman he had slept with? He had been involved with some of the most beautiful women in the world. She had seen photos of him with them. Not one of them looked anything like her.

'You don't have to be shy around me.' His tone was deep and gravelly and it made her blood heat hot enough to put the sun out of a job.

'This isn't easy for me…'

'Not much is the first time you do it.' His eyes held

hers in a funny little lock. A connection that felt almost audible like the click of a camera shutter.

Snap. Got you.

She swallowed and a flutter of something went through the network of her veins as quickly as lightning. 'Okay… I'll do it if you promise not to stare.'

'I can't promise that, *cara*.' The deep, dark velvet quality to his voice made her heart pick up its pace.

She walked backwards from the pool deck, still mesmerised by the magnetic potency of his gaze as it kept her entrapped. Ensnared. Enraptured. She knew she had to turn away at some point otherwise she might end up in the garden or over the edge of the cliff from where the pool was situated, affording it the most magnificent view of Lake Como and its surrounds. It was the most beautiful setting and of course it would make a spectacular hotel.

But a part of her still wondered why Vic was so determined to redevelop his childhood home where his earliest memories and only memories of his loving father echoed in the grand old place. Watching him in the pool playing with his little niece made her wonder if his father had played with him in the same happy and relaxed way. But in spite of the loving relationship he had had with his father, Vic insisted he didn't want a family of his own. But would he, like she had just minutes before when holding Katerina, feel a ripple of longing that couldn't be ignored? A desire for more than being on the earth to make more and more money but to build something for the future, a legacy of love and connection with a family of his own.

By the time she shed her clothes and put on her bright pink bikini and then applied liberal amounts of sunscreen and covered herself in a matching pink gauzy wrap, it was some time before she got back down to the pool area. But Katerina was nowhere in sight and only Vic was in the pool, swimming up and down in an effortless, graceful freestyle. He must have sensed her approach because he stopped at the end closest to where she was standing and scraped his fingers through his wet hair to comb it back from his face.

'Lucia has taken Katerina in for a bath and a snack,' he said, his gaze running over her long pink wrap. 'That colour suits you.'

'Th-thank you.' She was teaching herself to accept compliments from him rather than deflect them as had been her lifelong habit, but it wasn't easy. She hugged her arms around her middle, suddenly feeling shy and gauche. Her mother would have strutted all the way along the pool deck, removing her wrap to let it float to the ground in a silky whisper in her wake. She would have tossed the mane of her long blond hair over one slim shoulder and batted her eyelash extensions at whoever was looking her way, which was usually anybody with a pulse. Speaking of pulses… Addie's was going a little haywire. She had expected to come back down to have a quick dip with Katerina as a chaperone. But now she was intensely aware of being alone with Vic Jacobetti.

She looked at the clear blue water of the pool with a mixture of excitement and trepidation. She ran the tip of her tongue over her lips, then caught her bottom lip between her teeth, her heartbeat racing at the thought of taking off her wrap and uncovering her body to his appraising gaze. But then she somehow garnered a tiny remnant of courage and untied the wrap from around her waist and peeled it away from her body. She laid it with exaggerated care on a sun lounger next to the pool, but she was conscious of Vic's dark gaze tracking her every movement. She turned back to face him and took in a shaky breath.

'Okay, let's do this…' If only she sounded a little more confident. If only she sounded cool and sophisticated. If only she could get this over without making a complete and utter fool of herself. She inched a little closer to the pool's edge, feeling beads of perspiration between her shoulder blades, and her mouth was as dry as the flagstones she was standing on.

Vic held out a hand to her. 'Come on, one step at a time. It's shallow here, you won't be out of your depth.'

I've been out of my depth from the moment I met you.

She didn't say the words out loud but what if he instinctively knew that was how she felt? She put her trembling hand in the warm steadiness of his. His fingers closed around hers, gently but firmly and a lightning bolt of longing shot through her body. His touch was electrifying, the heat of his body sending arrows of lust to her womanhood.

Eek. Why couldn't she even name her own body parts without using old-fashioned euphemisms? For years, she had denied her feminine needs. She had ignored the primal hum and throb of her flesh, telling herself sensuality wasn't for her, that it would only lead to more shame and embarrassment.

But since she had met Vic Jacobetti, he had awakened something in her, stirring those sleeping needs into fervent, throbbing life.

She stepped into the silky warm embrace of the water, it rippled against her flesh and enveloped her up to her waist. She was standing so close to Vic, she could see the droplets of water in his hair, glistening like a scattering of diamonds on his broad and tanned shoulders.

'You don't have any freckles.' Arrgh. Why couldn't she think of something a little more sophisticated to say? But it was all she could think of at the time—his skin was perfect, not a spot or blemish anywhere.

One side of his mouth came up in a half-smile, his eyes glinting as bright as the sunlight on the water enveloping them. 'I happen to like your freckles.' His voice had lowered to a deep burr that made her skin tingle.

'You can have some of mine. I hate them.' She gave a self-effacing grimace and reminded herself to breathe. He was still holding her hand and she was secretly glad of it because right then she didn't think her legs were up to the task of keeping her upright. The sensation of his fingers wrapped around hers, his hard warm male body within a few millimetres of her, the potent heat of his gaze as it held hers made her feel as if she had entered an entirely different world. A world where she didn't have to hide or keep on the sidelines. A world where she was free of the shackles of the past, free to embrace the full expression of her humanity and her most earthy needs.

Vic's gaze meshed with hers and something hot and molten trickled down her spine. One of his hands came to rest on her right hip, the other in the small of her back, his body so close she could feel the warmth of his sun-heated skin. 'Aren't they supposed to be kisses from the sun?' he said.

'Yes, well, they're the only kisses I've had since I was sixteen so I supposed I should be grateful.'

His dark brows moved together over his eyes. 'Really?' His incredulous tone reminded her of what a misfit she was. What other woman of twenty-eight was so inexperienced that she had forgotten what a man's lips felt like? In fact, no man had ever kissed her, only a teenage boy.

Addie couldn't stop her gaze from drifting to Vic's mouth. Its sensual contours fascinated her, and she couldn't help wondering if his lips would be firm or soft or something in between.

Vic's eyes darkened to pitch and stayed focussed on her mouth. 'Addie...' He released a rough-edged sigh and his hand at her back pressed her inexorably closer. 'I shouldn't be doing this.'

'Doing what?' Addie breathed in the clean male scent of him, her senses spinning, her heart pounding with excitement and anticipation.

'I want to kiss you.'

A frisson skittered over her flesh. 'I'd like you to kiss me.' Her voice came out as a whisper. A fervent whisper of longing.

'But that's all we can do, okay?' His tone was firm, adamantine, but his eyes spoke another language—the language of desire and irresistible temptation. 'This can't go any further.'

Addie moistened her lips, her legs trembling with need. 'Okay.'

Vic lowered his mouth to hers in slow motion, or maybe it just felt that way to Addie. Time seemed to stand still, the garden around them cloaked in sudden silence, as if nature had taken a collective breath, holding it, waiting for this moment to happen. His lips touched hers in a light as air touchdown, the gentle imprint of his lips stirring hers into pulsing life. His lips moved against hers in a caressing motion, still soft, still gentle but she could sense the banked-down passion in every exquisite movement. His lips moved with increasing urgency against hers, drawing from her a response that was equally passionate—passionate and needy, as if his kiss had awakened something inside her. Something that would not be so easily ignored now it had taken its first breath, stretched and moved its cramped limbs. Desire moved through her body like flashing tongues of flame, igniting her, exciting her, delighting her.

Vic's tongue stroked the seam of her lips and she opened to him on a sigh of pure pleasure, hot tingles shooting down her spine as his tongue played with hers in an erotic dance as old as time. His kiss bore no resemblance to the rushed and clumsy kisses she had had in the past. Vic's kiss was leisurely and yet urgent at the same time, evoking a response from her that surprised and delighted her in equal measure. His hand on her hip moved to cup her face, his head angled to gain better access to her mouth, a soft but deep groan sounding at the back of his throat. It thrilled Addie to think she was having this effect on him, that her responses were inciting him to greater passion. She could feel the deep throb of his body as he drew her closer to his hard pelvis. The contact jolted her like a zap of high voltage electricity, sending arrows of heat straight to her core. The hollow ache between her legs became unbearable. A pulsing ache that begged for the possession of his hard male body. An ache that could not be satisfied by anyone but him.

No kiss she had ever experienced made her feel this level of excitement. Every one of her erogenous zones was eagerly awaiting his touch. Her feminine folds were swelling, moistening, the tingling sensation part pleasure, part pain, an intimate torture of primal need.

Vic dragged his mouth off hers but before she could express her disappointment, he lowered it to her neck, just below her ear. Her skin tingled as his lips moved across the sensitive flesh, her desire rising with every slamming heartbeat against her chest.

'You taste divine,' he said in a low, deep growl.

'So do you,' Addie whispered in delight.

Vic's hands held her by the hips, holding her against the potent throb of his arousal. The intimate contact was electrifying, and her body craved to be even closer. She murmured a plea for more and his mouth came back to hers, harder this time, the urgent exploration of his lips and tongue sending her senses reeling. Fireworks went off in her blood, explosions and flashpoints and fiery streaks of lust making her aware of her body in a way she had never been before.

Vic lifted his mouth off hers again but this time he

moved down from her neck to her décolletage, tracing his tongue over the gentle slope of her breast above her bikini top. Her skin tingled and tightened, her nipples budding into proud points, and she pushed herself into his erotic caress, arching her spine to gain closer contact to the magical stroke of his tongue.

He placed one hand just below her left breast, meeting her gaze with red-hot desire gleaming in his. 'May I?'

Addie was almost beyond speech, the sensation of his broad hand so close to the globe of her breast making it hard for her brain to function enough to produce an intelligible sentence. But somehow, she managed to whisper, 'Yes…oh, yes…'

Vic deftly but gently eased aside her bikini top and his glinting gaze devoured her. For a moment, a flood of self-doubts assailed her. Was he comparing her to all the spectacularly enhanced women he had dated? Was he disappointed she was only as nature had made her, and that nature had not been particularly generous?

'I'm not exactly swimsuit model material…' Addie filled the silence, her stomach prickling in case he agreed with her…or looked at her the way her teenage boyfriend had all those years ago. With disgust, with disappointment, with scorn.

Vic cupped her breast in his hand, his eyes locking on hers. 'You are beautiful, so natural and feminine.'

Turned out, her self-doubts weren't so easily put aside. She barely filled the cup of her bikini; she didn't have a cleavage because her breasts went outwards, not inwards. She was as small as she had been as a teenager—nothing had changed. How could Vic Jacobetti find her beautiful? 'You don't think I'm too…small?'

Vic stroked his broad thumb over her tight nipple, back and forth like a slow metronome, and she gasped in pleasure. 'I think you're perfect.'

Addie glanced at his olive tanned hand on her breast and something hot spilled in her belly. 'No one has ever told me that before. I've always been compared to my mother and found wanting.'

'Your mother is beautiful, but it's a surface thing. Your beauty runs deeper. It is a part of your nature, and it enhances your physical attributes in a way makeup and professional styling can never do.'

Tears prickled at the backs of her eyes and a lump formed in her throat. 'Do you really mean that?

Vic's mouth tilted in a sexy manner. 'You should know me well enough by now that I speak as I find.' His voice deepened and he began to caress her breast once more with his thumb. Then he bent his head and put his mouth on the soft skin of her breast, tasting her with his tongue, then using his tongue to circle her nipple, sending sparks of delight through her body.

Addie clung to his hips, needing an anchor as the tingles of pleasure flowed through her body. She had never thought her breasts could be so sensitive, so responsive to a man's touch. Vic continued his sensual exploration of her breasts, moving to her other one, subjecting it to the same spine-tingling caresses. Addie's inner core dampened with the dew of desire, her legs trembling with the overwhelming power of it.

Finally, he came back to press his mouth to hers, his

kiss long and deep and yet tender and worshipful at the same time. It was like he found her mouth captivating, exciting and thrilling to kiss. Addie had so little experience with kissing, but her lips and tongue seemed to know what to do without much thought. Her response to him was so natural, so uninhibited, so in tune with his movements it was like dancing with the perfect partner. You moved with them, not against them, your steps in perfect sync with theirs.

Addie wound her arms around his neck, one of her hands playing with the damp ends of his hair, her body pressed so close to him she could feel the potent ridge of his arousal against her belly. The water they were standing in somehow heightened the sensuality of the moment. She was aware of every point of contact with his wet skin, aware of the movement of the pool water each time he changed position to kiss her. The water became another caress, silky, warm, erotic. Vic kept kissing her, deeply, thoroughly, his murmurs of enjoyment like music to her ears.

Vic slowly lifted his mouth from hers, still holding her by the hips, looking down at her with a hooded gaze. 'If we don't stop, I won't want to stop.'

Addie didn't want to stop either. Her body was already feeling short-changed as he put a little distance between them. 'Do we have to stop?'

He closed his eyes in a slow blink as if trying to summon up some willpower. Then he carefully covered her exposed breast and let his hands drop from her body. 'You know we have to.'

Addie swallowed the bitter taste of disappointment,

her body still aching for him. But she decided against begging him to assuage her needs. She gathered some remnants of pride and affected a relaxed and casual attitude to what had happened between them. It was just a kiss after all. But, oh, what a kiss. 'Yes, of course we do.' She painted a smile on her lips and added, 'I've probably had enough sun for one day anyway.'

He gave a crooked smile, but somehow there was still a frown about his eyes. 'Go and have a shower. Later, I'd like to take you and Katerina for a walk to see the grotto.'

'There's a grotto?'

'It's not a natural one—my father made it out of some rocks. It's hidden away in the garden down near the water's edge.'

Addie climbed out of the pool and covered herself in her wrap, tying it around her waist. She turned and faced him, trying not to stare at his body as he launched himself out of the pool in one graceful movement, his biceps bulging, his abdomen ridged with taut muscles she ached to explore with her hands. 'What will you do with it when you redevelop the villa into a hotel? Will you get rid of it?'

A flicker of something went through his gaze and he looked away as he leaned down to pick up his blue-and-white-striped towel. He rubbed his face with the towel before he answered, 'The gardens will be relandscaped to suit the needs of the hotel.'

'But what about the sentimental value? Isn't that important to you?'

Vic's smile wasn't quite a smile, the hardness in his

eyes like a glaze of cynicism. 'Any decisions about the development will be financial, not sentimental ones. I would not be where I am today if I followed my heart instead of my head.'

Addie garnered some courage to hold his gaze. 'Do you ever follow your heart?'

'No.' His answer bordered on curt, his smile as brittle as his gaze. 'Never.'

Vic watched as Addie walked back inside the villa, torn between wanting to follow her and finish what he had started and the other part of him telling himself he was every sort of fool to give in to the temptation to kiss her. What was he thinking? Getting involved with Addie in any shape or form was dangerous. It would change the dynamic between them permanently and it would disrupt the balance of their other relationships—with Marcus and Isabella, and even with Katerina. He didn't know why he hadn't been able to resist her. She wasn't even his type. He normally steered clear of sweet and innocent unworldly women for those were the ones who wanted the fairytale, and he didn't believe in happy-ever-afters. Some people, if they were lucky, were happy for a time like his parents had been until death had snatched his father away. So many things could go wrong in a relationship even without illness and death. People grew apart, went in different directions, wanted different experiences and the other partner either had to compromise or be left behind.

But…kissing Addie had opened up a world of possibilities to him he was tempted to explore in spite of his misgivings. The passion she had ignited in him had stunned him. Passion that was more intense than any he had experienced in the last few years of his casual dating. Was it because she wasn't a stranger? A casual hook-up he wouldn't see again. Was it because he already had a connection with her through her brother and his sister and their little goddaughter? All of those factors changed the way he saw her.

The sun was warm on his back and shoulders, but it was nothing to the heat Addie had stirred in his flesh. He ached to explore the sweet contours of her body, to introduce her to the sensual world of making love. It intrigued him she was still a virgin and the more he thought about it, the more he wanted to be her first lover. He was shocked at himself for wanting it so badly. He wasn't a trophy hunter; he wasn't a man who treated women as objects rather than people. But he hated the thought of someone else sleeping with Addie without taking the care and consideration someone as unworldly as she would need. She had shyly offered herself to him and he had said no. But with their joint care and responsibility of Katerina to consider, the possibility of making love with Addie was something that had to be put to one side. For how long, he wasn't sure, and that was the thing that unsettled him the most. For while he wanted her, he could not give her what she truly deserved. Would it be fair to ask her to settle for less?

CHAPTER SEVEN

ADDIE HAD SHOWERED and changed and was playing with Katerina in the nursery when her phone rang. She glanced at the screen and saw it was Marcus on a video call and she grabbed her phone and answered it. 'Hi! I've been so desperate to hear news of you. Where are you?'

'Daddy!' Katerina piped up, trying to take the phone off Addie. Addie bundled her onto her lap and angled the screen so the little toddler could see both of her parents, as Isabella appeared in the frame too. 'Mummy!'

'Baby, we will be home soon. We miss you, darling. Are you having a nice time with Uncle Vic and Auntie Addie?' Isabella said, blinking back tears.

'Sorry it's taken us so long to get in contact, it's been wild here,' Marcus said, once he had spoken to his little girl first. 'But we're booked on a flight that leaves first thing tomorrow or at least that's what we've been told. The plans keep getting changed when there's a new weather report. Let's hope there aren't any further delays. How have you been managing?'

'It's been fine,' Addie said, trying not to think of Vic's kiss only half an hour ago. 'Katerina has had lots of fun with Vic and me, and of course Lucia has been invaluable if not a little exhausted at times.'

Isabella chuckled. 'Yes, well, Little Miss is at a very energetic age. Thanks so much for stepping in for us. I would have asked my mother but she's on a cruise with my father and Marcus wasn't keen on asking Solange.'

'Yes, well, I think you made the right decision,' Addie said. 'I've really enjoyed seeing Vic's villa. It's so beautiful here.'

Isabella's smile changed to a more wistful one. 'Yes, isn't it? I hope Katerina will remember it in the future. But Vic is determined to redevelop it and he's not one to change his mind once he decides on something.'

'Yes, I know,' Addie said, trying not to show how hard it was to accept that inescapable truth.

'How are you two getting on?' Isabella said with a twinkling light in her eyes.

Addie could feel a blush stealing over her cheeks, but there was nothing she could do to disguise it. 'Fine.'

Isabella arched a slim eyebrow. 'Just fine?'

'He's been a perfect gentleman and he's wonderful with Katerina,' Addie said.

Isabella put her head to one side in a musing fashion. 'I know what's different about you.'

Addie stiffened. Surely her sister-in-law couldn't tell she had recently been kissed. 'Different, in what way?'

'You're wearing colour, and it suits you. It makes your skin glow, and your eyes stand out.'

'Oh, yes, well, we went shopping. I packed in rather a hurry and—'

'We?' Both Isabella's eyebrows lifted this time. 'Did Vic spoil you?'

Addie was blushing so hotly she was worried she was contributing to climate change. 'Yes, he did but it was totally unnecessary, but he insisted. He can be very…erm…persuasive.'

'I'm so glad you two are getting along well,' Isabella said, smiling.

'Now, now, darling,' Marcus interjected. 'Don't go playing matchmaker. Vic's not the settling down type.'

Isabella gave him a playful shoulder bump, looking at him tenderly. 'And nor were you until you met me.'

Marcus smiled back in an indulgent manner and Addie couldn't help feeling a pang of envy. But Vic didn't believe in for ever love or at least not for himself. And Addie had never envisaged falling for anyone until now. Her feelings for Vic were confusing to her. She wasn't sure how to describe them. She had had a crush on him since she met him, but that wasn't love, was it? It was probably more along the lines of infatuation. Hardly a grown-up, mature love that would last. It was probably just a phase she was going through since she had not had much experience around sophisticated men.

And they didn't get more sophisticated and sexier than Vic Jacobetti.

A little later that day, Vic took Addie and Katerina to the grotto at the back of the estate. It had been years since he had been down to the hidden cave his father had built out of the natural rock face. When Vic was a child, they had spent many hours there together just hanging out. One of the last times he had been with his father had been the day before his father's death. If only Vic had known back then he only had a handful of hours left with his father…

Katerina had insisted on bringing a bunch of soft toys with her that she was now busily setting up along the rock ledges with painstaking precision. Vic remembered lining up his toy cars with the same focussed attention and smiled at the memory. But such memories were always tinged with sadness. His father had missed out on so many years of life. He had been Vic's age when he died—thirty-four. So young. So tragically young, his potential snatched away, snuffed out. So many milestones of his life to have missed, let alone those of Vic's. He thought of what a wonderful grandfather his father would have been…but why was he thinking about such things? Vic didn't plan on having a family, so it was a moot point. And yet, he couldn't help wondering if his father hadn't died, would he be so adamant about remaining single and childless?

Addie ran her hand along the wall of the cave, her features cast in lines of delight. 'This is the ultimate in cubby houses. What a wonderful place to explore.'

Vic had to stoop to enter the cave just as his father used to do, triggering another host of poignant memories. 'I used to spend hours down here with my father.' He too ran his hand over the cool rock, his heart squeezing as he recalled how it felt to have those special times with his father. Never once had his father made him feel as if he was taking up too much of his time or was in any way bored by the silly little games

Vic wanted to play. He wondered if he had children of his own would he be as present, as involved, as loving as his father had been with him. But he didn't want children, did he? It was a decision he had made a long time ago and it wasn't one he was going to revisit. He didn't want the responsibility of trying to protect those he loved. It was easier, safer not to love.

'So, what will happen to this place when you redevelop the villa?' Addie asked, helping Katerina prop up her floppy-eared rabbit on a little rock shelf on the back wall of the grotto. She turned to look at him and he found himself uncharacteristically lost for words. The light breeze had mussed her light brown hair giving her an untamed look that was mesmerising. Her tawny brown eyes were fringed with dark lashes and her lack of makeup only made her more attractive. He was used to being around highly polished women, groomed to the point of perfection. But he found Addie's natural and unadorned beauty totally captivating. Kissing her had been a mistake because now that he had tasted the sweet softness of her lips he wanted more. It had triggered a deep longing in him that he was finding hard to ignore. He was reassured to know Marcus and Isabella were on their way back to relieve them of their babysitting duties but another part of him was disappointed this time together was coming to an end. He had enjoyed getting to know Addie better. She had lowered her guard as indeed he had done his. It had created a different dynamic between them, so too had looking after their goddaughter together. Their team effort had helped the little toddler cope with the separation from her parents without too much drama, and that he believed was largely due to Addie. She was a natural nurturer, gentle and intuitive in handling young children.

'Vic?' Addie was frowning at him, and he suddenly realised he had been so lost in his thoughts he hadn't answered her question about what he planned to do with the grotto once he redeveloped the villa. What *had* he planned to do with it? It was well away from the villa and the formal gardens. It didn't need to be a part of the new development and yet why would he hold on to it? It meant nothing to anyone but him and he wasn't the sentimental type. And yet…and yet…closing it off, bricking it up or refashioning it into something else made him feel edgy, unsettled, rattled.

Vic glanced at his watch and frowned. 'I forgot I need to make a couple of calls. Are you okay with Katerina for a bit? I'll see you at dinner.'

Addie went back to helping Katerina organise her toys in the crevices of the grotto. The coolness of the little homemade cave was refreshing after the late afternoon heat. But she was puzzled as to why Vic had left without answering her question. He had mentioned his father had made the grotto for him when he was a child. She imagined it must hold a lot of memories for him. He was so determined to redevelop the villa, but would he keep the grotto as some sort of shrine to his father?

Katerina was tired after her busy afternoon of swimming and playing in the grotto, so Addie fed her early and tucked her in to bed and read her a story. The little toddler snuggled against the pillow, her lashes flickering as she tried to stay awake.

'Mummy come soon?' she murmured as Addie stroked her silky black curls.

'Yes, sweetie, Mummy and Daddy will be back soon. Now, close those eyes and dream lovely dreams. You've had a big day.'

Addie sat by her and watched as Katerina finally succumbed to the sleep she so desperately needed. Katerina gave a soft little sigh and drifted off, her little hand clutching her floppy-eared rabbit.

Addie leaned down and pressed a soft kiss to the little girl's forehead. 'Night-night, precious.'

CHAPTER EIGHT

ADDIE CAME DOWNSTAIRS a short time later to find Vic in the main sitting room, talking to someone on the phone in Italian. He was pacing the floor and frowning as if the conversation was a difficult one. He glanced at Addie and grimaced and then finished the call soon after. He slipped his phone in his pocket and smiled, but it didn't reach his eyes.

'Is Katerina down for the night?' he asked.

'Yes, sound asleep.' Addie said. 'Is Lucia about? I was going to see if I could help her with dinner.'

'I sent her home a few minutes ago. She wasn't feeling well.'

'I'm sorry to hear that. I hope she's okay.'

He pushed one of his hands through his hair in a distracted manner. 'I think your observation was right—she's too old to keep up with Katerina. But hopefully Marcus and Isabella will be back within twenty-four hours.'

Addie perched on the arm of one of the sofas, studying his tense expression. 'We can manage by ourselves until they get back. Katerina is completely at ease with both of us and only asks for her parents now and again.

I think it helped when she saw them on the video call earlier.'

'Yes, Marcus told me he'd called. I just hope there aren't any further delays.'

Addie rose from the sofa arm and smoothed her hands down the front of her linen pants. 'Was that a work call? You sounded a bit stressed.'

'No, it was my mother.'

'Is everything all right?'

He gave a shrug. 'According to her, everything is fine, but I can't help feeling she's not telling me everything about her relationship with my stepfather.'

'Perhaps she doesn't want to lose face by proving you right about him after all this time?'

Vic appeared to take on board her speculation, frowning as if deep in thought. 'Who knows? We're not particularly close these days.'

'When did you last see her? Alone, I mean, without your stepfather there?'

He rubbed at his face with one of his hands and released a sigh. 'I really can't remember. Years probably.'

'Maybe you could ask her to lunch or something when your stepfather is at work?'

He picked up a marble paperweight and turned it over in his hands. 'I'll give it a go, but she doesn't do much without him knowing about it.' He put the paperweight down again and looked at Addie. 'When was the last time you had lunch with your mother?'

Addie rolled her eyes like marbles. 'Arrgh. Sharing a meal with my mother is a form of mental torture. She tells me the calorie value of every single morsel

I eat, or she tells me she thinks I've put on weight, or my skin needs a special type of anti-aging facial—the list goes on. It's excruciating.'

'You do realise all of that comes from her own insecurity?'

Addie frowned. 'Insecure? She's the most confident person I've ever met.'

'People who are secure in themselves don't need to pull other people down. You probably threaten her with your natural beauty. I'd bet it takes her hours with a makeup artist and hair stylist to look as good as she does. You don't have to do anything to look gorgeous.'

Addie could feel herself glowing from his compliment. He thought her gorgeous? Naturally beautiful? She had spent her entire life feeling ugly and inadequate and yet Vic Jacobetti was telling her she was beautiful. 'I don't know about that…'

Vic gave a crooked smile. 'And you look even more beautiful when you blush.'

Addie could feel her face blushing all the more and quickly changed the subject. 'I—I guess you're keen to get back to work.'

'Yes, you are too, I imagine.'

'I miss it, but I've really enjoyed being here,' Addie said. 'I know most people wouldn't describe looking after a toddler as a holiday, but I can't remember the last time I had a proper holiday, so it's been fun. And this place is so beautiful.'

Vic came over to where she was standing, his gaze hooded, his expression now inscrutable. 'So, it's not been too much of a trial stuck here with me?'

She moistened her lips, not sure how to read his mood. 'I think you've helped me come out of myself. Not just with the lovely clothes you bought me but… other things too…'

He lifted her chin with the tip of his finger, locking his gaze on hers. 'What other things?' His voice was a low, deep burr of sound that sent tingles down her spine.

Addie disguised a swallow. 'Giving me compliments and…other things.'

His gaze drifted to her mouth, lingering there for a pulsing moment before coming back to mesh with her gaze. 'It was just a kiss, *cara*.' His thumb idly stroked her chin sending scorching heat straight to her core. His touch was electrifying, mesmerising, tantalising and she didn't know how to resist it. She didn't want to resist it. She ached for him and wondered if he felt the same. She found herself leaning into his caress, wanting more, needing more.

'Was it?' Her voice was not much more than a whisper.

He stroked his thumb across the curve of her cheek, his eyes still locked on hers. 'I think it would be dangerous to take things any further than we already have.'

Addie frowned. 'Dangerous? How so?'

He gave a wry smile and tilted her face upwards, his mouth only inches from hers. 'I think you know why.'

'I'm not going to fall in love with you from just a kiss or two.'

'But we both want more than that, don't we, *sì*?' He bent his head a little lower and pressed his lips to hers, igniting a spark of passion she couldn't control if she tried. It was a combustible reaction of male flesh on female flesh, hot, searing, irresistible. His tongue slipped between her lips and danced with hers in an erotic tangle that triggered molten heat in her core. Her lower body was on fire, aflame with need that begged to be assuaged. His kiss deepened even further, a low, deep groan sounding at the back of his throat, and he grasped her closer to the pounding heat of his body, leaving her in no doubt of his need of her. It thrilled her to feel the potent rise of his male arousal, the raw evidence of his lust exciting her beyond measure.

'You want me?' Addie said, against his lips.

Vic kissed the side of her mouth, his dark stubble tickling her smooth skin. 'I told myself this wasn't going to happen. It complicates things too much.'

'It's only complicated if we allow to be,' Addie said, leaning into his hard frame, relishing the strength of his arms around her.

'We can't allow any feelings to get in the way. If we do this, it's casual, no strings. That's the only reason I'd agree to it.'

'I'm not going to fall in love with you, Vic,' Addie said with far more confidence than she felt. Her crush had gone from seven to eight, who knew what it would go to if he made love to her? It was a risk she was more than prepared to take. If she didn't make love with him, she might never find anyone else she felt comfortable enough with to do the deed. Kissing him had shown her how wonderful he made her feel, how respectful and gentle he was with her. Why wouldn't she want him to be her first lover? He was the perfect candidate—the only candidate she wanted to give herself to.

Vic held her from him, his hands on her upper arms in a gentle hold. 'I think we should take things slowly. We'll have dinner and then see after that if we both still want to do this.'

How could he think of food at a time like this? All she could think of was the hunger growling in her body. But she realised he was giving her space and time to change her mind and she couldn't help loving him for it. *Loving him?* The thought slipped into her mind like a flashing light. Love? She had a crush on him, that's all. A silly little infatuation because she was so limited in her experience with dating men. How could she have fallen in love with him? Or was she just grateful for the attention he had given her, the compliments and kisses and deep conversations that had meant so much to her?

They sat down to the dinner Lucia had left for them a few minutes later. Addie tried to focus on the delicious beef cheek ragout, but her appetite was for Vic and Vic alone. She managed a few mouthfuls, watching him from time to time, wondering if he was feeling the same level of anticipation she was feeling at what might happen after dinner.

'You're not hungry?' Vic said at one point, fork halfway to his mouth.

Addie put her own knife and fork down. 'I'm worried you're going to change your mind about…us… you know…getting it on.' She cringed at how gauche she sounded.

Vic put his fork down and reached for one of her

hands, holding it in the gentle grasp of his warm fingers, his dark brown gaze meshed with hers. 'I should change my mind. I shouldn't be even thinking about making love to you, but I've thought of little else since I kissed you. But I don't want to pressure you in any way. It's your choice. It's a far bigger step for you to take than it is for me.'

Addie twisted her lips in a rueful smile. 'I guess I'm just another casual lover to you.'

His brows moved closer together over his eyes and he gave her hand a firm squeeze or reassurance. 'No, you could never be that. But I will always be your first lover. That's a big deal, especially since you're an adult who has waited for so long to get to this point.'

Addie looked at their joined hands, imagining their joined bodies in intimacy. A hot dart of longing shot through her at the thought of his limbs entwined with hers, his hard male body possessing hers. Her body was already secretly preparing itself, the silky dew of desire between her legs, the rush of blood and the swelling of her feminine flesh over which she had no control. She slowly brought her gaze back up to his. 'I want you to be my first lover. I don't want to do this with a stranger or someone I don't know and trust.'

'But will you be able to keep your feelings out of it?' He was still frowning in concern.

'I can't guarantee that any more than you can,' Addie said. 'No one can guarantee they won't be at risk of feeling more than they expected. People get blindsided by feelings all the time.'

His frown disappeared and his smile was confident

and cynical. 'Spoken like a true romantic. But I disagree. I decided a long time ago to never fall in love.'

'It doesn't mean it won't happen. It's not a mind over matter issue.'

'We'll have to agree to disagree.' He gave her hand another little squeeze and then released his hold and leaned back in his chair. 'Why don't you check on Katerina while I clear up here? I'll meet you upstairs in a few minutes.'

Addie placed her napkin on the table with a hand that wasn't quite steady. 'Erm…where will we meet? Your room or mine?'

His eyes smouldered as they held hers. 'Mine.'

Once Addie left the room, Vic let out a breath he hadn't realised he had been holding. He was at war with himself over whether he should sleep with her. He had a list of reasons not to but since kissing her in the pool, every one of those reasons was overruled by the pounding desire in his body. He wasn't the sort of man who couldn't resist his primal needs. There was a time and place for everything, and he had firm moral boundaries over consent. A fling with her would change everything, and not just between him and her but if Marcus and Isabella became aware of it, the dynamic between them all would be irrevocably changed. Never had he been so torn over a relationship. Even using the word *relationship* was alien to him when it came to his sex life. Those casual encounters were not strictly speaking relationships—they were hook-ups that had no future, no promises of anything but a good time. But now here he was with the prospect of becoming Addie's first lover. He had never been anyone's first lover. He had always been with experienced women, and he was a little overwhelmed by the responsibility, the enormity of what it would entail to be the first person to introduce Addie to physical pleasure. A part of him wondered if she would baulk at the last minute and not show up at his room. He would not pressure her. This had to come from her, there was no way he would coerce her into doing something she wasn't ready for. That's why he had suggested his room, to make sure she was one hundred percent willing to take this step. Would she have the courage, the drive and determination to follow through or would she shy away at the last minute. From what she had told him of her past, avoidance was her way of coping with things that threatened her, hence her still being a virgin at twenty-eight. But how long could she avoid the natural drives and urges of her body? She was a young and healthy woman—a passionate woman if those kisses he had shared with her were any indication.

Would she or wouldn't she follow through? And should he accept if she did?

Addie walked past Vic's bedroom door five times before she finally got the courage to knock. Her stomach was fizzing with a combination of nerves and excitement.

'Come in.' His voice was so deep it sent a shiver over her flesh.

Addie opened the door and stepped inside, softly

closing the door behind her with a hand that was trembling. She had nothing but her duckling pyjamas and refused to wear those for her first time with Vic, so had chosen to wear a plush bathrobe she had found in one of the guest bathrooms. She had thought about wearing underwear but changed her mind at the last minute. She had made the decision to sleep with him. This was what she wanted. How better to prove it to him than to be ready for him? And she was ready for him. She could already feel her body preparing itself, the secret scented secretions of female desire.

Vic was standing by the window that overlooked the lake and the distant mountains. The curtains were still open, revealing the long silver beam of moonlight across the water.

'Hi… Sorry it took me so long to get here.' Addie smoothed her damp palms over the soft fabric of the bathrobe. 'I wasn't sure what to wear.'

Vic came over to her and lifted her chin with his finger, locking his gaze on hers. 'Are you absolutely sure about this? It's not too late to change your mind.'

Addie kept her gaze on his, although her stomach was a nest of nerves of excitement. 'I'm sure that I want you to be my first lover. I can't think of anyone else I'd rather be with right now.'

Vic stroked his fingers through her hair, sending shivers coursing down her spine. His touch was so light and yet so enthralling, exciting, exhilarating. 'You know there's a part of me that still thinks this is crazy.' His eyes went to her mouth as if he had no control over their movement. 'Unwise and reckless, but I want to do it anyway.' And then his mouth came down and covered hers.

A delicious sensation rushed through Addie at the undercurrent of passion in Vic's kiss. His lips moved with increasing urgency against hers, drawing from her a response that was as heated and fierily passionate as his. How could she resist such an alluring kiss? A kiss that made every feminine hormone in her body shiver and shake with joy. Her body sprang to life when his tongue demanded entry, sending an electrifying shockwave of lust through her flesh, making her very bones shudder like someone rattling a loosely assembled cage.

Wasn't *this* why she had not made love with anyone else? No one had ever made her feel the way Vic Jacobetti did. No one had ever made her feel wanted for her, only for her body or because of who her mother was. But Vic made her feel not only truly wanted, but also safe and understood. His kiss deepened, his tongue courting hers in an erotic dance that sent her heart rate soaring. Desire shot through her with hot darting arrows, making her acutely aware of every secret curve and crevice of her body. Her female flesh swelled and moistened with longing, until the ache between her legs became unbearable. A pulsing ache that craved assuagement *now*. Addie had waited years for this moment, and it seemed her body was making up for lost time.

Vic lifted his mouth off hers, framing her face in his hands, his glittering gaze meshed with hers, his breathing as out of whack as her own. 'Are you still okay with this?'

Addie stepped on tiptoe to plant a kiss on his firm lips. 'More than okay. I feel like I've been waiting my whole life for this moment.'

Vic brought his mouth back down to hers in a lingering kiss that made the hairs on her head tingle at the roots. His lips were magical against hers, they cast a spell of sensual seduction that was irresistible. Each stroke of his tongue against hers set spot fires in her body. Each movement of his lips on hers was a caress and a promise of further pleasure. He walked her backwards to his bed, his mouth still fused to hers, the movement of his muscular thighs against hers making her insides coil in feverish anticipation. No kiss had ever made her feel this level of arousal, of excitement, of bone-deep longing. Every one of her erogenous zones had come to life like he had turned a switch. Her feminine flesh was tingling and fizzing, the sensation like a hollow spasm of part pain, part pleasure, the need so primal and strong she was driven by it in every cell of her body.

Vic laid her down on the king-sized bed and came down beside her, his hand moving down her body in one deliciously slow stroke from her breast to her thigh and back again. Even though she was still covered in the bathrobe, her flesh tightened and tingled under his tantalising touch. He was propped up on one elbow, his other hand moving to the V of her bathrobe near her breasts.

'May I touch you?'

His voice was husky with desire, and it made her own desire escalate. But then a tiny fear crept up on her...what if he was disappointed by her body? What if he compared her to all the other lovers he had had before? Vic must have seen the shadow of fear in her face for he brought his hand up to the curve of her cheek and cradled it gently.

'Hey, you have no need to be worried I won't find you attractive. Can't you already feel what you do to me?'

Addie could. His body was rock-hard against her thigh, his eyes glinting with unmistakable lust. She ran the tip of her tongue over her lips and gave a flickering smile. 'I've never felt beautiful in my life. It's hard to feel confident about my body when it's always been compared to my mother's perfect one.'

Vic's gaze darkened as he frowned. 'You are your own unique person. I find your natural beauty captivating. You don't need the enhancement of makeup or fancy clothes, although it has to be said at this point, I'm dying to get this bathrobe off you so I can touch you all over.'

Addie shuddered from delight at the erotic promise of his words. 'Touch me, please?' She gave her permission in a soft voice, but her body was shouting out for him in so many other ways. Heat pounded through her veins; the searing heat of lust let loose. Her breasts tingled behind the barrier of the bathrobe, her nipples hardening to peaks. Her flesh ached for his touch, her mouth longed for more of his passionate kisses, her inner core pulsed for his possession.

Vic slowly parted her robe, sliding his broad warm hand against the soft flesh of her breast, and she gasped at the expertise of his touch. He bent his head to her breast, his mouth moving around her tight nipple in a teasing touch that sent a shudder of pleasure through her entire body. His hand was gentle, so sensually gentle that she arched up to encourage more of his touch. He lowered his mouth to her breast, licking the circle of her areola and she whimpered as more tingling sensations coursed through her body. He took her nipple into his mouth, rolling his tongue over and around her tightened flesh, making her gasp and writhe with pleasure. Then he drew on her nipple with gentle little sucks that made her mouth drop open in a gasp of delight. He moved to her other breast, subjecting it to the same exquisite torture, sending riotous pulses of delight through her body. Her spine arched some more, her need for him rising like a tide. A flood of desire swept through her, making it hard to think of anything but the need clamouring through her body.

Vic lifted his head to gaze down at her. 'You are so damn beautiful, your skin is like satin, so soft, so smooth. I want to taste all of you.'

Addie blinked. Did he mean what she thought he meant? No one had ever touched her down there. She rarely touched herself as she had been too caught up in the years of shame she had inherited from her mother's comments. Her body, her needs had been poisoned by the shame of not feeling good enough, but with Vic, she could feel a few layers of that encrusted shame sloughing away.

She looked up into his eyes, amazed at herself for being so open with him, but hadn't he made her feel that way? Safe for the first time in her life. Safe to be herself, safe to express her needs and wants, safe to respond to those needs without shame or embarrassment. 'I'd like you to touch me…everywhere…' Her voice came out as a husky whisper, a plea for more of his sensual touch.

'I'd like you to touch me too, but I need to get out of my clothes first. Are you comfortable with me doing that?'

'Yes, I am. I want to see you,' Addie said, unashamed of how eager she was to see the male planes and contours of his body.

'How about you undo my shirt buttons.'

'Okay…' She lifted her hands to the front of his shirt, working on each of his buttons, but the task was made all the more complex because of the excitement building in her body. Her breath caught at the back of her throat as she exposed the sculpted muscles of his chest. His skin was like hot satin under her hands, and she wanted to caress his entire body, to feel it move and twitch with pleasure as hers had already done under his sublime caresses. Emboldened by every button she got undone, she leaned closer to brush her lips to his chest. He tasted salty and tangy, and she was instantly addicted as if she had just consumed a potent drug. She undid three more of his buttons, her heart rate pounding as she got closer to the waistband of his trousers. She glanced at the tented shape of him, her pulse racing to think of him so aroused for her.

'You can go further if you feel comfortable with that,' Vic said in a hoarse-sounding voice.

'Are you sure?'

He gave a wry laugh, his dark eyes crinkling at the corners. 'Absolutely.'

Addie tugged his shirt out of the waistband of his trousers, her gaze focussed on her task, the thought of uncovering him both exciting and nerve-racking. She was so inexperienced she didn't even know how to touch him. Would he think her ignorant and naive or would he find it refreshing to be with someone so new to intimacy? She undid the last of his shirt buttons and slid her hands over the broad expanse of his tanned and toned chest. 'I've never done this before,' she confessed, flicking her gaze upwards to meet his.

Vic captured one of her hands and held it against his chest. She could feel the hammer blow of his heart against the flesh of her palm, and it made her want him even more. 'Don't be nervous. I want you to be comfortable with every step we take. And remember, at any point you can say no.'

'Thank you for making me feel so…so safe and listened to,' Addie said, her gratefulness for his sensitivity to her needs making her crush on him move to another level—a level scarily close to love. She wasn't supposed to fall in love with him—those were the rules he had set down. This was a one-off affair that they would put behind them once they left Italy. But how could she not fall in love with him after he kissed her? How could she not fall in love with him after he touched her so tenderly, so passionately? The feelings she was trying to control were not able to be controlled. They were an unstoppable wave washing over her.

Vic lowered his head to kiss her once more, his mouth soft and yet insistent against hers. A drumbeat of lust pounded through her lower body, her female flesh on fire. His tongue touched hers and molten lava flowed straight to her core. She had no idea her body was capable of such rampant, rabid desire. It was like a wild thing had been unleashed inside her body, a wild energy that refused to be constrained any longer.

Vic raised his mouth from hers, his lips going to the side of her neck, caressing her sensitive skin until she was writhing beneath him. His mouth came back to hers with a hungry kiss that spoke of his own primal passion. With her mouth fused to his, she slowly peeled his shirt from his shoulders, and he did the rest by shrugging it off, tossing it to the floor beside the bed. Vic raised his head to look down at her and Addie feasted her eyes on the broad expanse of his chest, her hands moving over him, exploring the hard planes and contours of his body, her own body tingling with excitement.

'Don't be shy,' he said in a husky tone. 'You can touch me anywhere you want to.'

Addie put her hands to the waistband of his trousers, her fingers almost trembling as her need for him grew. Emboldened by her own desire and encouraged by his for her, she became more confident and unfastened his trousers. He helped her by sliding down his zipper but then left the rest to her. She drew in a skittery breath and stroked her fingers over the swollen length of him covered by his underwear. He sucked in a ragged breath and his eyes glittered with pleasure.

'Your touch drives me wild,' he said.

'That's only fair since yours does that to me.' Addie grew even bolder in her exploration of his form. She peeled his underwear away from the proud length of him and tentatively touched him along his shaft. He was satin-covered steel, potent and yet strangely vulnerable, strong, and yet sensitive. But didn't that describe not just his body but his whole personality?

Vic drew her hand away from his body but kept hold of her hand in the cradle of his, holding it against his abdomen. She could feel the ridges of his muscles beneath her hand, his strength exciting her even more.

He looked down at her with his dark glinting gaze, his features contorted by raw desire. 'I want to kiss my way down your body.'

'Okay…' Addie was barely capable of anything but that single word, her body on fire for more of his touch.

He worked his way from her neck to her breasts, kissing and caressing each in turn, sending her senses into a tailspin as her flesh came alive under his tantalising touch. He moved from her breasts to press soft barely touching kisses all the way down to her belly. She automatically sucked in her abdomen, hoping he didn't think she was judging herself for not being reed slim.

Vic propped himself up on one elbow to gaze into her eyes, his hand gently stroking her face. 'Hey, relax for me. You won't enjoy yourself if you're all tensed up.'

Addie slowly let out her breath and gave him a twisted little smile. 'Sorry. I can't help worrying you'll find me…unattractive or—'

He placed his finger against her lips. 'No more talk of me not finding you attractive. Can't you feel what you're doing to me?'

Addie could and it made her blood race and her heart pound and her desire for him to run wild. His body was rock-hard against her, and his breathing as hectic as hers. She could see the desire in his eyes, and it made her feel beautiful for the first time in her life. Beautiful and desirable.

He removed his finger from her lips and replaced it with his mouth, kissing her deeply and passionately. Addie's hands moved through the thick strands of his hair in a caressing motion, caught up in the maelstrom of physical need that was a force she could not control. She had no idea her body could feel this way, this primal drumbeat of lust that overtook everything else. Vic moved from her mouth back down her body, gently pushing the bathrobe out of his way, kissing every inch of her, sending her into new raptures of delight.

And then he came to the heart of her…

Addie held her breath, shocked at the intimacy but captivated by it too. His mouth moved over her female flesh, tasting her, separating her, allowing her time to get used to him being so close to the most intimate part of her body. He gently opened her with a stroke of his tongue, the erotic caress making her toes curl and powerful sensations to course through her lower body. He went deeper, tasting her essence, devouring her like he was addicted to the nectar of her female body. He flicked his tongue against the swollen nub of her clitoris, sending an earthquake through her flesh. She was riding a tidal wave, caught up in its powerful energy and momentum, tossing, turning and twirling her until she was gasping and crying out loud with noises so primal, they were faintly shocking to someone as shy as her. But she had no control over it. Trying to stop the forces moving through her body would be like trying to stop a hurricane. You couldn't. It would blow you away up, up, up into the atmosphere. Ripples of aftershocks pulsed through Addie's body, leaving her breathless until every muscle in her body relaxed as if her skeleton had been liquified.

'That was…' Addie struggled to find the words and looked at Vic in a kind of stunned wonder. 'How did you *do* that?'

He gave her a quizzical look. 'You haven't had an orgasm before? Even by yourself?'

Addie could feel a hot blush creeping over her cheeks. How naive and innocent and ignorant he must think her. 'I've always felt so much shame about my body that I haven't explored it properly. And it didn't help that the one time I was about to have sex with someone when I was a teenager, he told me he only wanted to sleep with me so he could boast about it to his friends that he had "done" Solange Featherstone's daughter.'

Vic's dark brows snapped together. 'He actually said that? What a jerk.'

Addie nodded, lowering her gaze to look at Vic's sensual mouth. 'I was lucky I had time to get away from him before it went any further, but the whole experience turned me off ever dating again. I could never decide if someone wanted to be with me for me or just because of who my mother was.' She let out a fluttering breath and added, 'It's been lonely to tell you the truth.'

Vic lifted her chin, so her gaze came back to his. His features were softened in compassion, and it made it even harder for her to keep her feelings out of their relationship. 'I'm so sorry you went through that. It was despicable of that guy to use you like that. It's dehumanising and disrespectful and he should have known better.'

Addie gave a tremulous smile, and he lowered his mouth to hers in a soft as air kiss, lifting off again to look down at her. 'Sex is complicated at the best of times, but it is particularly so when two people aren't meeting as equals in the relationship. I want us to be equally invested in everything we do together.'

'I want that too.' But how could she be his equal when he had sworn off ever falling in love? His heart was locked away, off limits, cordoned off because of the tragic things that had happened in his childhood. Was she being foolish to make love with him when he had already told her there was no possibility of them taking their relationship further than a short-term, perhaps only one-off event? She wasn't experienced enough in the rules of modern dating. All she knew was she was falling in love with him. It had started the first time she had met him, and it had grown with every subsequent meeting. But it had taken spending time with him, getting to know him, seeing him for the man he was behind the playboy supersuccessful businessman persona he presented to the world. He was sensitive, deep, caring and thoughtful. How could she not fall desperately in love with him?

Vic brought his mouth back down to hers in a longer kiss this time, his tongue calling hers into sensual play. She could taste the salt and musk of her body on his lips, and it excited her in a way she had never thought possible. It added another layer of intimacy that made her feel as if something had shifted in the dynamic between them. Something unique and special that could not be so easily undone.

Vic kissed his way from her mouth back to her breasts again, his lips and tongue teasing and tantalising her. Addie was aware of his arousal hot and heavy and hard against her and marvelled at his self-control. Or was he taking his time for her sake? Making sure she didn't feel rushed or pressured.

'Aren't you going to…?' She left the sentence hanging, suddenly too shy to say the words out loud.

Vic stroked a tendril of hair away from her face, his eyes bottomless pools of black ink. 'I want you so badly as you can probably tell, but I don't want to rush you. I want you to be ready for me, so you don't feel any pain.'

'I'm ready for you,' Addie said in a breathless whisper. 'So, so ready.' Hadn't she been ready from his first kiss? Her body had responded to his like a flower does to the warmth of the sun after a bleak and bitterly cold winter.

Vic kissed her again, deeply, urgently, his hands moving over her body in strokes and caresses that sent her pulse rate soaring. But then he pulled back again, his breathing uneven. 'I need to put on a condom.' He shifted away from her and stood from the bed to step out of his shoes and socks and trousers and underwear. They were such mundane everyday actions but in this context of huge significance to her. He was revealing all of himself to her as she had done to him. She drank in the sight of his tanned and toned and aroused body, her heart picking up its pace at the sheer beauty of him. He was a man in the prime of his life, athletic without being overly so. Toned and taut in a healthy, not obsessive way. He took a condom out of the bedside drawer and removed it from its wrapper, deftly applying it as if he had done it a thousand times before. But then, he probably *had* done it a thousand times before.

Addie was not aware of any change in her expression, but Vic must have read her mind, for he came back beside her, seated this time, and took one of her hands in his. He brought it up to his chest, holding it against the tum-tippy-tum-tippy-tum of his heart.

'I know what you're thinking.' There was a level of gravitas to his tone.

Addie held his gaze with an effort. 'What am I thinking?'

'That I've done this a heap of times, and you're just one woman in a long list of others who've shared my bed.'

Addie gave a tiny grimace. 'Okay, so you can mind read as well as kiss like a dream.'

Vic pressed her hand a little harder to his chest, his eyes warm and tender in a way that made her heart contract. 'This is a new experience for me, to be with someone who has never made love with anyone before.'

Addie tilted head at him. 'Are you nervous?'

His mouth twisted in a wry smile. 'A little.'

'But you're so experienced. Why would you be nervous about doing something that comes so naturally to you?'

He brought her hand up to his mouth and pressed his lips to her bent knuckles, his eyes still holding hers. 'I want this experience to be something special, not something you look back on with regret or shame. But you have to realise this is just sex. It's not a promise to be together for ever. You have to understand this is all I can give you.'

Right now, all Addie wanted was his body, but at the back of her mind a little voice was warning her that while this encounter would no doubt be wonderful, it wouldn't satisfy her need for the love and acceptance she had craved all her life. It was a one-off, a box ticked, a deed done, a goal accomplished. It was not a commitment to live in harmony for the rest of their days. 'I understand that.' She injected her voice with as much conviction as possible. 'This is just sex. My first, and your first with a first-timer.'

He kept her hand in his and came down on the bed beside her, propping himself up on one elbow, his long legs brushing against hers. 'Once we do this, there's no turning back the clock. It will permanently change our…relationship.' His hesitation over the word *relationship* made her wonder if he was concerned at how they would interact in the future. Was he worried she might embarrass him by following him around like a lovesick fool? Was he worried she would want more than this one encounter? That she would want commitment, marriage, babies, a future? That whenever they were in each other's company she might make a fool of herself fawning over him just because he had been her first lover?

'If you're worried I'm going to tell everyone we slept together, think again. I'm a very private person.'

'That's not what worries me at all.' Vic's voice contained a serious note, his expression reflecting his concern.

'Are you worried *you* might want more?' Addie wasn't sure why she asked such a bold question, but it came out before she could monitor her tongue.

His dark eyes were like a light flickering during a glitch in a power supply. 'Right now, I do want more. I want you.'

And his mouth came down and set hers alight all over again.

CHAPTER NINE

VIC PRESSED HIS mouth to Addie's and had trouble keeping a lid on his passion for her. Her lips were soft and sweet and supple and moulded to his as if made specially for him. Her tongue met his shyly at first, but then with growing confidence she kissed him back with an eroticism that threatened to blow the top of his head off.

Touching her skin was like touching the finest satin, her body was slim but curvy in the right places. And those places set him on fire. He was aching to be inside her, but he needed to take things slowly, to make sure she was adequately prepared. Being with Addie was so different from his usual hook-ups. There were even a couple of encounters where he hadn't even bothered to remember the person's name. It had only been about the physical release, mutual of course, because he was a giver, not a taker. Sex for him had to be a two-way deal, but it had never been this personal, intimate…undoable.

He was crossing a boundary he had never crossed before. A boundary he had never even considered until the night he had picked her up to bring her to his villa. Yes, he was aware of her infatuation with him at the engagement party and then the wedding of her brother and his half-sister, but back then it had mildly amused him. It had not been something he had thought he would ever act upon. Addie was so different from the women he dated in that she was unworldly, shy and totally unaware of how beautiful she was, not just in looks but in nature. There was a caring sweetness about her that was captivating. He had found himself telling her about his childhood, the loss of his father, the treatment of his stepfather, his difficult relationship with his mother—all things he had spoken to no one about before, not even Marcus, his closest friend. Somehow Addie had got him to open up about things he had shoved so deep inside him he had almost forgotten they were there. Almost.

Addie murmured her encouragement against his mouth and Vic deepened the kiss, breathing in the flowery scent of her hair and skin, relishing in the addictive taste of her. He moved over her, half across her body, conscious of his weight on her slighter frame. He raised himself up on his elbows either side of her body, his gaze dipping to her mouth, pink and swollen from his kisses. 'You have such a kissable mouth.'

She smiled and her tawny brown eyes shone. 'I like the way you kiss me.'

Vic smiled and leaned down to press another kiss to her lips. 'I enjoy kissing you.'

A little too much... a tiny voice said inside his head.

If he was having trouble resisting kissing her, what was it going to be like making love to her? It was a risk he was prepared to take. It was a little frightening how much he wanted her. He hadn't expected the chemistry between them to erupt as it had. It had flared like a match to tinder, sending flames of need through his body at their first kiss.

He lifted his mouth off hers, positioning himself close to the place he most wanted to be. His body burned with need, tight and hot with it and yet he was prepared to stop if she wasn't ready or changed her mind. 'Are you sure about this?' he asked.

Addie took his face in her hands and eyeballed him. 'I want you.'

'I want you too. So much.' Had he wanted anyone this much? Not in a long time.

She moved against him, instinctively offering herself to him. He slipped a hand down to the heart of her feminine form, sliding a gentle finger inside, watching her face for any sign of discomfort. 'Mmm...' She murmured in pleasure, her mouth falling open on a soft gasp. 'That feels so good...'

Vic positioned himself at her entrance, balancing his weight on his forearms, taking his time to move inside her, inch by inch, gauging her response every step of the way. Her body gripped him tightly and he shuddered with pleasure, desperate to glide faster but sensing she would need to get used to the heft of him inside her. He could be patient—sure he could. But, hot damn, how wonderful did it feel to be so welcomed.

'How are you doing?' he asked, his voice coming out hoarse from trying to maintain control.

'I'm doing fine,' she said, looking up at him as if in wonder, her eyes shining. 'It doesn't hurt at all.'

'I'll go slowly so you get used to me.' He did as he promised, slow shallow thrusts, gradually going deeper, faster, enjoying the tight grip of her body and the sounds of pleasure she was giving. She moved with him, catching his rhythm, her breathing as breathless as his as the tempo of lust climbed. He moved his fingers against the tender flesh of her womanhood, watching her come apart under his touch, feeling her contract and pulse around him. Her cries were wild and unrestrained, earthy, and raw and it sent shivers down his spine to see her so undone. He waited until she was through the other side of her orgasm before he let himself go. He surged forward with a low, deep growl of primal ecstasy, his skin tingling all over, his thoughts lost in the maelstrom, the expulsion of his essence sending him somewhere he had never been before.

Vic was unable to move for some moments, the aftershocks of his orgasm still rolling through him in blissful waves. He was aware of her arms around him, her legs still entwined with his, their bodies as closely connected as two people could be. He listened to her breathing slowly come back to normal, his own taking a little longer. His head was near her neck, and he turned to press a soft kiss to the scented skin below her ear.

'Am I too heavy for you?'

Her hands began to stroke his back and shoulders and he shivered in delight. 'No, not at all.' There was a tiny pause and she added, 'Was it…good for you?'

Vic raised himself up so he could see her face. He

brushed a wayward strand of hair away from her face and smiled down at her. 'You blew me away.'

Surprise and relief and delight lit her gaze. 'I did?'

'You did.' He pressed a lingering kiss to her lips, lifting off to gaze down at her again. 'How was it for you?'

A soft blush crept into her cheeks. 'I didn't realise it could be that wonderful, so enthralling that I'd completely forget everything but what was happening in my body.'

Vic was used to sex; he would even say he had lately become a little jaded about his numerous casual encounters, but nothing about what had just occurred between Addie and him had been mundane. It had been magnificent, magical, mind-blowing. And that was a huge concern to him. He wasn't supposed to be feeling anything but physical release. That was the deal. No emotions, just plain old sex. But how could he have fooled himself that having sex with Addie would be plain old sex? Was it because it had been her first time? That he was so conscious of her every response, her every breath and movement that it had somehow elevated the experience to something unique? Who was he kidding? Of course it had been unique. She had given him permission to be her first lover. He wasn't the sort of man to see a woman's virginity as some sort of prize or trophy to claim. It had certainly never been on his wish list of things to do. And yet, now that he'd made love with Addie, it felt like something different had occurred, something that had never happened to him before. Something shifted inside him, something that had been frozen, locked away, deadened. It had flickered, then taken a shallow breath, moved, stretched like something waking from a long hibernation. It was still quietly residing inside him, not asleep but not fully awake either. Somehow, he had to shut it back down, get it back into sleep mode because there was no way he was allowing it to come to life.

Addie was still stunned by the explosion that occurred in her body. She was lying beside him, one of his arms loosely around her shoulders, their legs touching. Vic had removed the condom and disposed of it moments earlier, then come back to her to lie down beside her. Was sex always that good? That amazing? Or had it been because Vic had taken his time with her, been so gentle and considerate, putting her needs ahead of his?

She was *so* grateful he was her first lover. So pleased he had agreed to making love with her so she could replace those embarrassing memories from when she was a teenager. Vic had made her feel wanted, desired and he had made her feel beautiful. She hadn't felt the need to cover herself, to hide her body from him; instead she had been open and uninhibited, his kisses and caresses freeing her from her prison of shame.

Addie turned her head to look at him. 'Vic?'

'Mmm.' He had his eyes closed and was breathing deeply and evenly, as if he had relaxed so much, he couldn't move a muscle.

'What was your first time like?'

Vic turned his head to lock gazes with her, his expression rueful. 'Rushed, embarrassing, awkward.' He ran a fingertip down the length of her sternum, his touch light but electrifying. 'I was seventeen and the girl who was nineteen was way more experienced. I made sure I worked on my technique after that.'

'It's certainly paid off.' Addie waited a beat before adding, 'No doubt there are a lot of very grateful women out there.' And now she was one of them. One woman in a long line of women. And she wouldn't be the last. Many would come after her, no pun intended. What right did she have to think his time with her would make him change his casual dating ways? Sure, it had been special for her, how could it not be? But to Vic Jacobetti it was probably just sex. But it wasn't just sex for her. Making love with him had shown her the depth of her feelings for him, the way they had grown from a crush to genuine love. She admired him, trusted him, wanted to be with him longer than this short time in Lake Como but how could she ask him to extend their time together? He had laid down the conditions and she had accepted them.

A frown formed on his forehead and his expression became serious. 'I know what you read about me in the press is entertaining and salacious at times, but a lot of it isn't true.'

Addie raised her eyebrows. 'Are you saying you're not a profligate playboy?'

Vic's mouth twisted in a rueful manner. 'I'm too busy running my hotel empire to have as many lovers as the press make out. I only have to be seen in the company of someone for the press to jump to conclusions.'

Addie thought about the women they had passed

while they were shopping and the comment one of them made about her. 'Not beautiful enough to be his lover.' But what if someone else had seen her with Vic and sent a photo to the press?

Vic reached up to smooth her frown away. 'What's that serious look for, hmm?'

Addie drew in an uneven breath. 'You know we're only a photo away from being exposed. Those women down when we were shopping—'

'Were wrong, for one thing,' Vic interjected. 'You are beautiful.'

As much as his compliment thrilled her, she still was worried about how the press would portray her. And if they realised she was Solange Featherstone's daughter, there would be comparisons for sure and not flattering ones towards her. 'But what if the press was to find out? And how will we explain it to Marcus and Isabella?'

He stroked his finger down the slope of her nose in a tender fashion. 'Let's not worry about things that might not eventuate. This is between us for now.'

Addie captured her lower lip in her teeth, her gaze slipping out of reach of his. 'I'd better go and check on Katerina. She often wakes this time of night.' She moved out of his loose hold and getting off the bed, slipped her bathrobe back on, tying it securely around her waist. Leaving to check on Katerina was an excuse to put some distance between them, to collect her thoughts, to reflect on her situation now that she recognised she was in love with him. She didn't want to make a fool of herself by suddenly blurting it out, especially so soon after making love with him. It would make her appear an even more naive and gauche person than she already was.

'Addie.' His firm deep voice sent her gaze back to his. 'The app on my phone will alert us to Katerina waking. Stay for a bit longer.' He patted the bed she had just vacated but somehow, she summoned up some willpower and resisted.

'I need to use the bathroom.' She gave a self-conscious smile and added, 'And I know this sounds terribly unsexy, but I'm starving.'

He gave a deep rumble of laughter and tossed off the sheet that was half covering him. 'You go and do what you need to do, I'll check on Katerina and then I'll make us some supper, okay?'

'It sounds wonderful.' And it did. But she was a fool to think this fairytale was going to last. A romantic location, mind-blowing sex, a handsome and tender lover, a midnight supper with only the moon watching on. It all sounded so dreamy, something she had never thought could ever happen to her. But the sooner she accepted this was temporary, the better. But oh, how she wished it could be for ever.

A short time later, Vic stood over Katerina's cot watching as she slept deeply. He could see his friend's features in his goddaughter's angelic face, but he could also see his half-sister's Italian colouring and even his mother. Genetics was an intriguing thin…how it passed on DNA from previous generations.

He had ruled out having children of his own because he didn't want any child of his suffering the loss he had suffered. Losing his father so young had made it impossible for him to envisage a life where he would be responsible for keeping his loved ones safe. Every day on the news, families of all shapes and sizes were shattered by tragedy. There was no escaping the vicissitudes of life and his only way to navigate through it was to control what he could. He could avoid grief by not loving someone the way he had loved his father.

But looking down at little Katerina, so soon after making love with Addie, made him begin to realise what he was missing out on. There would be no day in the future when he would look down at his own sleeping child. There would be no day when he would watch that child grow from an infant to an adult.

Those thoughts had never bothered him before. He had simply dismissed them, not allowing them any traction in his mind. But making love with sweet and innocent Addie this evening had triggered something inside him. A sliding doors moment. Something that made him wonder what his life would look like a couple of decades from now. Would he still be satisfied with the long hours he worked, the financial success he had accumulated, the no-strings casual dating he engaged in?

He had poured so much of his time and energy into his company, rebuilding it from the ruins his stepfather had left it in. He had thrown himself into the challenge, channelling his anger at his circumstances into producing one of the most luxurious hotel chains in the world. He had done it to honour his father who had not only missed out on seeing Vic grow from child to adult but had also missed out on seeing the business he founded grow into the successful empire it was today. This very villa was going to be Vic's ultimate achievement, to turn his family home into the most salubrious hotel of the Jacobetti chain.

But would he be satisfied at all he had achieved at the end of his life? It wasn't something he had dwelt on much in his quest to build the hotel chain into what it was today. He was not unaware of people's regret at the end of their life over the choices they had made, the things they would have done differently with the benefit of hindsight. Would he be one of them? Full of regrets instead of gratefulness? And why was he bothered by these thoughts now?

Making love with Addie had been a wonderful experience; he would even go as far as saying it was the best sex he had ever had. The chemistry between them was explosive, a slow burn that had fizzed and sparked into combustible heat. The sensual touch of her hands, the sweetness of her mouth, the tight wet warmth of her body had made him feel honoured and privileged that she had chosen him to be her first lover. His body was drawn to her by an irresistible force, like lightning was drawn to metal and his pleasure had been just as earth-shattering.

He couldn't remember feeling pleasure and satisfaction like it. It was like making love for the first time but without the clumsy awkwardness and embarrassment. His body still hummed with the sensations she had evoked in his flesh; the drumbeat of ongoing lust was rumbling like background thunder.

But what to do now? Was it fair to leave it as a one-off event? Surely Addie deserved more than a one-night stand? But if he continued their sexual relationship he would be drifting into dangerous territory. There were risks involved, risks he wasn't sure he wanted to take. What if she developed feelings for him? She was not a worldly type of woman; she had zero experience in the world of casual dating. She had a big heart and it would be bruised if not broken if she wanted more than he was prepared to give. And there were other risks, ones he didn't want to acknowledge existed, but he would be a fool not to factor them in. His relationship with Addie was unlike any other in his circle of friends, unlike any of his casual encounters. She was unique and therefore he had to be careful not to trigger feelings he didn't want to possess. He wasn't incapable of love; he loved his mother and his half-sister, he loved his friends, most particularly Marcus who was the closest thing to a brother he could get. But falling in love was not something he had ever done or ever wanted to do. Addie Featherstone was someone who deserved to be loved. She deserved to be treasured and adored for a lifetime, not a short time. But Vic wasn't the man to do it. Why then did that make him feel uneasy, unsettled, edgy?

Katerina murmured in her sleep and turned her head to the other side of the cot facing the wall, and Vic held his breath, hoping he hadn't inadvertently disturbed her slumber. But after a few more moments, she let out a sigh and settled back down again. Vic tiptoed out of the nursery, closing the door as he left. He wished he could close the door on his troubled thoughts just as securely.

* * *

Addie dawdled in the bathroom, showering, and changing into some casual clothes rather than putting the bathrobe back on. She didn't want to appear too desperate to make love with Vic again, but her body was still tingling from his possession and every now and again her belly would flip-flop as she recalled his thick presence inside her. She placed her hand on her stomach and stared at herself in the mirror. She looked the same and yet she felt so different from an hour ago. Her body was awakened to the needs she had ignored for years and it was hungry for more of Vic's touch. It was like she had tasted a potent drug and now craved her next hit. He was irresistible but hadn't she always sensed that? Her crush on him from the first time she met him should have warned her that he was danger personified. Dangerous because he had no intention of falling in love with anyone, much less someone like her. They moved in completely different worlds, he was a playboy everyone talked about, she was someone who avoided the spotlight. And she was glad not to be noticed, wasn't she? She didn't want to be compared to her gorgeous mother, nor did she want to be compared to Vic Jacobetti's gorgeous lovers. She wanted to stay out of the spotlight, to live her quiet uneventful life as before.

But…how could she now that she had tasted the delights of sexual intimacy? How could she turn the clock back and return to being that shy, innocent woman when Vic had awakened her to her sensual needs? Needs that still pulsed and throbbed inside her.

When Addie finally came downstairs, she found a light supper set out in one of the rooms off the kitchen. It had big windows that overlooked the lake and the moon high in the sky at this time of night sent a silvery beam across the water. Vic came in carrying a tray with a teapot and teacups and saucers on it and set it down on one of the side tables next to a brocade-covered sofa.

'There you go, tea for two,' Vic said, sending her a mercurial smile.

'You certainly know the way to my heart,' Addie said, then immediately wished she hadn't. It sounded like she was flirting with him, playing games of seduction she had no business playing. She lowered her gaze to the teacups on the tray, busying herself with putting milk in her cup, hoping her cheeks weren't as red as they felt.

'I was going to bring champagne but wondered if that would be appropriate.' He poured a cup of tea for her, the sound of the liquid filling her cup loud in the ensuing silence.

Addie took the cup with a hand that wasn't as steady as she would have liked. 'What would we be celebrating?' She still couldn't quite meet his gaze and carefully took a sip of the hot and fragrant tea to cover her embarrassment.

Vic sat opposite her, holding his own cup of tea, but he didn't take a sip. 'Addie.'

She slowly brought her gaze up to his inscrutable one. 'You don't have to worry, Vic, I'm not going to beg you to make love to me again.'

He frowned darkly and leaned forward to put his cup on the small table between them. 'You have regrets about making love with me?' His voice was full of concern.

'No, of course not. I just don't want you to think I'm desperate to continue our…association. I know the rules, you stated them clearly.'

There was a small pause while he stared at his cup sitting on the table as if it was completely absorbing, although the same frown was on his forehead. Then he drew in a breath, his eyes coming back to hers. 'I'm only thinking of you, *cara*. It would hurt you if we continued this for too long.'

How long was too long? A day or two? A week? A month…or more? But those were words she didn't have the courage to speak out loud. She didn't want to know the answer, was scared to hear it, so she stayed silent.

Vic rose from his chair and sent his hand through his hair, leaving wide finger trails in the thick black strands. He paced the floor a couple of times in an agitated fashion and then turned and faced her with a tortured expression on his dark features. 'It wouldn't be fair to you.'

Addie finally found her voice. 'What wouldn't be fair to me?'

'Asking you to have a fling with me.'

Addie stared at him for a moment, struck speechless all over again. Was he offering her a fling? And if he was, should she accept his offer? She tried to think through the repercussions: the possibility of the press finding out, what her brother and sister-in-law would think, what would happen when the fling ended as it most certainly would do. But then she recalled the magic of being in his arms and her body overruled the warnings of her brain. She sent the tip of her tongue out over her lips, her heart thudding in her chest like an out of rhythm drum. She put her cup down and rose from the chair and went over to him, placing a hand on his strong forearm. Her skin tingled as hers came in contact with his, her lower body smouldering with need.

'Is that what *you* want?' It was a bold question and Addie was proud of herself for asking it.

One of his hands came down over the top of her hand resting on his arm, his grasp warm and firm. His eyes blazed with heat, the same heat she could feel simmering in her body. 'I want you.' His other hand came to the small of her back and edged her closer to the hot hard heat of his body. 'I told myself I wouldn't get involved with you. I warned myself of all the dangers and yet, here I am, wanting you to say yes.'

Addie leaned into him, her excitement at being in his arms again making her almost giddy. 'I want you too. So, so much.'

He cupped her face in his both of his hands and bent down to press a lingering kiss to her mouth. She murmured her delight against his lips and his hands moved from her face to wrap around her body, holding her close once more. She could feel every erotic ridge and plane of his body against hers, and it fuelled her desire to fever pitch. A couple of hours ago she was a shy virgin, ignorant of the needs and workings of her body. But Vic Jacobetti had awakened her to a world of sensuality, an addictive world she wasn't yet ready to leave. His kiss deepened, became more urgent and passionate, and his tongue played with hers in a dance of desire that sent bubbles of excitement through her blood. She linked her arms around his neck, tilting her head to one side as he began to kiss the sensitive skin of her neck.

'Your skin tastes divine,' he growled and gave her earlobe a gentle nip that sent a hot shiver racing down her spine. 'I want to lick every inch of you.'

Addie moved her mouth to his neck, his skin raspy with its masculine regrowth abrading her softer skin in a deliciously arousing way. She stroked her tongue along his skin, tasting the salt and maleness and deciding it was her favourite flavour of all time.

Vic groaned and came back to her mouth with a kiss that set her senses on fire. His hands held her by the hips, holding her against the throbbing need of his body, so close to the pounding pulse of her own.

Later, she could barely recall how they got back upstairs but she remembered a lot of stopping and kissing along the way. By the time they got to his bedroom, she was half mad with lust and it was more than obvious so was he.

He undressed her as she undressed him, quickly, desperately. He knelt in front of her trembling body, tasting the humid heat of her and she whimpered in pleasure. He changed the speed and pressure of his tongue against that most sensitive nub of her flesh and her body suddenly erupted into a cataclysmic orgasm. An ocean broke over her, through her, within her. Waves washed, crashed, pounded and then cast her out the other side. She was breathless, panting, shaking with the delicious aftershocks that rippled through her.

Vic gently laid her back on the bed, looking at her with his dark eyes smouldering with lust. He sourced a condom and applied it, the action so stimulating to Addie, she was ready for him as soon as he joined her on the bed. He anchored his weight on his forearms, gliding inside her with exquisite gentleness but she wanted more. Much more. She gripped him by the buttocks and urged him deeper, groaning with pleasure as he responded to her encouragement with a guttural groan of his own. It was faster than the first time, fast and frenzied with electrifying fusion of their hungry bodies.

Vic lifted his mouth off hers to look at her. 'Are you sure I'm not going too fast for you? This is only your second time and I don't want to hurt you.'

Addie pulled his head back down so his mouth was close to hers. 'It didn't hurt the first time, so why would it now?'

'I just want it to be good for you.'

'It was brilliant for me before. I'm not sure how you can improve on that.'

He smiled a glinting smile. 'You just watch me, *cara*.'

CHAPTER TEN

Vic woke just before dawn and watched Addie sleeping peacefully beside him. One of her arms was flung across his chest, her head nestled against his shoulder. He breathed in the scent of her, the flowers of her perfume, the fruity fragrance of her hair, and the unique smell of her body.

These days he rarely spent the whole night with a lover because of the deeper level of intimacy it entailed. Waking beside a stranger was not something he enjoyed doing as much as he used to. But making love with Addie was nothing like a casual hook-up, far from it. It was intimate, erotic and tender in a way he hadn't expected. He had found himself offering her a fling even though he knew it was stepping over a boundary he never thought he would cross.

There were all sorts of complications in becoming involved with his best friend's sister. Keeping their involvement a secret was going to be difficult and he was uncomfortable insisting on it in case Addie thought he was somehow ashamed of their relationship. *Relationship.* That was the word he never used in the context of his sex life. But he was already in a relationship with

Addie and had been since he had been introduced to her at Marcus and Isabella's engagement party.

The weird thing was he was the reason Marcus and Isabella got together in the first place. He had never considered himself to be the matchmaking type and he had always kept his private life separate from his public life. But Isabella had been visiting him from Paris where she had been living and she was lamenting the poor state of her dating life. Vic invited Marcus over on a whim, thinking it couldn't hurt for his half-sister to meet his friend to show her not all men were bastards, and the rest, as they say, was history. Vic wasn't a believer in love at first sight, but even as cynical as he was, he had to admit his friend and his half-sister certainly fell for each other rapidly. They were only dating a couple of months when they announced their engagement.

And that was when Addie entered Vic's life.

He turned his head so he could plant a soft kiss to the top of her head. She stirred against him, murmuring something, then nestling back against him like a sleepy kitten. Something shifted inside his chest, a tightness loosening, a locked door cracking open to allow a tiny beam of light into the darkness. Vic gave himself a mental shake. He was getting sentimental over Addie allowing him to be her first lover, that's all it was. He was in new territory, unfamiliar territory where it was impossible to completely cordon off his feelings. He wouldn't be human if he didn't feel *something*, but what it was made no sense to him. He wasn't the falling in love type. He had never experienced the overwhelming sense of rightness other people talked about when they met their soulmate. He had bedmates, not soulmates and he didn't intend for that to change.

But...

Something stirred deep inside him as Addie lay sleeping in his arms. He fought against it, not wanting to allow his feelings to get out of control. He could not undo their lovemaking. And it had been lovemaking, not sex. Sex could be intimate and tender for him, but never had it been *this* intimate and tender. Their intimacy would always be something they had shared. Something unique and special, something she could never experience again and he suspected nor would he. The uniqueness of their physical union encased it in an impermeable membrane of memory. He would never be able to erase it from his mind. He could never erase it from his body, for even now, hours after they had made love, his body hummed with pleasure, with aftershocks and tingles that made his body feel alive and vital in a way it had never done before.

Addie moved again and opened her eyes, blinking up at him. A delicate blush formed on her cheeks and her smile was shy but it still was like a ray of bright sunshine. 'Good morning.'

Vic repositioned himself so he could press a kiss to her lips. *'Buongiorno, bella.'*

Her lips clung to his, so he went back for seconds, enjoying the feel of her soft lips moving against his with enthusiasm and stirring passion. He loved her responsiveness to him, the way she gave of herself so freely, so openly. Her mouth opened under his and he slipped his tongue through her parted lips, the eroticism of their tongues meeting making his spine loosen and his blood to pound in his groin. How was he to control this rabid rush of feeling? He wanted her like an addict wanted a drug. A drug they had not realised they had no immunity to its powerful potency. Vic was so hard for her he ached. He burned. His heart slammed against the wall of his chest as her lips and tongue kissed him back with equal passion. Her legs were entangled with his, her soft breasts pressed up against his chest. He removed his mouth from hers to kiss each breast in turn, stroking his tongue over her tightly budded nipples, delighting in the taste and texture of her body.

Addie arched her spine like a languorous cat and he moved his mouth down between her breasts, then all the way down to her bellybutton. Her skin was like satin, her soft whimpers of pleasure and encouragement sending him wild with desire.

He had to end this madness but how? He wanted her so much it was impossible to think of a time when he wouldn't want her. He knew he was wading in dangerous new waters, waters so deep and treacherous he could find himself in trouble—the sort of trouble he had thus far avoided. Attachment. He feasted on her body, enjoying every gasp and groan of pleasure she made. He couldn't allow himself to think of the time when they would no longer have the enjoyment of each other's bodies.

This was for now, not for ever.

Addie wasn't sure how she managed to do it, but when Marcus and Isabella finally arrived the following day, she acted as if nothing had changed between her and Vic. But in some ways, it was easier to do so because the parents were so desperate to be reunited with their little girl, their attention was on Katerina, not on Addie or Vic. She was secretly impressed with Vic's coolly impassive manner towards her considering the passion they had shared the night before, but she caught him looking at her when Marcus and Isabella were preoccupied with Katerina and his eyes glittered with raw longing. It triggered a flood of desire in her body, a tidal wave of lust that no number of sandbags of common sense could withstand. Her crush had moved from nine to ten as soon as he made love to her. She was madly, foolishly in love with him.

Vic had mentioned to her the night before that they would leave as soon as possible after Marcus and Isabella arrived, so Addie had already packed her things, including her new things.

Marcus came over when it was time to say goodbye and gave Addie a warm hug. 'Thank you so much for helping out. We knew our little angel would be safe with you and Vic.'

Isabella too, came to hug her. 'We can't thank you and Vic enough. I was out of my mind with worry until I knew you were coming to the rescue.'

Addie smiled and slipped out of Isabella's embrace, not wishing to reveal how emotional she was feeling about leaving, not just Katerina but this lovely old villa with all the beautiful moments she had shared in it with Vic. Moments that would never be repeated for soon it would be turned into a plush hotel, a showpiece for his chain of hotels, not the home she envisaged it as in her dreams.

Vic led her out to the chauffeur-driven car half an hour later. He waited until they were both seated and belted in and the glass partition closed before he glanced her way. 'There's something I want to ask you.'

Addie moistened her dry lips. 'Ask away.'

He reached for her hand and drew it towards him, resting it on top of his muscled thigh. 'Have dinner with me tomorrow night?'

Addie frowned. 'You mean in public? Like on date or something?'

A flicker of annoyance moved through his gaze, but he covered it quickly with a wry smile. 'Do you think it's too dangerous?'

Of course it was dangerous. She was at risk of spilling out her feelings for one thing. 'You're not concerned about being seen with me? I mean, we were lucky Marcus and Isabella didn't suspect anything, but if we were photographed…' She couldn't finish the sentence, not wanting to say out loud the scenario that played out in her head.

Vic gave her hand a gentle squeeze. 'Look at me, *cara*.' His deep voice had a note of command to it that made it impossible to do anything but meet his gaze. He brought her hand up to his mouth, kissing each of her stiff fingers. She could feel herself relaxing, melting like candlewax as his dark gleaming eyes held hers. 'I thought I'd made it clear I want to see you when we get back to London. We can keep it private. My staff will not breach my privacy or yours.'

Addie suddenly realised she was at a crossroads in her life. A turning point that would dictate how the rest of her life would play out. It was up to her to decide what would be the best thing for her to do. She could settle for a private fling or she could ask for the moon. There were no other options open to her. She wanted the fairytale. She wanted to be wanted for her. She wanted to be wanted for ever. Somehow, she kept her features neutral even though her heart was cracking like a porcelain egg. 'Do you really think it's possible to keep it private?'

One side of his mouth lifted. 'It's worth a try, *si*?'

Addie gently removed her hand from his hold, garnering as much resolved as she could to withstand the temptation of him. Of what he was offering. A fling. Who knew for how long? And how could it not become public? One whiff of their relationship and the world would be commenting on it, *on her* within seconds. She looked down at her hands clasped tightly in her lap, taking a deep breath for courage, for strength, for resilience. She had so much more to lose than him if their fling became public. He was used to being in the spotlight; she had avoided it all of her adult life. She would be crucified by the exposure. Why had she thought she could have any sort of involvement with Vic Jacobetti? It was madness on her part to dream of a happy-ever-after with a hardened playboy, a man who had sworn he would never love, never settle down, never have a family—the family she realised she wanted. Her maternal feelings could no longer be ignored. They had been stirred into life by caring for her little niece. She could not ignore them any more. She was twenty-eight years old. She didn't want to be on her own any more, her life containing nothing but her work and her hobby of knitting coats for cold old dogs. She had to get a life before it passed her by. She had to be realistic and accept that unless Vic returned even a fraction of her feelings there was no future for them.

'Addie?' There was a quality to his voice she had never heard before, an uncertain edge that made her wonder if she was wrong about him. But wasn't that her foolish heart trying to trick her into believing what she wanted to believe instead of what was true?

Addie turned to look at him. 'As much as I want to continue our…relationship, I can't.'

His gaze flickered like a computer screen having a momentary glitch. 'What?' The one word was so harshly delivered she jumped. 'Sorry,' he said, but continued to frown at her. 'Are you saying you don't want to continue our fling?'

She held his incredulous look with firm resolve. Firmer than she had ever believed herself capable of before. 'I want more than a fling, Vic. I want what most people want if they're honest with themselves. I want to be loved—I want to be in a proper committed relationship, one where I can look forward to the future. I want what Marcus and Isabella have. Love, a family, a future, security.'

She saw his throat tighten over a swallow and then his gaze shifted, his frown carving more deeply into his forehead making him look severe, unapproachable. He took a moment before he locked his dark and unreadable eyes back on hers. 'This seems rather sudden, does it not?'

Addie forced herself to hold his intimidating gaze. 'I know you don't want to hear this, but I've developed feelings for you.'

There was a beat or two of heavy silence broken only by the hum of the car's engine and the swish of the tyres on the road as a light shower of rain had begun to fall.

He seemed to be rehearsing his response inside his head before he actually delivered it. She saw the micro expressions on his face: irritation, frustration, impatience…and something else that looked faintly like acute disappointment. But again, surely, she was wrong about that.

'You're infatuated with me. Believe me, it will pass once you get to know me better.'

His coldly delivered statement was like a sledgehammer through the thin ice of her hope. Did he feel anything for her? Anything at all? 'I don't think you will allow anyone to get to know you, not really know you, especially with a time limit on our relationship. You can't offer your full self if you don't offer the potential of a future. I know you think I'm just crushing on you like the first three times I met you, but I know now what love is.' She placed one of her hands on her heart. 'I feel it here. I feel it with every beat of my heart.'

Vic reached for her hand and brought it to his own chest, placing it against the solid thump, thump, thump of his heart. His expression was less severe now, with a touch of sadness in his eyes. 'I never wanted you to get hurt, not by me, not like this. I can't offer you what you want.' He swallowed again and continued, 'I'm sorry, *cara*, but I don't feel the same way.' He gave her hand a gentle squeeze and added, 'Don't be insulted or hurt by that, please. It's just the way I am.'

Addie wondered if that was strictly true. He had loved and loved deeply as a child, but losing his father had torn his tender heart in two and now he was unable to allow himself to be vulnerable in any relationship, even that with his family members. But she had seen glimpses of his potential to be more than he allowed himself to be—the way he took care of Katerina, for instance, the tenderness in his smile, the laughter in his eyes when she did something cute or mischievous. Addie had even seen it in his treatment of her, the way he kissed her, touched her, looked at her, held her. But while Addie was patient, she did not want to take the chance and end up even more heartbroken when their involvement ended as it would certainly do unless Vic opened his heart to her. Or at least admitted there was the potential for his feelings to develop, rather than say he would never love anyone, including her.

'I don't believe that is just the way you are,' Addie said, taking her hand back. 'It's the way you are now, yes, but not who you are at your core. You're afraid to love in case you lose it. Like I've been afraid my whole life to be me, to stand up for myself and claim my space in the world. But I have you to thank for helping me come out of my shell. I think you made me see myself differently and I thank you for that and I hope we can always be friends, or at least be civil towards each other for the sake of Marcus and Isabella and Katerina.'

Vic gently flicked her cheek with a careless finger, his eyes softening. 'I want to be angry with you, but I find I can't.' He gave a lopsided smile and added, 'This is a new experience for me.' He looked at her mouth for a long moment. 'Unique, in fact.'

'What do you mean?'

His eyes came back to hers, a rueful expression on his face. 'I'm usually the one who ends a fling. I'm always the first to let go.'

'I guess that's a control thing, right? You've been traumatised by loss so young that you won't allow yourself to be again. It's completely understandable, but I'm not sure it's going to be good for you in the long term. I thought hiding away was good for me, or better than being out on show in case I was compared to my mother and found wanting. But that's another thing I have to thank you for. You said once that my mother's criticisms of me said more about her own insecurities than they did about me. I think I need to talk to her about that one day.'

His smile was still rueful; but his eyes lacked lustre; they were flat like deep empty pools. 'This is the most unusual breakup I have ever experienced.' He took her hand again and brought it up to his lips, kissing each of her bent knuckles, his eyes meshed with hers. 'Thank you for helping me with Katerina. I'm not sure I would've coped so well without you.'

'Nor me without you.' Addie smiled even though it hurt. Every part of her body hurt as if she had been battered. She loved him and yet he felt nothing for her other than physical desire, which would pass in time, no doubt. She couldn't imagine him longing for her touch the way she knew she would be longing for his for the rest of her life. He was perfect for her and she for him. She knew it on a cellular level. Why couldn't he see it? *Feel* it? Or was she just being a misguided romantic fool? Her lack of experience making her perceive things incorrectly.

Vic was the one to let go of her hand, but he frowned as he did it and then seemed to gather himself, turning to face the direction of travel. It was like a wall had come up between them, an invisible wall that she could not penetrate from her side.

Their arrival at the airport was brisk and efficient, but at the last-minute Addie came to another decision. 'Vic?'

He glanced at her as he slung his laptop bag over one of his broad shoulders. *'Si?'*

Addie steeled her resolve, wishing she could have spent more time with him on the journey home, but knowing it would only prolong her heartache. She had to make a clean break and take time to heal, if that was even possible. 'I want to travel back to London on a commercial flight, alone.'

A savage frown divided his forehead. 'That's ridiculous. I have a private jet. Why would you want to go on a commercial flight?'

Addie held his annoyed gaze with an effort. 'I need to do this, Vic. You can't force me to travel back with you. Besides, I don't want any more attention drawn to us being seen together. We've been incredibly lucky so far—let's not push it.'

His mouth flattened into a thin line. 'Fine. Do what you want. Clearly, I can't kidnap you, although I'm seriously tempted to.'

Addie crooked an eyebrow at him. A part of her wishing he would do exactly that—kidnap her and take her away to some place where they could be alone together. But how realistic was that? There was always going to be interest in who Vic Jacobetti was dating and her stomach churned at the thought of how soon it would be before she would have to see him with some glamourous starlet on his arm. She would have to be strong, stronger than she had ever imagined she would have to be, but she would do it.

She put out her hand to him. 'Goodbye, Vic. Thank you for a lovely time.'

He stared at her hand as if he was going to refuse to take it, but then he released a ragged sigh and grasped her hand in his. 'Take care of yourself, *tesore mio.*'

His voice had a gravelly edge that made her spine tingle, but she forced herself to pull her hand out of his and turn and walk away.

Vic stared at Addie as she walked to the service desk of a popular budget airline. He was so unfamiliar with the emotions running through him like shards of glass, ripping at his insides, tearing his flesh into ribbons of pain. He couldn't explain why he was feeling so surprised by her decision to end their fling. He had assumed she would want to continue it for a few weeks at least, not end it as soon as Marcus and Isabella returned to relieve them of their child-minding duties. He turned away, unable to watch her without the threat of acting on the pressing impulse to go after her, to beg her to change her mind.

Beg? Are you crazy? he mentally scolded himself.

He never begged. He never pleaded. He never changed his mind, so why would he expect her to? He was gobsmacked that the thought of begging her to change her mind had even entered his thoughts. And he was even more shocked at how much he had looked forward to continuing their relationship, which was why he was taken aback by her ending it. It was something he was totally unfamiliar with—the loss of control was anathema to him. He was convinced she was infatuated with him. She'd had no experience before sleeping with him. He was no egomaniac, but he knew his way around a woman's body and he knew when a partner was satisfied or not. It was sexual pleasure that had made her think she had fallen in love with him. He frowned and continued on his way to his check-in point. He didn't want to think too deeply about his own sexual pleasure with Addie. It stirred emotions in him he didn't want to examine. He pushed them down, down, down, to a place so deep inside him he could pretend it didn't even exist.

But all the way back to London, sitting alone in his private jet, all he could think about was Addie. Her touch, her taste, the satin of her skin against his. The way she smiled and the sparkle in her eyes that lit up the darkest room. He rubbed a hand down his face, angry at himself for ruminating over how things had panned out. A restless energy kept him awake, made him edgy and irritable. He clenched his hand into a fist and told himself to get a grip. To get control of his disappointment. But the feeling of emptiness inside him seem to widen with each interminable minute that passed.

Vic closed his eyes and leaned back against the headrest of his seat but all he could see in his mind was Addie walking away from him, reminding him of something he hated being reminded of—his loneliness. How could he have allowed anyone, much less Addie, the power to stir those painful feelings in him? Any feelings? But loneliness was one he hated the most.

CHAPTER ELEVEN

ADDIE SLIPPED BACK into her normal routine as if those wonderful days with Vic Jacobetti hadn't happened. Sometimes she caught herself wondering if she had dreamt it all—it was so far removed from her mundane pattern of going to work and coming home alone. She threw herself into her knitting, mindlessly watching series after series on television with her knitting needles softly clacking, her heart aching for the sound of Vic's voice.

Two, then three weeks went by, and she looked at her phone so often, but there was never a message or a missed call from him. She supposed she had herself to blame for that, insisting on a clean break, but how she wished he would contact her.

Her phone buzzed with an incoming call and her heart nearly leapt out of her chest, but when she looked at the screen, she saw it was her mother. She picked up her phone and pressed the answer button.

'Hi, Mum. I was going to call you to see if you were free for lunch or dinner next time you're in London.'

'Were you?' Her mother's voice sounded immensely surprised. 'I can't remember the last time you called me, other than for my birthday, even though I've told you I'm not counting those any more. Is there someone with you? I can hear someone talking.'

Addie shifted position on the sofa and reaching for the television remote, turned it to mute. 'It was just the television.'

'Addison, you really must try and go out more. How on earth are you ever going to meet someone by staying at home all the time?'

Addie ignored the critical parent tone of her mother's voice because she was starting to take on board Vic's insights into her mother's behaviour. 'Mum, I have met someone, but we recently broke up.'

'Oh, sweetie, that's too bad. Did he dump you?'

'No, actually it was me that ended it.'

'Was he a jerk?'

'No, far from it.' Addie paused for a nanosecond and added, 'I fell in love with him, but he didn't want to commit to anything other than a fling.'

Solange let out a sigh. 'Perhaps if you'd tried harder to please him, or lost a few pounds you might have—'

'Mum, is that what you do to keep a man? Twist yourself into whatever shape he wants to please him?'

There was a telling silence.

'Addie, I have twisted myself so much to please not only men, but the public and every brand I've ever represented that I no longer remember what my real self is.' She gave a half laugh that didn't sound humorous. 'I'm too scared to find out.'

'You have to find out, Mum, otherwise you'll spend the rest of your life inauthentically, like I've been doing for years.'

Her mother sighed. 'Yes, well, it's hard when the world expects you to look perfect all the time.'

'Maybe I'm lucky I didn't take after you, then.'

'Sweetie, I envy you. I always have to be honest. You don't have to work at looking beautiful. Do you realise the effort I have to put in to look this good? It's ridiculous and I'm getting tired of it. For once in my life, I want to eat chocolate, or drink a couple of glasses of champagne instead of counting the damned calories.'

Addie had never heard her mother speak so honestly before and it warmed her heart to think underneath all that brash bluster was someone as insecure as she was. Perhaps there was hope for their relationship after all. 'I can imagine how hard that must be, denying yourself the things you want most.'

'I wanted to be a better mother than mine, but I don't think I've done a good job,' Solange said. 'I haven't been there for you the way I should've been. The work always came first, or the current man in my life.'

'It's not too late to fix that.'

'Do you really think so?' There was an undercurrent of hope and vulnerability in her mother's voice Addie hadn't heard before.

Addie smiled. 'Of course because none of us are perfect. I have stuff to work on too. Getting over Vic is the first thing on my list.' She could have bitten her tongue for accidentally mentioning Vic's name.

There was another silence.

'Not Vic Jacobetti?' The element of gobsmacked surprise in her mother's voice would normally have annoyed Addie, but this time it didn't.

'Yes, Vic Jacobetti.' Even saying his name hurt inside her heart like a burning coal.

'Do you want me to talk to him? I'll set him straight. I'll tell him he has no right to break my daughter's heart and—'

'No, please don't do that.' Addie shuddered at the thought of her mother's version of what being an involved mother might be. 'I have to work through this myself, but thanks for offering.'

'So, about this mother-daughter lunch,' Solange said. 'Shall we go somewhere fancy and dress up? Or would you prefer something a little less exposed?'

'How about a compromise? A picnic in the park and a walk afterwards. How does that sound?'

'It's sounds divine.'

Vic went through the plans for the villa redevelopment with grim determination. He had been doing nothing but work to get this thing off the ground, but for some reason, every time he looked at those plans, he thought of Addie. He pictured her beautiful face with its sunny dimpled smile and those cute freckles. He thought of her tawny brown eyes that shone with delight when she looked at him…apart from the last time he saw her, of course. He rubbed a weary hand down his face, wondering if he was ever going to get these plans back to the architect with his final tick of approval. He kept stalling, finding details to be sorted out, minor things that he wouldn't normally make a big deal about, but he had turned into a pernickety person who found fault with everything and everyone. He was turning into a version of his stepfather.

Vic gave a mental cringe and looked back at the plans. He tried to ignore the heavy feeling in his chest, the weight of something pulling at his body like an anvil hanging from his heart. His heart. *Dio*, the last thing he wanted reminding of was his heart. He had no interest in dating. His playboy lifestyle had a pause button on it and he didn't see it switching on again anytime soon. He had lost all enthusiasm for anything but work, but even that was unsatisfying in a way it had never been before. It didn't numb the feelings of loneliness like it used to. He was worn out with trying to batter them into submission.

Vic turned his attention back to the architectural plans in front of him, but his gaze drifted to the grotto and something grabbed him in the guts like a clawed hand. It was one of the last places he had been with his father before he died. Memories of his father's smile came to him in a flood, ambushing him with their vividness. It was like travelling back in time, seeing himself as a young boy who idolised his father. Who loved his father with every cell of his body. And that love was returned. The love of his father had been his anchor, his guiding light, his everything…until his father died. Vic pushed the plans away in despair. He couldn't bring himself to work on them. If he was honest with himself, he was fast losing interest in developing the villa into a hotel. Those few days with Addie and little Katerina had reminded him of what his villa used to be like before his father was killed in an accident.

Back then it was a home full of love, full of laughter and fun and joy. Of course it was a big place, too big really for a family of three, but his parents had hoped to have more children.

Vic pushed back his office chair and got up from the desk and went to look at the view from his office. London was spread out before him in all its glory. The buildings and bridges, Big Ben, the river and parks and greenery all as familiar to him as his own features. Why was he feeling this wretched loneliness? He had ended so many flings and felt nothing. But now all he could think of was Addie. She was somewhere out there in this huge city, going about her life, just as he was trying to do. Was she missing him the way he missed her? Was she trying to distract herself with work and finding it impossible to remove the memories of their time together?

His gut cramped again.

Was she with someone else?

Vic was not a jealous man. He had no need to be. He had never wanted someone enough to trigger those feelings. Until now. He hated the thought of someone else being with Addie, giving her the fairytale she longed for and deserved.

You deserve it too.

Vic shook his head, wondering if he was going mad. There was a voice inside his head that kept prodding at him, but until now he had always been able to ignore it. A voice that told him he had got it all wrong, that he was ruining his life by not opening his heart to love. It was as if a vault inside him had been cracked open, shining light in all the dark places, revealing a truth that was worth more than anything else on the planet—love.

His love for Addie.

A weight lifted off him as he allowed himself to examine the feelings he had ignored and shut down before. He could not believe how foolish he had been to throw away a chance at happiness, at fulfilment, at finally being a whole person, brave enough to love someone even though he might one day lose them. That was the risk everyone who loved had to take. Addie had taken it and yet he had let her down, broken her heart by refusing to acknowledge his own feelings for her. Because of course he had feelings for her. Feelings that had crept up on him, surprising him by their intensity. Was that why he had fought so valiantly to ignore them? Feelings were something he had avoided since losing his father. He hated the thought of loving someone so much that they might be taken from him or he would fail to protect them from harm. But was it realistic to think that way? Life was unpredictable because life was out of his control. It was out of everyone's control. The only thing he could control was his response to what life threw at him. And life had thrown him a chance at happiness and he had pushed it away. Why had he been such a stubborn fool? He'd thought he was doing the right thing, the best thing by avoiding long-term relationships in order to protect his heart from further hurt. But hadn't the last few weeks shown him that it was more painful to stop himself from loving Addie?

Was it too late?

Vic arrived at her doorstep half an hour later. He took a deep breath and pushed the doorbell, but all he got was the sound of it echoing in the silence. His heart began to hammer. His stomach tightened. He had missed his chance. He had thrown away the one chance he had to be happy with someone who understood him, who got him, who was sensitive and kind and loving enough to see past the armour he had built around his heart. Vic pressed the doorbell again, his breath locked in his tight throat where his heart seemed to have climbed. When there was no answer his stomach plummeted like something falling from a tall building. He fished out his phone and called her but it went straight to message bank. He sent a text, but it showed her phone had switched off notifications. His heart throbbed in his throat like a wild creature. Where was she? He tried to get past the panic in his head to think clearly, to think rationally. There could be any number of reasons why Addie wasn't at home right now. His memory snagged on a conversation they'd had at one point when she'd talked about her work, how she worked extra shifts on weekends so others could be with their families. Her kind-hearted nature was one of the things he most loved about her. He hailed a passing taxi and got in, and then had to stop himself from asking the driver to speed to the after-hours veterinary clinic.

The taxi driver stopped at a red light.

'Come on, come on, come on...' Vic said under his breath, willing the traffic lights to change from red to green.

The lights reminded him of himself, how he had put a red light on his emotions. Stopping himself from feeling anything that could endanger his heart. But he had turned off the red light now and was allowing himself to feel the full depth of his love for sweet and beautiful Addie.

Addie was working overtime at the after-hours clinic because one of the other vet nurses had called in sick. It meant she wouldn't be home until late, which didn't normally bother her, but talking about Vic to her mother over their picnic in the park earlier that day had brought the pain back with a vengeance and she found the thought of going home to an empty flat depressing. She had to get over him. She had to move on. She had to stop clinging to the rope of hope, while swinging over a chasm of despair that threatened to consume her.

Addie distracted herself by checking on the new litter of puppies delivered that morning by an emergency caesarean. The mother, a gorgeous Cavalier King Charles spaniel, was still drowsy from the anaesthetic, but she was contentedly feeding her two puppies, a boy and a girl.

'How are you doing, Coco?' Addie crooned softly to the mother, while stroking the tiny backs of the puppies.

'There's someone here to see you.' Sanaya, the night shift nurse who was to take over from Addie's shift, popped her head around the door and added in a stage whisper. 'Tall, dark, handsome. Said it was urgent.'

Addie's heart skipped. Her skin tightened. Her pulse raced. Her dying hopes breathed in a breath of much-needed air. She moved back from the puppies' crate and tried to get her emotions under control. 'Thanks. I'll be out in a second.'

'A second is too long,' Vic said and strode in as if on a mission no force on the face of the earth could distract him from.

'Sir, you can't just storm in here—' Sanaya said, looking cross and flustered at the same time.

'It's okay,' Addie said. 'Can you take over reception for a couple of minutes?'

Sanaya nodded and giving Vic an up and down look, went back out to reception.

'It was rather rude of you to barge in here—' Addie began.

Vic took her by the upper arms in a grasp that was so firm it was almost painful. He looked haggard, his eyes had dark shadows beneath them, he had lost weight and his hair looked like it had been repeatedly combed with his fingers. 'Do you know the agonies I've gone through tonight? I've been waiting outside your flat, calling you repeatedly on the phone, sending message after message, but you didn't answer or show up. I thought something might have happened to you.'

'As you can see, I'm alive and kicking, well not exactly kicking but you get the drift.'

He pulled her against his chest, hugging her so tightly she thought he might crack a rib. 'Oh, *tesore mio*, I've gone through hell and back, not just tonight but the last three weeks.'

Addie eased out of his hold to look up at him, her heart beating so fast it was hard for her to speak. 'Y-you have?'

His eyes lost their look of despair and a smile turned up the corners of his mouth. 'It's so wonderful to see you. I've missed you so much.'

'Y-you have?'

'I have been a fool. A ridiculous fool to let you go. Can you ever forgive me?'

Addie was trying not to get too excited unless she was mistaken about his reason for coming here to see her, but how could she not feel anything but excitement? Nothing could have prepared her for this. It was like a miracle to see him standing before her, begging for her forgiveness. 'Of course I forgive you.'

Vic hugged her again, his chin resting on the top of her head. She breathed in the scent of him like it was a drug to ease her cravings. 'I can't believe I didn't realise what I felt about you until now.' He pulled back to look down at her with earnestness shining in his dark gaze. 'I love you to the core of my being.'

Addie's heart missed a beat, her stomach went into freefall and her hopes got out of a coma and did a happy dance. 'You do? Really?'

'I love everything about you. You have changed everything for me. You made me realise how locked down I was, how cowardly I was to block myself from feeling like this. I love you so much and want to be with you for ever.'

Addie blinked back tears. 'Are you…?' She couldn't finish the sentence because she was so overcome with joy.

'Yes, I am proposing, but I'll be damned if I'll do

it in an animal hospital in front of a dog and her puppies,' Vic said, smiling broadly.

'First time for everything,' Addie said, smiling back at him.

'I don't have a ring yet. The shops were closed when I finally came to my senses. I went straight to your flat, hoping to find you at home.' A flicker of anguish went through his gaze and his throat moved up and down over a convulsive swallow. 'I thought I might have lost you before I got to tell you how much I love and adore you. I can never forgive myself for being so stubborn and too proud to own what I felt.' His voice was rough around the edges and his eyes glistened with moisture. 'Will you marry me, *tesore mio*? Will you make a family with me and live part of the time at the villa?'

'Yes, a thousand million times yes,' Addie said, but then she gave him a puzzled frown and added, 'But isn't the villa going to be a hotel?'

He smiled and gathered her close again. 'That was another thing I was ignorant and stubborn about. The villa holds so many good memories after our time together there. I can't bear to part with it now. I want it to become a home again even though it's too big, but we can have a couple of kids, maybe more and—'

Addie's heart skipped and danced with joy. 'You want kids?'

'I haven't until now,' Vic said. 'But realising how much I love you has made me want the whole package. The fairytale as you call it.'

'You deserve it.'

He looked at her with such love it made her heart

contract. 'I'm not sure I deserve to be this happy, but I can't imagine living my life without you by my side. You have taught me so much about being true to myself. I haven't been living the life my father wanted for me. He would want me to find love like he did and support and protect my family to the best of my ability.'

Addie hugged him and choked back a sob. 'You are such a wonderful person, Vic. Your father would be so proud of the man you've become. It's so sad he isn't here to share our joy, but he lives on in you, in the qualities he gave you.'

Coco shuffled in the crate behind Vic and one of the puppies gave a little squeak as it came off its mother's nipple. Addie turned with Vic to look at the mother and babies, his arm firm around her waist.

'This has been rather an eventful day for Coco. She had an emergency caesarean this morning and now she has witnessed your proposal,' Addie said with a beaming smile.

Vic turned her in his arms, his eyes glinting. 'There's one more thing I have to do.'

'What's that?'

'This.'

And he leaned down and kissed her for so long Coco gave a contented sigh and went back to sleep.

* * * * *

MILLS & BOON®

Coming next month

TWINS FOR HIS MAJESTY
Clare Connelly

'The baby is fine?'

'Oh, the baby is fine. In fact, both babies are fine,' she snapped, almost maniacally now. 'It's twins,' she added, and then she sobbed, lifting a hand to her mouth to stop the torrent of emotion from pouring out in a large wail.

Silence cracked around them but she barely noticed. She was shaking now, processing the truth of the scan, the reality that lay before her.

'Well, then.' His voice was low and silky, as though she hadn't just told him they were going to have *two babies* in a matter of months. 'That makes our decision even easier.'

'What decision?' she asked, whirling around to face him.

'There is no way on earth you are leaving the country whilst pregnant with my children, so forget about returning to New Zealand.'

She flinched. She hadn't expected that.

'Nor will my children be born under a cloud of illegitimacy.'

Her heart almost stopped beating; his words made no sense. 'I—don't—what are you saying?'

'That you must marry me—and quickly.'

Continue reading

TWINS FOR HIS MAJESTY
Clare Connelly

Available next month
millsandboon.co.uk

Copyright ©2025 by Clare Connelly

COMING SOON!

We really hope you enjoyed reading this book. If you're looking for more romance be sure to head to the shops when new books are available on

Thursday 17th July

To see which titles are coming soon, please visit
millsandboon.co.uk/nextmonth

MILLS & BOON

FOUR BRAND NEW BOOKS FROM
MILLS & BOON MODERN

The same great stories you love, a stylish new look!

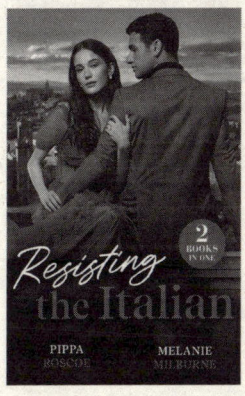

OUT NOW

Eight Modern stories published every month, find them all at:

millsandboon.co.uk

afterglow BOOKS

Afterglow Books is a trend-led, trope-filled list of books with diverse, authentic and relatable characters, a wide array of voices and representations, plus real world trials and tribulations. Featuring all the tropes you could possibly want (think small-town settings, fake relationships, grumpy vs sunshine, enemies to lovers) and all with a generous dose of spice in every story.

♪ @millsandboonuk
◎ @millsandboonuk
afterglowbooks.co.uk
#AfterglowBooks

For all the latest book news, exclusive content and giveaways scan the QR code below to sign up to the Afterglow newsletter:

SCAN ME

afterglow BOOKS

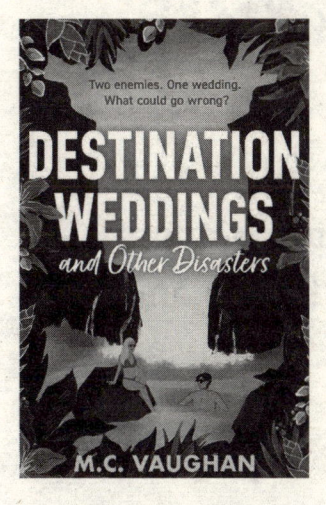

DESTINATION WEDDINGS and Other Disasters
M.C. VAUGHAN

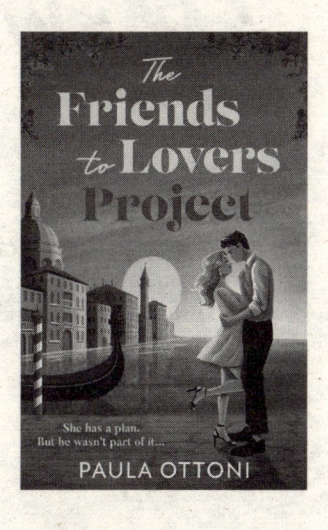

Two enemies. One wedding. What could go wrong?

The Friends to Lovers Project
PAULA OTTONI

She has a plan. But he wasn't part of it...

- ✈ International
- ♥ Enemies to lovers
- (((♥))) Forced proximity

- 👬 Friends to lovers
- ✈ International
- △ Love triangle

OUT NOW

Two stories published every month. Discover more at:
Afterglowbooks.co.uk

LET'S TALK
Romance

For exclusive extracts, competitions and special offers, find us online:

- **f** MillsandBoon
- **X** @MillsandBoon
- **◉** @MillsandBoonUK
- **♪** @MillsandBoonUK

Get in touch on 01413 063 232

For all the latest titles coming soon, visit
millsandboon.co.uk/nextmonth

OUT NOW!

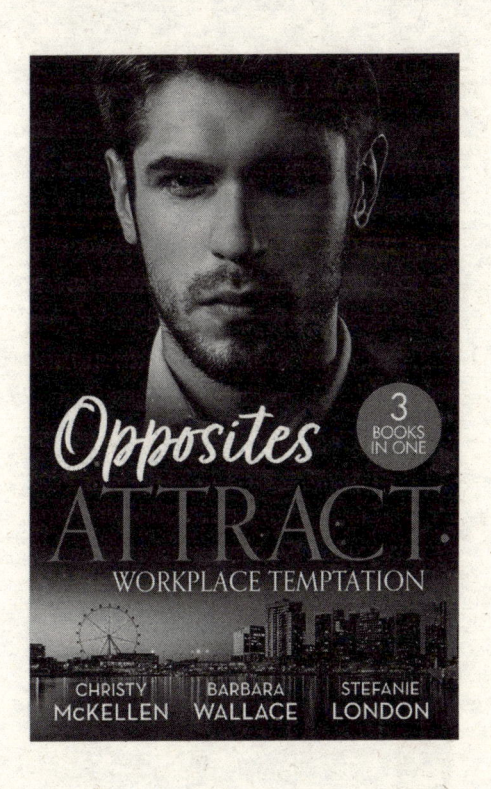

Opposites Attract: Workplace Temptation

3 BOOKS IN ONE

CHRISTY McKELLEN · BARBARA WALLACE · STEFANIE LONDON

Available at
millsandboon.co.uk

MILLS & BOON

OUT NOW!

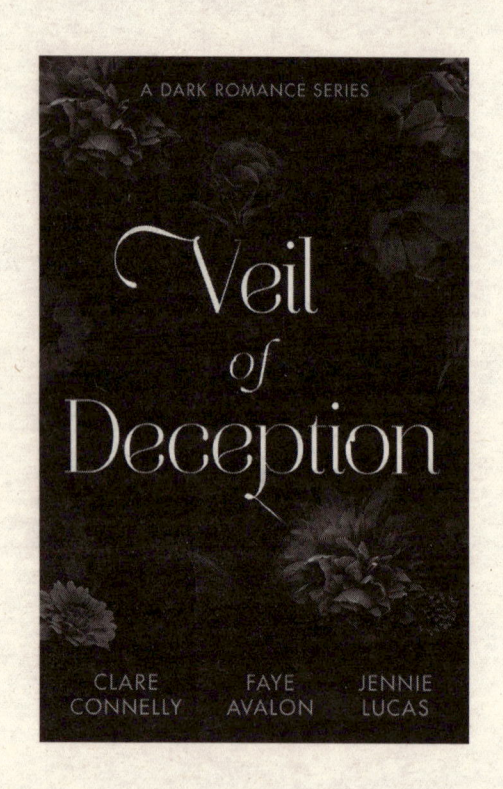

Veil of Deception

A DARK ROMANCE SERIES

CLARE CONNELLY · FAYE AVALON · JENNIE LUCAS

Available at
millsandboon.co.uk

MILLS & BOON